Acknowledgements

I should like to thank my family, my agent Laura Longrigg at MBA, my editor Sherise Hobbs, and the team at Headline for their encouragement and support.

FAMILY MATTERS

Also by Cathy Woodman

Under The Bonnet
Our House

FAMILY MATTERS

Cathy Woodman

headline

First published in 2006
by HEADLINE BOOK PUBLISHING

1

Cataloguing in Publication Data is
available from the British Library

ISBN 0 7553 2441 2

Typeset in Book Antiqua by Palimpsest Book Production Limited,
Polmont, Stirlingshire
Printed and bound in Great Britain by
Mackays of Chatham plc, Chatham, Kent

Headline's policy is to use papers that are natural, renewable and
recyclable products and made from wood grown in sustainable
forests. The logging and manufacturing processes are expected
to conform to the environmental regulations of the country of origin.

HEADLINE BOOK PUBLISHING
A division of Hodder Headline
338 Euston Road
London NW1 3BH

www.headline.co.uk
www.hodderheadline.com

To Nanna

Chapter One

My best friend Clare's fantasy is to wake up with Johnny Depp. Mine is to wake alone, spread-eagled across a sheet of fresh linen. Instead, I find myself sharing a bed with my husband and our two-month-old baby, three bodies hugged together like a row of steaming cannelloni.

The alarm clock bleats. Chloe doesn't stir. Tony sighs. I reach for his hand, link my fingers through his and give them a squeeze.

'It's time we were up.'

'I am.' He moves my hand behind my back and down between his legs where the evidence is quite clear.

'Not now . . .' I say wistfully.

'Tonight then?' he whispers.

My pulse quickens in response. Smiling, I wait for Tony to continue with, 'I can't believe it's been fourteen years,' or just plain, 'Happy Anniversary, my darling.'

Instead he grumbles, 'I can't remember when we last made love, Lisa.'

'You make it sound like it was thousands of years ago.'

'Well, it was sometime BC. Before Chloe.'

I *do* remember the last time we made love. I was forty-one weeks' pregnant – a whole week overdue – and we'd been trying to induce labour in the most natural way. It worked, although I'm not sure if it was the sex or the fact I was laughing so much that did it. Tony said it was like making love to a giant Space Hopper.

'Talking of Chloe, why did we waste our money on that new mattress for the carrycot when she refuses to sleep on it?' Tony goes on.

'I can't help it if she's hypnophobic. She's afraid to go to sleep in case she misses something.' Last night I spent hours sitting downstairs in the dark with the door shut and the radio on. I fed Chloe, changed her, rocked her in my arms, laid her down, and propped her up, but I couldn't stop her crying. She reminded me of that famous painting by Edvard Munch, *The Scream*.

'I'm not criticising you.' Tony pulls away and jumps out of bed. He stretches his arms above his head and peels his black T-shirt off over his broad shoulders, revealing the rippling muscles of his torso. Although he's no longer a competitive swimmer, he keeps very fit for a man of forty-two, doing lengths a couple of times a week at the local pool.

'Whenever I make any kind of observation, you seem to take it personally,' he goes on.

'I don't.'

'You do.' Tony screws his top into a ball and chucks it at my face, one of his more irritating customs that I've grown to expect, one of the many little things that keep us bound together in matrimony and make our relationship unique and special.

I throw it back, then close my eyes to snatch a few minutes' more sleep, while Tony disappears off to the bathroom.

'Mum. Mum!' I become aware of someone shaking my shoulder, of hair tickling my cheek. Light glints off an enormous gold hoop earring that dangles in my face.

'Mum, I can't find a shirt.'

'Is that all? I thought it was a real emergency.'

'It *is* an emergency.' My other daughter Jade is thirteen going on seventeen. She's sensitive about her appearance, yet she keeps dyeing her long straight hair this peculiar shade of pale chestnut so that I've almost forgotten what her natural colour looks like. It should be like Tony's – brown with blond highlights, as if it's been kissed by the sun.

'There are plenty of shirts on your bedroom floor. Use your eyes.'

Those eyes darken, turning shadowy blue like a summer's evening sky.

'I can't go to school in a dirty shirt. It's disgusting.'

'Tough!'

She stamps off, triggering a minor earthquake in the floorboards under her feet, and there's no way I can sleep now even if Chloe can, having finally dozed off at dawn. I leave the baby on the bed, slip into my dressing-gown and wander downstairs like a zombie. On my way through the hall, I stub my toe on a metal toolbox, but I am so tired that the pain barely registers. Tony's a plumber and he's had his tools nicked from his van so many times that he brings them indoors every evening. I'd like him to keep them locked in the garage, but you can't get into our garage for old kitchen units which are supposed to be going to Clare and her husband Jim as soon as they can afford to have them fitted.

Tony and I had our kitchen extended, and a utility room built on the back of the house while I was pregnant with Chloe. The Shaker-style cabinets looked great in the showroom, but I soon discovered that only cleaners with obsessive compulsive tendencies should buy white units.

In the kitchen, beneath the stalactites of dried flour and milk that adorn the ceiling – the consequence of Jade's enthusiasm for tossing pancakes with her dad – I make myself black coffee and toast with strawberry jam. However, my bum hardly makes contact with the stool at the breakfast bar before Chloe screams for attention. (I don't need one of those baby monitors – you can hear her at their maximum range and beyond without one.)

I whisk Chloe downstairs, snuggling her to me. 'Hi there, my darling.'

She yawns and smiles. She's beautiful – all blue eyes and a fuzz of blonde hair – until nightfall when she turns into the Baby from Hell. I don't remember Jade giving us so much trouble, but she's more than making up for it now, banging about in the kitchen cupboards, looking for breakfast. No cornflakes. No cereal bars. All my fault.

By the time I've organised Jade into making herself a sandwich instead – she chooses salad cream as the filling – Tony is down. He's a rarity, a man who can carry out more than one task at once: he has his mobile glued to one ear, a pencil over the other, a notebook in his left hand and a slice of toast in his right. I glance at my plate. Empty.

'Hey – that's *my* toast.'

'Finders keepers.' He grins and my heart somersaults.

'Anything special on today?' I ask.

'I doubt it.' He turns to Jade who's wearing a blouse undone to her navel, a skirt up around her buttocks, and no socks or tights. She's already slipped into her shoes, black clumpy ones with heels so high that you can see her calf muscles straining to keep her upright. 'Go and get dressed, Jade.'

'I am dressed.'

'Properly,' Tony insists. 'Take off that scarf you've got wrapped around your bottom and put on a skirt.'

'You can't make me do anything I don't want to,' Jade argues.

'Don't speak to your dad like that,' I say.

'I can't help being in a bad mood, can I? I haven't slept for weeks because of that,' she points at Chloe, 'that *thing*!'

'Chloe is your little sister. She's a baby.'

Jade isn't listening. 'Mum, you know you said I could invite a friend for a sleepover?'

'Did I?'

'I'm going to ask Kimberley, the new girl at school.'

'What about Alice?' Alice is – was – Jade's best friend. I like Alice.

'I'm trying to make Kimberley feel welcome.'

'Well, she can come to tea sometime, but you're not having a sleepover. The answer is no,' I add in answer to Jade's fierce scowl.

'You're always so negative,' Jade moans.

All in all, it isn't a promising start to what should be a romantic day, and I still have no idea of Tony's plans for our anniversary. When he leaves to take Jade up to the bus stop on his way to work, I try again. 'You haven't forgotten anything, Tone?'

He turns and frowns. 'Sandwiches?'

'They're in your hand.'

'And the van isn't going in for a service till next week.' He smiles and leans forward to kiss me. 'Bye, love,' he adds quietly.

Is that how you're supposed to treat the person you've been married to for the past fourteen years, when she's cooked for you, done all your washing and ironing, borne your children, and collected you and your mates somewhat worse for wear at closing time from just about every pub in South London with minimal complaint? Excuse me if I sound just a little bit resentful.

Ten minutes later, Chloe is fast asleep in her carryseat, which I've put down in the middle of our bed. My throat tightens like the tiny fist that grips the edge of her yellow blanket. I lean down, press my lips to her cheek and inhale her warm, milky breath.

'Love you,' I whisper.

She shifts slightly, rolls her eyes and yawns. Wind or a bad dream, perhaps? I turn my attention back to the mystery of the missing anniversary present.

Why is it I can never find anything in this house? Why is it that no one, apart from me, ever puts anything away? As I sort through the bits and pieces on my beside cabinet, a handful of receipts flutter down to the bedroom floor: nappies for Chloe; staples for Jade's science project; frozen bloodworms for Tony's tropical fish; cookies for me. All things that I bought on my recent foray into Croydon. Okay, so I don't put things away either, but is it surprising when I have so many people to think about, so much to do?

I open the drawer of the dressing-table and scuffle through the clothes. Nothing. No cute cuddly bear. No chocolates. Not a scrap of flimsy underwear. I cram the matronly bras and mumsy knickers back into the drawer and force it closed.

Where next, I wonder. I stand on a chair and sweep my hand across the top of the wardrobe. My fingernails catch on the edge of a piece of paper, an envelope. My sense of anticipation grows at the thought of a romantic evening out with tickets for a West End show, then shrinks like a punctured football. The envelope contains tickets for a match: Arsenal are playing at home.

Arsenal were playing at home in a crucial FA Cup match when Tony and I celebrated our fifth anniversary, yet he sacrificed his ticket to take me to Paris instead. I remember lying in his arms on a king-sized bed, watching the view from our hotel window of the Eiffel Tower illuminated in the night sky. I tried to ignore the faint smell of drains and the sound of traffic, while he spoke to Jade on the phone. It was our first night away together since before she was born and we'd left her with my parents.

'Jade wants to speak to you, Lees.' Tony handed me the receiver, but it was Mum on the other end.

'Your daughter has something to tell you,' she said.

I could hear Jade's snuffly breathing.

'Granny says you have something to tell me,' I said gently.

'I know,' she said, her voice taut with excitement.

'What is it?'

'Oh?' I pictured her tapping her knuckles against her forehead as she wailed, 'I can't remember.' I heard Mum prompting her. 'We had dog for tea.'

'She means cod,' Mum said in the background.

'Well, I tried oysters for the first time,' I told my daughter.

'Goodbye, Mummy,' Jade said, and the line went dead.

'She cut me off.' I turned to Tony who took the receiver and replaced it on its cradle on the bedside table. 'She isn't missing us.'

'You'd be more upset if she was.' Tony paused. 'Cheer up, love. Have a drink.'

We shared champagne kisses, the slow burn of Tony's lips against mine contrasting with the pricks of cold fizz popping against the roof of my mouth. Tony pulled me closer, crushing my breasts against his chest. He tugged at my French knickers, tearing the lace in his impatience to strip them down over my hips, and make love to me.

We didn't sleep much that night, or the next, but what I remember most about our second honeymoon, a memory that never fails to bring a smile to my face, is of Tony on a boat on the Seine, doing impressions of Inspector Clouseau.

Of course, much water has flowed under the bridge since then. My memories of our marriage are not all happy ones.

I glance at my watch. It's nine thirty. There's no time to continue my investigations right now. Clare's car, a battered but shiny green VW Polo, is already pulling up outside the house.

Clare, my business partner as well as my closest friend, double-checks the handbrake before she jumps out, and waits for a woman in a pale pink mac to bring a double buggy and a child on reins under control down the precipitous descent of York Road before she crosses the pavement. She looks up, raises her hands to her mouth and yells. I'm not sure whether it's Clare's voice that does it or a sneaky breeze that brings a shower of cherry-blossom down from the tree beside her.

'Lees, you lazy slapper, get yourself down here – and don't forget the baby!'

'All right, all right.' I close the window and check my make-up.

My bob of dark brown hair contrasts starkly with my pale complexion, and my eyes are puffy through lack of sleep. I am wearing a blue cotton surgical top with the company logo *Maids 4 U* embroidered to the left of the V-neckline.

The plastic apron and baggy trousers fail to disguise what is left of my figure, ravaged by pregnancy and childbirth. My breasts, belly and hips appear over-upholstered yet sagging, like a cheap and nasty sofa. The extra three stone that I fondly imagined was all baby turned out to be mainly me. Chloe was born eight weeks ago weighing just six pounds.

However, there are still signs of the woman I used to be. At thirty-eight years old, I have no need yet for hair-dye or Botox. My lips are full and, though I say it myself, very kissable. And my bum – I smile as I give it a wiggle – is neat and firm.

Clare rattles the letterbox. I grab Chloe's changing bag in one hand, the carryseat in the other, and make my way downstairs.

'Well?' Clare relieves me of Chloe as soon as I open the front door. While the uniform does nothing for me, Clare carries it off as if it's Moschino. The shape enhances her sexy curves, and the blue picks up the colour of her eyes which spark in anticipation of the question of the day. She can't wait to ask me. 'What did Tony give you then?'

'Nothing yet.' I follow Clare to the car, where she begins strapping Chloe into the rear seat beside her baby, Fern, a procedure requiring a degree in manual dexterity and bucketloads of commonsense, neither of which I possess.

'I expect he's planned something special for this evening – a meal at the Tapas Bar perhaps,' Clare says brightly. 'I'd like Jim to take me to that new Indian sometime, but spicy food gives Fern terrible colic,' she adds with the air of superiority that breastfeeding mothers can't help acquiring when speaking to their bottlefeeding friends.

I did try to breastfeed Jade and ended up with double mastitis. Tony said that I looked like a Cabbage Patch doll with red-hot cheeks and cabbage leaves spread over my boobs. I didn't care. I thought I was going to die. When Chloe was born, she went straight on the bottle.

'Tony didn't stop me taking the chicken out of the freezer for tonight.' I can't help noticing the dark roots in Clare's bottle-blonde hair as she fiddles around inside the car. She does her own. She's pretty handy with the bleach, in more ways than one.

'That would take away the element of surprise,' Clare observes. 'I can't remember exactly how long ago it was that you made me suffer the indignity of flouncing around in that pink dress as your Maid of Honour.'

'It wasn't pink. It was cerise.'

'Same difference. How many years have you been married?'

'Fourteen. We're way past the Seven Year Itch.'

Clare whistles between her teeth.

'If Tony did have an itch back then, I made every effort to ensure that it was me who scratched it,' I say mournfully. 'Maybe you do start to forget by the time you reach fourteen.'

'Don't be ridiculous. Tony hasn't forgotten.' Clare emerges from the car with a dry laugh. 'He wouldn't dare.'

I'd like to believe her. Clare's opinions are usually sound. In fact, I can hardly remember a time when I didn't depend on them. Clare found me hiding in the girls' toilets at primary school, bawling my eyes out because someone – I knew who it was but was too frightened to utter her name, let alone point the finger at her or confide in a teacher – had filled my satchel with water, ruining my reading book and turning the biscuits that I'd saved from break for my little brother Mal, into a sloppy gruel.

Clare helped me out. Even then she had a cleaner's eye, pointing out the limescale on the taps and the gunge in the sinks, as she bailed out the satchel and stuffed it with paper towels. With her on lookout, I swapped the bully's reading book for mine, and jammed her schoolbag into one of the cisterns. There were no repercussions. From then on, it was two against one. Me and Clare against the rest of the world.

I can rely on Clare to help me through a crisis. I've helped her through enough of her own – her numerous failed romances, for example, until she learned to distinguish love from lust, and settled for her husband Jim. Today though, her reassurance isn't quite enough.

Clare pushes the car door softly shut then goes round to the driver's side. She's taller than me and prettier in my opinion, with high cheekbones and a beauty spot above her upper lip. She says that if she could afford plastic surgery, she would have her nose made smaller, but it really isn't that big.

I slide into the passenger seat, arranging myself around the mop in the footwell. Clare turns the key in the ignition, releases the handbrake with two hands, and accelerates jerkily up the hill. Out of the corner of my eye, I see Fern's eyes widen. I'm surprised – I'd have thought that she'd be used to Clare's driving by now.

Fern is smaller and appears more delicate than Chloe. Her hair is dark and, like her dad's, there isn't much of it. She grins when I reach back to straighten her headhugger; unlike Chloe, she rarely cries.

Chloe remains asleep, unmoved by the bumpy ride up through Selsdon where we make a quick stop at the baker's for doughnuts.

According to the sign at the traffic lights on the High Street, this suburb of South Croydon is a village. Not any more. It doesn't have a village green, just a patch of mud and trees called The Triangle, in front of the new library. The Triangle boasts a useful Superloo, which will soon be replaced by a clock of cutting-edge design. I still can't understand why it cost thousands of pounds to create a piece of art resembling a sticky lollipop that's been kicked around in cobwebs, but then I didn't think much of Damien Hirst's dead sheep or Tracey Emin's tent. In my opinion, whoever made Clare's earrings had more taste.

'Those earrings are new, aren't they?' I ask.

'Jim bought them for me.' Clare fingers the mother-of-pearl-effect discs that dangle from her left ear. 'Do you think they're too big?'

'Size doesn't matter, when it comes to presents anyway, and neither does value. It's the thought that counts.' So why didn't Tony think of me, I wonder. 'The last thing Tony bought me was a tub of salt for the bath when my stitches broke down.'

'Tony's a practical man. You should be grateful that he has your welfare at heart.'

'I am. I'd just like him to give me something frivolous once in a while.'

Clare parks outside a block of maisonettes. 'Come on, let's get started.' She carries baby Fern in her seat and a bucket. I brush sugar off my front and take Chloe and the mop.

We set up *Maids 4 U* before the babies arrived, and our clients were none too keen on my idea of us both taking a year's maternity leave. Neither was Clare, considering it would be unpaid, so we compromised, sending apologetic, impersonal notes to those clients with the dirtiest homes, and keeping on the few who had slipped us the odd tenner or bottle of wine at Christmas.

Clare beats me to the front door of number 11A. She drops the bucket, not the baby, and pulls a bunch of keys from her pocket. She selects a key, slips it into the lock and jiggles it until it turns, then pushes the door open.

I follow Clare inside and up the stairs where a wall of humid air hits us. It's like getting off a plane in Majorca, but the air is laced with added notes of cold sweat and methane.

'You don't think . . . ?' I say nervously.

'I hope we're not going to regret stuffing those doughnuts.' Clare wrinkles her nose as we pass the bathroom door. 'Do you remember our first visit?'

'How could I forget?' It was like having morning sickness all over again. There was a carpet of nail clippings on the bathroom floor, mouldering tissues under the bed, and the most immaculate toilet brush that I've ever seen, still wrapped. An overlying scent of fresh Lynx failed to disguise the acrid odours of sour milk, uneaten takeaways and unwashed clothes. We booked three days to clear it up, and transformed the whole flat.

In the living room the curtains are closed and the lights are on. A CD is spinning, but not playing inside the mini hi-fi. Fragments of glass glitter from the laminate floor. The décor is – no, was – quite minimal; open beechwood shelving, and paper tube lamps hanging artily from the ceiling.

My mouth goes dry. Something is very wrong.

'Don't touch anything,' I warn Clare as she plonks Fern on the sofa. She tugs the curtains apart, throws a window open and takes the CD out of the player. 'This might be the scene of a crime.'

'It is. Look at this.' Grinning, Clare holds out the CD. 'The Opera Babes. *Beyond Imagination.*'

'That anyone should be interested in classical music is beyond *my* imagination.'

'Me too, except I do like that piece that Torvill and Dean used to dance to, "Bolero". Jim bought it before we met.' Clare colours slightly. 'He maintains that it's rather erotic. Have you and Tony you-know-what yet?'

I shake my head. As Tony pointed out earlier this morning, we haven't made love since before Chloe was born. I've been too sore, too weary, but I'm planning for tonight to be the night . . . A tiny quiver of anticipation runs down my spine as I imagine the pressure of Tony's hands on my back, his skin snagging on a pair of silk knickers, or more realistically a set of cotton/Lycra-mix pants because he hasn't bought me glamorous underwear for ages. He hasn't even bought me a tacky novelty item. He hasn't bought me *anything*.

I start to wonder if it might be my fault. I mean, I did lose it when he presented me with a waitress outfit one Christmas, but that's understandable when I wait on everyone hand and foot all day, every day. I don't need a uniform to remind me of my position as domestic servant because that's how I feel sometimes.

I change the subject. 'Do you think it's safe – hygienic, I mean – to leave the babies in here?'

'They'll be fine, Lisa. You know, I think we can justify charging Mr Harman for a couple of extra hours today with all this mess.'

'Two hours? I was hoping to be home early today.'

'It doesn't have to take us two,' Clare says wickedly, 'if we put our backs into it.'

'Oh, all right then.' I place my daughter beside Fern. 'I ought to wake Chloe up, otherwise she'll keep us up all night again.'

'If you wake her now, she's bound to want a feed—' Clare stops abruptly, interrupted by a bloodcurdling groan. 'Did you hear that?'

I tighten my grip on the mop.

'We are not alone,' Clare continues dramatically and some-what unnecessarily, I consider, from the soft thud that comes from the bedroom.

I head towards the source of the sound, then hesitate just out-side the open door, brandishing my mop.

'Show yourself, whoever you are!' My voice comes out as a squeak. I'm not sure who I'm expecting – a man in a striped sweater carrying a swag bag, or a youth in a black hooded top with a gun. It's neither of these. A naked man with wide, ice-blue eyes comes lunging at me full frontal, brandishing a truncheon.

11

I scream. The head of the mop makes contact with my assailant's forearm, knocking his weapon from his hand. He trips back against the bed, tries to regain his balance, fails and falls onto the mattress.

'Mr Harman?' Clare says from behind me.

'I didn't recognise him,' I bluster. 'He looks so different.'

'And so he would.' Clare throws him a duster. 'Last time we saw him, he had his clothes on.'

It's true. When we met to agree the terms of our contract, Mr Harman was wearing a suit with a lilac shirt and tie, which gave him an air of sophistication and maturity that he lacks just now. He's twenty-eight according to his passport, which he keeps in a small fire-safe but not cleaner-proof box, along with other important documents, and he's worth about ten thousand in savings and ISAs. He's tall and moderately handsome with flecks of grey running prematurely through short, mid-brown hair: not a bad catch.

Mr Harman slowly sits himself up on the edge of the bed with the duster clutched between his long thighs, and what I can now see is a wooden ceremonial truncheon at his feet. He groans, half-opens his eyes then closes them again. 'My head hurts . . .'

Clare moves round and shakes his shoulder gently. 'Mr Harman, it's Clare and Lisa here from *Maids 4 U.*'

'I'm sorry if I frightened you,' he says. 'I thought you were burglars.' His lips are encrusted with flakes of what could be dried baby rice, or something rather more unpleasant. 'What day is it?'

'Monday,' I say.

'Heavy night, was it?' Clare nods towards the empty bottle of vodka on the bedside cabinet, but Mr Harman seems preoccupied with some other concern.

'I should be at work.' He tries to stand up. 'What's the time?'

'Ten o'clock.'

'I'm supposed to be at a disciplinary hearing.'

'Is that your job, sacking people?' Clare likes to stick up for the underdog.

'They're trying to sack *me*.' He is on his feet. He sways, turns green and sits down again. 'You can stop all this Mr Harman nonsense – call me Neville.'

'I'll make some coffee,' I suggest.

'I'll get it,' says Clare.

'Oh no, you won't.'

'Oh yes, I will. What do you fancy? Espresso, cappuccino or latte? Red Monkey Blend, Organic Peru El Guabo, or Kenyan Elephant Ears?'

In spite of his hangover, Neville raises one eyebrow, while I flash Clare a warning glance. He has every right to be surprised at the depth of our knowledge of his coffee supplies. We might be strangers, but we are his cleaners, and therefore know far more about him than he would probably wish, or believe. We know that Neville owns a state-of-the-art coffee-maker with a frothing nozzle. We know that he collects ceremonial truncheons, but he isn't a policeman. We know that he's some kind of manager for a branch of one of the large supermarkets, but he shops at one of their competitors.

Within half an hour, we know quite a lot more.

While Neville's in the shower, Clare pops out to buy breakfast, and I shove his sheets in the washing machine on a hot wash. Then we sit him down in the armchair in the living room with a plate of fried eggs on his knees, while Clare and I put the babies on the floor and tuck into bacon butties.

'There's no need for you to do all this for me,' Neville keeps repeating. He looks more human now, dressed in a pair of navy track-pants and a grey sweat-top.

'It's all part of the service.' Clare wipes her face with a clean duster before hitting the rest of the doughnuts.

'I'm sorry about the mess, and look – your top's soaked,' Neville goes on. 'You haven't got the knack with the coffee-machine yet.'

'It isn't that. I'm leaking.' Clare picks Fern up then sits down again, cradling her in one arm while she lifts her top and unfastens her bra. 'You don't object?'

If Neville was going to protest, he changes his mind, looks discreetly towards me and continues to eat while Fern latches on with noisy snuffles and sucks.

'You should go back to bed while we clear up.' Clare relaxes back into the sofa and half-closes her eyes.

'I have to go to work.'

'You can't, Neville,' I say. 'You look terrible. Why don't you call in sick? I'll ring them if you like.'

'Would you?'

'I'll pretend I'm your mother.'

'My mother's Irish.'

'Oh, I'm sorry.' I am. 'Not that she's Irish – just that I can't do an Irish accent.'

'I can,' says Clare.

'My mother's in Ireland. You'll have to pretend you're my girlfriend.' Neville hesitates. 'Not that I have a girlfriend any more . . .' He sits back, tipping his plate so that his knife and fork fall clattering onto the floor, a noise which finally wakes Chloe from her slumber. Her head jerks, her hands open and close on the end of rigid arms, and her feet pummel the air. Her face turns red, her chest pumps up and down, and then she opens her mouth and lets rip with an earnumbing scream. Fern merely pauses from sucking just for a moment, more to catch her breath, I suspect, than because of the racket.

'There, there, my poppet.' I unstrap Chloe and pick her up. 'Did that scary man frighten you?'

'Lisa doesn't mean it,' Clare says to reassure Neville.

'I didn't mean to upset him.' Neville has a dribble of egg yolk on his chin.

'Chloe is a girl,' I say sharply, upset that anyone could possibly mistake my darling daughter for a boy. 'Her Babygro is covered in pink rabbits. Do I look like one of those politically correct mothers who dress their boys in pink?'

Neville apologises. 'I just assumed – her seat thingy is blue . . .'

Once we have all calmed down, apart from Chloe who is alternately sobbing and sucking on her tongue, I dig a bottle out from the side of her carryseat where I tucked it earlier, and sit down to feed her.

'Don't you warm Chloe's milk any more?' Clare asks.

'I warmed it before I came out and kept it in an insulating sleeve.' I tip a few drops onto the back of my hand, then slip the teat into Chloe's anxious mouth.

'Warm milk's supposed to be the perfect medium for bacterial growth,' Clare says.

'I steam the bottles and boil the water. It's completely sterile, isn't it?'

'Not in your kitchen, it isn't.' Neville looks up with interest,

14

and Clare retracts very quickly so as not to stain *Maids 4 U*'s reputation. 'Where's your phone?'

While Clare talks, Neville listens.

'Who was it? How did they sound?' he asks when she puts the phone down.

'It was your superior, who said that if you'd put as much effort into your work as you had making up that excuse for your absence, you might have had more chance of keeping your job, or words to that effect. Your ex-girlfriend blabbed. She said that you were quite well until you hit the vodka last night.'

'Josetta wasn't supposed to be in today.'

'She turned up to do an extra shift on the check-outs this morning.' Clare pauses. 'So who is she, this ex of yours?'

'Neville might not want to talk about her,' I cut in quickly.

Clare looks at me wearily. 'Sometimes it's better to get these things off your chest rather than brood. What's she like then?'

Nosy cow!

However, Neville is more than happy to oblige. 'She has the most amazing figure.'

'I meant, what is she like as a person? Is she funny, bubbly, generous?'

'Josetta is the funniest, bubbliest, most generous person I've ever met,' he says tearfully. 'I thought we were going to spend the rest of our lives together.'

'So what went wrong?' says Clare.

'It was my mistake,' Neville says. 'I gave her an engagement ring and asked her to move in with me, but it was too much too soon.'

'How soon?' I ask.

'We'd been together for three weeks and three days. I must have panicked her because she dumped me. She said I was too clingy, and that kissing me was like snogging a rollmop from the deli counter.'

'Did she give the ring back?' Clare says. 'You should have insisted on having it back,' she continues as Neville shakes his head.

'What for – next time?' he says bitterly. 'There won't be a next time.'

'You'll find someone else,' Clare comforts him.

'I don't want anyone else,' he says. 'I wanted *her*. Yesterday

15

I had everything. Today I have nothing, probably not even a bloody job.' He runs his hands through his hair. 'And all because I ordered too many yoghurts.'

'A couple of weeks ago?' says Clare. 'What, those vanilla ones that were on Special?'

'Trust you to notice,' I comment.

Clare ignores me. 'You couldn't arrange to do it again with the raspberry cheesecake desserts, could you?'

'I won't be given another chance,' Neville says glumly.

'No one's going to sack you over a couple of trays of yoghurt, surely?'

'It was half an articulated lorryload.'

Poor Neville, I muse when I'm back at home curled up on the sofa with Chloe, a mug of tea and a copy of *TV Quick*. It's tough when any relationship, however brief, comes to an end, and I'm not as confident as Clare that he'll find another girlfriend soon. Neville seems remarkably naive when it comes to understanding women.

I yawn. Chloe yawns too. When I've been cleaning other people's houses all day, the last thing I want to do is clean my own. I'm shattered and it's all I can do to cook dinner. Jade arrives home at the usual time, eats hers, then disappears into her room to do her homework to the beat of music by McFly. Tony doesn't turn up until I am in the process of emptying the dishwasher of yesterday's crockery so that I can refill it with today's.

'Hi, babe,' he says. 'I'm sorry I'm late. I had an emergency at work, a burst water tank.' He doesn't mention our anniversary even though I've left Clare's card on the kitchen worktop right in front of his face, so I'm glad that I saved him the smallest and ropiest piece of chicken. When I dish it up for him with oven chips, I stab it to check that the juices run clear – that's the only piece of breast he'll be getting tonight. As I dish up peas that have clearly suffered from a double exposure of microwave radiation, the phone rings.

'I'll get it,' Tony says quickly. He returns from the hall a few minutes later, by which time his dinner has gone cold for a second time. He looks a little sheepish.

'That was your mum wishing us a Happy Anniversary. You

16

didn't remind me,' he says accusingly. His voice softens slightly. 'You're always so excited. What happened?'

'I don't know.'

'I expect it's down to lack of sleep.' Tony moves up close and drops his arms around my shoulders. I slide my hands up around his neck, press my nose against his shirt and inhale his scent of musk and non-bio, and unfamiliar smells that he's picked up from the houses he's been working in today. His lips brush my cheek, and my body floods with heat. The hairs on the back of my neck prickle with a mixture of desire and antagonism. I should be able to forgive him for forgetting our anniversary – it's just one out of fourteen, after all – but it's difficult. I've already done more forgiving than a highly sprung mattress to keep this relationship together.

'Why don't you go and have a long soak in the bath, while I open a bottle of wine and spend some quality time with Chloe?' And then? Tony doesn't have to say it. 'I do love you, Lisa.'

'You haven't told me that for ages.'

'Well, when you're an old married couple like us . . .' He smiles.

'Jim tells Clare all the time.'

'You didn't marry Jim,' Tony points out. 'Go on, upstairs.'

I run a bath with a splash of Johnson's Baby Bath and light a cinnamon aromatherapy candle left over from Christmas. I strip off my clothes, lie back in the hot, foaming water, close my eyes and relax. I haven't had the luxury of a whole hour to myself since Chloe was born.

Tony brings me up a glass of lager because there isn't any wine in the rack, and neither of us has the energy to drive down to the offie. I slip into some clean underwear and head downstairs.

In spite of my resistance since Chloe was born, and the small matter of the forgotten anniversary, I find that I'm looking forward to renewing our marital intimacy in the fullest sense. I creep downstairs to find the living room in darkness, except for the blue glow of the fishtank and the flickering of the telly.

'Tone? Where are you?'

I am answered by a soft snore. Tony lies asleep under the baby gym with Chloe in his arms. So much for making it up to me. So much for a night of frenzied lovemaking. I feel hollow.

17

Empty. Angry with him. Angry with Chloe. Angry with myself for being angry.

I look down at where Tony sleeps, at the shadows around his eyes. A wave of exhaustion washes through me, and the anger saps out of my body as I crouch down beside them.

'I love you. I love you both,' I whisper.

Next year, we'll arrange a celebration of our fifteenth anniversary, hold a party and renew our vows. A tiny voice in my head, one that hasn't haunted me for a very long time, niggles: *if you make it that far* . . .

Chapter Two

Did I say yesterday that size doesn't matter? I didn't mean it. Tony has left me the Danny DeVito of all chocolate boxes.

'Dad went out early this morning to buy them,' Jade elaborates. 'He bought a box for Nan too.'

Nan is Tony's mum, Bunny – anyone less fluffy than a rabbit, I can't imagine – and any pleasure that I felt at Tony's belated gesture evaporates. Wouldn't it have been more tactful of him to forget our anniversary entirely, rather than place such an occasion on a par with my mother-in-law's birthday? How much is a box of Milk Tray compared with an Arsenal ticket?

'Where's your father now?'

'He's gone to work.' Jade pauses. 'I've put my clothes in the washing machine so that you don't have to, Mum.' Her soft smile doesn't fool me.

'If this is about the sleepover, the answer's still no.'

'Why do you always assume that I want something when I'm only trying to be nice?'

'And if you want a lift to the bus stop, the answer's no too,' I go on.

'Please . . .'

'You can walk.'

Jade's legs are long enough. She's tall and slim, verging on skinny, more Tony's build than mine.

'My bag's so heavy,' she moans. 'Just think of the damage you're doing to my spine.'

'Your dad's the soft touch, not me.'

'I'll end up like Quasimodo.' Jade flounces off. 'Like you!'

Do I really resemble that notorious hunchback? I twist myself up, trying to see my reflection in the microwave door. I haven't got a stoop, but there's a fatty hump across my shoulders. I look like a cantankerous old dromedary. To console myself, I eat all my chocolates – it doesn't take long – and drink a whole mug of coffee, uninterrupted, with the sun slanting through the window. Bliss. Well, almost . . .

It must be difficult for Jade to adjust to becoming one of two children, instead of the adored only child, and I suppose that I haven't been as sympathetic as I might have been. When I see her and Tony going off together most mornings, laughing like a pair of kookaburra, I feel as if they're almost ganging up against me because I was happier about Chloe's arrival than they were.

The sound of Jade's voice drifts through from the hall. At first I assume that she's commiserating with her baby sister – I've left her upstairs sleeping with Tigger, my favourite of all her soft toys – for their misfortune in being born to a mother such as me, then I realise she's on the phone.

'Yeah, they don't go out much. Yeah, sad, innit.'

I head for the hall, bend down to the skirting and pull the phone plug out of the socket.

'What did you do that for? You've cut me off!'

'You're supposed to be on your way to school.'

Jade reminds me of a prefect from St Trinian's with her glossy lips, dusky eyes and tie dangling around her neck. 'I was talking to Kimberley.'

'You'll be seeing her in less than half an hour.'

'If I had a mobile, Mum, I wouldn't need to use your phone, and I'd pay the bills with the allowance you refuse to give me.' I fold my arms as Jade continues, 'Kimberley has an allowance.'

'Bully for Kimberley. I'd have thought that your pocket money was more than generous.'

Jade stamps her foot. 'Mum, you are so old-fashioned. Kimberley buys all her own clothes and make-up. Manda believes that it's important to give her responsibility for managing a budget.'

'Manda?'

'Kimberley and her brother call their mum Manda.'

I am aware that I am not being fair on Jade. It isn't her fault that I've been reduced to a state of nervous exhaustion. It's Chloe's.

'I might consider lending you my mobile occasionally,' I offer.

'Yours?' Jade snorts with derision. 'It's bigger than a house and doesn't take piccies, or video clips.'

'I'm not aspiring to be the next Steven Spielberg. I bought it for emergencies.'

'I don't see why you wasted your money on buying a mobile anyway. You haven't got any friends except Clare, and you've no idea how to text.'

'Have you quite finished?'

Jade doesn't respond. I head off into the utility where the washing machine is strangely quiet. 'You haven't switched it on!' I yell, but she's already gone, her exit confirmed by the sharp slam of the front door, which sends Chloe off into a hissy fit that continues long after I've changed and fed her and packed the essentials that a baby requires for a single day: spare nappies, wipes, nappy sacks, bottles, muslin squares and soothers. I take just a purse.

On the way to meet Clare, I stop on the High Street so I can nip into the newsagent's. Chloe is snoozing. She looks so peaceful that I can't bear to risk disturbing her by lifting her out of the car. She hardly stopped crying last night and I just couldn't cope right now if she started up again. I know I shouldn't, but I leave her in the car, assuming that I'm more likely to be nabbed by a parking attendant for not buying a ticket than a health visitor for abandoning my baby in a vehicle.

'We've had a run on these today,' says the woman behind the till, when she hands over the last box of Milk Tray that was on the shelves. 'I'll have to send Ahmed down the cash and carry.' She looks me up and down as she hands me my change. 'Congratulations, by the way. I went right off chocolate when I was pregnant. My craving was for oranges.'

Pregnant? I'm tempted to rip the box open and eat all the chocolates right there in front of her, but I restrain myself. I don't want Tony going on at me about how I haven't saved the strawberry creme, his favourite. I stuff the box into Chloe's changing bag when I get back to the car, instead of stuffing the contents.

No one would mistake Mrs Eddington for being pregnant. She's in her eighties. She has knobbly, brown hands on stiff, skinny arms, and when she shuffles around her living room, reorganising her collection of ornaments, she reminds me of a wooden mug tree. At the moment, she's sitting in a fully adjustable armchair with Chloe on her lap. Chloe smiles, trying to focus perhaps on the grey hair that sprouts from a mole on Mrs E's chin. Mrs E didn't have any children because Mr Eddington died just six months after they married.

Clare sits feeding Fern on the sofa. 'How did it go last night, Lisa?'

'It didn't. Tony fell asleep.' A commemorative mug chinks against a Princess Diana doll as I dust. I don't like cleaning when the owner of the house is at home. It makes me clumsy. 'By the time we make love again, I'll have forgotten how.'

'You're going to do what now, dear?' says Mrs E.

'Nothing, Mrs E,' I say brightly. Clare and I can discuss the most scandalous subjects in front of Mrs Eddington because she has as much chance of hearing what we say as she did of marrying into Royalty. She claims to have danced with the Prince of Wales – we can't work out which one. She also claims to have been an atomic scientist. Her corgi, Prince, reputedly a descendant of the Queen's own dogs' bloodlines, lies curled up on a crocheted Union Jack blanket on the second armchair.

Mrs Eddington fiddles with the hearing-aid behind her ear. I relieve her of Chloe, afraid that she might drop her.

'How many times have we suggested that you go up to the Audiology Clinic?' Clare shouts, but it's no use. She ends up scribbling what she's trying to get across on a piece of paper. 'I'll ring to make an appointment for you.'

'Those clinics always run late. I have no desire to wait around with a bunch of old people.'

'Suit yourself.' Clare turns to me. 'I've been thinking about Neville and those strawberry yoghurts.'

'They were vanilla.'

'Camilla?' Mrs E leans forwards and screws up her face. 'I can't understand why Diana made such a fuss. Men have been unfaithful since Adam.'

'They certainly have,' I say, thinking of Tony.

'Not all men.' Clare corrects me. 'Not my Jim.'

I drop the duster and plug the vacuum cleaner in. This is an innovation for Mrs E, who had one of those pushalong carpet sweepers when she first employed us. Cleaning runs in Clare's family – Clare's mum used to do for Mrs E. I'd like to do for Mrs E's dog because he growls whenever I approach his chair. Eventually, he jumps down and aims a sly snap in my direction before heading off towards the living-room door where he pauses briefly to dig about in the top of Chloe's changing bag.

'How about Sue?' says Clare as I revert to the duster, misting the air with Pledge.

'What are you talking about?'

'Sue and Neville.'

'Your sister? What on earth has she got in common with Neville?'

'She likes real coffee.'

'You're clutching at straws. I don't see how you can expect to bring two people together just because they have a mutual love of real coffee. She's older than him for a start.'

'Only by three or four years, and he appreciates old things.' Clare grins. 'Those truncheons, for example.'

Sue is thirty-two and she followed the family tradition, taking on one of the dry-cleaning franchises in the High Street. You'd have thought she'd have met lots of eligible men working there, bringing their suits in, but Sue's very fussy. She has never been quite the same since Jennifer Aniston married Brad Pitt. (Mind you, she's back in with a chance now they've split up.)

'Sue's lonely. Neville's lonely. We'd be doing them both a favour,' Clare goes on.

'How are you planning to get them together?'

'If Mrs E managed to convince the Prince of Wales to dance with her, anything is possible. I'll think of a way.'

Later, Clare tests her powers of persuasion on me, wearing me down until I agree to attend the last postnatal class with her this afternoon. We settle down at the clinic, choosing seats side by side in the half-circle of plastic chairs that Patsy, the community midwife, has arranged in the large room at the end of the hall.

'You don't need instructions on how to be a good mum,' I say. 'You're a natural.'

'You overestimate my confidence,' Clare says before she turns to chat to Nadia, one of the eight regular attendees, strangers united by the trials of motherhood.

I hold Chloe in my arms while the sun streams hot through

the long windows, raising fumes of disinfectant. My T-shirt –
a navy one – sticks to my back. My body is melting in the heat.
Chloe smiles up at me, and my heart melts too.

Patsy pushes a trolley to the front of the class.

'Welcome to today's Parenting Class,' she intones. Her blue
dress is belted very tight at the waist, and her feet hardly
appear to fill her flat, black shoes, the kind Jade wouldn't be
seen dead in. Patsy wears a wedding ring, and I guess she's
in her thirties, but she comes across as being much older with
her hair scraped back into a bun. She stands straightbacked
and straightfaced, like an air hostess demonstrating emergency evacuation procedures, except that, instead of showing
us an oxygen mask, she touches a cuplike contraption to her
chest.

'Next, apply gentle suction to the breast by pressing the start
button.' She frowns. 'It helps, of course, if you plug the breast-
pump into an electrical supply.'

In silent protest, I take a bottle out of my bag.

Chloe takes a couple of gulps and drops off the teat. I try
again. Her stomach gurgles. She screws up her face and turns
her head away to one side. She's had enough already, which
means that I'll have to make up an extra bottle of formula tonight,
but it's worth it just to prove that, although breast may be best,
the bottle is good enough for me and my baby . . .

I put Chloe over my shoulder, supporting her head. As I rub
her back, she belches. Loudly.

'I beg your pardon,' says Patsy sternly.

Chloe burps again and shoots a string of white, curdled vomit
down my top. I dig around for a muslin cloth to wipe away
the sick. Patsy hands me a tissue with a weary, 'How on earth
is that child going to survive with a mother like you?' look on
her face. I wipe at the sick, spreading it around, while Patsy
lectures on the toe-curling subject of cracked nipples.

Every now and then a shrill whistle interrupts her – some
OAPs are waiting for their Audiology appointments outside in
the corridor. Chloe snuggles up against my shoulder, oblivious,
it seems, to the smell, as Patsy goes on to talk about incontin-
ence, explaining how to feel for our pelvic-floor muscles, which
is all very well if you have any left.

'Not now,' Patsy says quickly, in case Dippy Di as we call

her should start groping her nether regions in front of the group. 'In the privacy of your home.'

Privacy? What is that? When you have a baby you become so accustomed to exposing yourself to anyone who asks that you lose all inhibitions. Doctors, midwives, dustmen, come and have a butcher's . . . Clare even found herself baring her buttocks to her brother-in-law when the nurse on the maternity ward, assuming that he was Jim, carried on giving her an injection.

If Tony and I could have one night in private together – truly alone – I believe that I could make things right between us. I close my eyes as last night's lack of sleep starts to catch up with me. I picture a desert island, the kind you might see in a newspaper cartoon: a mound of sand stippled with pen and ink; in the centre an insubstantial palm tree. Me and Tony. Grains of warm sand trickling through his fingers, spilling down my front. His lips close to mine . . . We are about to kiss when an almighty bang brings me back with a jolt.

Like a herd of curious cows, we all look towards the window. Outside, a black Jeep has veered across two parking spaces and smacked straight into the side of a much smaller car. Patsy screams, and runs for the door. I assume she's seen something that I missed, that she's off to administer First Aid to the occupants of the stricken vehicle, but when we all reach the car park, Patsy is haranguing the Jeep driver who is still in the driving seat, her face as white as a baby's bottom.

'What have you done to my Micra? Do something. Back off. Put it in reverse! You have got reverse?'

'I'm not sure. I can't find it.' The driver scrunches the gears. The engine strains against the handbrake. Suddenly, the Jeep shoots forwards again, pushing the Micra sideways towards Clare's car.

'Stop!' yells Patsy. 'Stop!'

Too late. Patsy's bun has collapsed and her hair is all over the place. The Micra is a write-off.

'My foot slipped,' the driver wails out of her window. 'I'm not used to this machine yet. Greg – my husband – thought it would keep the baby safe. The roads are so dangerous around here.'

'So are car parks,' someone – Nadia, I think – mutters behind me.

'This is so exciting,' breathes Dippy Di.

Clare turns. 'You should get out more.'

The driver slides out hesitantly. She's tall and slim, with the tiniest bump of tummy visible beneath a pair of pink cropped chinos and spotted, ruched V-neck top. Her hair, strawberry blonde, is thick and lustrous. In fact, I can't believe that she's had a baby ever, let alone in the past few weeks.

'Patsy, I'm *so* sorry!'

'I'd like to say that I'm glad you could join us today, Jacqui,' Patsy says. 'Oh, come inside for some tea. I think we're both in shock.'

'What about my car?' Clare examines her paintwork. 'You've dented my panel.'

Tears catch on the long lashes that ring Jacqui's hazel eyes. 'I'll give you my address and phone number. I'll have to ask Greg for the name of our insurance company.'

'Oh, it's all right.' Clare grins suddenly. 'You've dented a dent that was already there.'

To my relief, because I don't like to see anyone upset, Jacqui's lips curve into a small smile. 'I'm having a hideous day. I've managed to get myself and Ethan out of the house before midday for the first time ever, and look what's happened.' She takes a couple of designer bags out of the Jeep, along with a handbag to rival one of those Hippo Bags that you can order instead of a skip to take your household rubbish away, and a litre bottle of Evian water, before she picks her baby out of the back seat. I say baby, but he's enormous. He has a big round face and rolls of fat around his neck. With his white tracksuit and hat, he looks as if he might have been fathered by the Michelin Man.

Back inside, Patsy winds up the meeting and directs us to the drinks machine so we can spend some time 'sharing our responses to what we've learned today' over cups of tea. Instead, Clare and I arrange to meet up with Nadia, Dippy Di and a couple of the other mums for coffee one morning next week.

'I wouldn't bother with the tea, Jacqui,' I advise when she stops scrabbling around in her handbag, looking, I assume, for change for the machine. 'It's revolting. I'm Lisa, by the way.'

'Hi. I couldn't help overhearing your plans to meet. I'm free next week. I could bring one of my cakes along.' Jacqui tips her head to one side. 'It would be great to meet a supportive group

26

of people who understand what I'm going through at the moment. None of my close friends have babies.'

'Come along and join us.'

'You're very welcome,' Clare backs me up.

'Thanks.' Jacqui seems distracted. 'I get here just as it's time to go home, and now I'm not sure what I've done with my car keys.'

'Are you three all right there?' says Patsy as we're sifting through Jacqui's luggage. 'Only I've got to get my car sorted.'

'We're fine thanks, Patsy,' I say at the same time as Jacqui confirms that she has lost her keys.

'If you want any advice, you have my number,' Patsy says. 'On looking after Baby, or how to drive. Or,' she adds, on making a brief return from the car park, 'where to find your keys. They're locked in the back of your Jeep. How did you manage that?'

'It doesn't matter how they got there,' says Jacqui, 'how am I going to get them out?'

'I'll leave that with you.' Patsy waves goodbye.

Jacqui makes a phone call. Her husband, Greg, has the spare key, and he's halfway up the M6 Toll Road with a set of dentures. 'Oh, he has all his own teeth,' Jacqui explains quickly. 'He's a courier. He's carried everything from gearbox replacements to hearts for transplants.'

'If Jim was here, he'd smash the window,' says Clare.

'I'll call Tony,' I offer. 'He'll know what to do.'

There are husbands who wouldn't consider abandoning their work to help a damsel in distress, but my Tony isn't one of them. Sure enough, before too much time has elapsed, my knight in shining armour comes whizzing up in his white van. The windows are down and the Black-Eyed Peas are playing "Hey Mama" on the radio. Tony slams on the brakes, flings open the door, and the throb of the engine is replaced by the thrill of my pulse as I watch him jump out and land catlike on the tarmac in battered brown workboots. He strides towards us in muscle-hugging jeans with rips and frayed threads of stonewashed denim at the knees, and a navy vest. In one hand he carries his keys, in the other a piece of packing tape. His eyes light up when he sees me and Chloe.

I suppose I shouldn't be surprised that, in spite of his messy hair and slightly crooked grin, I still fancy him after fourteen

27

years of marriage. It was love at first sight, after all.

I was twenty-three and Tony twenty-seven. I was working for a plumbing supplies company, based in an industrial unit off the Purley Way. As I was responsible for handling complaints, I'd been called downstairs to negotiate with a disgruntled customer. The sight of this tall, long-legged hunk of a man with a heartstopping smile wiped all thoughts of company policy out of my mind. He showed me where the joint had failed on one of the radiators he'd purchased.

'There.' He pointed to the split.

'There?' I said, and our fingers touched.

'It isn't hot.' He grinned as I snatched my hand away.

I was though. My face burned. My body was on fire.

'Would you like a refund or an exchange?' I asked slowly.

'I'd like your phone number,' he teased, but I refused to give it to him.

Either our radiators were rubbish, or Mr Anthony Baker was deliberately damaging them. He kept bringing them back with their white coating crazed, or their screw-ends cross-threaded, and then, when I finally plucked up the courage to ask him if he was taking advantage of my good nature, he said that he'd like to and asked me out.

'How's my little girl?' Tony bends down and picks Chloe up. He kisses her cheek, wrinkles his nose and hands her back to me.

'She's been sick.' I turn to our new acquaintance. 'This is Jacqui.'

A cloud passes the sun. The leaves on the trees darken a shade. Jacqui smiles at Tony, tucks a curl of loose hair behind one ear, and I suddenly feel rather dowdy in her presence.

'We've met already,' Tony says.

'Tony's a handy man to have around,' says Jacqui, addressing me. 'He changed my cold tank last night. I told him he could switch the water off and leave it till the morning, but he insisted.' She turns back to Tony. 'I forgot to ask you for your card. I wonder if you'd come round and quote me for a new bathroom. I'll be in desperate need of a plumber once I've finished with the kitchen fitter.'

Is it my imagination, or are Tony's eyes straying to the gold pendant that trembles in Jacqui's cleavage? Rain starts to fall. It stains his vest.

'Go back inside and wait,' Tony says. 'Leave this to me.'

Clare, Jacqui and I take shelter in the porch with our babies while Tony tries to break into the Jeep. From the opposite side of the car park rush a pair of feisty pensioners, brandishing their brollies.

'Stop that, young man! This is a citizen's arrest!'

'Leave him alone!' I dump Chloe on Clare and dash out into the rain as Tony's assailants force him back from the tailgate which is open now, towards the bushes at the edge of the car park. 'This is my husband.' I dodge between Tony and the OAPs. 'He's helping a friend of mine. She's locked her keys in the car.'

'You can't be too careful,' one says.

'It's very public-spirited of you to tackle someone you thought was a car thief,' I continue. 'You shouldn't feel embarrassed at making a mistake.'

'The youth of today,' sighs the other one before they walk away.

Tony winks at me. I can't help smiling.

'It's quite a compliment to be called a youth at forty-two.' Tony's vest sticks to his skin. His cheeks glisten. 'You're wet,' he adds softly, taking my hand. I can feel his blood pulsing hot in his fingertips, contrasting with the cool sting of the rain. My chest tightens. Tony might be no good at anniversaries, but he is a kind man, and I thank him for the chocolates with better grace than I was intending.

'Have you saved me one?'

'Of course.'

'Perhaps you'll give these to Jacqui.' He hands me a set of keys. 'I must get back to work. See you later, love.' He moves away swiftly, his buttocks rippling beneath his jeans, and his vest tucked up to one side, revealing a flash of lightly tanned loin. When he drives towards the car park exit, he leans out of the window and bangs on the door with the flat of his hand. 'You have remembered that we're going to my mum's tonight, Lisa? I said we'd be there at about seven.'

'How can I be expected to remember something when it's the first I've heard of it?' I complain to Clare after Tony's driven off, but she's in too much of a hurry to take any notice.

'Quickly, Lees.' She slips her shades on. 'Jacqui's loading her stuff into the Jeep. Let's hit the road before she does.' We accelerate out of the car park, faster than Thelma and Louise.

If I imagined that I could make up the best excuses for not going to Bunny's tonight, Jade surpasses me.

'I'd rather be stuck at the top of Dragon's Fury with Jack Hammond,' she rants.

Dragon's Fury is the rollercoaster at Chessington World of Adventures. I don't know anything about Jack Hammond.

'Who's he?' I sip my tea in the kitchen, trying to avoid looking at the splatters of ketchup on the units. I'll clean them some-time. Tomorrow . . .

'One of the boys at school.' She grimaces and gurns. 'He's minging.'

'Jade!' Haven't I brought her up to respect other people? Apparently not.

'In fact, I'd rather go to school than Nan's,' Jade goes on.

'I'd prefer to be at the dentist having all my teeth pulled out without anaesthetic, but it's Nan's birthday and she'll be upset if we don't go.'

'Why are you always doing things you don't want to do, Mum?'

A good question which I don't answer. I suppose that family life, like marriage, is about give and take, so I will give again, and go.

'What's this that Dad's scribbled on the calendar?' Jade says suddenly. 'I don't have to go to Granny's tomorrow night as well, do I?'

'Granny's coming here to sit with you and Chloe while we have an evening out.'

'It isn't fair. You're always going out.'

'I can't remember the last time I went anywhere special with your dad.' I pause. 'Have you finished your homework?'

'You're always going on about homework.'

'It's never too early to think about what you want to do when you leave school.' It is one of my greatest regrets that I didn't think about it at all. I knew from the age of five that I would marry and have kids, but I didn't plan a glittering career. It didn't seem important. My mother didn't have one.

'I'm going to work in a nail bar,' Jade says emphatically.

'You'll have to wear a uniform. You'd hate it. Don't you want to go on to higher education?'

'I'm going to apply to go to college to do a nail technician's course.' Jade smirks at me. She knows she's winding me up.

'A nail technician isn't likely to change the world. Why not consider something more rewarding?'

'Like cleaning, you mean?'

'No! Oh Jade, I mean a proper career.' I lower my voice. 'I only want what's best for you.'

'You don't know anything about me any more.' Jade's eyes flash with annoyance.

'We'll talk about it when you're not in one of your moods.'

'I'm not in a bloody mood.'

'Don't swear!'

'If you and Dad had your way, I'd be locked in a cell with bare walls.' Her eyes fill with tears. I hold out my arms to give her a hug, but she won't let me near her. 'You treat that baby better than you treat me. You're always dissing me.'

'Dissing? What language is that?'

'Disrespecting.' The door slams in my face. Footsteps hammer up the stairs. Another door slams. The house shakes.

At the noise, Chloe, who has been asleep in her carryseat with us in the kitchen, opens her eyes and cries. It's my fault. I'm the one whose actions have guaranteed that my marriage will be put through the hormonal hell that characterises adolescence for a second time. By the time I'm in my seventies, I'm going to give the same impression as Tony's parents: that I have suffered; that quiet fortitude is a virtue to be admired.

When Tony returns from work, he drives us to West Wickham. Bunny and Philip live in the same three-bed semi that they've shared all their married life; it's where they brought up the three daughters who arrived before their much-wanted son.

'Good evening.' Philip shakes my hand very briefly. His fingers are cold, his greeting frosty, and I've always imagined that the blood in his veins is the same consistency as a Slush Puppy. He is dressed in his customary outfit for these occasions of navy blazer and tie. The tie bears the logo of his local Allotment Association: an onion.

He shows us into the living room which is more packed than an Indian express train. Bunny is holding court with Tony's

31

sisters – Joanne, Bridget and Sally – and their families. When she stands to greet me, she towers over me, tall and elegant in an ice-blue skirt suit, her silver-grey hair set into waves, and reeking of violets and rose petals. She kisses the air to the left of my cheek. 'How are you, Lisa?' she says. Without waiting for an answer, she adds in the loudest whisper so that everyone hears, 'The button on your trousers is undone.'

'Your trousers will fall down,' giggles Kayleigh, one of Sally's kids. A ripple of mirth disturbs the sea of bored faces. Blushing, I tug my top down to cover my bulging waistline, and perch on one arm of the sofa. It won't break. It's made of solid wood. All their furniture is. They saved avidly for each piece. When I once mentioned that Tony and I might take out credit on a new leather sofa, Bunny reminded me that she and Philip sat on milk crates for the first ten years of their marriage. Philip began his working life as a milkman, and ended it as a civil servant in Immigration. Bunny never worked outside the home.

The atmosphere is like the one on Mars – almost non-existent – although Chloe is on top form. According to Bunny, Chloe is overdressed, and she is passed around the gathering, cooing and smiling, being stripped of her layers like a Pass the Parcel. Jade stands beside me.

'I'm so glad that everyone made time in their busy schedules to come and see us today,' Bunny says. 'And thank you so much for bringing me such lovely presents.' As she's running her eye over the Lilliput Lane cottage, an Oopsie Daisy Fairie and a new Coalport bone china figurine on the mantelpiece – at least one person in the family has a modicum of good taste – I glance towards Tony who's still standing in the doorway. He steps forward with a box of chocolates. A big box. Much bigger than the one he gave me.

'Oh, thank you, Tony and Jade. What a wonderful surprise. And Chloe.' Bunny sucks a tiny whistle of air past her false teeth. 'And Lisa.'

'Now that everyone's here, shall we cut the cake?' asks Philip, thawing slightly.

'Bridget made the sponge, Joanne iced the top and Sally arranged the candles.' Bunny oozes pride like the jam from the side of the cake. 'It's quite a family affair.' Bunny is a traditional housewife, not a Princess Style Domestic Diva. She's the only person I know who stews the chicken carcase after a Sunday roast.

After we've sung Happy Birthday, and Philip has relit the candles several times for the grandchildren to have a turn at blowing them out and spitting all over the cake, Philip passes round the tiniest slivers on white cotton napkins.

'Thank you, Philip,' Bunny gushes. 'I know you'd prefer to be at the allotment this evening.'

'Mum said that she'd rather be at the dentist,' Jade pipes up as she stuffs a piece of birthday cake into her mouth. The gathering falls silent. You can hear the crumbs dropping on the carpet.

'I didn't,' I say hotly. 'I just mentioned that I was rather tired.'

'I knew that going back to work so soon after the birth wasn't a good idea. None of my girls did – I wouldn't let them,' Bunny says. 'I don't suppose Chloe's sleeping through the night either, if the bags under Tony's eyes are anything to go by.'

I look to my husband for support, but he's nodding off in the corner on the floor.

Bunny purses her lips. 'Now I'd never interfere in the way you bring up your children, Lisa, but I used to have a strict routine with mine.'

My back is up. How many times have I heard this before?

'I'd bath Tony at six, give him a feed and settle him down in his cot in his *own* room before *The Archers*. If he cried, I left him to cry.'

'Oh, I've tried leaving Chloe to cry.' I'm not fibbing to please my mother-in-law. Twice I've walked out of the house with my head down and my hands over my ears, all the way down York Road and as far as Kingsway Avenue where my conscience got the better of me. 'I'll never do it again.'

'Mum doesn't mean to sound cruel,' says Joanne. 'She did it with all of us.'

'And look how you've all turned out.' My hand flies to my mouth. Tony's awake now and up on his feet. He turns to his mother.

'What Lisa means is that we're a credit to you, Mum. It can't have been easy looking after four children. Lisa's exhausted keeping up with just two.' He glances at his watch. 'In fact, it's time I took her home.'

33

Bunny frowns. I'm dragging her little boy away, breaking up her party.

'Before you go,' says Philip, 'you must have some rhubarb.'

Some people would consider that Philip is doing me a great favour. Fresh vegetables from the allotment grown without chemicals. Free food to supplement the week's groceries. Another flipping task for me. I have to chop it up and stew it, and I don't even like rhubarb, but before I can say, 'Please don't bother,' I find myself sitting in the car with an armful of stems.

'Couldn't you and Jade have been a little more tactful?' Tony says on the way home.

'I was,' says Jade. 'What Mum actually said was that she'd rather have all her teeth extracted without anaesthetic.'

'I don't understand why you dislike my mother so much, Lisa. Her advice must be worth listening to.'

'I don't dislike her. I just don't like her interfering.'

'Your mum's always around ours, monitoring my lager consumption to protect my liver. Do you hear me complaining?'

'Frankly, yes.'

'Not to her face.'

'At least she offers to babysit. Your mum never does.'

'Dad, have you thought about, you know, that allowance you might be going to give me soon?' Jade asks over the hum of the engine and the intermittent tick tick tick of the indicators. 'How can I learn to be responsible for managing my money if I haven't got any money to manage?'

'I can't think about that just now.'

'When then?' Jade wheedles.

'When I've talked to your mum.'

'Can't you talk to her now? She's right beside you.'

Tony ignores her request.

'You haven't seen any paperwork of mine, Lisa?' he asks.

'What kind of paperwork?'

'Just papers. An envelope.'

'Have you lost something?'

Tony shakes his head. If he can't be straight with me about those Arsenal tickets, why should I be straight with him? I let him stew. In fact, we all stew in a humid fog because the air conditioning's broken.

Chloe falls asleep just as we turn into the drive.

34

'She's gone, Tone,' I whisper.

'Thank goodness for that.'

'My allowance?' says Jade.

'Sh!' I try so hard not to wake Chloe, carrying her carefully up the stairs in her carryseat. In the bedroom, I unfasten the strap, sliding the two sections of the metal clip fastening apart very slowly. Praying, I slip my hands under her, one under her bottom, one behind her head. Hardly daring to breathe, I lift her, transfer her to the carrycot, and lower her down. When I was six, I had a doll whose eyes snapped shut as I laid her in a pram made from a cardboard box. As Chloe's back makes contact with the mattress, hers do exactly the opposite.

I force a smile to reassure her that I'm close by and she's safe. Her lips wobble, and her eyes fill with tears. She opens her mouth and lets rip.

'Leave her,' Tony says from behind me.

'She's hungry.' I pick her up. She sticks her fist in her mouth and sucks on it.

'Sometimes I think you do that deliberately,' Tony says. 'It suits you for Chloe to be awake just now, doesn't it?'

'Are you suggesting that I woke her up? I'm not a bloody masochist.'

'It's like the other night when it suited you for me and Chloe to be asleep so that you didn't have to go to bed with me.'

'Tony, that isn't true.'

Tony's arms slip around my waist, his body presses against my back and his lips against the side of my neck, and the hurt that I feel at his suggestion that I might be trying to avoid making love with him begins to fade.

'I'm sorry, Lisa. I guess tonight isn't going to be the night either.' With a sigh, he straightens. 'Hey, what's the difference between in-laws and out-laws?'

'I don't know.' I kiss Chloe's forehead. Tony's grinning. I can tell from his voice.

'Out-laws are wanted,' he says.

35

Chapter Three

Tonight is the night. I'm buzzing like the electric shredder in the spare room that we use as Tony's office. Tonight, Tony and I are going out on the razzle. We'll have a meal and a few drinks before we come home and make love, Chloe permitting. My mum jumped at the chance to babysit this weekend. I'm not sure why. She isn't usually quite so keen.

She did try to reassure me about Tony and the anniversary present, but when I asked if Dad ever forgot their anniversary, she had to admit that he hadn't. My parents have the perfect marriage.

Standing beside the desk with Chloe dozing in her carryseat on the floor, I shred an application for a credit card. I am a housewife, mother and cleaner. What point is there in using a shredder when I haven't got an identity to steal? However, it is satisfying to watch the curly strands of paper falling into the box beneath. Addictive. I shred a piece of blank printer paper then an old envelope. Hang on – the stuff coming out isn't just paper. It's card, printed card. My blood runs cold. Those Arsenal tickets. I've just shredded what remains of my marriage.

Tony pops his head around the door.

Do I confess? Ruin the evening? Grinning, Tony holds out a pair of pants – a posing pouch with *Horny Hunk* printed on the front. I decide that it can wait until tomorrow.

'These, or the shark?' He stuffs the pants into his pocket, and takes out another pair and slips them over his hand. When he spreads his fingers, the shark opens its mouth, revealing rows of white teeth.

'Surprise me.'

Tony grabs me, pushes me back against the desk. I put my arms around his neck, and wriggle round so that he can't see the contents of the shredder.

'Mum!'

'Jade?' Tony groans. We draw apart quickly, and Tony shoves his hand into his pocket. I'm not sure who is most embarrassed, me, Tony or Jade.

'What do you want?' Tony asks.

I find myself marvelling at how surprising life can be when Jade requests a binbag so she can tidy her bedroom. I marvel at how Tony and I had this house extended to give us more space, yet we are all assembled in one tiny room.

'I didn't know you knew what a binbag was,' Tony says, much to my annoyance.

'Don't discourage her. Would you like some help, Jade?'

'No way, Mum. I can do it. I don't want you throwing my stuff away, do I?'

She's referring to the pair of shorts that I contributed to Clare's most recent car-booting excursion – they were so faded and small that I assumed that they'd shrunk in the wash, but Jade said that she'd just bought them with a whole month's pocket money.

I'm relieved though, that she doesn't want my assistance. I have so much to do: make up Chloe's bottles for tomorrow – I don't want to be mixing formula milk at midnight; unload the dishwasher; bring the laundry in; shave my legs; find some clothes that still fit me.

Several hours later, as I finish applying a sachet of face-mask that smells like fresh gooseberries, the doorbell rings. Typical.

'Jade, you get it!' I yell, but she can't hear me over the bass beat of her music. 'Tone? That'll be Mum.' Tony is singing in the shower. The face-mask has dried from transparent to pale green, but there's nothing I can do about it. I head downstairs and answer the door. I am greeted by a small man with a big smile, bald head and goatee beard, who appraises my mumsy T-shirt and bare legs.

'If you've come for the Kleeneze catalogue, I left it out with my order last week.'

This man – in his early forties, I'd guess – gazes at me through prominent, bloodshot eyes. He's wearing the most unflattering poloshirt I've ever seen, all horizontal stripes in orange, cream and brown.

'It's Lisa, isn't it?' he says.

Do I know this man? Have I met him somewhere before? I tuck myself as far as I can behind the door, in case he's some kind of nutter, or a TV presenter who's been sent to declutter my house.

'Thanks so much for this,' he says earnestly. 'It's great to meet you after all that Jade's told us about you.'

'Er, who are you?' I scratch my forehead. My fingernails catch the edge of the face-mask and a strip tears away. I try to stick it back on. I feel like a fruit fool, trying to keep my face on in front of a complete stranger.

'Colin.' He holds out his hand. 'I'm Kimberley's dad. This is so kind of you, offering to look after Kimberley tonight. Manda and I – that's my partner – we haven't had a night out together for weeks.'

My lips start to form the words, 'And us,' but what I actually say is, 'Fine, it's no bother. We weren't doing anything special tonight.'

Colin digs around in the saggy pocket of a pair of fawn trousers and thrusts a piece of paper at me. 'That's my mobile number.'

The hairs on the back of my neck prickle. He's too familiar. Too pushy. However, I recall that my daughter has probably told him that I have condoned the arrangement, and then that it couldn't possibly have been Jade who planned this, but Kimberley.

'We'll collect her tomorrow afternoon. Jade says you often go up to the Harrow for Sunday lunch.'

'I don't know where she got that from. We've been once in the past five years.'

'As soon as Manda saw your daughter, she recognised a kindred spirit. They're both highly creative.' Colin turns. 'For the love of Mike, pick that up, Kimbo!' he yells at a girl who's staggering across the pavement with a sleeping bag, campbed and a sports holdall slung over her shoulder. Jade, who's been standing at my elbow, dashes out to pick up the clutch bag that the girl has dropped. How much luggage do you need for one night?

'Hi, Lisa.' The girl smiles, nervously perhaps, as she strolls up to join her father on the doorstep. Green eyes peer out from under a fluoro-pink cap. Black hair hangs loose over her shoulders and a skimpy vest top. Her feet are clad in what appear to be her school shoes which don't complement the retro print mini-skirt.

So this is the little minx who's been leading my Jade astray?

'We're making friends so quickly.' Colin smiles coquettishly. 'I didn't realise that this area would have such a lively scene.'

'I find that hard to believe.'

'Oh, you're being too harsh, Lisa.' Colin cocks his head to one side.

'I am. I mean, the people who've lived here for years do stop and chat in the street, but newcomers tend to keep their distance. I suppose it's the same wherever you go.'

'Indeed,' says Colin. 'Thanks again.' He takes a step closer and I can smell mint mouthwash on his breath. His gaze lingers on my breasts and I'm acutely aware that I'm not wearing a bra. I think he fancies me. I watch Colin trot off to his car, an old white Audi. I'm sure he does.

'What's going on?' Tony pads up barefoot behind me.

'This is Kimberley,' I say icily. 'She's come for a sleepover.' I flash him a glance. He knows what it means. *I want a word with you.* 'You take Kimberley's things upstairs, Jade, and don't you go thinking you've got away with this.'

'Got away with what, Mum?' she says innocently.

'You know what I mean.'

Tony turns me round by the shoulder. 'Why on earth did you say she could stay tonight of all nights?'

I can hardly speak, my speech inhibited by both the nerve of his accusation and the constraint of the face-mask at the side of my mouth.

'I didn't,' I say after a struggle. 'I'm assuming that you did.'

Tony frowns, then we both look towards the stairs at the same time.

'Jade!' Too late. Our daughter has scarpered.

'What are we going to do, Tone?'

'Send her home, of course.'

'Keep your voice down. I don't want Kimberley to feel unwelcome.'

'She is unwelcome.'

'I'll ring Mum and tell her not to bother coming. Perhaps it won't be so bad.' I run my hand down Tony's chest. 'Jade will have company while we snuggle up in front of the telly with a glass of wine.'

'And Chloe sleeps?' Tony curves his arm around my waist and gives me a rueful squeeze. You can't have everything.

At nine o'clock, I am kicking about in a jogsuit over a camisole, and knickers to rival Bridget Jones's. Tony and I have been banished to the kitchen with the portable telly, so that the girls can watch DVDs in the living room. I gave them crisps, sandwiches and soft drinks, but it doesn't stop them coming in now to share our takeaway.

Jade snatches a spare rib from the table.

'Hey, that's the last one.' I take a prawn ball instead and turn to Kimberley. 'Do you like your new school?'

'No,' she says bluntly. 'I hate it. I didn't choose to move here.'

Jade stares intently at a pot of sweet and sour sauce as if she's praying for me not to open my big mouth again, but Tony tells her that the price of food is conversation. Chloe is tucked in the crook of Tony's arm which makes her look very small.

'Why did you move then?' Tony asks.

'Oh, boring family stuff,' Kimberley says unhappily. 'Dad said that he and Manda – she's my mum – should make a fresh start.'

I am itching to find out more, but out of respect for Kimberley's feelings I keep my mouth shut as she continues, 'I hate school. So does Ali, my brother.'

'He's in the sixth form, and he's in a band,' says Jade, unable to disguise the admiration in her voice.

I start munching through the rest of the prawn crackers – there's a free bag with the order and it seems a shame to waste them. I feel bloated and fat, and I bet J-Lo doesn't stuff herself with Chinese when she's planning a hot night. I'd also wager that she doesn't have to wait for two teenage girls to fall asleep in the room next door.

When Tony and I do eventually go up to bed, Chloe is already sleeping. Tony kisses the tips of his fingers and lays them briefly on her forehead.

'Nighty night, angel,' he whispers before he jumps into bed

41

with me, dressed in nothing but his shark pants with its jaws open wide. 'I'm going to bite you, Mrs Baker.'

'Not yet.' We lie flat on our backs, side by side but not touching, wondering if we would be heard above the sound of Maroon 5 if we did make love . . .

Tony pinches me to keep me awake. I pinch him. I fetch coffee made with two teaspoons of caffeine per cup which has a disastrous effect on my bladder, necessitating several trips to the toilet. On my way back for the last time, I stop outside Jade's room. I can hear her and Kimberley giggling, but not what they're saying. I press my ear to the door.

'I don't fancy Jack Hammond.' Jade's voice. 'He has more spots than the 101 Dalmatians put together.'

'He wants you for his laydee,' giggles Kimberley.

The door flies open, bashing the side of my head. Jade's in full make-up and Minnie Mouse pyjamas. Kimberley wears a cow-print dressing-gown. She looks up from a copy of *Cosmopolitan*. Why do they want to grow up so fast?

'Mum! Are you spying on us?'

'I've just come to say goodnight.' I am still reeling. 'By the way, have you seen a box of Milk Tray anywhere?'

Jade frowns. Obviously not. I don't know what I did with it and I could do with a chocolate fix, albeit a small one. I retire to bed again and snuggle up with Tony. Dare we kiss? We fumble in the dark like teenagers trying to hide from their parents, except that this is the other way round.

Tony's lips smother mine, and my blood starts to thrill as he presses the hot, hard length of his body against my yielding curves, but before we can connect, male to female, Tony hesitates.

'Just a minute.' He reaches out to the bedside table then swears. 'I've dropped it. I ripped the packet open, and it pinged out.'

'Didn't you buy more condoms after Chloe was born? Haven't you got a spare somewhere?'

'No,' Tony says after a moment's hesitation.

I smile wryly to myself. 'Next time, choose some luminous ones like Chloe's dummy.' It glows in the dark at the end of Chloe's carrycot – we can find it when she spits it out, without switching the light on.

Tony slides out of bed onto the floor. I follow him, stifling a giggle as we crawl around on our hands and knees, searching for the lost condom.

'I'm going to have the snip, Lees.'

'That sounds a bit drastic. Isn't it painful?' I pause. 'We don't make love often enough to worry about using an irreversible method of contraception, do we?'

'I'm hoping we'll be able to get back to how we were, once Chloe's in her own room.'

'Shh! You'll wake her.'

'Jade slept on her own from a week after she was born. Ouch!' Tony curses out loud. 'I bumped my head.'

I hold my breath. Chloe snuffles then falls silent.

'Where are you?' I follow Tony's shadow in the line of light under the bedroom door.

'Over here. Come and kiss me better.'

'Have you found it yet?'

'No, but I've found you . . .' Tony takes me in his arms and finds my mouth with his. My elbow knocks against the dressing-table, sending packets of babywipes and tubes of heavy-duty moisturiser thumping down onto the floor.

Chloe cries out. Tony and I freeze. I can hear my heart beating. Chloe lets out a wail. It's like a question: Mummy, are you there? I bite my tongue, torn between my husband and my baby. Chloe cries again. It's no good. I can't leave her alone and upset. She wants me. She needs me. She comes first.

'Chlo—'

'Ignore her,' Tony mutters. 'She'll have to learn to wait.'

'She'll wake the girls.' I try to pull away, but Tony holds me tight. Chloe's cries crescendo and merge into a hell-raising scream. The door flies open. The room floods with light. Two faces gaze down at us.

'What's going on?' says Jade.

What does it look like? We're on our knees in an embrace on the floor, the lost condom now clearly visible at Jade's feet.

'We thought someone was murdering the baby, didn't we, Kimberley?'

My face flushes and my knees creak as I stand up and grab Chloe from the carrycot. Tony stands up too, turning away towards the wall to hide the shark's open jaws.

43

'Go back to bed, Jade,' he says. 'Now!'

For once, Jade, perhaps shocked by what she has seen, does as she's told.

'I hope that Kimberley doesn't report this back to her parents.' I hug Chloe against my breast. She's sobbing quietly.

'If she does, she won't be allowed to stay with us again.'

So it isn't all bad, I think, as I take Chloe downstairs and switch on the telly in the kitchen, letting the pictures flash mute. With Chloe still in my arms, I manage to extract a bottle from the fridge and feed her. Once she's fed, she lies back contentedly, picking at the strap of my camisole.

I love everything about her: the milk spots speckled across her nose, her tiny neck that's still too weak to support her head, the soft spot in the top of her skull . . .

I sigh to myself. It's true, what can happen to the best laid plans . . . I still haven't been laid.

'I can't stay at home with that wet, fallen leaf for one more minute, or I'll divorce him.' It's eight o'clock on the Monday morning after the sleepover, and my mum is standing on the doorstep. Next-door's ginger cat is rubbing its chin on the gate pillar.

I don't understand. I've been awake half the night. I have a toothbrush in one hand and Tony's lunchbox in the other.

'I'm talking about your dad. He's driving me mad.'

'Since when did he become a fallen leaf?'

'That's what the Japanese call retired men who hang around the house, irritating the hell out of their wives.' Mum pauses. 'Are you trying to tell Tony that he has smelly breath, Lisa, only you're trying to pack a toothbrush into his lunchbox.' She relieves me of both objects, leaving my hands free to give her a hug.

'I thought as it was such a nice morning that I'd walk over and sit with Chloe here while you go off to work,' Mum continues. 'She'll be happier in her own environment, and I can have the telly on without *him*, old Victor Meldrew, complaining about it.'

She looks a little too glamorous for the role of childminder in cropped navy trousers, a white shortsleeved blouse and flat gold strappy sandals. Her ash-blonde hair falls in soft curls to the nape of her neck and across her forehead that's hardly lined at sixty-five – the effect, she claims, of good genes and Yogalates. I do worry that looking after Chloe for me while I'm at work might conflict with some of her many pastimes, and that she might suggest that Dad, who has none, has the baby. Mum wouldn't let him do so much as change a nappy when my brother and I were babies, and his lack of hands-on experience would worry me.

'Hellooo, Tony, love.' Mum pushes past me. I close the door and turn to find Tony in the hallway with a towel around his middle and his hair wet and spiky from the shower. He backs away from Mum's embrace, rolling his eyes at me over her shoulder, like Jade does when she's in one of her moods, and Chloe when she has wind. Excessive mobility of the eyeballs is a Baker trait.

'Thanks for this, Mum,' I say.

'It's no trouble.' She smiles. 'You know that I'm more than happy to help. Chloe's such a darling. She sleeps all day.'

'Which is why she won't sleep at night,' Tony observes.

'I'll do my best to keep her awake,' Mum says. 'How's my favourite son-in-law?' (It's an easy thing to say when Tony's her only son-in-law.) 'I wish I could have sat with the girls on Saturday night – it was such a shame that you had to miss out on your anniversary dinner.'

'I didn't mind too much, Mum.' My maternal instinct kicked in, and I realised that I couldn't bear to leave my baby behind for a whole evening, even though I have complete faith in my mother. 'It meant that we could stay at home with Chloe.'

'She's still very young,' Mum agrees.

'I guessed you'd say you preferred Chloe's company to mine,' Tony says coolly.

'I didn't mean it like that.' He's annoyed because I didn't go back upstairs on Saturday night. I fell asleep with Chloe on the sofa when she wouldn't settle.

'I hope you're looking after him,' Mum says when Tony returns upstairs to dress. I want her to say that I look tired, but she doesn't. She goes on about poor Tony being so exhausted and having to look after a baby and work full-time, and could he just come round and take a look at the ball valve in their upstairs toilet.

'I work too.'

'I know, Lisa, but you do the kind of job that I'd have loved, something to get you out of the house and provide a little pin money to treat the family. You can hardly call a little light-hearted dusting hard work, can you? I expect you and Clare spend all your time gossiping.'

I can't win, can I? Having reminded Jade that she's grounded after school until further notice after the sleepover escapade, and begged Mum to keep Chloe awake all day, by fair means or foul, I drive into Croydon to meet Clare and Jim.

A short, broad-shouldered man, dressed in black T-shirt and jeans, is unloading Clare's car outside an Edwardian mansion. Beside the grey front door is a column of bell presses, indicating that the house has been converted at some time into bedsits.

'Hi.' I'm not really expecting a reply.

'Uhuh.' Jim nods to acknowledge me, and returns to his work, the back of his head bald and shiny, as if Clare has buffed him up with beeswax. Jim is forty-seven, five years older than Tony. He's been married briefly before, and vowed never to marry again. Meeting Clare changed his mind.

Jim lifts a vacuum cleaner in one arm and a loaded carrybox in the other, turns and limps towards the house. He glances around behind him, then bounds up the few steps and disappears into the gloom beyond. Before the motorbike accident that almost killed him three years ago, Jim was a caretaker, but he hasn't been able to work since. He does jobs like these, and helps Tony out from time to time, for cash in hand.

I hate these one-offs. Clare and I had to rearrange our week's schedule to fit it in. A mate of Jim's lets rooms. The lodgers are supposed to move on every six months according to their tenancy agreements, although they sometimes stay longer, until Jim's mate sends his heavies in. I can't understand why anyone would choose to reside in a house that has all the appeal of the Bates Motel for one night, let alone commit themselves to six months.

Clare emerges from the front door in a heavy-duty green boilersuit and mask. She's stretching and snapping the fingers of a pair of latex gloves.

'Jim says he finds latex rather sexy.' She grins. 'Are you ready for this, Lees?'

'As I'll ever be,' I say, distracted as always by the idea that Jim is some kind of super-stud.

'Before I forget,' Clare goes on, 'do you remember those chocolates you bought to replace the ones that Tony bought you?'

'Of course. I can't find them.'

'You left them at Mrs E's.'

'She isn't complaining, is she? I suppose she couldn't resist eating them.'

'The dog couldn't. He's at the vet's with suspected chocolate poisoning.'

'You're joking!'

'It's true. Prince should have stuck with doggy chocs.'

'Oh, poor dog.'

'You don't mean that, do you?'

'I know I've wished him dead, but I don't want to be the one who killed him. I couldn't live with the guilt.' I pause. 'I'll ring Mrs E.'

I was promoted to Customer Complaints at the plumbing company because I wrote friendly, conciliatory letters to make the customers feel better rather than being confrontational. This had a rebound effect – the number of complaints shot up because customers knew they'd get a good response compared with some other companies who never replied or gave satisfaction. I adopt my role as Customer Complaints Manager, shouting down the phone at Mrs E.

'This is *Maids 4 U* Customer Services Department.'

'Pardon? What, what, what? Speak up, dear.'

I repeat myself. Three times.

'Department? There are only two of you.'

'We're an expanding company.' I look down towards my belly. I'm not lying. Too many doughnuts and bacon butties with Neville. Corporate entertaining of a sort. 'How is Prince?'

It turns out that the dog is going to be fine. It's wonderful, the best news I've had for weeks. I offer to pay the vet's fees and deliver Mrs E a bunch of flowers. 'I take it that you won't be wanting our services any longer,' I add hopefully.

'I've employed Clare's family to do for me as long as I can remember. I shan't be giving her up yet, not after one minor oversight.'

With a terse, 'Good morning,' Mrs E terminates the

conversation and I head – very reluctantly – for the bedsit to find Clare.

'Did Tony take you to the Tapas Bar on Saturday night?' Clare asks. She seems rather anxious.

'Yeah, we had a great time,' I say sarcastically. I push a door open to reveal a bathroom. When I see the state of the floor, my knees lock. There's a sharp stink of men's pee that makes me feel sick. The carpet is stained and curled up from the skirting that might once have been white beneath the hair, and dust, and yellow splashes. 'You know, Clare, times like this make me wish that I worked in Woolies on the High Street. I can't do this. I just can't. I'm going to die.'

'Have you been sick? Do you think it could be food poisoning?'

'It's my knees. I can't bend them. I don't think I can get down there.'

'You can start on the kitchen then,' Clare suggests, her voice suddenly devoid of sympathy. 'It has an eye-level grill.'

I step through into the kitchen, fully armed with a mask and gloves, trying to avoid the carpet of what I assume at first are raisins or olive stones, but on closer inspection turn out to be rat droppings. A chop lies congealed, half hidden in a layer of rancid fat in the grill. Cigarette ends lie stubbed out in the sink alongside a filthy old sock. The swingbin overflows with rubbish – takeaway wrappers, slimy poultry bones, and half-empty jars of passata.

Suddenly, I feel a whole lot better. My home is immaculate compared with this.

'What kind of person lives like this?' I ask in a superior voice. Clare is behind me, already organising the ammonia that I'll need to soak the fat off the grill pan.

'I hate to tell you, but Jim says that he's the chef at the Tapas Bar.'

'In that case, Tony and I had a lucky escape! Jade ruined our night out by inviting her new friend Kimberley for a sleepover at ours. I couldn't leave Mum with two teenagers and a baby, so I cancelled.' I go on to tell Clare about how Colin didn't collect his daughter until three-thirty the following afternoon. 'He and Manda, his life partner, had a great time apparently.'

'Life partner?' Clare frowns.

'They aren't married. They don't even look like a couple.' I recall the woman who kissed me on both cheeks, taking rather a liberty, I consider, for someone who was meeting me for the first time. Her long, lean arms were draped in a striped poncho, her feet clad in green ballerina pumps, and she wore a wicker-weave hat over long red hair. 'Colin dresses conservatively. Manda does boho chic.'

'I hope they offered to return the favour so that you and Tony can go out.'

'They've invited us to their housewarming, but it won't be for a while. Colin's still decorating the bedrooms. Their new house is in too much of a mess for sleepovers.'

'Yo ho ho.' Jim comes stamping up behind us. His grey eyes glint wickedly, and he grins, revealing a missing upper tooth. He's standing on one leg, leaning on a mop, waving an artificial leg, complete with foot, and trying to balance a long dead, desiccated pigeon on his shoulder.

Clare bursts out laughing. 'Avast there, Cap'n Hook.'

Jim's shoulders start to shake. The pigeon falls off.

'I thought it would be difficult to leave a leg behind,' says Clare, when she and Jim have calmed down. 'Especially if you had to walk out. I bet the owner's really upset, and angry.'

'Mad,' mutters Jim.

'Hopping,' I say.

'I'll hand it in to a police station,' Clare says.

I don't add, 'If you can find one that's open and manned,' because if Clare says she'll do something, she'll do it. You can rely on Clare.

You're supposed to be able to rely on family too. I can rely on mine to be unavailable when I want them, and hanging around at my house when I could do with some space. For example, my brother Mal, who fitted the new kitchen, disappeared for four weeks when I pointed out to him that it still lacked pelmets and drawer handles.

When I return home several hours later, desperate for a shower, my dad opens the door. His hair – what remains of it – is combed precisely across the top of his head, emphasising rather than disguising the fact that his crown is completely bald. The pockets of his beige outdoor shorts bulge with keys, hankies and small change. He wears socks with sandals. To her

49

eternal regret my mother's sartorial elegance hasn't rubbed off on her husband. She says that I take after him. She considers that the clothes in the *Next* catalogue are for floozies.

There was a time when I disagreed with her. I mean, I could have gone to work dressed like my customers, workmen in jeans and overalls, but I liked to look feminine and up-to-date, which meant jackets with shoulder pads, blouses with outsized collars, and Vaguely Black sheer tights. Now, we have our uniform.

'What are you doing here, Dad?' I ask, following him into the living room. 'Is everything all right? Where's Chloe?'

'I was at a loose end so I strolled over to keep your mum company. Chloe's asleep.'

Tears prick my eyelids.

'I tried to keep her awake, love,' Mum says. 'I carried her around the garden and sat down on the old swing to sing to her, switched the television up loud, but nothing worked. I don't remember you being such a sleepyhead when you were a baby.' She sighs. 'I did some housework, made myself useful instead.'

Am I grateful? I don't care about the housework. All I want is one night of uninterrupted sleep . . . I'm shattered. My bones have turned to jelly, no longer strong enough to hold me up.

'I'll make us all a cup of tea,' Dad suggests.

'I'll do it.'

'No, no, you let him,' says Mum. 'He needs something to do.' Aside, she adds, 'He's driving me mad. He rang three times this morning, then turned up on the doorstep in time for lunch. We had that ham and loaf that you kindly left out.'

Did I? The ham was cold for tea with salad and chips, and the loaf was for Tony's sandwiches tomorrow. I start to question whether living ten minutes' walk away from the parents is such a good idea.

'Is Jade home yet?'

'We haven't seen her.'

'It's four o'clock. She should be home by now.' She doesn't usually put herself out to stay for the Homework Club, and I begin to worry. She's supposed to be grounded, so where is she?

On my way upstairs to change, I drop into her bedroom and wade through the piles of dirty washing that have appeared on the floor since the sleepover. I put my foot on the first rung of the ladder up to Jade's bed. It's a high sleeper which makes it almost impossible for me to change the sheets because I suffer from vertigo. Beneath the bed is a sofa with fluffy lilac cushions and a pink fleece throw, and a desk. On top of the desk is a chrome box with a lock that contains Jade's diary – a pink notebook and pen with a purple feather.

I close my eyes, clamber up the ladder and grope around under Jade's pillow for the key which she keeps on a piece of thin ribbon. I slide down again and stand in front of the box, dangling the key. The diary draws me towards it like a bar of chocolate. Just one square. Just one page. Not even that. A nibble. A single sentence . . . My conscience whispers that there are other, more honest ways to find out where Jade is and I force myself to retreat.

There's no point in ringing Tony. He'll go ballistic. I use the phone in his office to ring Kimberley's dad instead. The piece of paper with Colin's mobile number has escaped the shredder so far. In fact, talking of the shredder, I notice that it's empty. Mum must have emptied it in her assault on my housework, which means . . . Oh, I can't think about Arsenal tickets now.

I dial Colin's number, hoping that Colin won't go jumping to the wrong conclusion if he really does fancy me. It doesn't feel right, phoning a strange man, and by 'strange' I mean odd as well as unfamiliar. I remember his ringtone is swingtime jazz.

'Hail, friend! Colin Kennedy at your service.'

'Er, Colin, it's Lisa, Jade's mum.'

'Hello,' he says warmly. 'What can I do you for?'

'I wondered if you knew where Jade is, if she's with Kimberley?'

'I don't, I'm afraid. I'm at the office, but I can give you Manda's work number. She might have some idea.'

I call Manda. At first I assume that she's not going to reply, and I've forgotten what I planned to say by the time the inharmonious crashing notes of a piano assault my ear. It's as if someone's playing it by bumping their bum down on the keys, which is what Clare and I used to do at school.

'Just a mo.' The line goes mute then returns. 'Manda here.' She regains her breath, and I picture her in a leotard and stripy tights, leaping around like one of those kids from *Fame*.

'I'm sorry. You're busy.' I'd forgotten how physically demanding dancing can be, having done very little apart from the odd slow smooch with Tony since headbanging my way through my brother Mal's wedding disco along to Status Quo. It was his first wedding disco – there have been two more since, to different brides. 'I've lost my daughter.'

'How careless of you,' Manda says brightly. 'Just teasing. She and Kimberley are lending a critical ear to Ali and his band – they're practising in our garage today. We take it in turns to host them so as to offend the maximum number of neighbours.' She laughs. I don't. Why does this stranger know more about my daughter than I do? 'I'll give you my home number, but I can't promise that they'll hear the phone. I'll drop Jade back to you later.'

'Thanks.' My knees ache. I am wretched. Mum and Dad are still here, and I don't feel that I can kick them out because Mum's cleaned the kitchen and baked two kinds of flapjack. Mal drops in too, ostensibly to see his baby niece whom he has seen only once since she was born, but I know better. He's brought Carlton, my nephew, with him. He's three, and it's all I can do to keep him and his plastic hammer away from the fishtank. Okay, it's only a toy, but Carlton doesn't know his own strength. I half-carry, half-drag him to the kitchen where Mal is filming Chloe who's sitting on the worktop in her carryseat. I give Carlton a saucepan to bash while his dad fiddles with the camcorder, but Carlton starts thumping Chloe instead.

'Will you please keep your son under control, Mal!' I don't need this.

'Don't you want a record of your daughter growing up?' he says.

'Well, yes, but—'

'I'll have Carlton,' Mum interrupts. 'Come here, love. Let's take a turn around the garden. Chloe and I found some frogs out there this morning. They must have hopped across from next door's pond.'

Carlton grins. He looks just like Mal, even down to the blue jeans and open-necked short-sleeved shirt. Mal has dark hair, thinning on top, and a cheeky smile. He's Prince Charming. He wears his heart on his sleeve and woos women with promises that he can't keep. I know why he arrived at six. I usually have

Tony's dinner ready by then. He's out of luck tonight though.

So is Jade if she's expecting any tea. She saunters in, saying that Manda couldn't stop. I rip her off a strip.

'This morning you were grounded for one week. Now you're grounded for a month.'

'Every day? That isn't fair.' Her tie hangs out of her skirt pocket.

'If you're not careful, I'll ground you for the rest of your life.'

'Aren't you being a little harsh, Lisa?' Mal cuts in.

I cast him a look. Now isn't the time to mention that if our mum had been a little harsher with *him*, his life might have turned out quite differently.

'I can't have her disappearing off without telling me where she's going and who with. You wait until Carlton's thirteen.'

'I'm almost fourteen,' Jade says.

'You kept Mum up to speed with your movements, Lisa.' Mal's eyes twinkle with mischief. 'Don't tell me you've forgotten how you'd say you were going to the library with Clare so you could sneak off up the park with Peter Wrigley.'

'Mum!' Jade glows with self-righteous indignation. 'Who on earth is Peter Wrigley?'

'He was your mum's first boyfriend,' says Mal.

'He was the son of a pest controller,' I say. 'Perhaps that's why I went out with him, so he could rid me of my nosy little brother with a sneaky dose of Warfarin.' I stare fiercely at Mal. 'Will you please stop putting ideas into your niece's head?'

'There is an easy solution, Mum,' Jade says. 'If you let me have a mobile, you can call me to find out where I am.'

Out in the hall, the phone rings. I close my eyes. I've run out of energy. I'm having a hypo, like Tony sometimes has after swimming. My blood-sugar level is at rock bottom.

'Go and get that for me, Jade.'

Jade fetches the handset, throws it at me, and heads out to the garden to join Mum and Carlton. I put the receiver to my ear.

'Hi, love, it's me.'

'Who?'

'Your husband. I'm on the doorstep.' Tony lowers his voice to a husky whisper. 'I want to kiss you all over. I want to lick

53

chocolate ice cream out of your bellybutton . . .' Silence. 'Hey, I'm trying to be romantic,' he protests. 'I thought that's what you wanted.'

'I do, but not right now.' I head out to the hall to carry on our chat in private.

'Your mum's still here?' I can hear Tony's key turn in the lock. 'For goodness sake, Lisa, you know I don't like your mum being here when I get home from work.' He steps indoors, his mobile tucked under his chin, toolbox in one hand and a length of pipe in the other.

'Keep your voice down,' I warn. 'They're all in the kitchen.'

Tony frowns. 'All?'

'Mum. Dad. And Mal. And Carlton.' I watch him, expecting his expression to darken further, but his lips curve into an enormous grin.

'This is ridiculous.' He laughs. 'Do you realise that we're standing face to face on the phone to each other?'

We're both still laughing when I return to the kitchen with him.

'Anything for dinner?' Mal says.

How am I going to do dinner for seven, not including Chloe? From school assemblies, I recall the parable of the loaves and fishes on the shores of Lake Galilee, but what can I do with three fish fingers from the freezer, and half a loaf of bread? I need a miracle and I send Tony out to perform one.

He returns with fish and chips from McDermott's, one of the best fish and chip shops in the country, in spite of its being situated in the landlocked Forestdale Shopping Centre.

We sit and stand around in the kitchen, eating. Dad asks Tony if there's anything he can do around the house to fill in his time now that he's retired. Considering that he can't even fix a washer on his tap, I think he's being rather optimistic.

'Why don't you redecorate *your* house?' I suggest gently.

'Don't even think about it,' Mum says. 'Last time Don tried to put a mirror up for me, he drilled through a water pipe. Don't you remember?'

'It wasn't my fault. You insisted on having the hook in the centre of the wall. I thought it would look more aesthetically pleasing set to one side.'

'I told you we should have asked Tony.'

54

'Tony has his own house, and if Lisa's as demanding as you are, Jeanette, he has plenty of bits and pieces to fix,' Dad says sharply.

Mal and I look at each other. It's unusual for our loving parents to bicker.

I thought everyone would go home after tea, but Mum and Dad retire with Chloe and Carlton to the living room to watch the news, Tony escapes to his office, and Jade to her room.

'I'll help you clear up, Sis,' says Mal.

'I knew you didn't come here to play Happy Families.' I stuff the wrapping from the fish and chips into the pedal bin.

'I'm in a spot of bother.' Mal tips his head to one side, raises one eyebrow in supplication, and we're children again and he's begging me not to tell Mum that he's broken one of her ornaments, a green ceramic rabbit, playing football indoors. I'm not sure because that would mean lying, and then he smiles and says, *'Pleeease,'* and I'd do anything for Mal. So I tell Mum that I was doing some dusting as my Brownie's good turn every day, and I dropped the rabbit. Mum cries because it was an heirloom from her aunt who died of the big C – I didn't know what that meant for a long time – and I wish I hadn't given in to Mal after all, but he buys me a Sherbert Fountain with change he nicked from the piggybank where Mum saves for emergencies, and we share it up in the woods at the back of the house. 'You couldn't lend me a few quid?'

I fetch my purse. 'How much?'

'I'll pay you back. Promise.'

'Don't mention this to Tony, will you?'

'My lips are sealed.' Mal pretends to zip his mouth up.

The fact that I lend my little brother money and he never pays it back is another secret I keep from Tony. Ours is a marriage of secrets and inconsistencies. He bought football tickets without telling me. I shredded them without telling him. He knows that I conceived Chloe because I missed a Pill. He doesn't know that I did it deliberately, that I planned it without consulting him. My heart is heavy. My purse is light.

Chapter Four

'Greg is talking about part-exchanging the Jeep for something more manageable.' Jacqui leans forward in the armchair in Clare's living room, and a sac of swollen white breast falls out of her maternity T-shirt. 'I wish I could part-exchange *him*. In fact, I would if I could find a replacement – something sleeker, sportier and with a little more fuel in the tank.'

All conversation stops. Nadia and Dippy Di, the only other mums who managed to drag themselves out of their pyjamas in time for Clare's coffee morning today, forget about comparing the price of nappies and turn their eyes to Jacqui.

'Do you have a particular one in mind?' I ask. It's a light-hearted comment. Jacqui doesn't mean what she's saying, but Clare takes it seriously.

'What's wrong with Greg?' Clare says indignantly.

'He doesn't care about me or Ethan. When he's at home, all he does is watch Sky, sleep or play with his SatNav.'

'His what?' Nadia enquires.

'Satellite Navigation System. It's an electronic route-finder.' Jacqui smiles. 'Greg would be lost without it.'

'If I went to all the effort of ditching my other half, I wouldn't rush out to find a new one,' Nadia says lightly. Her short dark hair is sticking up as if she slept badly, and she's wearing a baggy T-shirt with MUM printed across the front, not that there'd be any mistaking her for anything else.

'I wouldn't dream of getting rid of mine,' says Clare.

'Oh Clare,' I cut in. 'Jacks doesn't mean it.'

'It's Jacqui – spelt q,u,i at the end.'

'That's you been told, Lees,' Clare says sharply.

'I didn't mean to be rude,' Jacqui says. 'I'm sorry.'

I accept her apology, but Clare is fuming. She is far more easily offended on my behalf than I am.

'You can't break up your family, Jacqui, not when you've just made that gorgeous baby together.' Clare glances towards me. She's exaggerating Ethan's good looks. I keep quiet. Unlike Clare, I know how the arrival of a baby can drive a wedge right through a marriage. Look at me and Tony . . .

All the babies except Ethan are lined up in front of Jim's motorbike: he keeps it in the front room beneath the window because the garage is *en bloc* across the road, and he worries about it being stolen. There are reusable cotton nappies draped over the handlebars and the radiator. The babies lie on muslin squares on Clare's rug on the floor, and I wonder if it is possible to feel different, to feel socially excluded at fifteen weeks of age? (Ethan is older than Chloe and Fern, and five times bigger.)

'Why don't you put Ethan down with the others?' asks Dippy Di.

'There's no need to worry about germs,' I add. 'What Clare doesn't know about cleaning isn't worth knowing about.'

'He's happy where he is,' Jacqui says. 'He adores reading his book.' So Ethan remains in his carryseat with Jacqui holding *Baby's First Book*, a series of black and white patterns on cloth, in front of his face till he goes cross-eyed. She turns the page. He goes cross-eyed again and blows bubbles which dribble down his chin.

'Ooh, you are wonderful,' coos Dippy Di.

At first, I assume that she must be praising Ethan's first attempts at literacy, but she's referring to Jim who has entered the room with mugs of tea and coffee, and a plate of the carrot cake that Jacqui has brought with her.

I thought Jim was immune to female charm, apart from Clare's, but his face reddens as he perches on the arm of the sofa.

'This is delicious.' Nadia bites into a slice of Jacqui's cake. 'Could I have the recipe sometime?'

'Of course.' Jacqui beams. 'I've been making bread at home too.'

There is an exhalation of wonder around the room. How does she do it?

'I couldn't live without my breadmaker. I'd recommend it to anyone. There's nothing better than the smell of fresh bread wafting upstairs every morning.'

I sip tea from a snowman mug that was on sale in Woolies after Christmas, and sit back in Clare's sagging sofa. She's covered it with a brown faux-suede throw and chintz cushions. Sounds awful, but looks great. Some people would pay a fortune for Clare's shabby chic look.

We can't wait to ask Jacqui more about her plans to find a new husband, but Jim's in the way, sitting there, listening to everything and saying nothing.

'Is that the post?' Clare says.

'Postman's been already,' Jim mutters.

'Did you phone the bank?'

'Uhuh.' Jim drops to his knees beside Fern who's dressed in a red and white Arsenal Babygro. Jim bought it, not that he wanted a boy particularly. He says that anyone can support Arsenal, and in his opinion, everyone should.

'Hello, my precioussss,' he whispers in a creepy voice like Gollum out of *The Lord of the Rings*. Fern kicks her legs. The other babies burst into tears. We all grab our respective children to console them.

'Jim, would you mind nipping down to the High Street to pick up some more biscuits?' Clare says once they've calmed down.

Jim grunts some protest.

'We're almost out of milk,' Clare pleads.

'Oh, all right. For you, anything.'

As soon as Jim's out of the room, the conversation returns to Jacqui's announcement, and soon we are competing like mad to prove who has the most inept and thoughtless partner.

'It has to be mine,' says Nadia. 'You say that men can't do two things at once – well, Simon can't do anything at all.'

'So what qualities should the perfect partner have?' I ask.

'He should be stinking rich,' says Jacqui.

'Oh, but he should be loving and kind as well,' says Dippy Di, 'and he should have lots of time to spend with the children.'

'But not so much that he's under your feet. Sometimes you can have too much of a good thing.' I'm thinking of my parents.

Clare suggests tenacity, strength and broad shoulders.

Nadia suggests staying power and an enormous . . . She giggles while those of us who had vaginal deliveries squirm.

'Someone who puts the lid down on the toilet.'

'Who enjoys ironing.'

'That's my Jim,' says Clare. 'Mr Perfect, but don't tell him I said that.'

'Someone who doesn't forget your wedding anniversary,' I add.

'Tony? Did he?' Jacqui's ears prick up. 'So did Greg, but he's going to make it up to me on my birthday. It's the big one this year.'

'The big three oh,' says Clare, but I know she's only being polite.

'Four,' Jacqui says.

'Thirty-four?' says Dippy Di.

'I'll make some more drinks.' Clare leaves Jacqui and Nadia to explain. I go out into the kitchen to remind her of the orders – water, tea with sugar, tea with sweetener, decaff . . . I watch her make the drinks with Chloe in my arms.

The kitchen units used to be beige, but Clare persuaded Jim to paint them burnt orange to give them a Mediterranean feel to go with the plastic lobsters she keeps suspended in a net across the ceiling. She forgot to tell him to prime them first, so now they look like the side of a weathered fishing boat. Hence the reason she's waiting for our old units.

She opens a cupboard door to display a new jar of economy coffee and dislodges three packets of Digestives.

'I thought you said that your cupboards were bare.'

'I had to find some reason for Jim to go out.' Clare smiles. 'I can't have him hanging round here, reporting all the gossip back to Tony.'

'Do they speak to each other when they're together?'

'Tony doesn't stop talking.'

'He's stopped talking to me,' I say gloomily.

'Don't be silly.'

'It's true. I don't blame him. I'm always sniping at him – I can't help it.'

'It'll get better,' Clare says reassuringly. 'Chloe will sleep through the night soon. She'll get so tired that one day she'll have to.'

'I'm not interrupting anything, am I?' Jacqui swans in with Ethan.

'Here comes Superwoman,' Clare whispers.

'I was just about to tell Clare about my visit to the doctor's on the way here,' I say.

'Was it your poor perineum again,' says Clare, 'or your knees? Did Dr Hopkins agree to write you a sicknote?'

'He told me that the odd twinge in my knees was only to be expected at my age.' You'd have imagined that Dr Hopkins would have a little more sympathy, that he'd polish up his bed-side manner for me, but he didn't give any indication that he recognised me as a patient, let alone one of his cleaners. Doesn't he realise how hurtful it is to remain invisible? I've been regis-tered with him for over twenty years.

I parked Chloe's pram in front of the couch in his consulting room, and my bum on the seat beside his desk. Dr A. Hopkins (A for Andrew, not Anthony), a tall man with bloodhound jowls, looked past me. He can't be more than forty.

'It's my knees,' I said. 'They ache.'

'So do mine.' He rested his chubby hands on the barrel-like swell of his stomach. 'It's a common affliction of middle age.'

Middle age? I seethed as he declared that I had nothing to worry about, providing I refrained from jogging, pounding the pavements. I assured him that I would.

'However, a little exercise would do you good,' he added, straightfaced. 'A thirty-minute brisk walk three or four times a week.'

'Of course.' I nodded smugly, recalling how I had pushed Chloe up the hill from the car park without running out of puff until I reached the top of the disabled ramp into the surgery. I doubted that the doctor could walk from one side of his con-sulting room to the other without suffering a coronary.

'Is there anything else, Mrs Baker?' Dr Hopkins looked at his clock. His nails, I noticed, were bitten to the quick. 'Any prob-lems with the baby?'

There might be, in as long as it takes to incubate a cold, I thought. Babies are like magnets, attracting all kinds of people to pull faces and make silly noises. Just about every patient in the waiting room had cooed and sneezed over Chloe, and I wished that I hadn't brought her with me.

My librarian was more helpful than Dr Hopkins. I call him 'my librarian' because I've become a little possessive of him; he's a man a few years younger than me, who gels his dark hair into tidy spikes. I'm careful to time my approaches to the desk because the other librarians are rather intimidating. 'My librarian' has a friendly smile. He knows that I have a conservatory, aspire to owning an indoor water feature, and that before Chloe was born, I had a problem with excessive sweating.

Today I borrowed books on *Living with a Troublesome Teen* and *My Baby Won't Sleep*. It was difficult to decide between the two ends of the spectrum of the baby self-help books. Should I select the one which advises you to let your baby choose its own sleep pattern – somewhat inconvenient when your baby has decided that she is an honorary Antipodean – or the alternative, which must have been written by someone like my mother-in-law, which suggests that you force the baby to fit in with your routine? I took them both to the BOOKS OUT desk.

'You might find this useful.' The librarian pointed one stubby finger towards the information board. At first, I assumed that he wanted me to buy a book called *The Vale of the Black Crocus*, which turned out to be *not* a story of witchcraft but a pocket-sized history of Croydon.

'No, not that, the other ad,' he said. As he wrote down the phone number for the helpline for desperate parents of babies who won't sleep, I noticed how his bright orange shirt – far too loud for working in a library – was stretched so tight across his chest that I could see his nipples.

'Thanks,' I said. 'Thanks a lot.'

People are always offering me advice.

'You should try shark cartilage or extract of green-lipped mussel for your knees,' says Jacqui, now that we are back in Clare's sitting room with mugs of fresh coffee and tea.

'I wonder who discovered that eating sea-creatures was good for your joints,' says Nadia.

'Someone who lived near the coast?' offers Dippy Di.

'I'll let you have some when you come round to my house, Lisa,' Jacqui says. 'You will all come round to mine next week, won't you?'

There is general assent, and an exchange of phone numbers and addresses.

'I can hardly believe that we've all come so far in the last few weeks,' says Nadia, 'especially when I didn't think I was going to survive childbirth. I lost over a litre of blood,' she adds, leading the conversation towards the subject of 'most gruesome labour'.

'That's nothing,' I say. 'I lost two litres and had to have a transfusion – that was after deciding that I couldn't go through with labour for a second time. After a couple of mega-contractions, I told Tony I was leaving the hospital. He said, "You can't." I said, "Watch me," but I only got as far as the door of the labour room when the next contraction caught my breath and shut me up.'

'I planned a low-tech birth,' says Clare. 'I wrote a birth plan – would you believe that it was eight pages long?'

'I typed mine,' Dippy Di interrupts. 'It came to ten pages, but I used a large font.'

'I said I wanted to keep as active as possible, using breathing techniques to control the pain, as well as delay going to the hospital until the last minute,' says Clare.

'Did you stick to it?' asks Jacqui.

'The excruciating pains that I interpreted as full-on labour were just twinges. I was one centimetre dilated when I arrived at the hospital. I stayed for forty-eight hours on gas and air, then pethidine, till I was begging for an epidural.'

'What happened next?' says Dippy Di, although we've all heard this story several times before.

'I had a Caesarian, and Jim fainted exactly as Fern was delivered.'

'I had a water birth,' Jacqui says. 'It was the most natural and wonderful experience. You can see it on my website – Greg photographed it, tastefully, of course – and it's going to be published in one of the parenting magazines next month.'

There are gasps of admiration and amazement.

'And then, immediately afterwards, I ate the placenta.'

There are more gasps – this time, of horror.

'It was cooked,' Jacqui elaborates. 'Lightly fried in that low-cal spray-on fat. We froze the rest.'

Top that, I think, looking around at Nadia and Dippy Di. They don't even try.

'My story should be in print at about the same time as I go back to work. I've bought a franchise from a Health Supplement company with one of my friends who doesn't have children. We're going to run it from an outlet in Caterham,' Jacqui goes on. 'Greg and I don't really need the money, but I have no desire to be a stay-at-home mum. I love to work.'

'Lisa and I run our own cleaning company,' says Clare.

'Oh?' Jacqui's eyebrows almost hit her hairline as if she assumed – from our homely appearances, perhaps – that we had no other role in life apart from those of housewife and mother.

'I'm General Manager, Accounts and Payroll, and Lisa is Customer Services. Not that we have any complaints,' Clare adds quickly. 'We provide a personal and professional service.'

'That's handy,' says Jacqui. 'I'll need a cleaner.'

'We weren't going to take any more clients on until the babies were older,' I cut in before Clare can say anything.

'You could bring them along. My nanny can look after them with Ethan.'

'Your nanny?'

'I'll need a nanny. I can't rely on Greg to share the childcare. He has to be available at all times. He never knows when the call will come.'

'We'll certainly consider it.' Clare is wearing earrings that I can only describe as corrugated slices of beetroot. They shake furiously from her earlobes.

I've considered it, I think. Jacqui and I might share the bond of being married to forgetful and neglectful husbands, but I don't need, or want, to clean her house. I won't argue with Clare now; I'll save it for later.

'How can anyone say they'd rather be at work than with their baby?' Clare says once Jacqui, Nadia and Dippy Di have left.

'Jacqui didn't say that exactly.'

'And that she's looking for a new hubby?'

'She was joking.'

'I don't think Greg would find it very funny.'

'Not all jokes are.'

Jim returns from the High Street with Sue, Clare's sister. As she greets me, I can't help noticing that she bears the unmistakable scent of dry-cleaning chemicals. In appearance, Sue and Clare are peas out of the same pod, whereas my brother and I look very different. I am a broad bean compared with Mal, who is tall and stringy like a runner bean. Sue preserves her individuality by not bleaching her hair.

She walks up to the fireplace in the sitting room and runs her finger along the mantelpiece – unconsciously, I believe. Clare does the same whenever she goes into my house.

'How's Chloe?' Sue blows invisible dust off her fingertip.

'Fine, and you?'

'Fair to middling.'

'You're looking very . . . muscular.'

Sue's wearing a white vest that shows off her upper arms.

'I've been spending every spare hour I have down at the gym. I've heard that it's the place to meet eligible men, although the only ones I've met there pounding the treadmills have been too in love with their own bodies to give me a second glance.' She hesitates. 'I'm thinking of applying for one of those American husband-hunting seminars. You have to clear your life of anything that might be keeping you single, apparently, then you have to throw yourself in the path of as many men as possible, in case one of them turns out to be your future spouse.'

'How are you supposed to do that?' Clare asks. 'Stop them in the street?'

'Almost. You eat out, hang out in cafés and take the bus everywhere instead of driving.'

'That's no good. You'll end up marrying someone like Jim,' Clare says. She sounds harsh, but she's smiling fondly when she turns to her husband. 'What took you so bloody long?'

'I dropped in at the Sir Julian Huxley for a swift half.'

I guess that he's had a lot more than a half because he's considerably more garrulous than he was before.

'Here's me working my fingers to the bone and you go and spend it all at the pub.'

'Come here, love. Give us a kiss. You don't begrudge your old man the odd drink now and then?' Jim hands over party rings and a packet of pink wafers, then picks up Fern and blows a raspberry on her tummy. Her eyes widen with surprise and concern. A couple more raspberries later and she's chuckling out loud. Soon, we are all laughing.

Jim turns to Chloe. 'You want a turn?'

She gazes at him, then yawns. I yawn too. I pick her up, determined not to let her go to sleep. Clare makes cheese and tomato rolls, and Jim goes upstairs to watch *Neighbours*. As soon as I bite into my roll, Chloe starts to wail for food. Not only will she not let me sleep, she won't let me eat either. I feed her, bottle in one hand, roll in the other.

'Do I get a discount if I recommend your services to a new customer, Sue?' says Clare.

'I thought you'd stopped trying to fix me up with a man. There hasn't been anyone since you married Jim.'

'I don't have any more cast-offs, but there is someone I'd like you to meet. He's young, free and single. He's tall – not as tall as Tony, but taller than Jim – and he likes to talk.' Clare omits the fact that Neville is also unemployed, untidy and thoroughly depressed.

'Is he goodlooking?'

'On a scale of one to ten, I'd say he was an eight.' Clare glances at me for confirmation.

'Seven and a half.' I'm comparing him with Tony who is most definitely a ten.

'Not bad.' Sue does a twirl on one heel. 'Is he an owner-occupier?'

'Mortgaged.' Clare pauses. 'Are you mucking me about here?'

Sue grins.

'I'm serious, Sue. If you want to grow old alone like Mrs E, go ahead.'

'I'm not desperate,' Sue says. 'Not really. But I'd like to meet this guy to see if he's as amazing as you're making out.'

'I'll suggest that he brings some dry-cleaning to you, so you can give him the once-over.'

'You can tell a lot about a man from the state of his suit,' Sue says wickedly.

And from the state of his flat, I muse. Neville and Sue? Not one of Clare's better ideas.

Jade says that the most embarrassing occasion in her life was when Tony and I sat her down and told her that I was pregnant. What I am about to do now is going to run a close second.

Halfway through the afternoon, I drive Chloe up to the school. I have to park some way away and carry her up the road. I begin to wonder if I've been foolish, expecting to find Jade in a crowd of fifteen hundred kids dressed in grey, white and black, but suddenly, I catch sight of her. In fact, she might have caught sight of me first, and turned against the tide of pupils to head back towards the school gates.

'Jade!' I call after her. 'Jade Baker!'

Kimberley's with her. She comes towards me, struggling with a bag and a bulky black instrument case.

'Jade, it's your mum!' she shrieks happily. 'She's brought your baby sister with her. How sweet.'

Jade's face is scarlet when she reaches us. Her eyes spark and her teeth glint as she vents her fury. 'This is so humiliating!'

'Well, if I can't trust you to do as you're told ...'

'I'll go straight home on the bus, if you'll just go away,' she begs. 'I promise.'

'You're coming with me. Would you like a lift too, Kimberley?'

'Yes, please. I hate carrying my euphonium on the bus.' In the car she tells me that she wishes her mum would come and pick her up from school, and I find myself warming to her.

'Mum's always too busy,' she sighs.

'When will she be home?'

'Not till six or seven. She leaves a key.'

Poor little thing, a latchkey child. My mum was always at home when I returned from school, even during her brief spell as a dinner-lady. She was sacked after three warnings for persistently handing out sweets in the playground, forever branded a pusher of Tutti-Frutti chews and liquorice laces.

'Come home with us,' I say. 'You can stay for tea.'

'You can borrow some of my clothes. Well, you could if I had any. The Grinch – that's my dad – won't let me have an allowance,' says Jade.

'Is that surprising when you behave like a three year old?'

'Can we go up the park, Mum?' she says, ignoring my comment.

I haven't read the chapter in the library book that gives tips on maintaining the consistency of one's approach to parenting a troublesome teen yet, so I give in. 'Oh, all right, but I haven't forgotten that you're grounded.'

I walk up to the park behind Jade and Kimberley and perch on a swing with Chloe on my lap, watching them discreetly from a distance. Anything for a quiet life.

I have to drop Kimberley home after tea. Tony is back, so I take Jade, and leave Chloe with him. Kimberley's house, a semi in Hamsey Green, has an unattractive grey render and a new sign, *Villa Colanda*, up beside the door. There are stone – no, plastic – lions rampant on the gateposts. I walk Kimberley up the short cobbled driveway to the front door and ring the bell.

A man opens the door. I see his feet first, hairy toes protruding from leather sandals with laces that criss-cross up his shins. Chubby thighs disappear inside a scarlet tunic that's tied around his middle with a rope belt. It takes me a moment to recognise that it's Colin.

'Hi, Dad,' Kimberley says, apparently unperturbed that her father is dressed like some creature from Middle Earth. Manda strolls up behind him in a long, flowing kaftan.

'Meet Marcus Aurelius,' she says.

I pinch myself discreetly on the forearm. It hurts, therefore I am not dreaming.

'Jade and I hung out at the park,' Kimberley says. 'It was cool.'

'I was there too,' I say hastily. 'I took Chloe into the play-park.' I smile. 'I'd forgotten how much fun swinging could be.'

Manda raises one eyebrow. She does that quite often, I notice, and I wonder if she has a tic.

'Come in and share a drink with us to celebrate.' As Colin holds out one hand to me, his tunic slips off his shoulder, revealing one heavily tufted armpit.

'Er, what are you celebrating?'

'My promotion to Centurion.' Colin beams.

'Colin belongs to a Roman re-enactment group,' Manda adds in explanation.

I relax slightly. How silly of me not to have realised . . .

'I'm afraid that I can't stop,' I say. 'It's Chloe's bathtime.'

'You and Tony must come to our housewarming party,' Manda offers.

'If you know any other likeminded couples in Selsdon, do ask them along too,' says Colin.

'I'm not sure – I haven't seen any Romans on the High Street.'

Colin bursts out laughing. I didn't realise I could be that funny.

'So you will come?' he says.

'Well, yes. Thanks.' This isn't the first time I've been forced to fraternise with people who aren't my type. It's true that you can't choose your children's friends, and Jade has picked on some peculiar acquaintances in the past. There was Taz, whose mother ended up in prison. There was Emma, whose parents were born-again Christians. Emma's mother did her best to save my soul. She hosted a party-plan evening with an evangelical theme, promoting candles and tea-lights alongside the teachings of the Bible. Why can't Jade stick with being best friends with Alice? Alice's parents are completely normal – they keep themselves to themselves.

'I hear from Jade that your husband Tony is Corgi-registered,' Colin goes on. 'We could do with someone running their expert eye over our boiler.'

Manda gives Colin a look.

'We'd pay, of course,' he stammers, 'and if you ever want to submit a planning application, I'm your man in the Planning Department. If you chuck us a couple of quid, I'll see that any decision swings in your favour.'

'He's joking,' says Manda. 'Colin's a jobsworth.'

'It's Marcus Aurelius, if you don't mind.'

'Everything has to be correct, right down to the colour of the ink on the reports,' Manda goes on.

'It's important to follow procedure,' says Colin. 'It must be true of cleaning too. Don't you always clean from the top of a room down?'

'Oh Colin, don't be boring,' Manda sighs. 'Thanks for looking after Kimberley, Lisa. She and Jade are getting along so well. Jade's a lovely girl. I wondered if she'd be interested in having a go at dancing. I'm willing to give her a trial lesson – free, of course.'

I turn towards Jade. She's leaning against one of the stone pillars, chatting to Kimberley.

'I said that I'd ask you,' Manda continues.

Why does Jade listen to this woman, when she won't take any notice of me? Are things so bad that we have to converse through an intermediary?

On the way home, I mention the subject of dancing lessons to Jade. She jumps at the opportunity.

'Oh please, Mum. If I was dancing, you'd know exactly where I was. *Pleease.*'

'I'll think about it.'

When Jade and I reach our doorstep, it appears that Tony has acquired an enthusiasm for dancing too. I can hear the thud of feet and the beat of music slightly out of phase. Jade raises one eyebrow. I raise my finger to my lips. We creep through the hall and peer around the living-room door.

Tony is flushed and breathless, as if he's about to have a heart-attack. He's holding a baked-bean can in each hand and waggling his booty to one of my exercise tapes. Chloe is in her bouncy chair, gurgling and opening and closing her fists on outstretched arms with excitement.

Jade grins at me. We both start laughing.

'Gotcha, Dad!'

'Are you having a midlife crisis or something?' I ask.

'What's so funny?' Tony stops, mid-move, one foot off the ground. 'You do these exercises, Lees.' He takes one hop to the sofa, turns and perches on the arm.

'Actually, I don't have the time, or more accurately, the energy.'

'You should have a go.'

'What – and damage my back? Don't tell me what to do, Anthony Baker. I'm just too busy.'

'You've been out for coffee this morning, and lunch. I'm the one who's been working!'

I change the subject. 'Manda's invited us to a party. I said we'd go. I couldn't think of a good excuse.'

'You're so negative all the time.'

'I'm not.'

'There you go. Listen to yourself. It would be great for us to go out and make new friends.' Tony massages the small of his back with one of his baked-bean cans. 'I think I've pulled a muscle.'

'Serves you right.'

Tony puts the cans on the mantelpiece and steps towards me with his head tipped to one side. 'Oh, come here, love.' He wraps his arms around me, holds me very close and presses one prickly cheek against mine. I am vaguely aware that Jade has left the room.

'You've been thinking about sex too often.' Smiling, I look up at his face.

'What makes you say that?'

'They say that each time you think about sex you have a rush of testosterone that makes your beard grow faster.'

Tony kisses me then rests his chin on the top of my head. 'I dropped by at your friend Jacqui's on the way home to look at her bathroom.'

70

'What's her house like?'

'Oh, I didn't take much notice.'

'Well, was it modern? Has she got good taste?'

'I don't know, do I? It looked like any other home, I suppose.'

'Don't you realise how irritating that statement is? What about the bathroom? You must have noticed that.'

'It had a brown corner bath.'

'Go on.'

'The tiles were mouldy just like ours.' Tony pulls back slightly. 'Why did you let Jade bring Kimberley home tonight when she's supposed to be grounded? How is she going to learn if you aren't consistent?'

My body stiffens at Tony's criticism. I'm a good mum. *I am.* And I'd be an even better one if I wasn't tired all the time.

'Tony, you know what Jade's like.'

'Yes, and she's got you wrapped right round her little finger.'

I might have my breasts pressed against my husband's chest, his musky scent up my nostrils, his salt taste on my lips, but I feel as if we're half a world apart. I try to explain about Kimberley and the euphonium, but Tony interrupts.

'I have to lie down.' He takes a sharp intake of breath, and clutches his back.

'Now you have a better idea of how painful it is to give birth.' I am filled with sympathy! 'What you're experiencing is a mere twinge.' I fetch him some water and painkillers, not because I'm Florence Nightingale but because I'd like him up and about to put the bins out later. Then I feel a twinge myself – of guilt for being so mean because he's lying, white-faced, flat out on the floor – so I sit with him for a while with Chloe still in her chair, making eyes at us. Jade pops back in, determined to discuss the subjects of dancing and her allowance. Tony shades his eyes.

'Go on then,' he sighs. 'Make your case.'

Tony and Jade agree on a trial dancing lesson, and settle on a figure for a monthly allowance.

'That much?' I say. 'Now who's giving in to Jade's demands?'

'Anything to get her out of my hair,' Tony smiles when Jade skips – yes, I haven't seen her so lightfooted for weeks – out of the room.

'Would you like Chloe and me to leave you in peace as well?' I ask.

'No, stay.' Like a small boat trying to moor, Tony stretches his hand out to touch me, but he can't quite reach. He tries again, winces and fails. He drops his arm to his side. It's my fault though that we can't connect, not his.

I let the Pill slide, envious of the idea that Clare might have a baby and I wouldn't. Tony always wanted to concentrate on Jade whereas I had an ache for another child. I didn't feel that rush of love for Jade that I felt for Chloe when she was born. Conceiving Jade really *was* an accident. I chose to have Chloe.

'Have you ever done something terrible, Tone? Something really bad that you didn't dare confess to anyone else?'

'Let me guess.' Tony smiles. 'You've sold the baby – no, you'd never do that. You're having an affair. No, you don't have time . . .'

'There's something I have to tell you.'

'You've found my tickets.' He brightens.

'I shredded them.'

'Lisa!'

'I didn't mean to.'

He tries to get up. 'It isn't as if I go to every match.'

'When you bought those tickets, you assumed that I'd be here to look after the girls. Didn't it occur to you that I might like to spend a Saturday afternoon out enjoying myself?'

'If I'd known, I would have ordered a ticket for you as well as Jim.'

'I didn't mean that I wanted to watch football.'

Tony grins. 'Can't you tell when I'm pulling your leg any more?'

I shake my head as Tony goes on, 'I'll ring the Club and ask them to send replacement tickets. Sorted.'

If only the rest of our lives were as simple as that: one phone call – problem solved.

Why didn't I tell Tony the truth before Chloe was born? Why didn't I use that brief window of opportunity when he was so relieved at her safe delivery that he wouldn't have cared if I'd told him that I'd sold the house to buy a Ferrari? Why do I leave the conversation I should be having with him lying around like the duster I left on the windowsill the other day with all good intentions, unused yet gathering dust?

72

Chapter Five

'Do you think a jury would let me off on the grounds of diminished responsibility?' Clare's extendable pink feather duster hovers above books on Pathology and Toxicology on the shelves in the doctor's study. Thinner tomes, including *Bereavement Counselling* and a children's book, *Owl Babies*, lie on their side. The Abba song 'Money Money Money' blares out from the hi-fi system.

'That depends on what crime you're planning to commit.' I draw a circle in the dust on the computer screen on Dr Hopkins's desk with the folded corner of an alcohol-free wipe.

'I'm going to kill Jim.'

I add two dots for eyes and an upside-down smile.

'He's only been down to Allders on the tram and bought me a breadmaker after Jacqui talked about it yesterday,' Clare continues. 'What do I want a breadmaker for when I have a supermarket less than five minutes from my doorstep? Oh Lisa, here I am scrimping and saving while he spends all the money we have, and more, as if we've won a million on the Lottery.' Clare's shoulders sink. 'What can I do?'

'Can't you return the breadmaker?'

'Jim's already baked a loaf in it.' Clare pauses. 'It was harder than his head – he forgot to add any yeast.'

'I don't think you'll ever change Jim. He's always been a generous soul. I'll ask Tony if he can find him some more work.'

'Would you? As soon as I suggest that he looks for a proper job, he starts hobbling around the house, so I've told him that he'll have to sell his bike. He had it repaired, but he'll never ride it again. He's keeping it because it reminds him of his lost youth.'

'He's having a midlife crisis like Tony,' I say, trying to imagine Jim clad in black leather and roaring down the M23 on a motorbike.

'It's getting a bit late for that, isn't it?' says Clare. 'I mean for Jim, not Tony. Jim's forty-eight next year.'

'If you want some space, you could come up and babysit for us sometime. I promised Colin and Manda that Tony and I would go to their housewarming party. In fact, it was an open invitation, so if you and Jim—'

'No, you could do with a night out,' Clare interrupts. 'I'll bring Fern over. Jim can do what he likes. We haven't had such a dust-up since Jim decided that he wanted to name the baby after his mother. I said, no way was I going to call her Edith.'

'You ended up calling her after one of his mother's dogs though.'

'A pretty name like Fern is wasted on a miniature poodle, and we couldn't be like the Beckhams and use the name of the place where she was conceived.'

'I don't know. Sandy Bay Caravan Park has quite a ring to it.' Smiling, I pick up a magazine from the floor. *Practice Nurse.* I hope that Mrs Hopkins is qualified, not merely practising, since I shall be relying on her to give Chloe her immunisation jabs soon. She's definitely slacking. When we started cleaning here, the house was always immaculate with the toilets clean and the sinks swished out. Today, we've had to clear the floor of the children's bedrooms of toys before we can run the vacuum over the carpets.

'Have you checked behind the computer, Lees?' Clare says. 'I found some rubbish there last week.'

Feeling a little sheepish that Clare has caught me out not keeping up to her high standards, I slip my hand behind the monitor and pick up a fistful of confectionery wrappers.

'Why leave these here when there's a bin under the desk?' I think for a moment. 'Unless you want to hide the fact that you've been secretly bingeing on sweets.'

'I found half a packet of Chocolate Digestives in the doctor's bedside cabinet last week, and some fruit pastilles in his sports holdall.' Clare grins. 'I ate those.'

'You didn't offer to share them with me!'

'There weren't many left.'

'What a hypocrite!' I continue, dropping the wrappers into the bin. 'Not you, Clare. I'm talking about Dr Hopkins and his advice for a healthy lifestyle.'

'You are going to empty that bin now, aren't you?' Clare says. 'I wouldn't like to get the doctor into trouble with his wife.'

'Give us a chance, will you?' I grumble.

'We'd better draw up a contract for Jacqui,' Clare says, changing the subject as I collect up my box of wipes. She pronounces 'Jacqui' with a soft J and qui like *queen*.

'Do you have to?'

'There's hardly any travelling involved, and it doesn't look as if she lives in a grotty house, does it?'

'I'm not worrying about my knees – it's just that I don't like the idea of being employed by a friend.'

Clare raises one eyebrow.

'I know you aren't keen on her, but I'm prepared to give her a chance,' I continue. 'She's lonely, she's just had a baby, and her husband's a complete bastard. She seems nice enough – she's invited us back round to hers.'

'There's something odd about her though,' Clare says thoughtfully. 'Why does she want to swap her husband?'

'We talk of changing ours sometimes,' I point out. 'You did when Jim turned up with that fifteen-foot outdoor paddling pool, and then paid out another forty quid for an electric pump.'

'In jest.'

'As I recall, you were deadly serious. You said you hoped he'd drown in it.'

'Did I?' Clare grins, and grabs my arm. 'It's "Voulez-Vous".' She holds the duster to her mouth and sings into it as if it's a microphone. I join her, Anni-Frid to her blonde Agnetha. All our worries disappear. Clare's that Jim is going to bankrupt them. Mine on the state of my marriage.

We're going through a bad patch, that's all. So are Clare and Jim. My mum and dad. And Neville too.

We find him slumped in front of the telly, watching *Teletubbies* in the dark. Clare pulls the curtains and opens a window.

'Cheer up, Neville,' she says. 'Life can't be like Teletubbyland where the sun is always shining.'

75

'No babies?' he says gloomily.

'Not today.' We left Chloe with my mum, and Fern with Jim. 'Coffee?' I suggest.

Neville requests something stronger like vodka, but I don't think that's such a good idea. I don't want to be drunk in charge of a Dyson. I head for the coffee machine, while Clare feeds Neville on cream horns from the baker's. We sit together on the sofa, and Neville informs us that he did lose his job.

'It was time I moved on anyway. Not only were the management stifling my talents, but I couldn't go anywhere – pubs or parties – without someone complaining that we didn't stock the right kind of grapes or crisps or jam.' By the time Neville's finished, he's managed to convince us that it was more like taking redundancy than being given the sack. Almost.

'So what are you going to do?' I ask.

'Chill for a bit? Travel the world? Make myself interesting to women?' He stretches his legs. 'I shall acquire a history, some amusing anecdotes and spellbinding stories. How I, Neville Harman, subdued a poisonous snake by giving it a ferocious glare then sucked its venom out of the long, slender leg of the sultry beauty I was escorting through the rainforest. How I led some gorgeous well-endowed blonde safely from the Outback and into civilisation.'

'The one thing that's guaranteed to turn a woman off is listening to a man bragging about his previous conquests,' I say. 'How about "How I rescued a child from the jaws of a tiger"?'

'You mean, in front of his or her gorgeous, and unmarried mother?' Neville grins. He's winding me up. 'I get your point.'

'It isn't a good idea to run away,' Clare says. 'Someone accustomed to all your luxuries won't enjoy bumming around, living out of a rucksack. You must apply for another job. Think of this as an opportunity to take up a new challenge. If you really hate being a glorified grocery assistant, try something different.'

Neville sits forward, smiling. 'Have you two ever considered a career change? You could write an agony column, or set yourselves up as lifestyle gurus.'

'I wouldn't want to be anything but a cleaner,' says Clare. 'There must be something that you're passionate about.'

'Apart from women,' I add.

'Whatever you decide to do, Neville, there'll be interviews.

You'll need to smarten yourself up. What state is your suit in?' Clare winks at me. 'Go and fetch it. I'll have a look.'

'What are you doing?' I mouth.

Neville brings the suit. Clare deftly points out the creases, the stains, and the fact that one of the buttons is missing from the jacket.

'You must take it to the dry-cleaners,' she says. 'My sister Sue works there – she'll fix the button for you. I'll call her and tell her that you're coming, shall I? Or I can drop you there, if you prefer.'

'I can manage,' says Neville. 'I have plenty of time on my hands.'

'You don't have to practise your mothering skills on Neville, Clare,' I say on the way home. I find it a little embarrassing.

'He's like a lost boy,' she sighs.

'It's kind of you to help him out, but there's no need to adopt him.'

'I'm helping my sister at the same time.'

'Well, I hope Sue's tempted by the idea of a bit of rough, because that's what Neville looks like at the moment – rough.'

'He scrubs up quite nicely though.'

'I don't see how you can make someone fall in love with someone else, especially Sue, she's so fussy.'

'I'll find a way,' Clare says firmly. 'I should add "Head of Innovation" to my list of executive and non-executive titles within the *Maids 4 U* corporation. What do you think?'

The company that Jacqui has a franchise with is keen on innovation too, and Jacqui decides to innovate by changing the venue of the next coffee morning. Instead of meeting at her house, we are to assemble at a local farm.

'Do you think Jacqui's so ashamed of her home that she prefers to meet us in a pigsty?' I ask Clare on the way.

'It isn't really a farm that we're going to. It's more of a theme park. I think that it's a great idea to take the babies out for the day.' Clare's lips curve into a sly smile. 'However, it would have been interesting to have had a good nose around Jacqui's house, wouldn't it?'

'Well, yes.'

'Oh, I know I wasn't keen on her at the beginning, but perhaps she isn't so bad. She has quite a sense of adventure. She might shake us up a bit.'

Clare parks what she considers is a safe distance away from Jacqui's Jeep, and we wait while she unloads Ethan and his pram. 'If you're not sure you'll need it, throw it in anyway,' seems to be Jacqui's rule of thumb. I am more minimal. I've already had a baby, and I know that you don't need the kitchen sink for a daytrip.

'The babies will love this,' Jacqui enthuses. 'It'll be an educational experience for them.'

'I thought it was supposed to be a bit of a laugh,' says Clare.

'And that too.'

'Don't forget your keys, Jacqui,' I remind her.

She jangles them at me and drops them into one of her bags. 'Where are the others?'

'They couldn't make it,' I say. 'Nadia was still in her dressing-gown and slippers when I rang her to remind her of the arrangements, and Dippy Di's staying at home to do her pelvic-floor exercises.'

'Pity.'

'You'll have to make do with us.' Clare releases the brake on Fern's pram and pushes it along behind Jacqui, who heads off towards the turnstile at the entrance with Ethan. Jacqui looks very glamorous in a lilac vest top, short flouncy skirt and high-heeled wellies.

We head for the rabbits first. Clare doesn't like animals, even though she often boasts that Jim is an animal in bed. (I can't help imagining him as a gentle sloth, not the untamed stallion that Clare hints at.) Clare is more than happy to watch the rabbits through the wire netting, but Jacqui's in the run with them, shoving Ethan's face up close to their twitching noses, and showing him off to each and every rabbit. Chloe isn't impressed and, having decided that one rabbit is very much like another, she closes her eyes and falls asleep in her pram.

There's a sign on the door to the run: *Baby Rabbits for Sale, Please See Keeper.*

'I wonder how you choose one,' I muse aloud.

'By assessing all the facts – like how fluffy, how cute, how old they are, and then making the final decision on instinct.'

Jacqui tosses her hair. 'I should know – I've been trying to choose a nanny.'

'I thought there were agencies to help with that.'

'They can't tell you which one to choose.'

'Have you chosen one?' Clare asks.

'Not yet.'

'Haven't you got family nearby who could help out?' I ask. 'My mum has Chloe when I'm at work.'

'My mother works full-time – she's in sales.' Jacqui kicks a stone with the toe of her welly. 'And you know what Greg's like. He hasn't been terribly supportive recently. He doesn't get home until after nine most nights.'

I feel so sorry for her. Tony might not be with me in spirit in the evenings when he's watching telly, but at least he's there in body, and when he's late, it's because he's working, or he's down at the pub with Jim. I know that he's not getting up to anything else – at least, I don't think he is . . .

I try to suppress that little voice in my head. It was years – no, a lifetime ago. A minor indiscretion. Forgiven and forgotten.

'Greg doesn't like the idea that I'll be earning more than him in three or four years' time,' Jacqui continues. 'It takes a while to build a successful business – as you must know. Anjula and I have to establish a broad customer base before we can start paying off the loan we've had to take out to buy the franchise in the first place.'

Jacqui cleans Ethan's hands with a wipe when we leave the rabbit pens. The packet is labelled *Inaglow Products, Impregnated with Aloe Vera*.

'I've brought a couple of travel packs with me if you'd like to try them,' Jacqui says. 'They're three pounds each. I can't give them away – I'm sure you understand,' she adds, after I've agreed to sample them. I hand over the cash. Clare declines.

We move on to watch a man mucking out a horse.

'I'm still looking for a cleaner if you're interested,' Jacqui says. 'Greg's very keen – he wants the best for me.'

'So he isn't all bad?' says Clare.

'Of course not. Whatever gave you that idea?' Jacqui dashes off with Ethan across the yard to the field beyond, leaving me and Clare to struggle on behind her. I wish Tony would employ a cleaner for me, just while Chloe is so tiny and dependent. Some people have it so easy . . .

'Hurry up, you two!' Jacqui calls over her shoulder. 'I'll race you to the tyres.'

'Now I can see the advantage of an all-terrain pram,' Clare grumbles.

I take a little persuading, but soon we are taking it in turns on the play equipment, riding tyres suspended on chains from one platform to another at great speed. Clare screams with delight. Jacqui is more restrained, and looks far more elegant clinging to a tyre than either Clare or myself. Clare balances with one hand, then no hands. Egging me on. And I wish that Tony could see me now so I could prove that I can still let my hair down.

Jacqui proposes lunch. I hesitate, knowing that Clare has no money, but she says, 'What the hell,' and we sit down in the shade of a tree with cheese salad baguettes. Jacqui picks the cheese out, making a small heap on the ground.

'I'm detoxing,' she explains.

'Is that okay when you're breastfeeding?' says Clare.

'I bet that I expressed more milk this morning than the farmer got out of that cow over there.' Jacqui points towards the mock-up of a milking shed. She sits back with Ethan cradled in her arms. 'I took Ethan to the health visitor yesterday, and she says he's growing well.' She bites at her lip. 'She also said that his head's too big. Well, bigger than it should be at this age.'

'They said that to me about Jade, my eldest. I told them not to worry – they should see the size of her dad's.'

'It isn't funny,' says Jacqui. 'It could be serious.'

'I know, I'm sorry. When will you know if he's all right?'

'The health visitor's going to recheck him in a month.'

A mobile rings, interrupting our conversation. I look at Clare. She shakes her head and looks at Jacqui.

'It isn't mine,' she says.

'It must be yours, Lisa.'

I retrieve my mobile from the bottom of my handbag. It's Colin, confirming the date of the housewarming soirée. I switch off Colin's heavy breathing. 'That was Colin – he and Manda wanted to make sure we had plenty of notice to find a babysitter for this party of theirs.' My face burns hot – I don't know why. There's nothing wrong with Colin ringing me, is there?

We walk around a little longer, seeing who can oink the loudest beside the pigs, who can cluck most like a hen, and who can run fastest away from a quartet of bossy geese who hiss at us for wandering too close to their pond. We pop into the shop. Clare keeps her purse firmly shut. Jacqui buys Ethan a cardboard book about farm animals. I buy a set of yellow ducks for Chloe's bathtime.

'It's my turn to host next week's coffee morning,' I say as we head back to the car park.

'That's very kind,' says Jacqui, as Clare butts in with, 'No, not next week.'

'It must be.'

Clare scowls at me and then I realise why she's making such a fuss. My house is not a great advert for a cleaning company. It's more of a 'before' scenario than an 'after'.

'I can't make next week anyway,' says Jacqui. 'I'm interviewing my shortlist of nannies so that Ethan can have his girlfriends round to play while you're cleaning.'

'What are you grinning at?' I ask Clare on the way home.

'I can't help picturing Jim's face at the idea that Ethan, with his squiffy coiffure and boss-eyes, would ever make a suitable match for his baby girl.'

'Clare, you are mean sometimes. The boy can't help it.'

'I wonder if you shouldn't be a bit more careful, Lees.'

'With what?'

'With Colin.' Clare pauses. 'I know that there's nothing between you and Kimberley's dad, but it might appear that there is to an outsider.'

'Jacqui, you mean? She isn't an outsider. She's a friend. A mate.' I smile. 'I think Jacqui has enough on her plate with Ethan and a new job without dreaming up an affair between me and Colin, and anyway, he reminds me of that flashing gnome Tony bought me one year.' (When I say 'flashing', I don't mean one with a light.)

'It's all right – you don't have to convince me.' Clare glances in the rearview mirror. 'Chloe's beginning to resemble a garden gnome too. Have you noticed how red her cheeks are?'

'She's teething.' I sit back, basking in a rare moment of maternal one-upmanship. Chloe is about to cut her first tooth – before Fern and Ethan.

* * *

'You're my clever little girl.' I am trying to soothe Chloe later the same evening, when she's grizzling and dribbling and chewing her fingers. I am trying to persuade Jade that cold chicken and salad is a tasty alternative to beefburgers and chips. I am trying to do one hundred things at once when, at six, the phone and the doorbell ring at the same time.

'Hi, Tony.' I answer the phone with Chloe in my arms.

'It's Bunny.'

'Oh? This isn't a good time. Can I ring you back?'

'I wanted to speak to Tony, but I assume that he isn't home yet. I wonder if he'd have time to call in tomorrow. Our shower's sprung a leak and I can't bear bathing. It's so unhygienic, lounging around in your own detritus.'

'I'll ask him.'

'Very well.'

The doorbell rings again. And again.

'I'll have to go.' I throw the receiver down and answer the door.

It's my mum. She looks terribly tired with dark circles around her eyes and lipstick on her teeth.

'Can I come in for a while?' she says. 'It won't upset Tony, will it? I know how hard the poor lad works.'

'He isn't here.'

'Working late again?'

'No, he's at the pub.'

'He deserves some time out. You should be grateful that he doesn't want to be home under your feet all the time.'

I'd like him to be under my feet some of the time though, I muse. I'd like him to want to be with me.

Mum takes Chloe from me and gives her a cuddle. 'Hello, my darling. Oh, your poor little face. She's hot, isn't she, Lisa?'

'It's her teeth.' I take her back. 'I was just about to give her a bath.'

Mum brings two cups of tea upstairs, where I have Chloe in the bath, propped up on a sponge slope and surrounded by yellow ducks and bubbles. Mum perches on the edge of the bath, clutching a fluffy white towel. She keeps sighing very loudly, and I'm beginning to realise how Tony feels when he comes home to find my family here. It's getting me down now.

82

'I can't understand why, when your dad claims to be so bored, he refuses to switch the telly on,' Mum says.

'Daytime TV isn't that gripping.'

'There's only so much two people can talk about though: the state of the pavements; speed cameras; funerals. When you retire, your friends start popping off.' Mum sighs again. 'Dad wanted to come over here with me, but I said we'd be having a girlie chat.'

'Have you tried telling him how you feel?'

'How can I when I've spent years going on about how much I was looking forward to him retiring so that we could do more together?'

Later, once Mum has gone home and I've put Chloe to bed in her carrycot, I notice that the bath is split. I'm the only person in the world who is married to a plumber and has no bath. And I wanted a long soak in my own detritus, just to spite the mother-in-law.

Instead, I go to the kitchen, pull out a big tin from the cupboard, lever the lid open with the end of a knife and release the sickly-sweet scent of milk powder. I dig around for a while for the scoop with the knife, so as not to contaminate it, before I remember that I've left the scoop in the dishwasher, which is on. I yank the door open, stopping it midcycle. Steam pours out, like the steam that's beginning to pour out of my ears at the thought of Tony sitting in the pub – if that's where he is – enjoying a few beers and some adult conversation with the lads. That may be a contradiction in terms: can 'lads' talk' about Arsenal, Rachel Stevens and motorbikes be described as grown-up?

I pour boiled water up to the level in each bottle. I make up seven, plus one spare, because Chloe sometimes catches me out. She suggests that she's starving, then falls asleep on the teat, having drunk no more than an ounce. I line up the bottles and get scooping. Scoop, level and tip without chucking it all over the worktop. How easy is that? Try it when you can't recall the last time you had a good night's sleep.

One. Two. I yawn. Three.

'Lisa! I'm home!'

Tony joins me in the kitchen. Was that three or four? I can't remember.

'I've lost count, thanks to you.'

'Is that any way to treat your loving husband?' He steps up behind me and rests his hands on the curve of my waist.

'I've stayed in all evening, while you've been out enjoying yourself.'

His fingers stiffen. 'You said I could go out tonight. I asked you this morning.'

'I know.' I clutch the knife tight. 'Oh, what am I going to do with this bottle?'

'It doesn't matter if it's out by a scoop or two. Even I've miscounted occasionally.'

'You?' I try to recall when Tony ever made up Chloe's bottles. 'You must be remembering doing Jade's.'

'I've done Chloe's a few times.'

'When?'

'If you're that worried, tip it out and start again,' Tony says testily.

'I'll have to boil more water and wait for it to cool. I'll be here all night.'

'So?'

'I've got too many other things to do.' I look up at the clock. The hands blur. 'I'm so tired.' I push Tony away, and turn to face him. He's looking a little the worse for wear, but that doesn't make him any less attractive. 'How's Jim? What did you talk about?'

'Do I ask you what you talk about with Clare when you go out together?'

'No, because I tell you.'

'Do you want to ring Jim to check?'

'No, no.' I wipe my face.

'Do you realise that you've just wiped your face with the floorcloth?'

I frown.

'I don't suppose you knew that we had one.'

Tony's teasing, but I don't think he realises how mean that sounds. I haven't had the time or energy to whizz round with the Hoover, or mop the kitchen floor.

'Come on, love,' he goes on. 'This won't last. Yes, Chloe was a mistake, but these things happen. Before you know it, she'll be like Jade.'

84

'That's what I'm afraid of.'

'Oh, don't be silly, Lisa. We have two beautiful daughters. You should be very proud of them.'

'I am.'

'Come on, we'll be all right. We'll get through it. Let's go to bed.'

'I can't.' I'm close to tears. I don't need reminding that the house is a tip. 'I've got to do the ironing.' I gaze at the cloth. 'And clean the bloody floor.'

'It can wait.' Tony takes my hand. I snatch it back, my heart mean and small. 'Let *me* finish the bottles.'

'Go on then.' I stand and watch as Tony spills milk powder over the floor. He's slow and clumsy. I push him aside.

'For goodness sake, let me do it.'

'I was trying to help.'

'You can help by getting out of my way. Go and take a look at the bath – it's sprung a leak. Or go and watch a film or something. Go and sit on your bum and let me do everything, like you normally do.'

'I can't help you unless you tell me what you need help with.' Tony sounds aggrieved, but so am I.

'If I ask you to do anything, you accuse me of nagging.'

'Okay,' Tony says flatly. 'Goodnight.' He closes the door behind him. A draught chills my feet. I don't do the ironing. I don't clean the floor. I head upstairs, change and slide into bed. I lie very still, listening. Tony is already snoring. Chloe starts to snuffle about. I guess it's getting boring in that carrycot, staring up into the dark, wondering if anyone's ever going to come over and speak to you again, musing over why you've been dropped into a place of solitary confinement when you're in the mood for conversation. She chatters to herself for a while, and I recognise her growing frustration at not being answered. She's going to cry any time . . . I hold my breath . . . now!

'Tone?' I nudge him in the ribs, but he doesn't stir. After all that beer, he's sleeping like a baby – but not our baby. I struggle out of bed, pick Chloe up and carry her downstairs.

'Hush, don't cry, darling.' I walk her up and down the kitchen. I can't shut her up. I want to throw her against the wall, or dump her in the wheelie bin with the lid shut, but I don't. I wouldn't. Really.

85

In desperation, I call the helpline number that the librarian pointed out for me. The phone rings for ages before a message cuts in. 'This is the Infant Sleepline. There is no one here to take your call. Please leave a message and we will get back to you as soon as possible. You might like to avoid calling at our busiest times, which are between ten p.m. and two a.m.'

My teeth ache. My head pounds. I know my mum says that you shouldn't cry over spilled milk, but I do tonight.

Chapter Six

'Milky pops? I'll fetch your milky pops, Chlo.' How can I expect Jade to do well at English when our household communicates through babyspeak?

'I bet that Ethan's nanny has a cut-glass accent so that Ethan learns to speak posh.' I fasten the poppers on Chloe's sleepsuit, a yellow one covered with red elephants that used to belong to Jade. (Tony never complained about me hanging on to Jade's baby clothes for sentimental reasons because we had room to store them in the loft.) 'It'll be Mama and Papa, not Mummy and Daddy. Do you think she'll be in uniform?'

'She'll wear a jacket, buttoned up to the throat, a skirt, black stockings and kidskin gloves.' Clare keeps glancing out of my living-room window.

'If you'd forgotten to leave the handbrake on, your car would have rolled down the hill by now.'

'I'm keeping an eye on Fern. I didn't bring her in because I thought you'd be ready.' Clare jangles her keys impatiently, and I find myself wishing that I was as keen to get to work as she is.

I pick Chloe up and sit her in her carryseat. She isn't impressed. She arches her back, flaps her arms and kicks her legs. Her face reddens. 'Please, Chloe,' I beg. 'Clare's in a hurry.'

'I'll carry her. You bring the seat and we'll put her in it once she's in the car.'

I hand Chloe over to Clare. She smiles and burbles with joy. It's amazing how quickly a girl learns how to get her own way. Jade's known exactly how to twist my arm since I can remember.

'I've agreed to let Jade have dance lessons with Manda.'

'I shan't encourage Fern to take up dancing.'

'She'd look very cute in a tutu, although I don't suppose that Jim would approve. I doubt that anyone makes ballet dresses in Arsenal colours.'

'I don't want her having thick calves like mine, or hundreds of verrucas,' Clare says protectively. 'Come on, Lees. Let's get going.'

Although I'd expected a mansion from the way Jacqui described her home, it's a modest three-bed detached modern house tucked away in a development of similar houses in a close on the far side of the recreation ground.

We pile our gear on the doorstep and fetch the babies from Clare's car. We have no key – Jacqui hasn't provided us with one yet – and we have to wait for some time after I've rung the bell for the nanny to open the door. He – yes, it's a he – is beautiful. Even Clare is gobsmacked.

'Hi, I'm Peter.' He flashes a mouthful of white teeth. Anyone less like Mary Poppins, I can't imagine. Clare starts stroking her hair and fluttering her eyelashes.

'Peter, who is there?' A woman's voice. Not English. A blonde in her early twenties appears behind him and rests one hand on his shoulder in a gesture of possession.

'These must be the cleaners that your employer warned you about, Katya,' Peter says.

'Warned?' I can't help noticing the close-fitting white shorts – Tony used to wear shorts like that.

'A figure of speech, I assume.' Peter goes on to introduce us to Katya, his girlfriend, who is looking after Ethan. He is helping her with her studies before she returns to Latvia in September. She has an English exam at the end of the week.

'Does Jacqui know about this arrangement?' Clare enquires.

'Do not tell, please,' Katya says nervously. 'I do not wish to lose my work.' She looks down at the step and her face relaxes into a smile. 'Oh, you have bought the babies.'

'It's "brought",' Peter corrects her. 'They've brought the babies with them.'

Peter and Katya take the babies and whisk them off to the dining room where Jacqui's set up some kind of play area. There's an alphabet frieze on the wall, and the table stands to one side, covered with a plastic sheet. There's also an upright piano with Easter Eggs lined up on top of it.

'Easter Eggs in June? How can anyone save chocolate that long?' Clare exclaims. 'It's a sign of a highly controlled personality.'

'Sh.' I am aware that Katya and Peter are listening.

These are no ordinary three-for-two eggs from Woolies, but personalised Belgian chocolate eggs. There is one in the shape of a heart with *To My Darling Wife* written around its circumference in white fondant.

'I shouldn't think that they taste anywhere near as nice as Cadbury's,' I say enviously.

'It isn't normal behaviour.' Clare lifts the lid off the piano keys. 'I wonder if Jacqui plays, or if it's for Ethan to help him realise her dream of raising a child prodigy. Shall we play "Chopsticks"?'

'I'm rusty.' I sit beside her and soon we're playing like we used to at school.

'Can you play, Katya?' says Clare.

'No, no.'

'We'll teach you some traditional songs,' Clare continues regardless. I nod in agreement, assuming that Katya is here to experience English culture as much as to look after other people's children. However, she isn't very forthcoming. I don't know if it's because she's shy or she hasn't acquired enough of the vocabulary yet. I ask her if she's done any training, if she's a Norland Nanny, and Peter tells me that she isn't a nanny at all. She's an au pair.

We sit in a circle with the babies on our knees and sing 'Wind My Bobbin Up', 'Pop Goes the Weasel', and 'Three Little Men in a Flying Saucer'. Peter holds his hands up in surrender when I suggest 'Humpty Dumpty' next.

'That's enough. Really. Let Katya take care of the babies. You go off and clean.'

'I have to mind four children at my other place,' Katya says. 'It is too quiet at this house.'

'Oh, it isn't quiet with us around,' Clare assures her.

'We've noticed,' says Peter.

Clare and I wander out into the hall, wondering where to start.

'I think we should take a recce first,' Clare says, 'then we'll take some swabs to send off to the lab.'

'What do you mean?'

'I've acquired some Germ-busting Test-kits.'

'Aren't you rather taking advantage of our friendship?'

'Isn't Jacqui? She charges us full price for her products, and probably a bit extra, judging by the cost of those babywipes. We charge the going rate for our services and, if that isn't adequate justification for you, Lisa, I'm desperate. I can't pay the bills.' Clare hesitates beneath an enormous picture in a gilt frame – I don't know how we missed it when we came to give Jacqui a copy of our contract, terms and conditions. 'Hey – I imagined from the way Jacqui talked about him that Greg was no oil painting.'

'It is an oil painting, isn't it?' I examine the picture more closely. 'No, it's one of those wedding photos altered to look like one.'

'I was expecting to see someone with heavy brows and a sour face,' Clare says. 'Greg isn't unattractive. In fact, he reminds me of Kevin Costner.'

Slightly disappointed that Jacqui hasn't conveyed the correct impression of her husband's appearance, we move on through to the kitchen.

'Why on earth would anyone even consider chucking all this in?' Clare runs one fingertip across the sleek stainless-steel finish of the fridge door. Everything looks new, right down to the apples in the fruit bowl on the worktop. I can't see any mouldy oranges or black bananas, which suggests that not only does Jacqui buy healthy fruit but, unlike mine, her family eats it as well.

'You can't equate money with happiness.'

'You can when you haven't got any. I've just received a bill for a credit card I didn't know I had. Jim says he's been consolidating our debts. How am I going to stop him?'

'I don't know. Nobody's perfect. All husbands have their faults.' When I'm in Tony's company, all the niggles and irritations of everyday life – his being overprotective about Jade, his criticism of my housekeeping skills, and his staying out late with Jim – come to the surface, yet while we are apart like this, I find that my memory fails. It must be love . . .

'Jim's having his bike serviced so we can advertise it.'

'You twisted his arm then?'

'I gave him a choice. Me and Fern, or a longterm relationship with a motorbike. Hey, this is for you.' Clare picks up an invoice from a heap of brochures for bathroom suites on the kitchen table. 'Twenty-eight quid for some reconstituted sharks' cartilage and extract of green-lipped mussel?'

'Jacqui hasn't forgotten about my knees,' I say gratefully.

'Neither have I, because you won't let me.' Clare grins. 'It seems a bit of a rip-off to me, but if you're in that much pain, I suppose that you'll pay anything.'

I grab the tubs of supplement. I'll give Jacqui a cheque next time I see her.

'Let's see if we can find some real grime.' Clare takes a swab from the fridge doorhandle, wipes it down with a sterile wipe then takes another. (I'd swear the second swab didn't touch it.) 'It looks clean, but you can't be too careful.' While she's scribbling the details on a form, looking very much more like a nurse than a cleaner, I check the fridge contents. There are stacks of those little pots of good bacteria.

'Everyone has a dirty corner somewhere, a place where they chuck their old receipts, cottonbuds and crisp packets,' Clare says when she's finished. 'Let's find it.' She slips into her favourite pair of rubber gloves – pink ones with fake fur edging – grabs a multipurpose spray and cloth, and we search for a crack in Jacqui's façade. Zilch. Apart from a week's accumulation of dust and a few splashmarks of limescale on the bathroom tiles.

'I can't believe it,' Clare says. 'The toilet seats are down – all three of them.'

Ethan's nursery is perfect too, with a changing-station at waist height with raised surrounds, shelves and dividers. There's a place for everything, from barrier cream to Baby's *first* First Aid Kit. Clare gives the changing mat a quick squirt and wipe. I vacuum underneath the cot, and we're finished.

With the Hoover silent, I can hear the sound of people playing tennis, not on the courts at the recreation ground, but on a television downstairs. Clare and I follow the noise to the sitting room where the babies are lined up on their backs on the floor. I poke my head around the door. Katya and Peter are snogging on the sofa.

'What do you think you're doing?' I rip them off a strip, while

Clare does a hammy impression of looking appalled.

'We really should tell Jacqui,' I say in the car on the way to Clare's house where we'll have lunch, watching Wimbledon. 'She's paying Katya to cuddle up with Ethan, not Peter.'

'Yes, but I bet that she's paying her peanuts,' says Clare. 'Why shouldn't Katya take a break now and then?'

'You're siding with Katya to get one up on Jacqui,' I suggest. 'I know you're not keen on her.'

Clare doesn't respond to my opinion which means that I'm right, but she's too stubborn to admit it.

'I don't think they'll do it again,' Clare says eventually, 'not in front of Ethan anyway.'

'I'm not worried that they're going to corrupt our babies' young minds. Katya is supposed to be responsible for Ethan – and Fern and Chloe. Anything could have happened.'

'Give them a chance. Don't you remember when you were going out with your first boyfriend? I remember mine.' Clare raises one eyebrow. 'I didn't have a clue what a sub-woofer was until I met Trev.'

'Keep your eyes on the road!'

Clare brakes sharply as a car pulls out in front of us and gives the driver a two-fingered salute as he roars off in a souped-up BMW. 'Where were we?'

'In the Audiovisual department at Dixons.' Clare persuaded me to accompany her there several times before she plucked up the courage to open a conversation with Trev. We spent ages comparing cassette-players, but never bought one.

'Oh yes,' says Clare. 'We were talking about young love. Are you sure you can't remember the first flush of passion when you and Tony couldn't keep your hands off each other?'

'It was a long time ago,' I say grudgingly. I can recall when Tony first kissed me – the anticipation, the glint of his eyes in the dark, and the heat of his breath . . .

'There are times when you should keep your gob shut, and this is one of them,' Clare says firmly, and I make up my mind not to say anything to Jacqui about her neglectful nanny. 'Now, will you keep an eye on the wing mirror your side?' Clare is trying to manoeuvre the car between a row of stationary traffic and a van that's pulled in so that its offside wheels are on the pavement.

'You won't make it.' I wince as Clare sticks out her chin and slams her foot on the accelerator. The mirror catches the side of the van, but we're through and out on the other side of the traffic lights before Clare slows down.

'Your mirror's smashed,' I observe.

'Oh, I never use it anyway.'

I smile to myself. Clare might be a useless driver, and we might have the odd disagreement now and then, but she is the *best* best friend I could possibly have.

'How about a picnic?'

When Jacqui mentions the possibility of us all meeting up at the weekend, I wish that I'd suggested it. I'd like to have impressed her with my sociable personality and organisational skills. We arrange to assemble in the park on the Saturday at noon.

The recreation ground is a windswept open space with views of the tower blocks of New Addington and the hills beyond. There's a tatty pavilion where the council wages constant war with graffiti artists. Behind that is a tall wire fence with ivy growing up through it to give some privacy to the houses that back onto the park. At the far end is a small car park and a children's play area.

Today, the sun shines from a clear blue sky. You can see the glint of planes, six or seven at a time – the Heathrow stack, the jets flying north from Gatwick, and smaller planes flying in and out of Biggin Hill.

Tony, Jade, Chloe and I catch up with Clare, Fern and Jim at the park gate. Clare and I arrange picnic blankets and cool boxes on the grass nearby before we sit back to watch Tony and Jim kicking a football about. They're both wearing Arsenal shirts.

Tony is running around, keeping possession with Stop Turns and Outside Hooks. Jim limps along some way after him.

'Tone thinks he's Thierry Henry.' I smile and carry on rocking Chloe's pram gently with my foot. 'Jade's disowning him.'

Jade sits on a bench under one of the trees in the corner of the rec, holding a notebook open in one hand and chewing on the end of a pencil.

'It isn't fair, is it?' Clare says. 'Kids have so much homework nowadays.'

'Oh, she isn't doing her homework. She's writing lyrics for this band she sings with.' I look up. Jacqui is walking towards us, her hips swaying in a pair of tight white jeans. Some way behind her on the path is a man attending to the front wheel of an all-terrain pram.

'Hi, everyone.' Jacqui smiles. 'Greg's mending a puncture. He won't be long.'

'There's room for a small one.' I shift up towards Clare on the blanket.

Jacqui sits down. 'I feel as though I haven't seen you two for ages. You made a great job of the housework, by the way.'

'Thanks,' says Clare.

'What did you think of Katya? A gem, isn't she? I was so lucky to find her.'

'She seemed very pleasant.' I try desperately not to mention Peter, having decided after a battle with my conscience not to get Katya into any trouble. If it happens again, of course, if I feel that Ethan is in any danger, I will tell her. Secrets between friends are like secrets between spouses. They fester.

'I thought you were going to employ a qualified nanny,' says Clare.

'Katya might be an au pair, but she's had more experience of looking after babies than I have,' says Jacqui. 'She won't spend much time alone with Ethan anyway. I'm sending him to a gymnastics club and, as soon as I can find one, a music-based activity session. It'll have to be local. I don't think Katya can drive.'

Neither can Jacqui or Clare, I think, trying not to laugh.

'Unfortunately, that means you won't be able to bring the babies to work with you, because Katya won't be there to look after them,' Jacqui goes on. 'I hope you don't mind.'

Clare does. I can tell from the expression on her face.

'My mum will be delighted,' I say. 'She's desperate to come over to our house to look after Chloe.'

Greg turns up with his fingers black with grease. Jacqui makes the introductions, touching Greg's shoulder. He's younger than Jacqui but, in my opinion, the age difference isn't enough to qualify him as her toyboy. His hair is brown and wavy, and brushed up into a Hoxton fin, his eyes are dark like Ethan's, and the red logo on his T-shirt coordinates with Jacqui's red

94

scoop-neck top. He sits down alongside his wife.

Tony strolls, and Jim limps, over to join us. Tony offers Greg a beer. Jacqui asks him if he'd prefer a glass of the chilled white wine that she's brought with her, but Greg declines and snaps the lid off a can of lager. Greg props his son up between his outstretched legs so that Ethan can reach the fringe at the edge of the picnic blanket. He fingers it, and wobbles forwards, trying to stuff it into his mouth.

'Jade, our eldest, is over there.' Tony nods towards her. 'She's writing lyrics, and one day she'll buy us a Spanish villa with the royalties.'

'Not if you won't buy her a mobile phone,' I say.

'Don't let Ethan eat the grass, Greg.' Jacqui sighs wearily. 'No, don't just rub his fingers on your shorts. Use a wipe.'

Greg frowns. 'I'm not sure that I put them in the bag. I counted out four nappies, like you said.'

'Oh, that's so New Man of you,' Jacqui says scathingly.

'Have one of mine,' I offer.

'At least I was trying,' Greg says.

'You certainly are that.' Jacqui takes a wipe from the packet that I find in Chloe's changing bag, and cleans Ethan's hands. 'I don't know why I ask you to do anything. It's always easier if I do it myself.' She looks at me and Clare, and gives a smile that says, 'You know what I mean. You understand.'

In a spirit of mutual understanding, Clare, Jacqui and I unpack the food. Tony calls Jade over so we can eat.

'I hate picnics, they're so not cool.' Jade rolls her eyes. She's dressed up as if she's going clubbing, in a black vest-top and low-slung hipster jeans with a mesh insert full-length down the seams. They're black too.

'Can I see your lyrics?' asks Clare.

Jade flashes a page of her notebook. It's blank.

'Ali says that he can find inspiration anywhere,' she says. 'I don't think he can have tried Selsdon Rec.'

'What's he like, this Ali?' says Clare.

Jade glances towards me. 'He's all right.' She blushes and changes the subject. 'Mum, can we go on holiday this year? Everyone goes on holiday.'

'Not this year, darling, not with Chloe.' We went last year with Clare and Jim, and shared a caravan in France. The weather blew hot and cold, and the mosquitoes treated our lodgings as if it was a giant lunchbox. In my opinion, the purpose of a holiday is to remind you how wonderful it is to be at home. I know it sounds sad, but I like my home comforts.

However, Jade looks so disappointed that I find myself promising to book us a holiday in the sun next year.

'Your dad deserves a break,' I add, nodding towards Tony who is already muching his way through a third sandwich.

'Can I borrow your phone then, Mum? Please . . .'

I hand it over – there's only a couple of quid left on the card – and Jade returns to her seat under the tree with a sandwich and my phone, and starts pressing buttons.

Jacqui nibbles at a cheese scone and leaves it on the side of the plate. She's still detoxing, I suppose.

'Are these homemade?' she asks, taking a sip of wine instead.

'Yes,' I say proudly.

'I thought so. They have a certain rustic charm.'

'You must take that as a compliment, Lisa,' Greg says supportively. 'I think they're delicious. It isn't often that I enjoy some home cooking.'

'That's because you're always eating in motorway service stations,' Jacqui grumbles. I find myself wanting to tell her to give him a break, poor guy.

Immediately after lunch, we're back onto comparing labours, this time from a male perspective. I don't know why I should be surprised. It is the one thing that our husbands know for certain that they have in common.

'Jim,' Clare speaks for him, 'said that the build-up was as stressful as watching an Arsenal match; then, when Fern came out two weeks after her due date, he said it was like winning the FA, European and World Cups all at once.'

'Ethan was early,' says Greg.

'Unlike his father, who's always late,' snipes Jacqui.

'I made it to the birth in time.' Greg rubs Jacqui's back. 'It was an amazing experience.'

'It wasn't for me,' Tony grumbles, but a smile plays on his lips. 'Lisa bit me.'

'I don't remember that.' I sit up too quickly, my face burning.

'Labour obviously brings out the animal in you,' Jacqui teases. 'I'll give you the number of the birthing-pool company for next time – if there *is* a next time,' she adds, glancing in Tony's direction.

'No way,' says Tony. 'There won't be any more babies for us. I've booked an appointment for the snip.'

'You're having a laugh, mate.' Jim goes pale.

Greg hands Ethan over to Jacqui, and crosses one leg over the other.

'So many people end up having reversals nowadays – it costs a fortune and isn't always successful. Oh, you mustn't have a vasectomy yet, not until you're completely sure,' Jacqui says, wide-eyed.

'Oh, I'm sure,' Tony confirms.

Jim stands up. He shuffles one hand discreetly about in the front of his shorts, then kicks the football in Tony's direction.

'Do you fancy a game, Greg?' Tony gets up too.

'Oh, I don't know . . .'

'Go on.'

'I haven't played for years.'

Tony kicks the ball to Greg. Greg goes in goal between a cool box and a pram. I make daisy-chains, and drape them in Chloe's and Fern's hair. Jacqui says she prefers that Ethan doesn't have one.

'I don't want there to be any confusion about his gender orientation.'

'So you wouldn't dress him in pink, or give him a doll to play with,' Clare says.

'Do you think anyone dressed Tony or Jim in pink when they were babies?'

'No.' I smile at the thought.

'There you go then. Boys are supposed to be boys. There's no need to confuse the issue by giving them girlish toys.'

A ladybird lands on Chloe's nose. She sits there, slowly going cross-eyed as she tries to focus on it. I laugh. She blows bubbles of spit. I wipe her mouth with the corner of a muslin cloth, then squeeze some teething gel on her gum where a second tooth is about to break through beside the first. Jacqui looks on enviously. I was right – Ethan has no teeth yet.

'We used to make daisy-chains, didn't we, Jade?' I call across to her. She's scowling at her notebook, and I suspect that her songs are going to be more like Morrissey's than Cliff Richard's.

97

I wish I hadn't mentioned the daisy-chains though. She glares at me until a thumping, thrumming bass beat from the direction of the car park distracts her attention. It vibrates along the surface of the ground, and I feel as if I'm sitting on a washing machine at full spin.

'It's Ali!' Jade squeals as she jumps up. 'He's brought Kimberley and Shifty with him.'

In the distance, two boys and a girl get out of a yellow convertible.

'Where are you going?' I stand up and intercept Jade as she heads off towards them. 'Jade, stop!' She glowers at me. 'Is Ali old enough to be driving that thing?'

'He's passed his test. Mum, he's eighteen.'

I am appalled. The car bears an old registration plate.

'He's just bought the car,' Jade says.

I have to say that I'm surprised. It looks as if he should have had it for years.

'Manda calls it The Yellow Peril,' Jade goes on.

'You're not going anywhere in that car!'

Jade ignores me. I can only watch her go off to the playpark with the others. They hang off the swings. The two boys smoke. When Jade sees that I'm still watching, they slope off through a gap in the fence beyond, to hide among the trees and bushes that grow around the site of what I believe is a bomb crater from the war, a bowl of chalky soil riddled with fox-holes. Clare and I used to hang out there with our friends. Our boyfriends used to come up here and play football, just as our husbands are now.

Greg is still in goal, standing with his hands at his sides and his knees apart, looking rather despondent. Jim jogs up, his limp miraculously absent, and kicks a ball at him from an imaginary penalty spot. He doesn't put much welly into it. Perspiration drips off his forehead, and his shirt sticks to his back. Too many nights down at the Sir Julian Huxley are taking their toll.

Greg saves the ball as it rolls slowly towards the cool box.

'Oh, well done, Daddy.' Jacqui claps Ethan's hands together. 'What's the score, Greg?'

'I've given up counting,' he says rather sheepishly.

'He's saved two and we've put nineteen past him.' Tony is grinning.

'Isn't it time you swapped over?' Clare suggests. 'Hasn't Greg suffered enough humiliation?' she adds aside to me. But Tony comes chasing up and passes the ball to Jim who knocks it into the air. Tony's head makes contact. The ball soars past Greg's ear.

'Goal!' Tony strips off his shirt, whirls it around his head and tosses it towards us. Jacqui catches it. I notice how she folds it neatly, compelled by her maternal instinct, while Tony's jumping all over Jim, hugging him and planting kisses on the top of his shiny pate.

'One more,' Tony says.

'It's your turn in goal.' Greg picks up the ball. 'I've had enough.'

Tony misses Greg's first ball, and his second shot at goal.

'You're pretty good at this, Greg,' says Jim.

'I used to play as a kid. I was signed by Millwall, but I couldn't take the pressure, all the training. My fault really.'

Jim and Tony's jaws drop. Greg has just shot up in their estimation. He isn't just another dad with a boring job. He could have been a famous striker.

'I could have been a footballer's wife,' Jacqui says.

'As you never fail to keep reminding me,' Greg says quietly.

I recognise the competitive glint in Tony's eye. He hates losing. You can almost hear his frustration as he thumps the ball back out to Jim. Jim passes to Greg. Clare winks at me. Greg dribbles up again, feints to the left, and whacks the ball. Tony dives the wrong way this time. Either the ground isn't so forgiving, or he's trying too hard, because he lands awkwardly on his hand.

'I'm fine,' he yelps. 'Really.' He stands, clutching his fingers. Jacqui jumps up, thrusts Ethan into Greg's arms and inspects Tony's injury.

'You should get that checked,' she says. 'What do you think, Lisa?'

'I wouldn't take any notice of Lisa's opinion,' says Tony. 'She made Jade do Games at school with a cracked bone in her wrist.'

'It wasn't hurting her that much, and you know how she makes a fuss over nothing.'

'I know.' Tony winks at me and I know that he's teasing.

'Can you wiggle your fingers, Tone?' I ask.

99

'A little . . .'

'I think you've broken them,' says Jacqui. 'I mean, I haven't got a medical qualification but I've done a Saint John Ambulance First Aid course. I didn't learn how to repair broken bones, but I'm told that I shone at mouth to mouth.'

She gazes up at my husband, and I feel as if I've just had a football booted at my chest. She fancies him, doesn't she? I tell myself I'm being silly, that if she hadn't joked about looking out for a new man, I wouldn't be in the slightest bit bothered. She's had one too many glasses of wine, and what's wrong with some innocent flirting, after all?

'Jacqui's right – you should see a doctor to be on the safe side,' says Greg.

'Make sure you see the right kind of doctor though,' Jim mutters.

'There are good ones and bad ones,' says Clare. 'When Jim had his accident, the consultant in Intensive Care said that he had no more than a couple of months to live. He was wrong. Jim's had three more years, and the doctor's dead.'

'I'll see how it goes,' Tony says manfully. By 'manfully' I mean that he's biting his lip and clutching his hand, as if he's about to die in agony himself.

'We should be going, Greg.' Jacqui gives me a key for her front door. 'Turn up when you like – I shan't be there.'

'And neither will Ethan now,' Clare says rather acidly, as we watch Greg and Jacqui walking purposefully up the path towards the opposite end of the rec. 'I suppose he has to be seen to be mixing with the right babies. Did you notice how Jacqui was flirting with Tony?'

'Of course I did.'

'Don't you mind, all things considered?'

Tony interrupts my opportunity to ask Clare what she means.

'Are you talking about me?' He sits down on the picnic blanket with a can of lager, tips his head back and drinks. The muscles in his neck tauten, and his skin shines with sweat. He crumples the empty can in his good hand, drops it on the picnic blanket and picks Chloe up.

'Be careful,' I warn. I don't know why. Chloe is in no danger. She smiles and coos at her daddy.

'You know I'd never hurt her,' Tony says sharply.

'I know.'

We sit side by side in warm sunshine and a word-stealing wind. Jim offers to buy ice creams from the van that's just pulled up in the car park.

'Anyone would think you'd won the Lottery,' I say.

'He did – ten pounds last Saturday.' Clare smiles.

I thank him, but decline. It's time we were going home too. Tony fetches Jade, but she doesn't want to come with us.

'Please let me stay, Dad.'

Tony shakes his head in response to her fluttering eyelashes.

'Why do you keep treating me like a little kid? Don't you realise how embarrassing it is to have parents like you?' Jade's lip trembles. She squeezes a tear from the corner of one eye.

'Perhaps it would be all right as long as you promise not to go anywhere near that car of Ali's,' I suggest gently. I can see that Tony is torn.

'Okay, Jade, you can stay for a while,' he sighs. 'You've got to promise you'll be back by five. That's when the long hand's on the twelve and the short hand's—'

'Dad,' Jade interrupts. 'I've never owned a watch with hands. I live in the digital age, not the Early Jurassic like you and Mum.' She doesn't say 'goodbye', or 'see you later', but turns and waves from halfway across the field.

I link my arm with Tony's.

'You can't protect her for ever, Tone. We don't want her to be tagging around with us when she's forty because you wouldn't let her have any friends.'

'I suppose not.' He smiles ruefully and we head off across the rec with Chloe.

When we arrive home, Tony's fingers have become very swollen. 'Look at my hand,' he says. 'What do you think?'

'As you said earlier, my opinion isn't worth anything.'

'Would you mind driving me to the hospital?'

I try phoning Jade on the house phone, but there's no answer. I try texting on Tony's.

Answr fone!

She responds immediately.

'Why didn't you answer it in the first place?'

'I thought it would be someone for you. I went through your last number redials – Kimberley says her dad's number is there, lots.' Her voice is laced with suspicion, but I can't worry about that now.

'I'm taking your dad to hospital. We'll pick you up on the way.'

'I'll stay with Kimberley.'

I am about to argue when I realise that it would be easier. When I phone Colin to check, he says it's fine for Jade to stay overnight. This is irritating, since for the payback for Kimberley's sleepover with us, I am not being taken out to be wined and dined, I'm going to be sitting in A&E for hours with nothing but a cup of hot muddy water from a drinks machine and half a molten KitKat, dredged up from the fluff at the bottom of my handbag.

Mum has Chloe while Tony and I sit in a corridor in Mayday Hospital. The reception area is full, every seat taken. Expected waiting time, six hours.

Tony pats my knee with his good hand. 'I'm sorry, love.'

'At least we're having an evening out together, even if it is with half the employees of an NHS Trust.'

Tony smiles ruefully. 'If this is half of them, they need to take on some more.' He stretches out his legs. 'You know what would be fun to do when we get home, apart from the obvious?' he whispers. 'Imagine jumping into a hot Jacuzzi in the garden . . .'

I frown, not seeing the appeal. I'd have to take all my clothes off.

'It would be too much like having a pond,' I say. 'I'd worry about Chloe drowning in it.'

'Oh Lisa, it would have a secure lid. You don't think Jacqui would be considering one if there were any safety issues?'

'Is she? I didn't know.' I notice that Tony's nose is bright red under the striplights in the corridor. He's caught the sun, and the junior doctor who eventually sees him asks if he's seeking treatment for sunburn.

'Any previous medical history?' he asks.

'Concussion once. A bad back last week.'

'*Relevant* medical history,' the doctor says. He books Tony for an X-ray and, after another long wait, he confirms that there is no fracture, just wrenched ligaments. All he can do is strap the fingers together, which is something I could have easily done at home while watching *Casualty*.

102

'Are you going to be able to work?' I ask on the way home. Tony is self-employed and, like Clare, he can't really afford to take off more than a couple of days sick.

'I told Jacqui that I'd make a start on stripping out her old bathroom,' he says. 'I'll have to ask Jim to do it instead.'

I am reassured.

'I've given her a fifty per cent discount as she's a friend of yours.'

Silence.

'I thought you'd be pleased.'

'I wish you'd asked me first. Never mind, it doesn't matter.' I mean, Tony does do work for friends and family at reduced prices, but I haven't been friends with Jacqui for that long, and I doubt very much that she reduced the price of those supplements by half for me. It's a bit of a cheek, but Jacqui's a woman who knows what she wants and how to get it, and I can't help but admire that.

I hug my generous husband who smells of grass and lager and sweat and hospital disinfectant.

'Ouch.' He whimpers just like a baby, but I can't help smiling to myself. So what if Jacqui flirts with him? Tony is adorable. That's why I married him. What woman would wish to marry a man that other women didn't want?

Chapter Seven

I've made the instantaneous transition from text virgin to text maniac. It's addictive. I am itching to text the answer to the competition on early-morning TV. You know the kind: *What animal is Disney's famous creation, Mickey? Is it A: Louse B: Moose or C: Mouse?* I don't suppose that everyone who enters gets the answer correct. It's easy to make a slip, and I have the same chance of winning as anyone else. I don't have to justify the £1.50 entry fee to myself, but I might have to to Tony, if he ever finds out.

I peer around Jade's door. She's admiring herself in front of her bedroom mirror. I know she's my daughter, so I might be a tiny bit biased, but she is becoming a very beautiful girl, and I wonder how Ali will be able to resist her. I clear my throat.

'Jade? Could I have my phone back, please?'

She turns to me. 'I really need a phone, Mum.'

'Dad and I have agreed that we'll consider it for your birthday.'

Jade takes it out from under her pillow and hands it over. All my Pay As You Go has, not surprisingly, gone so I have to top up with my credit card before I can use it, and it takes me as long as Jade is in the bathroom to text the answer to the competition.

When Jade comes down for breakfast, she's wearing a cap. A black ponytail protrudes from the gap above the adjustable strap at the back.

'Jade, what have you done to your hair?'

'Nothing,' she says lightly. 'Have we got any chocolate spread?'

'No one eats chocolate spread for breakfast.'

'Ali does. And Kimberley.'

'You shouldn't do things just to be like other people.' I pause. 'Jade, look at me when I'm talking to you, will you?'

She looks up at me for the first time. Her eyes are black too.

'Make sure you take that make-up off before you go to school. You look like a panda with a sleep disorder.'

Once Jade's left for the bus, and Tony's headed off down the road for a paper to read while he's off work nursing his fingers, I text Colin.

Thnks 4 lkng rfter Jade @ w/e. Wil brng Kimbalee home 4 T 2nite. L.

I'm proud of my abbreviations even if they aren't very good. It's like learning a new language.

Colin rings back almost immediately.

'Hello, Lisa. I didn't realise you were into textual intercourse. I thought I'd ring you though, rather than text back, as I have something I'd like to firm up.'

'Er?'

'For the party, the housewarming.'

Can we make it? he asks. Me and Tony, not me and Colin – at least, I hope that's what he means.

'Tony and I are looking forward to it.' I make it perfectly clear that I am one of a couple to avoid any misunderstanding. I'm not sure whether Colin means to be suggestive, or not.

'That's fantastic,' says Colin. 'I don't know if Manda mentioned it, but we'd like everyone to turn up in fancy dress.'

'Oh? I'm not sure . . .'

'There's no need to worry. We've chosen a theme for you. Ancient Rome.'

'I wasn't much good at history at school.'

'If you need inspiration, think of Antony and Cleopatra.'

'Will *Up Pompeii* do?'

Colin laughs. 'I can tell you're getting into the swing of this, Lisa.'

'Can we bring anything?'

'A bottle of wine, or bunch of grapes would be most acceptable. And I'd almost forgotten – thanks for offering to have Kimberley after school today.'

'No problem.' I'd rather have the girls at my house where I

can keep an eye on them. Who knows what moral danger Jade may be exposed to at Colin and Manda's with Ali there?

I return to Jade's room and sit myself down on her sofa with Chloe, my face close to hers. Jade's diary is on her desk, not in its box. I lean towards it.

'What do you think, Chloe?' She grabs my cheek and twists it. It's painful. Very painful. And so is temptation. Very slowly, I open the book at the first page. *Diary of Jade Lauren Baker. Private. Open on Pain of Death.* There's a sketch of a skull and crossbones too, a little at odds with the fairy theme of the rest of the page. I flick through to today's date, turn back a couple of pages, then close my eyes, aware of the butterflies dancing in my belly.

The consequences of reading this book *may* be more painful than death. How am I going to tell Tony that his daughter's lost her virginity? How can I tell my mum that her granddaughter's pregnant at thirteen? I realise that Jade's not showing signs of morning sickness – she looks more vibrant than ever – but there is that small question of her craving for chocolate spread.

I'm being ridiculous. My Jade is a good girl. Although she is easily led . . .

I open my eyes, and force myself to look. The pages are blank.

Chloe tips forward. I catch her. Drops of dribble patter onto Sunday's empty page. Jade hasn't written anything for the past week. Her attack of writer's block has extended beyond struggling to find lyrics for Ali's band.

I feel angry at myself for succumbing to temptation, and at Jade for not bothering to write anything. I try to wipe Chloe's saliva away with the cuff of my sleeve, but it scuffs the lines on the page.

'Come on, Chloe, darling.' I slam the diary shut and drop it back into the box, hoping that Jade won't notice. 'Your dad had better be back soon. I've got to go to work. If I don't, there won't be any more cuddly caterpillar toys for you.' I give Chloe's cheek a gentle tweak. 'And no monthly allowances for Jade.' The extra cash that I bring in from my cleaning job isn't merely handy. It's often essential.

Neville doesn't appear to need to earn a living. He's still kicking around at home, and you would have thought that with all this time on his hands, he could at least make an effort to keep his flat clean and tidy.

All he does is sit in the dark, listening to music or watching television.

'Didn't you book yourself that round-the-world ticket?' I ask him as Clare pulls the curtains open.

'I read the health advice for world travellers – it scared me.'

'You wimp!' I observe.

Clare smiles. She's up to something.

'Your curtains are filthy,' she says. 'It says on the label that you can machine-wash them, but I always think that this kind of cotton-fibre mix looks so much better dry-cleaned, and you don't have to iron acres of material before you rehang them.'

Neville frowns. 'I'm not taking them down the High Street. That place took me to the cleaners over my suit. In fact, it would have been cheaper to buy a new one.'

'I'll have a word with that sister of mine for you, and see if I can persuade her to give you a discount. Maybe she'd do a three-for-two deal on the curtains.'

'I don't know who you're talking about,' Neville says blankly.

'My sister Sue at the dry-cleaners.'

'Oh?' He gives no indication of having noticed her – Clare has her work cut out if she really believes that Sue and Neville are made for each other – then his lips curve into the cheekiest grin. 'Your sister ought to volunteer for the Samaritans – she's a great listener. In fact, she knew exactly what was bothering me, as if she'd already been told – which, I guess, she probably had.'

Clare remains uncharacteristically silent.

'If you'd really like to do me a favour, you could drop these in the postbox on your way out.' Neville picks up a pile of envelopes from the sofa beside him. 'They're application forms,' he explains. 'It's taken me a week to make my CV sound interesting.'

'Oh, cheer up, Neville,' says Clare. 'It might never happen.'

'That's what I'm afraid of,' he says morosely. 'I won't get a job, or another girlfriend.'

'You won't if you mope about here all day. Go on, get out of here. You're spoiling the look of the place. At least you will be, by the time Lisa and I have finished with it.'

It takes us a couple of hours to clean Neville's flat once he's taken the curtains down and left us to it. After that, we're off to Mrs E's where there's a strange smell.

Mrs E insists that she can't smell anything except her eau de cologne.

'You're making a right royal fuss about nothing,' she says.

I agree. I plug the vacuum cleaner into a socket and am just about to switch it on when Clare screams at me to stop.

'There must be a leak,' she says. 'I'm going to call the Gas Board.'

'What will the Good Lord be able to do?' Mrs E adjusts her hearing-aid.

'The Gas Board!' Clare turns to me. 'We can't just leave it. If the silly old thing switches a light on tonight, she'll blow the place up.'

'Along with the dog,' I note.

Prince is lying, unusually quiet, on his Union Jack blanket, his belly bloated and rumbling and his tongue lolling out.

'Poor Prince is exhausted.' Mrs E rubs her hip. 'So am I. My friend and I slipped up to see the Princess Diana Memorial in Hyde Park. Some ignoramus gave Prince a sausage sandwich. I told them, "That dog has blue blood in his veins – he only eats chicken, lightly boiled, and biscuits".'

'We can't ignore it,' I say. 'The dog's almost unconscious. What effect will the gas have on Mrs E?'

We evacuate the house, and Clare calls British Gas who send an engineer out as a matter of urgency. Within twenty minutes, a van pulls up outside.

'We'll see you next week, Mrs E,' Clare says.

'I didn't meet the Queen. She wasn't in residence at Buckingham Palace.'

'You should have given her notice of your visit,' Clare says cheekily.

'Pardon?' Mrs E squints as if she can't see Clare either.

'You really should have that hearing-aid fixed,' Clare adds.

'I do wish you young people wouldn't mumble so. Your mother never mumbled. Always very clear, she was.'

'We'll leave you to it,' says Clare.

When I look back, Mrs E is checking the man's credentials. There's no need to worry about her. She can look after herself.

However, once we've nipped into the supermarket to pick up a few bits and pieces, we drop by on the way back to mine to check that she is all right. The engineer is coming out of her front door as we arrive.

'Hi, we're her cleaners.' Clare leans out of the car window. 'We rang you to report the leak. Is everything okay now?'

'It wasn't the boiler. It was the dog.' He grins. 'Flatulence. It's happened before.'

We don't stop.

I can't wait to get back to see Tony. It isn't often that he's waiting for me to come home, but when I get there, he's sitting down on his bum with Chloe, watching some television programme about smartening up a house, and chatting on his mobile with the paper open across his knees. He has done nothing. How annoying is that? There's no lunch prepared, no tidying done, and the post is still inside the front door, where it fell through the letterbox.

'Hi, Chloe.' I whisk her off Tony's lap. She beams and I can't help grinning back.

'Who's that on the phone?' I ask when Tony switches off.

'Jacqui. Bathroom talk.'

'What have you been doing all morning, apart from chatting to Jacqui?' I ask crossly.

'I haven't done anything.' He waves his sore fingers. 'I couldn't.'

I raise my middle finger behind Chloe's back in mock insult.

'My mum dropped in to see if I was all right. She was worried about me.'

'She didn't offer to help out then?'

'I don't see why she should.'

'She does the housework for your sisters.'

'If she did it for you, you'd accuse her of interfering.' He pauses. 'I'll have a tea, if you're making one.'

'Tony!'

'Only joking,' he grins. 'I'll do it. By the way, Mum's left some of Dad's veggies from the allotment. They've had a glut.'

I follow Tony into the kitchen and find a bag of vegetables on the draining board. Just the sight of the spring onions is enough to reduce me to tears, and the cabbages are so big that I half-expect to find a label with *Exported from Sellafield* attached to them. I should be grateful, but I'm not. Why does everyone keep giving me more work to do? Can't they see that I have enough on my plate? I hide the veg under the sink, and make cheese and pickle sandwiches before leaving Chloe with Tony so that I can fetch Jade, and Kimberley and her euphonium, from school.

Jade takes full advantage of her dad being at home to ask for her allowance early, after softening him up with a show of concern for his injured hand.

'Kimberley and I are going shopping this Saturday.'

'I'll come with you,' I say quickly. 'You're not hanging out as you call it in Croydon all day on your own.'

'Mum, there are two of us,' Jade says. 'I need some clothes. All my jeans are like, cropped, and you're always complaining that my tops are too revealing. It isn't surprising that I've outgrown them though, is it? I haven't had new clothes for ages.'

'I could take you to Bluewater,' I say.

'There won't be time.' Tony reminds us of the fact that it's Jacqui's birthday party on Saturday. 'You and Kimberley can take the bus into town in the morning, and I'll pick you up at lunchtime.'

'There's no point in me going if I haven't got my allowance.'

'I'm broke,' says Tony.

'You can't be,' I say. 'You took some cash out at the end of last week.'

'I went to pick up some plumbing supplies, didn't I?'

'I thought you usually paid on your business card.'

'I had the cash in my pocket.' He scratches his head. 'I didn't think.'

I wonder which of us is going mad, him or me?

First thing in the morning three days later, I catch Tony in the hall, toolbox in one hand and lunch in the other.

'Where do you think you're going?' I ask as he heads for the front door.

'I've got to get back to work, babe.'

'Hang on a mo.'

He hesitates. 'I don't know how you do it. I mean, I adore Chloe but sitting at home all day with her and Bid-Up TV because there isn't anything else to watch is driving me bananas.'

I know that: Jim came round to see him and ended up buying a kid's bike that he's going to put aside until Fern's old enough to ride it, and yet another pair of earrings for Clare.

'Have you rung my mum?' I go on.

Tony raises one eyebrow. 'What would I want to do that for?'

'I'm working today. Who's going to look after Chloe?'

'Oh? I'm sorry, I didn't think . . .'

'Okay, leave it to me.' I flounce off to the phone. Luckily, Mum's at home, and delighted to have an excuse to come over before Clare picks me up on the way to Jacqui's. There's a sporty silver Hyundai and a skip outside Jacqui's house. I'm surprised that the skip hasn't been disguised with stick-on flower decorations to match her wheelie bins.

'You don't think she's having an affair?' says Clare.

'Don't be ridiculous. She wouldn't ask us to drop round any time, would she?' I ring the doorbell.

'Hello,' says Jacqui when she eventually opens the door. She's wearing an ice-blue jogsuit, and full make-up.

'Who's that?' a female voice shouts from the kitchen. No affair then.

'It's only the cleaners,' Jacqui calls back.

'I thought you'd be at work,' I say.

'Katya has caught chickenpox from that other family she works for. I can't cope with Ethan being ill, as well as work and everything else.'

We step inside the hall. Clare is turning red, and about to explode like an overblown balloon.

'Only the cleaners?' she whispers. 'Did you hear that?'

'She was merely explaining who we are,' I argue softly. 'Come on, Clare, you're always telling me to act like a professional.' I head for the kitchen where a woman sits perched on a stool with Ethan in her arms. She turns towards us, her long black hair floating around her shoulders as though she's just stepped out of an advert for a salon shampoo. She smiles, revealing a mouthful of stained teeth.

'This is Anjula, my partner in the franchise and a friend of mine from way back,' says Jacqui, reminding me that she had a life before she met us, and I don't know much about it.

'Call me Anje,' she drawls. 'I was just saying to Jacks here, how she and Greg seem to be doing well for themselves with a new bathroom and a hot tub on the way.' Anje's short white denim-style jacket contrasts with her deeply tanned complexion, and I can't understand how anyone can wear leather trousers in this hot weather. Her earrings are too big, and her strappy red heels too high. 'I hope we're all invited to try it out. It would be such a laugh.'

'I suppose so,' says Jacqui.

'Do you remember when we last went skinny-dipping?'

Jacqui glances towards me and Clare. 'No.'

'You must do. Brighton, last summer. You, me, Greg and Mitch. Jacks, you stripped right down to your birthday suit. When you realised that that old bloke was watching, you tried to run down the beach to the sea, only it was pebbles, and you hadn't got anything on your feet, so he copped quite an eyeful.' Anje's voice is husky and deep. So is her laugh. It makes Ethan sit up in her arms.

'If you keep cuddling Ethan like that, you'll fall pregnant,' Clare smiles.

'Oh, you don't believe in that old wives' tale,' says Jacqui.

'I picked up a friend's baby on my way round the supermarket. The next day, I fell for Chloe,' I say.

Anjula passes Ethan back to Jacqui as if he's a hot potato. Silence falls, and I realise that we're out of luck. Jacqui isn't going to offer us coffee and a chance to sit and chat. I wonder if it's because she's worried about what other revelations Anje might come up with.

'We'd better get started. I'll go and strip the beds,' I say.

'Before you go,' Jacqui hugs Ethan tight, 'I don't know what you used on the kitchen floor last time, but it was very sticky . . .'

Did we use anything, I wonder, glancing at Clare.

'It was Flash,' she says. 'Perhaps I didn't use the correct dilution.'

'And *do* remember to clean behind the bathroom doors this time.'

'Of course,' Clare says icily.

I fear that our friendship with Jacqui is like one of Clare's many love affairs that she had before Jim, a brief fling, instant irresistible attraction followed by rapid disillusionment.

'I don't have to clean for the silly cow.' Clare beats up a pillow in the marital bedroom.

'Oh, come on, Clare. Jacqui's showing off in front of Anje. I bet she hasn't got one cleaner, let alone two.' It's a fact of life – Jacqui has to be tactful, but firm. The distance is important. Once you allow your cleaner to become too familiar, you've lost control. At least, that's the theory. I reach out and run my fingers down the contours of the post at one corner of Jacqui's fairytale four-poster bed.

Clare throws herself down on the bed. I sit on the edge.

'Make some noise, Lees,' Clare hisses. 'We don't want anyone accusing us of slacking.'

I pick up a broom, tap the end of the handle on the floor and knock it against the skirting, while we speculate on the state of Jacqui's marriage. Jacqui's dressing-gown, made from lilac satin, hangs from a hook on the back of the bedroom door, and Greg's pyjamas, which are blue and traditional like the ones my dad wears, are folded on a chair beside the bed.

'Greg isn't a passionate man then,' says Clare. 'Not like my Jim. He never wears anything in bed.'

'Coffee?' Jacqui offers when we return to the kitchen, having attended to the rest of the house, paying particular attention to the areas we missed last time. However, as we sit with Jacqui and Anjula in the living room, I catch sight of a couple of bathroom brochures lying on the floor. I must have missed those when I whizzed around with the vacuum cleaner, pretending that I was Michael Schumacher doing a couple of circuits around Silverstone. I kick them under the rug.

'How's Tony?' Jacqui asks.

I wonder why she's suddenly so interested in my husband's health before I remember his footballing injury.

'Oh, you know what men are like – you would think he's at death's door to hear him going on about it.' I smile. 'He's managed to drag himself back to work today.'

'I'm so sorry if all that about you being my cleaners sounded bad – Anjula said that it sounded terribly superior.' Jacqui glances towards her. 'I didn't mean it to come out like that and I apologise. I'm planning to book Ethan in for swimming lessons – I'd like you two to come along too. It would be a laugh, wouldn't it?'

'All right then,' I agree. 'Tony will be pleased. We took Jade swimming a few times, but she doesn't have the same affinity for water as her dad.'

'I suppose that being able to swim is useful,' says Clare.

Anje seems to have gone very quiet, and Clare mellows under the influence of a slice of Jacqui's wonderful cake. She must have made it yesterday, because I noted that the oven was cold and there were no tins in the dishwasher.

'Are you going to go to Jacqui's birthday party?' I ask Clare on the way back to her house.

'I wouldn't miss it for the world.' Clare grins. 'That Anje is a bit of a slapper, isn't she?' She puts her foot down and turns left onto the main road, not right.

'Clare, where are we going?'

'Mrs Ramsay's, a prospective client. She lives opposite the Bird Sanctuary.'

'I thought we'd agreed not to take on anyone else.'

'Did we?' Clare parks outside a semi with a scruffy front door and a desiccated hanging-basket suspended from a rusty hook. This isn't looking good.

'Where did this Ramsay woman find our number?' I ask suspiciously.

'Don't worry about where she came from, Lisa.' Clare rings the bell.

'Did someone recommend her? Neville, or Mrs E?'

'Shut up, Lees.'

The door opens, and a petite blonde welcomes us.

'Leave your shoes on the mat,' she says. 'This way.' She shows us into the sitting room where Clare and I sit, one at each end of the sofa. 'Coffee?'

'Please,' I says. Too much caffeine gives me palpitations, but it's about the only thrill I get these days. Clare declines, which is probably a good move because there is no coffee machine, just the clink of a teaspoon against a jar of instant.

When Della Ramsay returns from the kitchen, she sparkles. If she was a cleaning product, she'd be one of those tablets that fizz when you drop them into the toilet to remove limescale. She is also immaculate, dressed in an olive vest, gold bracelet and khaki cropped trousers, which coordinate with the sage and cream décor.

'We need to discuss hours, exactly what you expect us to do

115

and our fees,' Clare says. 'How about Thursday mornings?'

Della pads up to the window and peers out past the voile drape.

'It doesn't matter which day. I work irregular hours.' She fingers the chain at her neck. 'I'm a mystery shopper.'

'How exciting,' I say. Why do other people's careers always sound so much more fun than mine?

'I love it, although Reggie, my husband,' she points towards a photo of an older man in a black suit on the mantelpiece, 'would prefer me to work in an office.'

'I'll write you down for Thursdays then.' Clare ticks a box on the sheet of paper on her clipboard.

'Discretion is very important to me,' says Della.

I'm all ears. What does she want us to be discreet about?

'*Maids 4 U* pride ourselves on our discretion,' Clare says.

'It's my husband, you see. I prefer him not to know that we have a cleaner. I don't see why I should stay at home all day, bored out of my skull, polishing taps and disinfecting handsets. You *do* disinfect phones?'

If we didn't, I think, glancing at Clare, we do now.

'I can't do everything to the standard that Reggie expects.'

We agree terms. Della signs, without reading the contract.

'It's so difficult to find the right people,' she says. 'I hope this is the start of a long relationship. I've sacked four cleaners in the past six months.'

This isn't a revelation that I wanted to hear.

Clare drives faster than usual on the way home, jolting over the speedbumps along Sundale Avenue, which means that I'm getting more of the hump every few seconds. I am not happy.

'You knew she'd sacked her previous cleaners, didn't you?' I can't contain myself any longer.

'She did mention it,' Clare admits. 'I met her in the newsagent's the other day. She was behind me in the queue.'

It never ceases to amaze me how Clare can strike up a conversation with anyone, anywhere.

'What did she sack them for?'

'Oh, various reasons – using the phone for ringing premium-rate numbers, and pilfering teabags.'

'You're a sucker for a sob story, Clare,' I sigh. 'I hope you're right.'

'Let's go and hit the bottles.'

I probably spend more time in Clare's kitchen than I do in my own. I am standing beneath her net of plastic lobsters, filling bottles. It's one of Clare's sidelines. We buy cleaning products wholesale, repackage them and resell. I always feel a sense of unease, but Clare swears that no one is going to bother us when there are coke dealers and armed robbers on the streets. It might be illegal, but it's a great moneyspinner. I have bottles of all kinds of chemicals that Clare has recommended for the removal of various kinds of dirt, lying all over my house – unused, like the smellies that Bunny buys me every Christmas.

'Has Jim had any interest in his bike?'

'Not yet, but he's put it in the paper for three weeks.' Clare pours bleach into a funnel. 'A couple of grand is going to make all the difference to us, and I've told him that it isn't cash in hand, his or mine, because we've already spent it.'

The smell of bread wafts over the scent of bleach. A machine bleeps.

'You kept it then?'

'Jacqui was right. We wouldn't be without it.'

'It smells delicious,' I say hopefully.

'It's chocolate chip. You can't have any, and neither can I. It's for Jim. I'm going on a diet, and you're going to join me.'

I stare at her.

'You can't deny that you've been feeling incredibly tired.' Clare picks up what might be a packet of crisps, and holds out a clear cellophane bag with one of those drab, health-food shop labels, as if the plainer the label, the better the contents are for your constitution. 'They're pumpkin seeds. Try them,' she offers. 'They're full of zinc to boost your sex drive.'

I nibble on a single seed. Clare grabs a handful and stuffs them into her mouth. She screws up her face as she chews. She's still chewing ten minutes later, when she's trying to demonstrate a pedometer to me.

'I bought two,' she says. 'One for you and one for me.'

'Why the health kick?' I ask.

'I'm looking after my preconceptual health.'

'Already?'

'Jim and I aren't getting any younger, and we want a brother or sister for Fern. There'll be no more doughnuts or cream horns. The baker's is an exclusion zone from now on. I'm going to have to persuade Jim to cut down on his alcohol intake too – he couldn't raise more than a smile last night.' Clare continues to pour very precisely. She doesn't waste a drop.

'Well, don't drag me into it.' I take the bottle that Clare has filled, screw on the lid, and stick a label onto it. 'I don't want another baby.'

While Chloe drifted off to sleep in my arms last night, I was browsing Teletext – how sad is that? A poll has shown that 42 per cent of parents believe that their quality of life would be better without children. It's one of Nature's many deceptions, isn't it? I couldn't resist the drive to have babies. I wanted two, and then, when the second arrived . . . No, I'm being mean.

Chloe is at her best right now. I might occasionally resent her arrival when she keeps me awake for no obvious reason, but I can't imagine my life without her. She's lying on her hooded towel, the one that has a smiling strawberry face with a green topknot. While bathwater and bubbles gurgle down the plug-hole, I pat her bottom dry so that she can lie naked on the bathroom floor, kicking her chubby legs. Why does cellulite suit her better than it suits me?

I try brushing Chloe's hair down flat with a soft brush. It stands up on end with static.

'You are my little sunshine.' I smile and take her foot gently between my hands, run my fingertip around the soft pads at the base of her toes. 'Round and round the garden, like a teddy bear.' She knows what's coming. She wriggles, and huffs and puffs. 'One step. Two step . . .' I waggle my fingers over her tummy. 'Tickle her under there.' She giggles.

I am aware of Tony's shadow at the door.

'Daddy's home. Come here, darling.' I scoop her up in my arms.

'You don't call *me* darling any more,' Tony observes.

I resolve to try harder. Falling in love with your baby is like having an affair – at least, I think it might be, not having had one. You fall in love to the exclusion of everything else for a while . . .

'Let me take Chloe,' Tony says.

'While I cook your tea, you mean?' I say sharply. I'm being

118

unreasonable, I know, but I want to spend as much of the evening with Chloe as I can, quality time to assuage the guilt of the working mother.

'I didn't mean that I was going to sit about, watching you do all the work,' Tony says. 'Whatever I say, you take it the wrong way.'

'I'm sorry.' I straighten, my knees creaking, and walk towards him.

'Jacqui's bathroom is going to look amazing.' Tony holds me, and drops a brief kiss on the top of my hair. 'She has sophisticated taste.'

I wonder if he's criticising my seahorse and starfish theme, accessorised with plastic dolphins that I bought from the Bettaware catalogue; the blue one filled with genuine seashells that dangles on the end of the light cord.

'She wants it to be very minimalist,' Tony goes on.

'I suppose that means no seagulls.' I bought mine in one of the cheapie shops in Selsdon. It's full-size and has a furred, not feathered, finish.

'And no laminate,' Tony adds.

'Have you noticed how our floor is bowing even though it was supposed to have been made for bathrooms? If I put Chloe on the floor in front of the door, she slides down towards the sink.'

'I'll have to lay something else.'

'Me!' I squeak.

Tony stares at me, then frowns. 'Do you mean that?'

'Yes.' It must be that pumpkin seed. 'Why don't we hire a video, cuddle up on the sofa like we used to, then . . . ?'

'I thought you didn't like the idea of Chloe watching violence,' Tony says.

'I was thinking more romantic.'

'I didn't think you'd want Chloe watching sex either.'

'Well, I don't see any point in curling up with *Shrek 2* – we've already seen it twice.' I pause. 'I know, I'll cook your tea; you feed Chloe and put her to bed. We'll tell Jade we're having an early night, so she won't disturb us.'

'We'd better tell Chloe that too.'

By ten, we're all in bed. Chloe is asleep in her cot. Tony lies with his back to me.

119

'Are you playing hard to get?' I reach my arm around him. 'You're wearing pyjamas.' I'm disappointed. I slip my hand inside the waistband of his shorts. Tony's breath catches, and I smile to myself.

'Wait a minute, Lees.' He grabs my wrist and grips it tight. 'Listen.'

Chloe starts to snuffle. Tony's body tenses.

'I'd better get up,' he says. 'You've always said that we should respond quickly, before she gets a real scream going and wakes Jade.'

'Leave her, Tone.' I tug the hem of his top. 'I want—' I bite my lip. 'I'd like us to make love, to be close again . . . I thought that's what *you* wanted.'

'Not with Chloe awake.' Tony pauses. 'Oh Lisa, I don't know where I am with you. My hand hurts. I'm tired. You keep pushing me away, and then you expect me to turn it on when you want me to make love to you. I'm sorry, it doesn't work like that.'

'Is it me? You don't find me attractive any more? Tone, do you think I'm fat?'

'Cuddly.' He frowns in the dark. 'It doesn't matter though. You are the same person, however heavy – or light – you happen to be.'

'So I'm as big as a house?'

'It isn't you. For goodness sake, why do you imagine everything's down to you? Aren't I allowed to have an off day once in a while?'

Chloe is crying now, and so am I, inside.

'I'll see to her.' I slide out of bed.

'I can do it,' says Tony.

'You get some sleep.' I pick her out of the cot. I won't be able to sleep tonight, even if Chloe lets me. I sit downstairs with her, pigging out on a packet of out-of-date crisps and a minibox of Smarties, and I'm almost tempted by half a limp cucumber from the fridge.

Doesn't Tony fancy me any more? Does he know I'm holding back? Or is there another, more sinister reason? It would be so easy to run upstairs and say, 'Is anything bothering you?' But the questions I don't ask him hang about like wet washing. Unsaid in the dark.

Chapter Eight

I am a milliner's nightmare. I hate hats. I have worn one twice in my life: once when I dressed up as a highwayman at the age of ten; the second time at my grandmother's funeral, when I wore a furry black number because the forecast was for snow. I should have worn a hat today. The occasion seems to demand it.

'Who does Jacqui think she is?' Clare rocks Fern in her arms. 'The Queen?'

'Mrs E would appreciate it.' We're standing on Jacqui's immaculate lawn, and I feel decidedly underdressed in a cream blouse and beige linen trousers. Jacqui is swanning in a black and white floral dress with a scalloped hem, organising her guests. I tried on the dress that I wore for Clare's wedding, and Jade told me that I looked about sixty, and wished I was more like Manda who can make orange tights and striped woollen ponchos look stylish.

'You look great, Lees,' Clare says. 'All right, you don't have to believe me.'

'Tony put his own washing in the machine for the first time that I can remember, *and* asked me if I'd pluck his eyebrows. Can you believe *that*?'

'At least he's taking an interest in his appearance. Look at Jim.' He's standing in the shade of a gazebo that takes up most of the garden, inconspicuous in dark trousers and grey shirt, and clutching a glass of Pimms and lemonade as if it's poison. 'He can't wait to get to the pub,' Clare goes on. 'Where is Tony?'

'He's changing Chloe.' I relax slightly. 'He bought me flowers when he took Jade and Kimberley into town this morning.'

'How romantic,' Clare sighs.

'Buying his way into my good books, I suspect.'

'Lisa, you are so cynical. You complain that Tony never buys you anything, then when he does, you start looking for ulterior motives. Accept them with good grace.'

'Oh, you're right as usual.' I can't help smiling. 'I hope Tony doesn't graduate onto breadmakers. This diet?'

'The one you aren't going to join me on?'

'I'll do it. Just to help you out.'

'Our hostess is heading our way,' says Clare, and we both shut up – unwilling, I guess, to admit that we're both dieting in case she should try to sell us more of her Inaglow products. 'Happy Birthday, Jacqui.'

Jacqui arrives beside us with a pair of designer shades on top of her head, at the same time as a woman dressed in a turquoise blouse and short, shiny skirt that ruckles across her generous hips. Stepping rapidly from one foot to the other as if she's treading water, she thrusts two plates in front of my nose.

'Can-apes?' She smiles, revealing a row of gold crowns. Her coppery hair is brushed up to make it appear thicker than it is, and her scalp is clearly visible. She wears more jewellery than you'd find in a branch of H. Samuel. Her complexion is freckled, right down into a generous cleavage to rival Jordan's. She might be about fifty, but her boobs defy gravity like a twenty year old's. 'Hurry up, loves, I can't hang about here all day.'

I hesitate, eyeing the rather mangled offerings. I doubt that Michael Winner would stand this level of insolence from a waitress. If I were Jacqui, I'd be having words with the outside caterers.

'Move your arse, will you, Jacks!' The waitress pushes past, drops the canapés on the table under the gazebo and blows on her fingers. 'Those plates are bleedin' hot.'

'Mum, can I have a word?' Jacqui draws the woman aside. I strain my ears; Clare winks at me. 'I didn't want you here, and Greg invited you on condition that you keep your big gob shut. This is *my* day. I don't want you ruining it, like you've ruined the rest of my life.'

Jacqui's mother heads off back across the patio to the kitchen. I realise why she couldn't stand still: if she had, she would have sunk. Her stilettos keep catching in the lawn on the way back.

'Jacqui?' I hand over a pretty carrier bag, one of those you see in gift shops that cost more than the present inside, except that, in this case, it was free. Clare salvaged it from when Jim gave her perfume – *Eternity* by Calvin Klein.

'You shouldn't have.' Jacqui glances inside at Clare's bottles of stain remover and fridge deodoriser, done up with coloured labels and ribbons. I know what she's thinking. You *really* shouldn't have. 'Everyone's so generous.'

'So what did Greg buy you?' I ask.

'He's agreed to the hot tub.' Jacqui is like a little kid. 'I can't wait.' She lowers her voice. 'We'll be able to have a girls' night in.'

'In the tub,' Clare finishes for her, and the three of us are laughing at the very thought.

'My Greg is the most imaginative person that I've ever met for choosing presents.' Jacqui tips her head to one side, a far-away look in her eyes. 'I suppose that the contents of the packages he has to deliver for work give him ideas.'

'Jim's pretty original too.' Clare is not to be outdone. 'He wanted to hire the Red Arrows for a flypast outside Mayday Hospital when Fern was born, but they were fully booked.'

'As you've probably guessed, the outside caterers were too,' says Jacqui. She isn't smiling any more, distracted by some new arrivals. 'Oh no, Greg's invited Uncle Roger, and he's brought Gran. What did he do that for?' She slips her shades over her eyes. 'Help yourself to food,' she adds.

'What's in those things?' Clare pokes a canapé once Jacqui has gone to greet her guests.

'Mushrooms? Prawns?' I am just about to sample one when I remember Jacqui's story of after the birth and the afterbirth. 'I wonder what happened to that frozen placenta?'

'She wouldn't have . . .' Clare recoils.

'I doubt it very much.' However, I pinch a Dorito instead, wishing that I'd eaten breakfast, not saved up my daily calorie allowance for Jacqui's party. I should have waited to start this diet on Monday. Monday is always a good day to start something new. 'The class of guests isn't what I'd expect at a "do" at Buckingham Palace,' I continue.

With Anje and gaggles of Jacqui's relatives present, it is as if her past is oozing out of the woodwork, like the sap that forms

123

an ugly encrustation on the teak table. In the centre of the table, surrounded by food and drinks, is a display of Inaglow products, and Jacqui is soon back, rearranging them for her uncle's benefit.

He gives Jacqui a big smile.

'How's my favourite niece?' he says. 'Happy Birthday, gorgeous.' He's one of the skinniest men I've ever seen. Tight trousers hug his narrow hips. Black boots slop around his ankles, and he carries a brown leather shoulderbag. His cheeks are red, his lips wet and his dark hair, coarse and sparse. He runs his eyes over the Inaglow display. 'Anything for the old soldier?'

'Roger by name, Roger by nature,' Jacqui says rather stiffly.

'Oh, I've brought your gran with me,' he says. 'Here she comes. Make way . . .'

She must be in her eighties, yet she walks upright, almost as broad as she is tall. It looks as if she might be wearing the marquee that Jacqui talked about hiring when she first mentioned her party; a polyester dress in lime-green with short puff sleeves and a pleated skirt.

'Gran, how lovely to see you.' Jacqui moves towards her. They embrace.

'You haven't brought Ethan over to see us yet,' the old lady says.

'We will soon, I promise.'

'Call me Pat,' she says, when Jacqui introduces us. She takes a packet of cigarettes and a lighter out of her handbag. Clare and I move upwind with Fern, while Pat puffs on a fag.

'Our Jacks is moving onwards and upwards.' Uncle Roger pats her on the back. 'Ever since she was born, she's been trying to move out of New Addington, and up the hill. I don't know why.'

'She thinks she's too good for us.' Gran blows rings of blue smoke that float up towards the clouds that are assembling in a darkening sky.

'Of course, Greg's a generous geezer,' Uncle Roger says. 'Better than her last husband.'

'Last husband?' I look towards Jacqui. 'You didn't say.'

She flushes scarlet. 'We were married a week so it doesn't count.'

124

'I never did like that Steve,' Pat says. 'He thought he was going to get the market pitch off of your Uncle Rog.'

Clare glances towards me. We've heard more revelations here than on a set of Princess Diana tapes.

'Will you two shut the fuck up?' Jacqui says in exasperation. 'No, not you and Clare, Lisa.' She swears again. 'Wouldn't life be so much easier if you could choose your family as well as your friends?'

Uncle Rog grins at her outburst. 'There you go,' he says. 'You can take the girl out of New Addington, but you can't take New Addington out of the girl.'

'Hey, where's the food Greg promised us?' Pat says, apparently oblivious to any offence she's caused.

'That's it,' Jacqui says sharply, 'on the table.'

'Oh? I was looking forward to a good nosh.'

'The kebab shop on the High Street should be open by now.' Jacqui looks at her watch. 'You and Uncle Rog can go down there for lunch, and take Mum too.'

'Oh no, we wouldn't want to miss anything,' Pat grins. Her teeth slide around on her gums. Her cheeks hollow as she sucks them back into position.

Someone yells across the lawn that the karaoke machine has arrived, and Jacqui excuses herself, leaving Uncle Roger to us. He doesn't stop talking. He tells us that, if we want any watches, batteries or items of jewellery, he is our man.

'My mate sells ladieswear from the stall next door to mine. Tasteful stuff, mind you.'

'I can imagine,' says Clare.

'This couple of young ladies decided they wanted to try some leggings on, so he says, "Nip in the back of the van". Anyway, I was just about to drive off in mine when I heard all this banging and yelling. I opened the back and found these two dippy birds naked, and then they had the barefaced cheek to ask me if I fancied a bit of that ... Well, I told them toot sweet that they'd chosen the wrong one to take a ride with when they picked on me.'

'What did he mean?' I ask Clare, when we finally manage to retreat.

'He's gay, isn't he, can't you tell? He's more camp than Pat's tent-dress.'

I'm beginning to understand why Jacqui's so sensitive about Ethan's sexual orientation.

The sky has almost disappeared. There's a spit or two of rain and a distant roll of thunder. Clare and I shelter under the gazebo while Uncle Rog fingers the Inaglow products and Pat grazes on the canapés. Tony joins us. He hands Chloe over to me.

'What took you so long, Tony?' I ask. 'Have you discovered that changing a nappy takes practice which you haven't had?'

'I've always been a hands-on dad.' He looks a little hurt. 'It's difficult to deal with those poppers when your fingers are strapped together.'

Rain starts to drip through the roof of the gazebo and we are forced to retire inside Jacqui's house. No one takes off their shoes. I watch them tramping wet grass and mud across the carpets, and I want to ask them to be more careful because it won't be Jacqui who will be clearing up after them.

'The mud'll be dry by next week – we'll brush it off with a stiff broom,' Clare tells me. Someone switches music on and we head for the living room. 'It's karoake time!'

Anje sings the first number, a rendition of Johnny Nash's 'I Can See Clearly Now' which is clearly inappropriate for, far from being gone, the rain is tipping it down. She almost succeeds in emptying the room before Clare and Tony take up the microphone. They turn to each other and sing.

'They make a lovely couple,' Jacqui observes from beside me. 'They remind me of that singing duo, Renée and Renato.'

'Is that supposed to be a compliment?' I say.

Someone – Pat, I think – shushes us and I hold Chloe a little tighter. She is transfixed throughout Clare and Tony's rendition of 'Endless Love'. As the last note fades out, Tony kisses Clare on the cheek, then gives me and Chloe a wave.

I don't mind Clare and Tony gazing into each other's eyes – Clare is my best friend and Tony has known her for years – but I'm not so comfortable when Jacqui snatches the microphone and begins her version of 'I Will Always Love You', her voice sounding more like Dolly Parton than Whitney Houston. She keeps slinking towards Tony and fluttering her eyelashes, and from the grin on my husband's face, he's enjoying the attention.

I take a step back. I'm being paranoid.

Uncle Roger is just about to take over the microphone during the introduction to 'Sex Bomb' when Greg switches him off and calls everyone together to toast his wife.

'Lambrusco, anyone?' Jacqui's mother brings round a tray of flutes of sparkling white wine.

'It's champagne, Cheryl,' says Greg.

'Same difference, isn't it?' Her voice is harsh and screeching, and I half-expect the glasses to crack. 'It makes me fall over.'

'Jim doesn't appreciate it either,' says Clare.

'Where is Jim? I haven't seen him for a while.'

'He's gone home. Someone's coming to look at the bike, although why it had to be now, I don't know.'

I smile to myself. Chloe is trying to reach out for my glass. I hand it over to Tony. Jacqui holds hers in two hands at her waist, and twists her heel into the carpet. Her face is flushed. She won't look at Greg.

'Now,' Greg begins, 'I promised that I wouldn't go on about Jacqui's age, but I have to say it – Happy Fortieth! To my wife!'

Everyone raises their glasses – Tony raises mine for me – and Jacqui's mum and Gran carry in a cake with forty candles aflame. They lower it onto the top of the karaoke machine. Jacqui blows the candles out, and makes the first cut. Greg takes a photo while Uncle Roger pops streamers. They land on the cake, leaking lines of coloured dye across the white icing.

'Thank goodness that's over,' Jacqui says quite clearly. She gives me and Clare a small, almost apologetic smile.

'One last thing,' Greg says. He takes a red, plastic-bound book from the top of the television and opens it. 'It was Jacqui's mum's idea to present her with a photographic history of her life so far.'

'No!' Jacqui tries to snatch the book from him. Her moves are playful, yet the glint in her eyes and the vertical lines between them suggest that she is furious.

Greg keeps hold of it and displays a page above his head. 'It's okay, Jacqui. Your family didn't have a camera when you were a baby, so there aren't any of you naked in the bath.' He's laughing. 'This is you at Butlins though, winning the prize for best Disco Diva, and this is one of the photos from your modelling portfolio.'

Jacqui turns like a cat. Her teeth flash. I can see her chest heaving up and down. 'Give that to me!' She grapples with Greg for the album. Jacqui's gran joins in, flapping her handbag at Jacqui.

'Oh, you were so proud of those topless shots,' Jacqui's mum shouts over the fracas. 'You still have a lovely figure.'

Uncle Roger pushes into the fray. As he calms everyone down and takes hold of the offending album, his shoulderbag sags open, revealing several bottles of Inaglow products, which I imagine will end up on his stall next week. I don't think that Jacqui notices. Greg is trying to appease her . . .

Clare winks at me. I feel sorry for Jacqui for having the Relatives from Hell, Greg included, this time.

I turn to Tony. 'Promise me that you'll never do that to me.'

'I never make promises I can't keep.' He gives me a wicked smile. 'I need another drink, a proper one this time. Greg's stashed some lager in the cupboard under the stairs. Jacqui doesn't know about it.'

'Haven't you had enough?' I run my hand down his back and slip my fingers into the belt loop on the back of his trousers as if to restrain him.

'I'm making the most of it. You should too, seeing we can walk home.'

'Someone has to be sober for Chloe.'

'A couple of glasses aren't going to matter, are they?' He smiles though, and pinches my bottom. 'Party pooper.'

'It's stopped raining, so I can show you where I thought we'd put the hot tub, Tony,' Jacqui interrupts. She's clutching the album under her arm. 'I won't keep him long, Lisa.'

I wait inside with Chloe who is becoming restless in my arms. I'd like to find somewhere she could lie down and kick her legs, but there isn't room indoors and the grass is wet outside. Jacqui is outside on the patio, pointing here and there, nodding and smiling furiously. Tony stands back with his hands in his pockets. Her enthusiasm is infectious, and Tony is soon strolling up and down, marking out the boundaries of a rectangle with party streamers. Jacqui keeps taking her sunglasses on and off, and resting them on top of her head.

Greg joins me and Clare at the window.

'Save me,' he says warmly. 'Jacqui wants blood because I invited her family, and the mother-in-law wants my body. I should have remembered how she was at our wedding.' He falters. 'I did remember. I just hoped she'd changed.'

'Mother-in-laws never change,' I say, thinking of Bunny.

'Cheryl wants to. She's saving to go to Poland for liposuction and a facelift. I asked her which one, and she thought I was joking, that I was giving her the come-on.' Greg shudders. 'She wants me to persuade Jacqui to help run the stall while she's away – it's a joint venture with Uncle Roger – but there's no way that Jacqui will consider it.'

'I don't understand why anyone subjects themselves to cosmetic surgery. True beauty comes from within,' Clare says.

I press my nose to Chloe's forehead.

'I told Cheryl that, but she says that people who say that are ugly and kidding themselves.' Greg pauses. 'Jacqui's offered to go with her, but we haven't got the money. This franchise isn't doing very well – she earns just about enough to pay Katya to look after Ethan.'

'Is it worth it?'

Greg sighs. 'It's a few years until Ethan goes to school, and then it'll be so much easier.'

'The school day isn't very long,' I say, thinking of how Clare and I cut our cleaning jobs short so that I can be home for Jade. 'That cake looked lovely, by the way.'

'It's Lisa's way of saying that we haven't had a piece of it yet,' Clare says. 'Did Jacqui make it?'

'Oh no. My wife has many talents, but she doesn't bake,' Greg says with a dry laugh. 'Whatever gave you that idea?'

I hardly have time to digest this information, as Tony returns indoors.

'Let's go home.' He puts his arms around me. I am aware that Jacqui, still hanging on to her photo album, is looking at us through the French doors.

'Who's the party pooper now?'

'Jacqui keeps on at me about the bathroom and the bloody hot tub. Please, let's go.'

We walk home via Clare's to make sure that she finds her way back safely – she failed to realise that Pimms is alcoholic. She's going to have one hell of a headache, especially as she refuses to take anything for it because she's breastfeeding.

*　　*　　*

Headaches aren't always a nuisance, of course. They can be quite useful, especially if you adopt the label of 'regular sufferer'.

It's the Sunday afternoon after Jacqui's party, and I've taken advantage of a migraine to have a quick snooze. It's been very peaceful. Tony used emotional blackmail to persuade Jade to keep her music down, and he's looked after Chloe for two whole hours. In fact, I think I'll have to have a migraine more often.

When I open my eyes, disturbed by the faint scent of vomit, I find that Chloe is on the bed, and Tony is changing his shirt.

'Feeling better, Lisa?'

'Slightly.' 'Now that I've seen you' is left unsaid, because it's true. I feel a whole lot better. The mattress sinks beside me as Tony sits down. I reach out one hand to the ridges of muscle that run down each side of his spine. He turns in to me, cups my chin, then leans down and brushes my lips with his, sending tiny shivers down my spine.

'Isn't it time Chloe slept in her own room?' Tony says softly.

'You read my mind.'

'It seems mad to have decorated the nursery with pink fairy princesses. She'll be wanting black walls and posters by the time she moves in there. She'll be a bloody teenager.'

'Did you say black walls?'

'Jade's been asking if she could buy paint with her allowance. It's all right – she hasn't got any money left.'

I yawn. I can't help it. It is as if all the past weeks of sleepless nights have caught up with me at once.

'You've been overdoing it – too much socialising.'

'We've been to one party!'

'We shouldn't have gone. It wasn't that much of a party, was it?' Tony smiles.

'What do you think of Jacqui?'

'She's okay.'

'I thought you felt a bit more than that, the way you kept gazing down her cleavage and slipping outside to discuss hot tubs.'

Tony wipes the palms of his hands on his thighs. 'I was being polite.'

'Is it polite to stare down at someone's tits?'

'I wasn't.' He fumbles for an alternative.

130

'Don't tell me that you were admiring her necklace.'

'Well . . .' He cocks his head to one side.

'She wasn't wearing one,' I say sternly.

Tony tries not to smile. 'How about – I was pursuing my interest in wildlife?'

'What's that? Birdwatching?'

'Moles.'

I can't help laughing.

'Have you noticed that Jacqui has lots of moles?' he goes on. 'I'm not keen on them.' He pauses. 'I think there's something very odd about her.'

'She's all right.'

'I don't quite trust her,' he tells me.

'Well, we know where she is if she doesn't pay you.'

'I don't need this job.'

'You can't back out now. Both Jim and Clare need the money. I wonder if Jim sold his bike yesterday?'

'Oh no, that was just a ruse to leave the party,' says Tony. 'He won't ever sell it.'

'It's in the paper!'

Tony smirks. 'Jim's advertised it for twice what it's worth. It'll never sell at that price.'

'You shouldn't have told me that,' I say. 'I'll have to tell Clare.'

'Can't you keep anything secret from her?'

'Friends don't have secrets, just like husbands and wives.' Except that, as I'm saying this, I'm aware that I'm lying to myself.

Tony picks up his shirt and chucks it towards the corner of the room.

'Aren't you going to put that in the washing basket?'

'So you don't have to, you mean? This place is a tip.' Tony slips down to the floor on his knees, picks up a pound coin and places it on his bedside cabinet. 'Just look at it.'

'I'd rather not.' I'd *really* rather not. I feel bad enough about not having managed to clean our house within living memory, without Tony reminding me.

He starts scrabbling his fingers across the carpet under the bed. With a low growl, he brings his hands out covered with fluff and hair, and bares his teeth in an imitation of a werewolf.

'Oh, I'm scared,' I laugh.

'I think you're more frightened of the Hoover than mythical dogs with big fangs.'

'We need a cleaner.'

'You *are* a bloody cleaner,' says Tony.

His mood has changed. A storm is brewing, I can tell. The air is hot and close. In the distance I can hear a roll of thunder, or a low-flying jumbo jet. Still silent, Tony turns his back. There is a terrible heartstopping thud. Sickening. I race to the other side of the bed, swipe Chloe up from the floor and hug her, while Tony stares, his face white.

'Don't just stand there!' I am shaking. 'Call an ambulance.'

Chloe's eyes are glassy, unseeing. Her lips are taut. She takes tiny sucks of air in through her mouth, but doesn't breathe out. Her chest expands as if her lungs will explode. Then the cry comes, and my body goes weak with relief. She's alive. I stare at her. Her skull isn't dented – no more than usual anyway. There's no blood.

I hold her close and lose track of time. When her sobs subside, I turn on Tony.

'I thought you were watching her.'

'I was. I wasn't. I turned away. It was an accident. One minute she was in the middle of the bed, the next she was on the floor.'

'So it's her fault?'

'She must have wriggled. Oh Lisa, I'm sorry. I feel as bad about this as you do. Worse.'

'I don't think you do. I don't think you have any idea about how I feel about anything any more.'

Tony approaches me, his arms outstretched as though he's trying to take Chloe away from me. I step back until I'm pressed against the wardrobe. Tony gives me a hard stare, then turns away and starts sifting through the ironing on the bed to find a clean shirt.

'What are you doing?' I say.

'Going out. I promised I'd meet Jim.'

'You're not going anywhere. You can't go out when your daughter's just cracked her skull.' I go ballistic. 'Look, Tony, she's losing consciousness!'

'She's going to sleep!' Tony reaches towards me and tweaks her toes. Chloe wakes up, rolls her eyes and closes them. 'You can rouse her, see? She's fine.'

'What about delayed shock? Bleeding?'

'She's all right. She doesn't look concussed to me.'

'Since when did you qualify as a doctor?'

'I was concussed once when I nutted a goalpost instead of the ball. I kept throwing up.'

I convince Tony to ring the doctor, who suggests we'd be better off going straight down to Mayday Hospital than waiting at the surgery. I tell Jade that she'll have to go up to my mum and dad's.

'I want to go to Kimberley's.'

'Not today.'

'You can ring Colin and Manda and ask them. It *is* an emergency.'

'No, stop arguing.' Jade's selfish attitude infuriates me. 'Your baby sister is about to die, and all you can worry about is whether or not you're going to Kimberley's.'

Jade's face pales, but before I can retract my dramatic pronouncement and apologise for frightening her, she's off to grab a few things to take with her to my parents' house.

It's all becoming rather familiar – the drive to Mayday Hospital and the wait to see a doctor, although Chloe is fast-tracked because she's under one year old.

'Keep your hand in your pocket, Tone,' I warn. I'm nervous that the staff might spot a link between Tony's injured hand and Chloe's fall, but no one mentions it. Tony reaches an arm to my shoulder. I shrug it off. I know it's an accident, that it could have happened to me, that I'm just as guilty as Tony of leaving Chloe on the bed while I nip out to grab a clean Babygro from the airing cupboard, or pick up the phone.

'Don't be angry with me, Lisa,' Tony says quietly. 'I'm feeling bad enough as it is.'

After twelve weeks of perfecting the art of persuading Chloe to sleep through the night, I have to pull out all the stops to keep her awake. The hospital sends us home with instructions to keep a close eye on her. She's bruised, nothing worse, but we have a nerve-racking twenty-four hours' wait to be absolutely certain she's okay. I do it. I can't trust Tony to look after her.

I carry her into the living room and lie her under the baby gym. She whimpers. Cries. Screws her face up with rage as I try to keep her awake. I pinch her toes – gently, of course – change her nappy, offer her the bottle, tickle her tummy, and play her some of Jade's Green Day album. I've never wanted her to stay awake any more than I do tonight.

Chapter Nine

I have no eyes. This morning, they are buried somewhere beneath my eyelids. I grope around the fridge to find the sandwiches that I made for Tony last night, open the bag, and remove two cucumber slices. This is an emergency, and he won't miss them. I stick them on the bulges where my eyes should be for five minutes, then rinse the crumbs off my face with cold water at the kitchen sink.

Chloe snoozes in her carryseat on the worktop. Streaks of sunlight creep in through the window, highlighting her snub nose and smooth forehead, and I feel a sharp pain in my chest. Indigestion? A heart-attack? No, it's love. I adore her.

Tony was right – there's nothing wrong with her. I over-reacted, and I should apologise.

'I'm sorry, Tony,' I say, as he wanders into the kitchen. 'Chloe's fine.'

'Thank goodness for that.' Tony kisses her forehead. She stirs then settles once more.

'Would you like coffee?' I offer.

'I'll make it. I didn't sleep much last night. I don't suppose you did either.'

'No, I'm completely shattered.'

Jade flies into the kitchen, fastening the buttons on her blouse. Her hair is still very black. She leans anxiously over her baby sister.

'Her eyes are closed. She's brain damaged then.' Jade's voice wobbles. I reach my arm around her shoulders.

'She's fine,' I repeat.

'That's cool.' My older daughter smiles with relief.

135

'I didn't think you'd miss her,' Tony says.

'Course I would!' Jade whizzes past me and opens a couple of cupboard doors.

'I bought chocolate spread,' I say.

She glances up at me, her brow furrowed. 'For breakfast? I'd prefer a chicken and mushroom Toast Topper. Oh, before I forget . . .' Jade scuttles off to the hall and returns with a muddle of papers and a pen. 'Can you sign this? It's permission to go on the school trip.'

I'm aware that Tony is reassembling his sandwiches which I left out on the worktop, and Chloe is awake. Any minute now, she'll start whingeing to be fed.

'Sign there, and there.'

'Okay.' I scribble my name twice.

Jade grabs the papers back and stuffs them into her bag. I don't even ask her where they're going, or how much – because it always costs. 'Can you give us a lift, Dad?'

'If you're ready in ten minutes.' Tony's face breaks into a grin. 'If *I'm* ready in ten minutes.'

Half an hour later and they've gone, along with the cucumber slices that I used on my eyes. Tony must have put them back into his sandwiches. I change Chloe, load the pram then head off down the York Road, bumping the wheels over where the roots of the trees have forced the asphalt up into mounds across the pavement. I cross Sundale Avenue, resisting the temptation to divert to Clare's, because if I stop there, I'll never go anywhere else today.

I saunter around the shelves in the library. Chloe stretches one hand and starts grabbing at the books on the shelves. I suppose she's attracted by their brightly coloured spines. She fails to reach them and starts to cry. A couple of people reading look up and scowl at me. I can't help it. What am I supposed to do? Suffocate her, so that they can read their newspapers in peace?

I move away to the section on Self-Help. I pick up books on *Men: Understanding the Impossible, 365 Ways to Spice up Your Sex-life* and *Making Your Marriage Work*, hoping that somewhere within their pages lie the answers to all my difficulties. I hide them under a book on *Practical Fishkeeping* and take them to the desk.

'Morning.' The librarian takes my card. 'How's the baby

today?' He smiles and says, 'Coochy coo,' at which Chloe bursts into tears again. He and I apologise at the same time.

Why are children so embarrassing? Why is the librarian so embarrassing? He strokes the book on sex, reads the dustjacket and leaves it in full view on top of the others, so that everyone knows that my life is in crisis. Mind you, they can probably tell that from my appearance. My hair is frizzy, my blouse creased with a splash of coffee down the front, and I've chosen the wrong shoes – winter moccasins, not sandals.

On the way out, I check the noticeboard, pop back and ask the librarian if I can borrow a pen so that I can scribble some phone numbers down. *South Croydon Meteorological Society*: New Members welcome. *The Poetry Workshop*: no experience necessary. *Watching Wildlife*: friendly local group seeks associates. I return the pen.

'You keep yourself busy, don't you?' the librarian says. His tone is filled with admiration. I don't like to disillusion him.

I head off for the High Street and cross over to the newsagent's for a paper – some of us don't have the luxury of time to read them for free in the library. As I leave, I run my eye down the Adverts board. Shouting out in red lettering from among the ads for old sofas, roofbars and clarinets, is one for *Maids 4 U Domestic Technicians and Hygiene Operatives*. It's better than the first ad that Clare placed – *Maids 4 U for a Personal Service*. More people with dirty minds than dirty houses contacted us in response to that one. However, I am not impressed. I grab my phone out of my bag and text Clare.

Y the ad? We don't need NE mor work. Wot r u up 2 this am?

She texts back when I'm in the chemist's.

Havent U got NEthing better to do? (Me & Jim mkng baby) Nsy cow!

I check my shopping list. It's true what they say about your brain shrinking when you've had a baby – I have to write everything down. A new lipstick isn't on the list, but I choose one anyway. When did I last have a new lipstick? When did I last have something for me?

I park the buggy beside the seat that is reserved for the infirm who are waiting to collect their prescriptions, and test several sticks on the back of my hand, rubbing the pigments with my thumb. Why is it that the most delicious colour is the most

137

expensive? Fourteen quid. I add a tube of mascara, which means that I have to pay with a card, not cash. Then I remember that I missed the last and most important item on my list – silicone teats – and have to pay for those with the cash I can scrape together from my purse.

While I'm waiting for my change, I do a few quick pelvic-floor squeezes. According to Patsy, you're supposed to be able to do these exercises anywhere – on the bus, in the library, in the car – without anyone knowing that you're doing them, but the chap waiting in the queue behind me gives me a funny look, so I stop, just in case.

I wander back out onto the pavement. The sun stings the backs of my eyes. I pause, blink a couple of times then stride out down the hill for home. I am aware that someone is shouting, but not for me. I picked up my shopping, didn't I? And my receipts. I pat my plastic bag to check. There's more shouting. What's wrong with people? Selsdon used to be such a quiet place. And I smile to myself because I'm beginning to sound just like my mother, which is something that I promised myself I'd never do.

There's a hand on my arm. I try to shake it off. I haven't the time to stop and fill in a questionnaire from some charity blogger.

'Stop! Stop!' someone yells. I hesitate. A young woman in a white coat steps across in front of me, blocking my way. At first I wonder if she's coming to put me away, then that I may have inadvertently pocketed something off the shelves in the chemist's shop.

'You've forgotten something,' she says breathlessly.

'I don't think so.'

'Your baby.'

'Oh no!' My hand flies to my mouth. My legs turn to jelly. My heart explodes. How could I have done such a thing? Everyone is watching me – from the corgi that's tied up out-side the estate agent's, to the traffic warden. Even the Group 4 man pauses on his way back from the bank to his van, with his helmet and briefcase. A second woman in a white coat – the pharmacist herself, I think – wheels Chloe's pram down the High Street. I beat my brow with my fist. What an idiot! Anything could have happened to her!

'Oh Chloe, my darling.' I grab her out of the pram, hug her, make sure she's all right, that no one's touched her. I apologise for being a bad mother. She looks at me with an air of mild surprise at being woken up, then breaks into a smile and grabs for my nose.

'At least she's none the worse for being abandoned, poor little scrap,' says the pharmacist, and my relief that she is okay turns to panic. Do these people believe that I left her deliberately?

My knees tremble. The gaggle of strangers assembled around me begin to float and spin. My body grows hotter and hotter. Someone takes Chloe. Someone else, a woman, with a perfume of sandalwood and oranges, leads me a few steps to a bench beside a giant tub filled with summer flowers, and sits me down.

'Put your head between your knees, Lisa.'

It's all very well, but I can't contort myself into that position; I haven't been able to see my knees, let alone put my head between them, for months. The flowers go black and swimmy. The traffic quietens. It's so peaceful that I could stay here for ever . . .

I don't know how long it is before I come round.

'You fainted.' It's Manda.

Why did it have to be someone who knows me? Tony is bound to hear of this now, how his wife, who criticised him for turning his back on Chloe for no more than a minute, left her alone in a public place.

'I popped out between classes to do some shopping.' Manda is wearing a blue and white tie-dye sundress and red mules.

'I feel such an idiot.'

'It's easily done. I left Ali at the launderette when we lived in London. I was back at the flat, putting my feet up with a soup in a cup, when a policeman knocked at the door. I can remember exactly what flavour it was – minestrone. I haven't touched it since.' She pauses. 'Oh, you're shaking.'

'It's delayed shock, I suppose.'

'Come back with me and I'll make you a cup of tea at the dance school,' Manda suggests. 'We can chat.' She smiles as we stand up together. 'Actually, you'll be doing me a favour. I don't like going back into the premises when there's no one else there.'

'Oh?' I walk with her, pushing the pram up the hill. 'Have you got a resident ghost?'

'I suppose you could describe it as the Ghost of Christmas Past. Last year, I met this man, a friend of a friend, at one of our parties. He flirted with me, said I reminded him of Kate Bush – he'd had a crush on her when he was a teenager – and we went to bed . . .'

'Oh Manda.' We walk on together in silence while I wonder how to handle this revelation. I suppose that I'd like to be able to understand why Manda did such a thing, whereas Clare would give her a piece of her mind, and sever all ties immediately. It's what she did to Tony, although they're reconciled now. She can't stand to see anyone wronged. 'What about Colin?'

'I still loved him.' Manda bites her lip. 'He knew that, but he was terribly hurt.'

'I'm not surprised. I know exactly how it feels,' I say hotly.

'I broke the rules,' says Manda.

'So did Tony once, but it was a long time ago.'

'I told this man that we had no future.' Manda unlocks the front door to the dance school, a hall that was built some years ago on a section of car park, sold off by one of the local churches to raise funds for a new roof. She hesitates on the front step. 'He couldn't accept that our relationship, if you can call it that, was over, and wherever I went, he'd be there. I'd be at the check-out at the supermarket – any supermarket – and he'd be there behind me with a trolleyful of exactly the same items that I'd picked up, the same brands of margarine and toothpaste, even pantyliners.' She shudders as she steps inside the door. 'One night, he broke into the dance school – I rented a room in a leisure centre back then – and lay in wait . . .'

'Oh my goodness,' I squeal. 'What happened?'

'He attacked me.' Manda flicks the switches and turns all the lights on, even though it's daylight. 'For once, I'm grateful that Colin takes things more seriously than anyone else. He'd been following the man who'd been following me. He saved my life.'

Manda makes tea, and we sit down at a small table in the corner of the hall. Although she has opened the windows, the room still smells of sweaty bodies and old shoes. Manda tops up my mug with liquid from a small plastic flask.

'Brandy for emergencies,' she says. 'I believe that every relationship needs to go through testing times – it makes you appreciate the good ones so much more. Colin is my rock. My refuge.'

No one – Tony excepted – has confessed to having an affair, let alone a stalker, to me before. One confidence deserves another and we're soon trading them like two small boys trading football cards. Mine are more two-star plains, hers are four-star shinies.

'How's Jade doing with the dancing classes?' I ask.

'She's a natural. You should come up and watch her sometime.' Manda smiles. 'Jade is really bringing Kimberley out of her shell. She used to be so shy, she wouldn't say a word to anyone.'

Voices at the door disturb us.

'That's my next class,' Manda says.

'I'd better go then. Thanks for rescuing me.'

'I'll see you on Saturday, at our housewarming party. I'll have my eye on your husband. He's lovely.' When Manda compliments Tony, I try to compliment Colin, but can't think of anything to say. 'Don't forget the baby on your way out.'

'There's no chance of that.' I have the pram parked across the door, so I can't possibly leave without tripping over it. The dancers can't get in for their lesson, either.

'Are you going to take Chloe up to the park on the way home?' Manda goes on. 'I used to love taking my children out on the swings and slides when they were small.'

'Oh no, she's far too tiny to swing,' I say.

Manda grins. 'I suppose she is. Bye, Chloe!' She waves.

Chloe raises her hand, but she can't wave very well yet, so I wave back for her. She is still perfecting her waving technique when Jade returns home after school and her dancing lesson.

Jade walks in, chucks her schoolbag on the floor and kicks off her shoes, breaking down the backs without untying the laces.

'Have you had a good day?' I say.

'You always ask me that. Can't you think of something more original, Mum?' She turns to Chloe. 'How are you, chubby cheeks?'

Chloe smiles. Jade is being unusually solicitous over her baby sister. She picks her up and fetches her bottle, then sits down in the sitting room with her. I follow, concerned that Jade might have experienced some life-changing event today, that perhaps Ali's asked her out . . .

'Are you sure that everything's okay?'

'Yes,' she says impatiently, 'except I've lost my games kit.'

'Where?'

'How do I know? I've just said that I've lost it. If I knew where I'd left it, it wouldn't be lost.' She sighs loudly. She's become quite theatrical recently, a side-effect of the dancing lessons, I suspect.

'When did you last see it?'

'On the bus.'

'I'll ring the bus company.'

'It was a couple of weeks ago.'

'Why didn't you tell me before?'

'Because you never listen to anything I say, and I hate sport, and I hate that poxy games kit.'

'Well, you can buy a new one with your next allowance.'

'That's not fair.'

'Tough. You had one and you lost it.' I'm so tired that my self-control is fraying like the tassels on the curtain tie-backs. 'If you go on being rude to me, I'm going to tell Dad to stop your allowance.'

'I'm not the only person who loses things,' Jade says icily. 'I lost a games kit. You mislaid a baby.' Chloe sucks on the bottle in the ensuing silence. 'Manda told me.' Jade's glossy lips curve into a sly smile. 'Does Dad know about you, like, abandoning my little sister in the chemist's?'

My face burns. Is she blackmailing me? I really ought to sit her down for a proper chat, but the doorbell rings.

It's Mum and Dad, and I was about to start on the dinner.

'Do say if this is inconvenient,' says Mum.

How can I? I don't want to hurt their feelings.

'We thought we'd stroll over and see you,' Mum continues.

'I tagged along too,' says Dad.

'I've got some information for you.' I find the phone numbers for the various clubs and organisations from the library noticeboard at the bottom of Chloe's changing bag. Mum peers over my shoulder as I show them to him.

'Not the Wildlife Association,' she says. 'He can't bear seeing the foxes going through our bins.'

'How about a Poetry Workshop, Dad?'

'I quite enjoy Spike Milligan,' he says.

'I think you have to create poetry yourself.'

'Oh no, I couldn't write in rhyme.'

'Poetry doesn't have to rhyme nowadays,' says Mum. 'How about joining the Meteorological Society? I imagine that they'll have lots of meetings, and field trips, and you're always interested in the weather.'

'Anyone would think that you two were plotting to get me out of the house more,' Dad says. He heads off to the kitchen to make some tea, giving me the opportunity to ask Mum how she is.

'Can't say too much.' She lowers her voice to a whisper. 'Your dad's finished all the little tasks I'd been saving up for him. Are you absolutely sure that there isn't anything he can do for you here? He could put up a couple of hanging-baskets to brighten the place up,' Mum goes on hopefully.

'No, I don't think so.' I recall the shelf that Dad put up to display Mum's ceramics. When she placed the last piece, a Toby jug worth forty pounds that she had picked up for 50p at a car boot sale, the shelf crashed down from the wall. Never one to allow anything to go to waste, she decorated some pots for the garden with mosaics of the fragments that were all that was left of her collection.

'There must be something he can help out with,' Mum says.

'If I think of anything, I'll let you know,' I say firmly.

'Is Chloe sleeping through yet?'

'No,' I sigh. 'She's better, but—'

'I expect she's hungry,' Mum cuts in. 'Why don't you start weaning her? You were feeding Jade on baby rice by now.'

'The advice has changed – no solids until the baby's six months old.' I do wonder though. I started Jade on solids when she was about twelve weeks old, and it hasn't done her any harm, has it?

'Poor Tony. Your marriage will suffer if you carry on like this.'

'Shh.' I glance towards Jade. She's playing with Chloe and the mirror on the baby-gym, but I'm sure she's listening. 'Tony's fine. He knows what it's like to have a baby. We've had one before. We survived.'

Is survival enough though, I muse. Shouldn't we be happy too?

I hear Tony's van pull onto the drive. He isn't happy when he puts his head round the door. I'm dealing with my parents, and his dinner's in the freezer. I guess from the look on his face that he'd prefer it to be the other way round.

'How are you, love?' he asks.

'I've got a bit of a headache.' I'm not lying.

'When did that start?' Tony says sympathetically.

I glance at the clock. 'About ten, fifteen minutes ago.'

'What Mum's trying to say is that she wants you to go home, Granny,' Jade says brightly.

'Jade, I don't mean that at all.'

'Well, she's right. We're intruding,' Mum says. 'I should have thought—'

'Tea?' Dad enters the living room with a tray of steaming mugs.

'We're just leaving, Don.' Mum takes the tray and puts it on the coffee-table on top of a heap of newspapers and post. 'I've just remembered that I've left the back door unlocked.'

'Oh Jeanette, you said you'd checked,' Dad grumbles. 'I'm beginning to wonder if you're losing your marbles like your mother did.'

Mum winks at me. Like Clare, she understands the value of being able to economise with the truth.

'Mum has a confession to make,' Jade says with a wicked smile on her face once my parents have gone. 'It's really funny.'

'Will you stop poking your nose into matters that don't concern you? Go and do your homework.' I turn to Tony who stands with his arms folded. 'I left Chloe in the chemist's this morning. I forgot her.'

'Oh, so you *are* a mere mortal like myself after all!' Tony's eyes narrow. 'I can't believe that you left our daughter in the middle of the High Street.'

'Not in the middle exactly,' I point out. 'I think I'd have realised if I'd parked her in the road.'

'Who knows what you might do next?' He is angry with me! The sausages are too salty, the mash lumpy and the beans the wrong brand, and after tea, he disappears off to the shower faster than a bottle of Radox when Jade gets her hands on it.

I make Chloe's bottles up for tomorrow, try to help Jade with her homework – a project on Healthy Eating for PSHE, Personal,

144

Social and Health Education – and answer Tony's mobile which he's left on the kitchen worktop.

'Mr Baker?'

'It's Lisa.' I pause. 'Hi, Jacqui, how are you? And Ethan?'

'Actually, I was ringing to speak to Tony – in a professional capacity, of course.' She giggles, and I wonder if she's drunk too much Chardonnay from her understairs cupboard.

'He's busy. I'll ask him to call you back.'

'Thanks.' She doesn't stop to chat. I press the off button on the phone, and stand looking at it for a while. If it's a bathroom-related call, why didn't Jacqui contact Tony during the day? Why wait till after six for the cheaper phone tariff? She and Greg aren't hard up. Unless. Unless . . . I've been watching too many soap updates. I'm being silly, aren't I?

There's a message written in lipstick on the bedroom mirror when I drag myself out of bed on the following morning.

I'm sorry. Love you. Lots of kisses. Tony.

Does he know how much a stick of longlasting lippy costs? I'm being mean. His sentiments are all the more heartfelt for being expressed in a medium that cost fourteen quid of our household income, although I think it's better that I don't enlighten him.

Make time for each other. Choose a venue conducive to romance. The library book on the subject of marriage says that the marital bedroom should be a place of escape: calm, private and seductive, with freshly laundered linen and flowers.

I can't see our bed for clutter. Would it make any difference to our marriage if we decorated this room? Started afresh? Is a lick of paint, or a new duvet cover really going to spark the flame of passion?

And yet I am feeling more optimistic today. Tony's words on the mirror suggest that romance isn't quite dead after all.

If the flame is rekindling at ours, it may have been completely extinguished at Clare's. She doesn't turn up at mine until eleven because she overslept. Apparently, Jim didn't sell his bike on Saturday. There wasn't anyone to sell it to. It *was* all an excuse to leave the party and head home the long way round, via the pub.

'He had a cracking headache that night. I'm not sure if it was the drink or the rolling pin that I beat him with.'

145

I raise one eyebrow, recalling how Clare has already vowed never to smack Fern under any circumstances. I told her to wait until Fern hits the 'terrible twos', and she's throwing herself at the floor beside the sweets in Woolies like Jade used to. Clare just might change her mind.

'I thought you were opposed to physical violence of any kind,' I say.

'I used a metaphorical rolling pin,' Clare enlarges. 'I've taken Jim's credit cards, chequebook and his cash – there was only 50p left – so he can't spend any more money. He begged me for a couple of quid for a beer, but I told him that there's no more until he gets a job. A proper job.'

'He can't work,' I say, aghast. 'He's on the sick.'

'Jim breaks the World Land Speed Record each time he goes off to the pub or the shops. He can climb up inside doorframes and perform handstands to amuse Fern. I'd say that he's fitter than I am, but he doesn't want to work. He likes his freedom. He likes looking after Fern. He likes to be available to help out when Tony needs him.'

'I thought you enjoyed having him at home.'

'I do ... I did when he wasn't well. Now I'm starting to wonder if he's taking advantage of my generous nature. I'm having to work more and more hours to pay the mortgage when he's perfectly capable of working himself.'

Clare changes the subject as we head off to drop Chloe at my mum's. 'Have you decided what you're wearing to the party this weekend?'

'I'm going in a sheet.'

'Tony won't let you buy anything?'

'It isn't that. I told you before – it's a fancy-dress do.'

Once I've apologised to my parents for making them unwelcome last night, Clare and I head off to Dr Hopkins's house where we discover that Dr Hopkins is one step ahead of us when it comes to dieting. I have a nasty suspicion that it may be partly my fault, but I decide against mentioning this to Clare. As far as she's concerned, I emptied that bin of sweet wrappers and kept Dr Hopkins's unhealthy vice a secret. I jeopardised *Maids 4 U*'s reputation when I poisoned Mrs E's dog, and I wouldn't like Clare to think that I've done it again.

There's a Man of the Month certificate from a slimming organisation, displayed in a frame alongside a weight chart in the cloakroom. There's salad, low-fat cottage cheese and low-calorie tonic in the fridge, and new gym equipment in the utility room.

I have a go on the exercise bike. Clare tries to keep up with the treadmill, but can't work out how to change the speed.

'Stupid thing.' She's gasping when she finally manages to turn it off again, and I start to wonder if Dr Hopkins has a defibrillator in his study. I know that he keeps a selection of stethoscopes about the house. 'Hasn't anyone told Dr Hopkins that it's dangerous to become obsessed about your health?' Clare complains. 'That machine could kill someone.' Her cheeks are still pink when we've finished the cleaning.

Dr Hopkins isn't alone in having obsessive tendencies. Della Ramsay is out, giving us the opportunity for a thorough nose. Clare calls it 'orientation'. Having checked the kitchen where Mrs Ramsay was supposed to be leaving us some cash – there isn't any – we head for the master bedroom. It's always a good place to begin when you want to learn more about a client's character and habits.

There is a range of built-in wardrobes and a king-size bed. The duvet is pulled up over the pillows to hide a pair of crumpled pyjamas and a long black nightie, nothing unusual in that, but the cupboard doors are all firmly closed, a phenomenon that is more uncommon than you might imagine.

Clare opens the bedside cabinet. A pile of underwear swells up out of the drawer. Clare picks up a couple of bras from the top.

'Della hasn't cut the price tags off yet,' she says. 'They're designer label.'

I tug open a wardrobe door. It's shelved, and stacked with T-shirts, not one of each style but several of the same style in different colours. Alongside them hangs a row of ponchos.

'Someone likes shopping almost as much as Jim does,' Clare observes drily.

'Della must be a shopaholic. She can't possibly wear all these outfits.' I start rifling through the ponchos. 'You'll have to drop by on the way home and see what Jade's got in her wardrobe. I knew that giving her an allowance was a mistake – you should see her taste in clothes.'

Clare is deep in thought. 'You'll have to deal with this, Lisa,'

147

she says. 'Ring Mrs Ramsay and ask her to leave the money out for us to pick up next week, otherwise . . .'

'Otherwise what?'

'I'm not sure yet.' Clare rubs her chin. 'Am I getting a beard?'

I examine her follicles. 'No, don't think so. Hang on a mo . . .'

Clare shrieks.

'Just winding you up.' I take out a poncho and slip it over my head. 'I used to have one of these. Do you remember?'

'It looked just as unflattering then,' says Clare. 'What is the point of a poncho? It doesn't keep your arms warm and it makes you look as if you've lost your sombrero on your way through the Mojave Desert.'

I take it off quickly, and we make a start. During the two hours that we've allocated, we discover that Mrs Ramsay possesses all kinds of cleaning materials, various telescopic dusters for those hard-to-reach places and not one, but four vacuum cleaners, hardly used. I suppose that I shouldn't be too hasty in my judgement. I have a single vacuum cleaner at home, and I haven't used it often enough to have had to empty its cylinder, or unclog its cyclones. In fact, I'm not even sure where it is.

Clare and I collect our babies from Jim and my parents, and head to my house. I make two coffees – no milk, no sugar – and we go upstairs to Jade's room. Clare sits down on the sofa beneath Jade's bed and starts feeding Fern. Chloe doesn't see why she can't be fed too.

'You've just had a bottle and some baby rice,' I tell her. 'You can't possibly be hungry.'

Chloe sucks her lips for a moment then stops.

'Has reason prevailed this time?'

She yawns and rolls her head to one side, so that Jade's diary on her desk is in her line of sight. I sit her up on my knee and turn away slightly so that I can't see it, recalling one of my mum's trite sayings, 'What the eye can't see, the heart can't grieve over'. Would I grieve if I read it? Would I pine for Jade's lost innocence?

'Jacqui phoned Tony last night,' I say.

'And?' says Clare. 'Jim says that Jacqui's driving Tony mad over this bathroom. She keeps calling him to make changes to her design.'

I suppose I should be happy with that explanation, but I continue to probe the subject, like a dentist driving a metal pick through a hole in a tooth.

'Do you think I should be worried? Jacqui doesn't just fancy herself as an interior designer – she fancies Tony too. And Manda thinks he's attractive.'

'So do I,' Clare says cheekily. 'Your husband is a goodlooking guy. Women adore him. So what?'

'I just wondered if I might have given Jacqui the impression that my marriage isn't so good. In our "complaining about the husband" sessions, I might have inadvertently given her the wrong idea.' Clare gazes down at Fern. She isn't getting it, is she? 'Do you think Tony might be having an affair?'

Clare looks up. She's grinning. She isn't taking this seriously.

'When you suspect your husband of having an affair, you're supposed to send your lover out to follow him and find out.'

'This isn't a joke.'

'It might as well be, Lisa. Tony made one mistake a long time ago. He'll never do it again.'

'How can I be sure of that?'

'I know him almost as well as you do.'

'Do you think I should say anything?'

'Absolutely not. If Tony thought you suspected him of sleeping with someone else, he'd be devastated. He might never forgive you.'

Clare's right, I think. It's a matter of trust – like not reading Jade's diary. My eyes wander back towards Jade's desk. Clare follows my gaze.

'I'd have read that by now,' she says.

'Would you feel comfortable if it was Fern's?'

'She'll be online when she's old enough to write a diary. I won't have a hope of reading it. I'm more of an it-girl than an IT-girl.' She grins and swaps Fern deftly onto her other breast. 'Where are these clothes of Jade's that you wanted to show me?'

I prop Chloe up on the sofa beside Clare with a pillow, and open Jade's wardrobe. I pick up a tiny skirt and skimpy top.

'This is what she spent last month's allowance on, and this . . .' the hangers clank along the rail '. . . is this month's, a black T-shirt and jeans.'

'That's horrible.'

'I know. She's turning Goth on me.'

'The clothes we wore in our day were so much more femi-nine and sexy,' says Clare. 'Do you remember how we went New Romantic with Spandau Ballet and Duran Duran? I used to adore Gary Kemp, and you were in love with Simon Le Bon.'

I offer her a muslin square.

'What's that for?'

'You're dribbling.'

'We had frilly blouses and big hair,' Clare sighs, 'and matching jelly bags and shoes.'

I hold up the skimpy top – it just about covers one boob.

'Try it on,' Clare says.

'I can't. It's too small.'

'You've lost a couple of pounds recently.'

'Do you think so? I haven't had time to stand on the bath-room scales.'

'Go on,' Clare urges.

I slip out of my *Maids 4 U* top and squeeze myself into Jade's. It must be made of 100 per cent Lycra.

'There you go,' says Clare. 'Britney Spears, eat your heart out.'

I start a rendition of 'Toxic', sending Clare into hysterics.

'Stop. Stop! You'll curdle my milk.'

I am laughing fit to burst and can hardly contain myself . . . I *can't* contain myself, and have to dash off to the bathroom. I've been slacking on those pelvic-floor routines that Patsy advised, and now I'm slacker than ever.

Chapter Ten

'Dad didn't try to come with you tonight then?' I give Mum a hug when she drops round to look after Jade and Chloe.

'He's busy, thanks to Al Qaeda.'

'He hasn't joined a terrorist organisation, has he?'

'He's making up packages of emergency supplies to help us in the event of a terrorist attack, in accordance with that government leaflet that arrived the other day.' Mum smiles. 'He's also bought himself a weather-station for the garden, and a notebook in which to record his observations, after that talk that you saw advertised in the library.' Mum looks me up and down. 'You aren't dressed yet. Aren't you going to be late?'

'This is my outfit.' I'm wearing a pristine white sheet, wrapped around my body like a sari and fastened with a brooch. (I had to buy a new sheet because all of ours are fitted.)

'Hallowe'en isn't until October.'

'I'm not a ghost. I'm supposed to be a Roman. And before you say anything, no, I didn't bathe in asses' milk. I smell like this because I tipped half a bottle of formula down my front. I should have dressed after I made up the bottles, not before.'

Tony appears in a sheet and beach sandals.

'I wonder if you'll be expected to play party games,' Mum says.

'I don't really want to go,' I say.

'You never want to go out anywhere any more,' Tony says coolly.

'I've just had a baby. Some couples don't go out together for years afterwards.'

'Well, we're going now,' says Tony.

151

'Don't forget your chariot,' Jade taunts.

'Have a lovely time,' says Mum. 'I'll keep Chloe awake for as long as I can.'

I drive. We park around the corner from Manda and Colin's house because there are already three cars on their drive. We walk back towards Villa Colanda, stopping the traffic. The grey render has a warmth about it tonight, from the golden light of the sun low in the sky, and the flaming torches on each side of the porch. The door is wide open, but Tony knocks anyway, bringing Colin tripping down the hallway in a purple toga to greet us.

'Welcome. Welcome.' He grabs me and plants wet kisses on my cheeks. 'Get your asp in here, Lisa, and you, Tony.'

Tony takes a firm grip on my hand, and leads me through the hall into the kitchen. I forget that he doesn't know the Kennedys as well as I do, so they might appear a little peculiar to him. I smile to myself. They're nice people. Even Bunny would approve of them. Maybe not . . .

Colin and Manda don't appear too bothered about showing off their new décor. The house is almost dark, the corners of the rooms illuminated by candles and tealights. The kitchen bears an air of bohemian neglect. It has a Tuscan theme with bare plaster walls and a blue and white mosaic floor.

'This is very . . .' I search for the right words to convey my opinion of the Kennedys' sense of style, but I'm floundering.

'What Lisa is trying to say is that it's very kind of you to invite us,' Tony finishes for me.

Manda, who's stirring something in a saucepan on the cooker, smiles warmly. 'It's our pleasure.'

Colin sticks his finger in the pan and licks it. 'More chili required, Manda.'

'Sod off,' she says gently. 'The rule in this kitchen is that the chef is always right even when he – or she – is wrong.'

'I hope you and Lisa don't mind indulging in my passion.' Colin turns to Tony. 'I was born into the wrong century. I missed my millennium. I might be a planning officer, a dad and much maligned partner, but first and foremost, I am a Roman.'

'Do you believe in reincarnation?' Manda asks.

'I swim a couple of times a week, if I'm lucky,' says Tony, 'but not because I was a dolphin in a previous life.'

152

Manda laughs. Colin doesn't.

'I used to compete,' Tony continues. 'Now I do the occasional charity fundraiser, or friendly gala.'

I just know that Colin's going to ask me. 'What do you do in your spare time, Lisa?'

'What spare time?' I say, trying to laugh it off.

'You have to remember that Lisa has a baby, even if she forgets that sometimes.' Manda winks at me, then Colin offers us a glass of wine before he introduces us to their other guests.

'It's our own vintage,' Colin says. 'We grew a vine at our last house.'

'Just a very small one then,' I say quickly. 'I'm driving tonight.'

'I can drive, Lisa,' Tony says hopefully.

'No, it's what we agreed. I insist.'

'Our plonk is rather potent,' Manda says.

'It isn't plonk.' Colin opens a bottle, pours a small one and samples it. 'Bloody Norah,' he gasps. 'Here, have some of this – Casa Kennedy, two years old.'

Potent? It's like bleach on the back of the throat. I choke on the first sip. Tony rubs my back. I notice that he doesn't try any himself.

'Colin, will you go and fetch that ice?' says Manda. 'How many times have I asked you?'

'Ali can do it,' says Colin, nodding towards the back door. 'Kimberley is staying with a cousin tonight. My son refused to go with her.' A youth steps inside with an unlit roll-up between his lips. 'This is Ali, my son.'

I'm not sure if his complexion is unusually pale, or whether it's the contrast with his scraggy black hair and clothing. A black cord hangs around his neck. The crotch of his trousers dangles level with his knees which makes his legs look very short, and his body incredibly long, as if I'm seeing his reflection distorted in a hall of mirrors. My heart sinks. I'm sure that he's wearing black eyeliner.

'Are you off out?' says Manda.

'Yep,' he mutters.

'Give me that cigarette first.'

Ali screws it up and throws it into the sink.

This isn't the kind of lad I'd choose for my daughter's first love affair. I'd like someone clean-cut like Ronan Keating, but younger, of course, no more than fourteen. A boy who can communicate in a polysyllabic language, not primitive grunts.

'He's saving his voice for his singing,' Colin says proudly. 'If you're all right out here, Manda, I must take Lisa and Tony to mingle with our other guests.'

I follow Colin into the living room where there is a large dark coffee-table covered with books, a battered green three-piece suite, and yet more candles in the stone fireplace. Colin stands with his back to the flames and raises his glass.

'Friends, Romans, Countrymen, lend me your ears.'

'Hail Julius,' comes a murmuring of voices.

'I've had a rapid advancement to the position of Emperor at long last,' Colin says aside to me and Tony before he introduces us to two other couples, Spenser and Victoria, and John and Elaine. I guess that they are all in their forties.

'We all met several years ago through the Roman Re-enactment Society,' Colin says. 'These are our new friends, Lisa and Tony, all dressed up and throwing themselves into the spirit of the party.' He smiles encouragingly. 'I think role-playing helps break the ice. Having been boring old Colin,' he says in a tone that suggests that he's convinced that he's anything but, 'down at the office all day, it's great to step into someone else's shoes' – he glances down at his feet and gives a little laugh – 'or should that be sandals?' There is a chorus of polite laughter. He gestures grandly to the last couple. 'This is Ted and his girlfriend Lucy.'

My friendly librarian greets me with an enormous smile. 'Lisa and I have met many times before,' he says, then goes on to list the books I've borrowed in reverse chronological order over the past three months. *Men: Understanding the Impossible, 365 Ways to Spice up Your Sex-life, Making Your Marriage Work* . . . 'I have a photographic memory,' he adds during the silence that follows.

I glance at Tony. He's frowning. I can understand his confusion when I'm always telling him that I don't have time to read.

'Manda's organising some food,' Colin says. 'There's plenty of it, but go easy – we haven't mocked up a vomitorium, ha ha.' He goes on to explain, for my benefit, I suspect, about the room that the Romans would have set aside for throwing up in after gorging themselves, but there's not much chance of anyone eating too much. She may be highly creative and able to dance, but Manda can't cook.

I find myself standing beside Lucy, picking at chicken legs served pink, and steaks served black. She seems like a child with her big innocent eyes and easy smile, yet she must be at least twenty-five. I'm getting old. Soon I'll be wanting to mother the baby policemen you occasionally see around here, usually three or four days after you report a crime. How sad is that? How sad am I?

Lucy is slim with straight, bobbed chestnut hair, and she wears a sheet, tied around her middle with what looks like a curtain tie-back with tassels, and jangling bracelets on both fore-arms. Her lashes are thick with mascara, and her lids are black with eyeliner and shadow. She looks more like an Egyptian than a Roman to me, but I might be mistaken. My view of the Ancient Egyptians is coloured by drawings of Tutankhamun that Jade did at school when she was about eight.

Lucy doesn't speak. I don't know if she's painfully shy or whether she simply doesn't wish to talk to me.

'I've left my mum babysitting Chloe – she's my youngest,' I begin. Big mistake. Nothing is more boring than the subject of other people's children.

Lucy smiles encouragingly, but just as I'm about to launch myself into the story of how I left Chloe in the chemist's, I realise that she's smiling at Colin. He wanders over to join us, a bunch of grapes in one hand.

'Thanks for inviting me and Ted. I haven't been to a party like this one before.' Lucy slips her arm through Colin's and I feel rather awkward, as if I'm intruding on a private conversa-tion. 'I don't know much about Romans – they're all Greek to me,' she adds in a coquettish tone.

'I thought Ted might have borrowed some books for you from the library.' Colin pats Lucy's hand. 'However, I'll be delighted to enlighten you on the customs of the Roman race. They created a civilised society where eating and drinking well, and free love were the norm . . .' He whispers something into Lucy's ear, making her giggle and blush. I make to turn away, but Colin stops me.

'How's Jade?' he asks.

'Oh, she's fine. We've given her an allowance like Kimberley.'

'How much?'

I tell him.

'Gordon Bennett! Kimbo gets half that if she's lucky. She earns it for good behaviour, and for practising her euphonium.'

'Jade didn't mention that there were conditions attached.'

'That's teenagers for you. Have a grape, Lisa.' Colin plucks one from the bunch in his hand and raises it to my lips. 'Open wide.'

I shake my head. He reminds me of the dentist. Colin pops the grape into his mouth and chews, spattering tiny drops of juice. 'I can see that you're new to this.'

'I haven't been to a fancy-dress party for years. The last one was tarts and vicars.'

'I bet you made a delicious tart . . .'

I think he's being rather rude, ignoring Lucy, so I try to involve her in the conversation.

'Are you going to join this re-enactment group?' I ask her. 'I've been thinking of suggesting it to my father.'

'Oh, I wouldn't recommend it,' says Colin. 'It's quite a physical hobby.'

'My dad's pretty fit.'

'We need more female members really, and there are certain rules of engagement.'

'I suppose you can't be too careful when you're carrying a sword.'

'Oh, I remove that and lay it down by the bed first.' Colin leans closer to me. 'Can I be your slave?' He's joking, of course. I find myself looking for Tony, someone else to share the joke with, but he's preoccupied, deep in conversation with Manda.

'No one's offered to be my slave before,' I say lightly. I have Colin all to myself – Lucy has rejoined Ted on the sofa. She slips her hand up inside his toga. Young love, I think with a pang of regret. 'I have to wait on everyone else.'

'You don't strike me as the subservient type,' Colin says.

'You misread my character then.' I'm laughing now. 'You've drunk too much wine.'

I'm not sure how it happens, but Colin's wine ends up down my sheet, a dark purple stain spoiling its way across virgin-white polyester.

'You're sloshed. You've sloshed me.'

'I'm so sorry.' Colin grabs my arm. 'I'll wipe you down. Come with me into the kitchen.'

I obey his imperial tone. In the kitchen, beside the sink, he looks me up and down then moves very close, so that I can feel the pressure of the shaft of his spear against my thigh. The air foments with the scent of hot pickles on his breath, and rotting leather from his feet.

'*Veni, vidi, vici.* I came, I saw, I conquered – then you conquered me,' Colin murmurs. He reaches one hand out to the brooch at my neck. His fingers brush my skin. The hairs on the back of my neck prickle with confusion.

'What do you think you're doing?'

'I thought it might be easiest to take it right off.'

'You thought wrong. Give me some kitchen towel or a cloth. I'll do it.' I scrub fiercely at the stain, my face burning.

'Can I have a word with my wife?' Tony interrupts. He moves round and pats my bum in what some anthropologists might describe as a mate-guarding display. 'We're going home.'

'So soon?' Colin's face falls. 'It isn't midnight yet.'

'We have to get back for the babysitter. Come on, Lisa.'

'I'm having a good time,' I protest. I can hardly believe it, but I'm actually disappointed. I mean, I've hardly spoken to anyone apart from Colin. I wanted to chat to Manda.

Tony guides me out past Colin, and then Ted who is snogging Victoria. At least, I think it's Ted, although it should be Spenser. I'm confused. Perhaps I've had too much to drink. Tony drives, in case my second drink, grape juice, has been spiked with Roman vodka. I slide into the passenger seat.

'I was just beginning to relax and enjoy myself.'

'Couldn't you see what was going on?' Tony touches my knee briefly. His eyes flash in the dark. 'Colin tipping wine down your front, and getting up close and personal in the kitchen? Don't try to deny it. I saw him.'

'It was an accident. He was having a laugh.' I hesitate. 'Are you jealous?' I start laughing myself. 'You are, aren't you?'

'Manda and Colin are swingers.'

I catch sight of my reflection in the rearview mirror. I look like one of Tony's fish out of water.

'Manda propositioned me,' Tony goes on. 'She offered to take me up to the bedroom.'

157

My immediate reaction is, 'How dare you allow yourself to be asked!' then I realise that Tony wouldn't have told me if he'd had any idea of going through with it.

'I thought swinging was something the newspapers made up to sell copies. I didn't believe that real people did it.' It takes a while to sink in. 'Not in places like Selsdon and Hamsey Green too.'

'It's disgusting, isn't it?' Tony huffs.

'I don't know why you're making out that you're so shocked. Isn't it a popular male fantasy?'

'That your teenage daughter's friend's parents are swingers?' Tony crunches the gears. 'It isn't mine.'

As we're on the subject of relationships, it seems like a good time to ask. 'Tone, could you fancy someone other than me?'

'That isn't a fair question.' He gazes towards me, his skin green in the light of the traffic lights. 'Do you have the hots for Colin?'

'Are you referring to Manda's Colin, or Colin Firth?' I find myself laughing again, but this time, my laugh is hollow. 'Give me some credit.' My voice softens. 'I love you,' I say, but I don't think Tony hears over the throb of the engine.

'I don't want Jade mixing with Kimberley any more.'

'We can't stop them seeing each other at school.' I am torn. I like Manda, in spite of the fact that she isn't quite the person I thought she was. I like Kimberley too.

'I don't want Jade going to that house.'

'You'll tell her then?'

'I shan't let her back into that den of vice,' Tony says adamantly. 'Colin lets his partner sleep with other men. He lets her do what she likes. I don't understand how he can appoint himself Emperor. If anyone wears the toga in that relationship, it's Manda.'

Manda and Colin's hobby is wife-swapping, while Jacqui wants to swap her husband. Life is full of surprises, isn't it? And my mum tries very hard to hide her surprise that Tony and I are back home before ten. Which is the least embarrassing admission? Confessing to having attended a swingers' party, or to fancying an early night? I choose the latter.

'Jade and I had a lovely talk,' Mum says. 'She told me all about Kimberley and this boy, Ali.'

158

'He's almost a man,' I sigh. 'I imagine that she made him out to be a paragon.'

'She says that he's going to university in October, if he hasn't signed a record deal first.' Mum smiles at me. 'Oh Lisa, Jade's growing up so fast.'

'I know. That's what I'm afraid of.'

'I shouldn't think anything will come of it, considering the age gap,' Mum says reassuringly. 'Jade's gone up to her room, and Chloe's tucked up asleep.' She winks towards Tony. 'I should make the most of it, if I were you.'

It's a tempting thought, but by the time I've showered away the scent of wine on my skin, Tony is in the bedroom, singing 'I Wanna Be Like You' from *The Jungle Book* (the song with the King of the Swingers' Ball), which can only mean one thing: that Chloe's woken up.

I'm up with her three times during the night and, on the fourth occasion that she wakes, I can't see any point in trying to go back to sleep. I take her downstairs to watch me stew apples to stick in ice-cube trays in the freezer. I pick up and put down the phone a couple of times, then try to concentrate on a book, but by six, I can contain myself no longer. I phone Clare.

'This had better be good,' she groans. 'What is it?'

'Manda and Colin are swingers.'

Clare isn't impressed. I don't suppose I would be at this time on a Sunday morning.

Tony has a go at Jade about not seeing Kimberley any more, on Sunday morning after I've finally got to bed for a couple of hours. They continue arguing on Monday, and the subject's still current on Tuesday morning.

I'm sitting on the edge of the bed with Chloe propped up on my lap so that she can see her reflection in the mirror with mine. I pick up my mascara and twist the wand out of the tube.

'Ma,' Chloe says. 'Ma, ma, ma, maaah!' She takes a swipe.

'No, that's mine.' I'm too late, and anyway, Chloe works on the principle of what's mine is hers, and she catches hold of the wrong end of the wand. By the time I've extricated it from her grasp, we are both sticky with dark-brown mascara.

'Mummy's trying to make herself look pretty, Chlo.'

159

Thwarted, Chloe strikes out for the lipstick on the dressing-table.

'Oh no! Oh, what's the point anyway? If you want me to go out and about *au naturel*, who am I to argue? What difference are cosmetics going to make when I need a face transplant? Let's go downstairs.'

'You can't tell me who my friends are!' Jade screams from the kitchen.

'On second thoughts, Chloe.' I rest my lips on the top of her head. 'Let's stay here.'

'How can you ground me for something I haven't done?' Jade storms upstairs and slams her bedroom door. Her anger and devastation is evident in the creaking and thumping as she climbs up the ladder and throws herself onto her bed. If I'm upset that she and her dad are at each other's throats, she must be doubly so. Poor Jade.

I can remember when Clare's next-door neighbour invited us to his sixteenth birthday party. It was a political decision. He wanted to make sure that Clare's parents wouldn't feel able to complain about the noise that night.

Clare and I were going through our punk phase. Clare dyed her hair black with a blonde streak across the top of her head, and pierced her ears with safety pins. I was more moderate, too scared to have my ears pierced because of my mum's doom-laden warnings of death through septicaemia as a consequence. I contented myself with black jeans, a temporary colour rinse which gave my hair a subtle, auburn tinge, and a bracelet of safety pins. We thought we were the bees' knees, and, although Clare was in love with the lead singer of Sham 69 at the time, she hoped to charm her next-door neighbour into asking her out.

He didn't, and we lost all sense of time, drinking Pernod and Black – it's strange how everything was black back then. My dad turned up to find me asleep under the table in the kitchen. I was alone, but he didn't see it that way when there were two couples in the same room, snogging each other.

It was all Clare's fault. She was the baddie. She led me on. I was never to see her again.

I take Chloe with me and knock on Jade's door.

'Jade?' I say softly. 'Can I come in?'

'What do you want?'

'To see how you are.' I open the door.

'I'm fine.' Her eyes are red, but defiant.

'It might seem as if Dad and I are trying to spoil your fun, but we want to keep you safe. You do understand?'

Jade sniffs then gives me a slow smile. 'Of course, Mum.'

I think I detect a note of condescension in her voice, but I give her the benefit of the doubt. 'Are you ready for school?'

'Almost.' Jade slides down off her bed without using the ladder. She picks up her school bag from the floor. She could do with a bigger one, considering how many books she must have stuffed in there. 'I'm going to walk to the bus stop. I'm not asking Dad for a lift, the way he treats me.'

'I'm glad you're happier about going to school.'

'As you keep saying, Mum, a good education will stand me in good stead. If I want to be a lawyer rather than a nail technician, I'll need to pass some exams. I'm going to stay on for Homework Club, if that's all right. And no, I'm not making it an excuse for going to Kimberley's house.' She comes up to me, kisses Chloe's forehead and my cheek. 'See you both later.'

I grow warm with pride. Jade suddenly seems so much more mature and sensible than I ever imagined she could be. Chloe and I wave her goodbye as she saunters down the drive, weighed down by her bag. Tony walks up behind me, rattling his sandwich box. He's wearing a new shirt and has been rather heavy-handed with the aftershave.

'I hope you're not letting her play us off against each other,' says Tony. 'We must stick to our guns.'

'I don't want her to hate us.'

'Most teenagers hate their parents.'

'They say they do, but they don't mean it, and it's all very well telling her not to see Kimberley, but we haven't told her why.'

'I'm not going to.'

'We can't protect her for ever, Tone.'

'I'll do my best. Jade doesn't need to know about wife-swapping just yet.'

'She probably knows more than we do,' I point out. 'She sees all kinds of sensational stories in the papers, and I expect that she and her schoolfriends have already done sex and drugs.' I notice how Tony's knuckles blanch as he takes a tighter grip on his lunch. 'I meant that she's probably learned all about them in PSHE. Anyway, I think she's seen sense and realised that we're only looking after her interests.'

'I don't believe she'll give up on seeing Kimberley that easily.' Tony's lips brush my cheek. 'I'm off. I'm going to drop into the barber's on the way to work.'

'Will you be late home?'

'I've got a lot on. Someone wants me to give them a quote for replumbing an entire house, but they're not back from work till after six tonight.' He strolls towards the van. 'I'll let you know.'

His hair gleams in the sunshine. His trousers – fawn chinos today – hug his long thighs.

'Tony,' I call out. 'Love you . . .'

He looks up and gives me a small smile. 'Keep an eye on Jade. I think she's up to something.'

I hug Chloe tight as a dark thought crosses my mind. The new clothes. The fact that Tony has suddenly discovered how to work the washing machine. The trip to the barber's. Is Tony up to something too? Am I missing the signs?

Tony does his best to miss my mum, who is walking up the hill towards the house. He shoots out of the drive in the van and tears off up the hill away from her, driving the long way round to the main road in order to avoid having to stop and talk. Mum insisted on coming over here to sit with Chloe while Clare and I go to work.

Neville hasn't gone to work. When Clare and I arrive, he's wandering about with his suit on, eating toast and scattering crumbs all over the place.

'Can't you be more careful?' I grumble. 'I have to clean up after you.'

'Okay, I'll sit down.' A slice of toast falls from his plate and lands butter side down on the carpet.

'We should charge you more for that.'

'Don't worry about the floor. Look at my trousers!' Neville rubs at a smear of jam with a tissue. 'I've got an interview today. What am I going to do?'

'Haven't you got another suit?' I ask.

'You don't need a new one,' Clare interrupts. 'Sue will get that stain off for you. I'll drive.'

Neville squeezes into the back of the Polo and we head up Addington Road at high speed. Neville is clutching my shoulder, not the back of the seat.

'Shouldn't you slow down, Clare?' he says. 'I wouldn't like you to break the law on my account.' He pauses. 'After what you said about taking up a new challenge, I applied to join the police.'

'You what?' Clare brakes sharply and continues at a sedate pace.

'Why?' I ask. Neville seems such a wimp.

'I want to make a difference to people's lives,' he says earnestly.

'You only have to watch one episode of *The Bill* to see that being a police officer is a very dangerous occupation,' I say. 'Wouldn't you be afraid of getting hurt?'

'Somebody has to do it,' Neville says. 'I'm halfway through an assertiveness training course to prepare for facing up to violent criminals.'

When we reach the High Street, Clare parks on double yellow lines because there isn't a free space. Neville doesn't comment in the face of Clare's stern frown, which suggests to me that his course hasn't done him much good yet.

We all jump out and run into the dry-cleaners, where Clare explains the problem to Sue. Sue flips the sign on the door to *Closed* and shows us through to the back room, which is crowded with ironing boards, sewing machines and clothes rails. Virgin FM is on the radio and Clare switches it off quickly. I know why. It's because she's worried that Neville won't appreciate Sue's taste in music.

'Now, how are we going to do this?' Sue rests her hands on her hips.

'Drop your trousers, Neville,' Clare orders. 'Don't be shy,' she goes on. 'We've seen it all before. We're women of the world.'

We all stand there, watching Neville step out of his trousers. With a flash of his pale, lanky legs and Homer Simpson pants, he dodges behind a wedding dress that's draped over a clothes rail. Sue takes the trousers away and works on them at a table.

'I've fixed it,' she says a few minutes later. She hands them over the clothes rail to Neville. I've never seen anyone put on a pair of trousers so quickly.

'Thanks,' he smiles. 'You've saved my life. What do I owe you?'

'You can buy her dinner,' Clare cuts in.

'I can speak for myself, Sis,' says Sue. 'You don't owe me anything.'

'How about coming along to the Tapas Bar with me?'

'Sue's not keen on tapas,' says Clare protectively.

'Clare!' I cut in. She's trying too hard.

'How about some modern continental cuisine? Monkfish, capers, that kind of thing?' says Neville.

Sue seems impressed.

'Tonight?' Neville asks. 'I'd like to have someone to celebrate with, or help me drown my sorrows, depending on the outcome of this interview.'

'Call me later,' says Sue. 'Here's my number. Good luck.'

It's our lucky day, I think. Not only isn't there a single traffic warden on the High Street, but Neville sets off for his interview with a smile on his face.

'It'll never work,' I say, relaxing back into the sofa once he's gone.

'Never say never,' says Clare.

'You just did.' I grin. 'Sue and Neville – it's like pairing chocolate cake with cheese.'

'They'll be ideally suited. Sue's always loved men in uniform, and Neville doesn't realise it yet, but Sue is exactly the kind of woman he's looking for.'

Clare and I go looking for Della as soon as we've finished at Neville's. We drop in unannounced at her house to pick up the money that she promised me when I phoned to chase her up the other day.

'Can't this wait?' says Della at the door. 'I'm in a hurry.'

'Are you going shopping by any chance?' I ask.

'The summer sales. How did you guess?'

'We've dropped by for our cash,' Clare says.

'Oh, I'd forgotten. Just a minute.' Della shuffles about in her handbag and pulls out a chequebook. 'Can I pay in instalments?'

'We don't do credit, or cheques.' Clare glances at me to back her up. Clare has first-hand experience of the perils of a cheque. Jim, having received a new chequebook in the post that Clare didn't know about, has just bounced three.

'We agreed that you would pay up on time.' I smile sweetly. Inside, I am seething. I'm not spending hours on my knees for nothing.

'It's no skin off our nose if your husband finds out that you've employed a cleaning company,' Clare goes on. 'We have a waiting list of clients as long as your arm.'

'We'll drop by again.'

'Promise me that you'll ring first,' says Della, 'then I can have the cash ready.'

'At *Maids 4 U*, we don't make promises we can't keep,' I say, 'but we'll do what we can.'

'Thanks.' She gives a weak smile. 'Look, I really must go. I'm meeting someone in town . . .'

'I wonder if her husband knows about that as well,' Clare says thoughtfully, as we watch her head for her car.

From her appearance and lifestyle, Della must have money, but I'm not sure how fluid her assets are.

'Shall we give her the push?' I ask hopefully.

'Not yet,' says Clare. 'We'll give her another couple of weeks. If she doesn't pay up then . . .'

'What's it to be? Blackmail or payment in goods?'

'It's all very well providing references to prospective clients,' Clare grumbles. 'They should be obliged to provide them for us. I don't think she sacked her previous cleaners. They sacked her!'

That's rapid disillusionment, even for Clare, I think. She looks pasty, as if this diet she is following is doing her more harm than good.

'Right then, let's go and burn a few calories,' Clare goes on.

'I don't think we'll burn that many calories taking the babies swimming,' I argue, as we collect Fern from Jim, and Chloe from Mum. Mum is reluctant to let Chloe go. She doesn't approve of Chloe learning to swim, but I've read all the literature I can possibly find. I know that chlorine kills germs, and that it's safe to introduce a baby to the pool as soon as you feel ready. Grandparents exist to give advice. It's up to parents to decide whether or not to follow it.

The pool is hired out to the Mini Dolphins' swimming classes by one of the local private schools. Jacqui is already in the changing rooms with Ethan.

'I thought I was going to be late.' She smiles, as Clare and I start changing Chloe and Fern. 'I told Anje that she'd have to hold the fort at work because I didn't want Katya to be the one who sees Ethan take his first strokes.'

'I don't think that the babies will be swimming on their first attempt,' I say. 'It took me years to learn.'

'Oh, you'll be surprised,' Jacqui says. 'Zara's supposed to be an excellent teacher.'

When we emerge from the changing rooms, Fern is dressed in a Mini Dolphin swim nappy and a Mini Dolphin T-shirt – Jim wanted her to look the part. Ethan is sporting a swim nappy with a go-faster stripe. Chloe is wearing a swim nappy and vest.

All three babies have grown. Fern's hair has thickened up into dark waves, Chloe's face is leaner and Ethan is bigger than ever. In fact, he's so enormous that I can imagine his bulk displacing all the water from the pool.

Our class is taken by Zara, who looks like a model out of a sports catalogue. Her hips, shown off by a high-leg blue costume, are narrow. Her shoulders are broad. She jumps into the pool.

'In we go!' she yells.

'You first,' I say to Clare.

'No, you.'

While we're deciding who braves the water first, Jacqui climbs down the steps in her pink floral bikini. I follow with Chloe in my arms, and my cellulite all a-quiver. I shudder as the water creeps up around my midriff. Chloe wriggles up as high as she can go, up to my shoulder, and clings on tight to the strap of my swimming costume.

'We should have waited until they were old enough to go in the pool without us,' I observe.

'It's too late then, Lisa,' says Jacqui. 'Babies are like sponges. They can absorb everything and anything at this age. Come on, Clare. Don't be chicken.'

'Let the babies feel the water,' Zara says. 'Float them on their backs.'

As I lower Chloe into the water, she cries and grabs at my necklace. She yanks it so hard – I didn't realise there was so much strength in that tiny arm – that a link breaks and the chain slides off into the pool.

'What's wrong, Lees?' Clare asks from the poolside.

'I've lost my chain. Chloe's pulled it off.'

Zara dives a couple of times, but she can't find it. I hold Ethan in one arm and Chloe in the other while Jacqui has a look. I can't put my face underwater without closing my eyes so I'm no help.

'It must have gone into the filters,' says Zara.

'It doesn't matter. It wasn't expensive.' The only value it had was sentimental. 'Tony gave it to me when I told him that I was pregnant with Jade.'

'Perhaps he'll buy you a new one,' says Jacqui.

'I doubt it.' I watch Clare negotiate the steps into the pool. Fern loves it. She giggles as she slaps at the surface. Her delight is infectious. Soon, we're all giggling – except Zara.

'Now, trickle water on their faces,' she says impatiently. 'We've wasted enough time.'

I trickle a few drops onto Chloe's forehead. She screams. Her skin is turning blotchy.

'Well done, everyone. That's it, now push Baby's face under the water,' says Zara. I hesitate. 'It's all right, infants of this age automatically hold their breath.'

'How do you know?' I want to ask. 'How do you know that all babies are the same?'

Clare ducks Fern underwater and Zara catches her.

'She swam, did you see that?' cries Clare. 'Oh, I wish Jim had been here to see it.'

'I should have given him a break from stripping out the rest of my bathroom, and brought him along too,' Jacqui smiles. 'Come on, Ethan, darling. It's your turn.'

Ethan bobs down and up with flying colours because he's so fat. He's a star, according to Zara. When I refuse to do it to Chloe, Zara does it instead. It stops her screaming, I'll give her that, but I've had enough.

'Come here, my little ice cube.' I drag myself out onto the edge of the pool like a walrus. I'll get Tony to bring Chloe next time. He likes swimming.

'I'm also starting some classes for mums,' Zara starts hopefully as I wrap Chloe in her towel, and mine. (If she had top teeth as well as the two in her lower jaw, they'd be chattering.)

'What are you going to call that then?' I ask. 'The Old Whales Club?'

'Regular swimming is great for getting your pre-pregnancy figure back,' Zara says, 'and it's fantastic exercise if you have back or joint problems.'

'There you go, Lisa,' says Jacqui.

'Oh, my knees have been much better since I started taking those supplements.' There's no way that I am going to let Zara rope me into regular swimming. Actually, I'm not sure the tablets are doing any good or not but, if I come off them, I fear that my knees will be worse. I recall that I haven't taken them for a few days. I started out with good intentions – as I did with the Pill. 'I could do with some more.'

'I'll let you know as soon as we have some in stock.' Jacqui wraps Ethan in a white towelling robe that matches her own.

'How is the business going?' Clare asks.

'It's more difficult than I imagined,' Jacqui confides. 'Katya isn't very reliable. She passed her English exam.'

'That's wonderful,' I say.

'If she'd failed, she'd have a reason to stay on. As it is, she's planning to leave next month. I don't know what to do. Anje doesn't understand. Greg refuses to take any responsibility for childcare.' Jacqui looks up from drying Ethan's creases. As when we first met in the car park at the clinic, I see her vulnerability. She's close to tears. 'I might have to give up my share of the franchise.'

'Give it a chance,' says Clare. 'It's early days yet.'

'Oh, I get so tired, trying to do it all,' Jacqui sighs.

'So do I,' I agree.

'I don't see why you two are always complaining about your husbands,' says Clare. 'You should be thankful that they're out there working at all. They're doing it for you, and your children, not because they don't want to spend time with you.'

I hope she's right. I really do.

Chapter Eleven

Scorpio: passionate, ruthless and dangerous. That's me. Master of her emotions, but not today because it's Friday, the end of an exhausting week when the temperature has been hitting 28 degrees every day, and Jade is winding me up.

'You've had my phone all week, Jade, and I want it back.' I'm not sure why – texting isn't that exciting when you haven't got anyone to have textual intercourse with.

'You've received another message from Colin.' Jade hands it over.

I frown. Colin's left three messages on the landline too, to the effect of *I hope you enjoyed the party, and the next one is at Ted's.*

'Is this why you and Dad won't let me go to Kimberley's? Is this why I've had to stop dancing lessons?' She glowers at me. 'I think it's pathetic.'

Suddenly, I realise what she's getting at. I snatch the phone. 'Are you and Dad going to divorce?'

'Of course not.'

'You're always arguing.'

'Arguing is part of being married,' I point out. 'Even if you're in love with someone, you are allowed to disagree with them now and then. Go on, you'd better go down for breakfast.' I flick through Colin's messages that have become increasingly desperate.

No reply? R U OK? Colin x

No Jade @ dancing. Call me? Colin.

Mand sez u mite b offended. 1000 Apols. Plese get in tuch. Colin.

I wander into the living room where Chloe is batting the

baby gym. I flick the switch on the light in the hood of the fishtank and open the lid of the fishflakes. I don't suppose that Tony has remembered to feed them. All the fish but one come swimming up to the glass. The remaining one floats upside down. I remove it on a piece of tissue, and throw it in the bin in the kitchen – Jade is too old for the fish funerals which I used to have to conduct with great solemnity in the garden.

I suppose the fact that Colin has sent me so many texts does look fishy, and Jade does have a particularly active imagination. I head off to find her to set her straight about me and Colin, but she's in a hurry to leave for school and I ask her if she's remembered to pack her homework instead.

'Bye, love,' I say.

'Bye,' she says distractedly, slamming the door behind her.

Once Jade has gone, I text Colin back.

Insist u do not contact me agen. Lisa. Do u no how much it costs to receve a txt?

I call Della Ramsay to warn her that Clare and I may be dropping round today for our money, but there is no answer. When I return from the supermarket later, there's a message on my answerphone, not from Colin or Della, but school. Can I call them to explain Jade's unauthorised absence? Suddenly, the room seems very cold. I ring back straight away.

'It's Mrs Baker. How can my daughter not be at school when I waved her off to the bus this morning?'

'She's been absent all week,' the school secretary says firmly. 'We assumed that she was off sick and you'd forgotten to contact us. She hasn't had a very good attendance record so far this term. The odd day off here and there.' She lists Jade's reasons for absence: gastric influenza; abscessated verruca; migraine with aura and visual disturbance.

My forehead tightens. Jade is the healthiest person I know, and those afflictions could have been lifted straight from the medical dictionary that I keep in the front room in case Dr Hopkins should start using terms more complex than headache, rash and boil.

I promise to let the school know as soon as I find her. *If* I find her . . . I'm beginning to panic. I call Clare first to tell her that Jade's gone missing.

'Calm down,' Clare soothes.

'Oh, stop it. This isn't a commercial. It's real life.'

'I'm sure Jade'll be fine,' Clare says. 'I'll come round.'

I can't get hold of Tony – he's switched off his phone. I try ringing Colin – he's in a meeting. I try Manda – no answer. I wish I'd bought Jade her own mobile. I wish I'd let her hang on to mine.

'She's bunked off school,' says Clare when she arrives with Fern. 'Don't you remember that's what we used to do sometimes? Mitch. Skive. Whatever you like to call it.'

'For the occasional day, and with good reason – like Duran Duran coming to London – not a whole week.' I pause. 'Her bag was stuffed with clothes and shoes, not books.' I slap my cheeks as if to wake myself up from the daze that I must have been wandering about in.

'We used to change on the way to the bus stop, and hide our clothes in the bushes. Do you remember how your mum tackled the bag lady who used to push her barrow up and down the High Street, when she discovered her wearing your school cardigan?'

'She was furious when you told her that I'd given it away to help the homeless.'

'I wonder if Jade's fallen out with one of her teachers.'

'She hasn't mentioned any of them particularly.'

'She might be meeting someone, Ali perhaps? Could she be practising with the band?' Clare pauses. 'What about her diary? Have you looked in there? That's the first place I'd look to find out where Jade is.'

I hesitate, unwilling to betray Jade's trust.

'I wouldn't be searching my conscience if I was in this situation with Fern,' Clare goes on.

'That's because you haven't got one.'

'If Jade's keeping something from you, you need to know what it is.'

We go upstairs, leaving the babies under the baby gym. I clamber up Jade's ladder, oblivious to my vertigo. I extract the key, come down and unlock the box. I take out the book and open it. Jade has apparently solved her problem of writer's block, and caught up with writing her diary. Every page is marked, scribbled and blotted with black ink. My face burns. My eyes flood with tears. It reads like Dave Pelzer's memoirs.

'Read it out loud,' Clare begs.

Mum is wearing her sad, sloppy T-shirt today. I don't see how Dad could ever have fancied her, and anyway, she doesn't love him any more. She goes on at him all the time, like she does me. I think Mum and Dad will divorce. Mum's always too tired to listen to me, and the baby's always crying. I wish I never had a sister. She has ruined my life.

I thrust the diary at Clare. 'You read the rest.'

'*Everyone in the world has a moby, except me* – she means a phone, not a whale.'

'I know, I know. Go on.'

'*I well fancy Ali,*' Clare pauses. '*He touched my breast.*'

'How dare he!'

'I don't think he meant to,' Clare says. '*Ali brushed against me on the stairs* – a trivial incident embellished with great significance.'

'And?'

'I'll summarise. She wants to lose her virginity to him in the most graphic way.'

I try to snatch the diary back, but Clare holds it above her head.

'She's only thirteen.'

'Almost fourteen,' says Clare. 'Here we are. At the Whitgift Centre in town, there's some kind of talent show, sponsored by a local radio station. First prize, a session in a recording studio.' She snaps the diary shut. 'That's where she'll be. Let's go.'

We take my car; Clare is being so frugal with fuel that she has barely enough in the tank to get as far as the petrol station, if that. Twenty minutes and three potential road-rage incidents later, I'm walking – no, running – with Clare puffing along behind me. What do we look like? Two fat ladies with prams, whizzing past Dorothy Perkins and the Disney shop, towards the source of a noise: unharmonised drumming, strumming and wailing. Around the corner, the wide corridors of the shopping centre open up into a tall atrium with a glass roof. In one corner, beside Woolies, is a stage, hardly visible

172

behind a throng of people – proud grannies and grandads, mums and dads.

A band is playing on stage. They're all dressed in black, with black hair brushed forwards over their faces. There's a mutant playing drums like one of the Muppets, looking through a black fringe with crazed black eyes. Another, with black lipstick, plays electric guitar. The singers, two girls in black cropped tops over coloured bras, and hipster trousers that don't pull up over their knickers, seem familiar . . .

'It's a Black Sabbath revival,' Clare gasps.

'It's Jade, and Kimberley!'

'Ali's band? They sound terrible considering the amount of practice they're supposed to have been putting in.' Clare puts her hand on my arm. She's trying to tell me to keep calm, but I can't hear her properly. My eardrums are already under pressure from 120 decibels of bass guitar.

'Look after Chloe for me.' I tear myself away from Clare's restraining grasp and force myself through the crowd to the stage. A security guard steps in front of me.

'Out of my way.' I duck past him – he's a trainee, apparently, as I take him completely by surprise – and run up the stairs onto the stage. All that lies between me and my daughter is an orange compère in a suit and bow tie.

'You can't come up here.' He tries to keep smiling in front of his audience. His white teeth make an extraordinary contrast with his complexion. 'See one of my girls.' He points behind him. 'You'll have to wait your turn if you really want to show yourself up like the rest of the dross I've seen today. We've already had the Pam Ayres impression, and if you're thinking of rapping, forget it,' he adds rudely.

'I'm not an act,' I insist. 'Who do you think you are – Simon Cowell?' I tell him where he can stick his microphone, and pull out the amplifier lead. The music, if you can call it that, stops. Jade and Kimberley's voices fade. I'm not sure if the audience is clapping me for stopping the racket, or the band for their performance.

Jade can't work out what's gone wrong. 'Is it the amp again, Ali?' Then she sees me. 'I am going to die,' she says dramatically. 'I'm going to kill myself.'

The audience cheer her on, assuming, I suppose, that I'm part of the performance.

'Only if I don't get to do it first,' I yell at her. 'What do you think you're doing?'

'I knew you'd go ballistic. That's why I didn't tell you. You never give me a chance. Manda lets Ali and Kim do what they want. I'm *soooo* embarrassed.'

'So am I.' The last time I went on stage was in a school play – I was the Bong Tree in *The Owl and the Pussycat*.

The compère's assistant ushers us into the wings.

'My daughter's supposed to be at school. Don't you know how old she is?'

She looks at her clipboard. 'Sixteen, and you gave your consent to her taking part.'

There is my signature, in duplicate, and obtained by deception. That school trip . . . I look for Jade, but she's staring up at the stage where the compère is giving his opinion of Ali's band.

'It's a no,' he says. 'I can't put you forward to the final. The nearest you lot come to having the X factor, is that you're Xtra bad.'

'We've worked so hard,' Ali pleads. 'Give us a chance.'

'Hard work isn't enough.' The compère is unmoved. 'You need talent.'

'A great confessional helps too,' the compère's assistant says aside to me. Jade must have heard her because she interrupts with, 'I'm a kid from a broken home.'

'Jade!' I glare at her.

She has the grace to correct herself. 'Well, almost.' She looks round frantically. 'Kimberley's been scared out of her life by her mum's psycho-stalker.'

Kimberley can't confirm this because she has sensibly sloped off, leaving Jade to face the music and Shifty to pack up the drums.

The security guard escorts Ali off the stage, and another group sets up, a gang of sporty, clean-cut, fresh-faced girls, revealing a discreet amount of belly, but not their pants. Why can't Jade aspire to be like one of them? I am gutted. Parental disappointment does indeed cut deep.

I frogmarch Jade away to rejoin Clare and the babies beyond the crowd.

'I can't believe you did that. The school have been on at me this morning because you haven't shown your face there for a week, yet you've shown just about everything else here. What did your dad say about not seeing Kimberley again?'

'Kimberley didn't want to do it,' Jade says. 'Ali wants the band to be a success. I persuaded her.'

I realise now that it isn't Kimberley who leads Jade on, but the other way round.

Jade won't look at me, yet I know from her reflection in the shop windows that the panda shadows around her eyes are streaked with tears. What have I done? Have I been too harsh? Should I have let the band finish their audition, then taken her to one side? Hindsight, in spite of what my mum says about it, is not a wonderful thing. It's bloody irritating. I've embarrassed her in front of hundreds – well, fifty maximum – of people but, more importantly, in front of Ali and her peers.

What's more, she's been brooding over those text messages that I've received from Colin, and imagines that her parents are on the verge of divorce, which we aren't, unless I discover that Tony's been up to something that he shouldn't. I need to talk about it, but Clare for once isn't talking, and I can't approach Tony because Clare, as usual, is right. If I tackle Tony on the subject of infidelity, and he isn't having an affair, I don't think he'll ever forgive me.

Clare nips into the Disney shop with Fern before we head back to the car, and, by the time we reach the multi-storey, I'm in such a state that I can't remember where I left it.

'Didn't you take note of which level we stopped on, Clare?' I start losing my grip on the pram.

'I assumed that you did – *you* were driving.'

'It isn't here.' We take the lift up one floor. It isn't there either.

'I can't believe that someone is so desperate that they'd steal your car,' Clare says.

'Well, they'll soon discover that the air conditioning unit's broken in this weather.' I report it missing, calling up a car-park attendant on the intercom on the ticket machine. He finds it on the next floor up. Luckily, he has a sense of humour.

'My wife had a baby recently,' he says understandingly. 'Her brain's gone soft, but I've reassured her that her wits will return, eventually.'

'Lisa's didn't,' Clare grins.

'Thanks a lot.'

175

'Soon, you'll both be back with the rest of us, all neurones firing,' he adds.

'All what?' I ask, as his walkie-talkie crackles into life.

'Look, I can't go into the intricacies of neurophysiology right now. Someone's stuck at the ticket barrier. Goodbye, ladies.'

'What was he saying?' I ask Clare as we watch him march away, his shoes clacking on the asphalt floor.

'I think he was saying that he's overqualified to be a parking attendant,' Clare says. It's a concept that Jade won't let go of when I tell her that she's going back to school.

'What's the point,' she says, 'of learning lots of, like, stuff, when all I wanna be is a star?'

'It's always useful to have something to fall back on, if your dreams don't work out,' Clare says, helping me out.

'Like cleaning, you mean?' Jade says scathingly. 'Well, you don't need exams or a degree for that.'

'I don't care,' I snap. 'You're going straight back to school.'

We divert to Della Ramsay's on the way. She isn't at home, so Clare lets us in with her keys. We take Fern, Chloe and Jade into the house with us.

'What are you two doing?' Jade asks nervously.

'Looking for money,' says Clare.

'She hasn't left the cash where she said she would.' I pick up the biscuit barrel in the kitchen to check underneath it. 'I think it's time that we had another look through her wardrobe.'

We head upstairs and open the doors.

'I don't like this,' Jade says, as Clare pulls out a neat stack of jumpers and starts checking the price tags. 'You tell me off for missing one poxy day at school . . .'

'I think it was more than that,' I interrupt, but Jade ignores me.

'. . . Yet you're here in someone else's house, stealing their stuff,' she goes on.

'Exchange is no robbery,' says Clare. 'We're only taking goods to the value of what we're owed.'

'Those clothes won't fit you.'

'We can sell them on,' I point out.

'These earrings will,' says Clare, taking a pair of pearl-effect studs out of a box on the bottom shelf.

'What if this woman calls the police?'

'She won't.' Once we've selected a few bits and pieces – some earrings and a gorgeous pink mohair polo-neck for Clare, and a couple of T-shirts for me – I leave a note under the biscuit barrel.

Maids 4 U contract terminated on full payment – goods in kind. Don't try anything stupid. We have your hubby's contact numbers from address book.

'It isn't blackmail,' I try to reassure Jade on our way to school after dropping Clare and Fern back home. 'It's insurance.'

'Oh, stop blagging, Mum.'

'Okay, but you'd better start doing some,' I say. 'Here we are.'

I walk Jade up to the school gates with Chloe in my arms, and watch her wander morosely up the drive, her head down and shoulders collapsed with the weight of more than her school bag. She glances behind her. I turn away and head back towards the car which I've parked exactly where I can find it this time, but around the corner from the school . . .

My brainpower might be temporarily lessened by the effect of my maternal hormones, but I'm not completely stupid. Before I reach the corner, I dodge into the bushes at the side of the pavement to hide. Chloe frowns at me.

'Think of it as a game of boo,' I whisper.

She smiles expectantly and coos.

I tickle her cheek. How long do I give it? A few cars go by. A white van like Tony's, except it isn't his. I wish it was. I wish I could jump out and stop him, and share the responsibility. The traffic falls silent. I can hear the clump clump of feet heading back towards us.

I creep forwards. As Jade draws level, I leap out. 'Booo!'

Jade jumps out of her skin. Chloe laughs. I'm laughing too, although I shouldn't because Jade has disobeyed me yet again. Jade flushes scarlet at being caught out.

'The school office is that way.' I point. Chloe tugs on my hair. 'Chloe and I are coming with you this time.'

'Oh Mum, you can't.'

'I trusted you. From now on, whenever you go, I shall have to come with you.'

'Muum . . .'

'I don't know what your dad's going to say about all of this.'

177

'You're not going to tell him?'

'Of course I am. In spite of all this stuff about me not loving your dad any more, which is totally untrue, and him maybe not fancying me like he used to, we are not planning a divorce.'

Jade's eyes narrow. A shiver runs down my spine. I have betrayed myself.

'You've been reading my diary.'

'Only the bit about the talent contest,' I say quickly.

'It's private, personal stuff.' Jade bites her lip. 'How could you?'

'I'll never open it again,' I promise, for my own peace of mind rather than concern for Jade's privacy.

'It's because of what I said about Ali, isn't it? That's why you don't want me staying with Kimberley or dancing with Manda any more.' Jade stamps her foot. 'Well, you're too late. Ali's my boyfriend, and you can't stop me seeing him.'

'What do you mean?'

She looks down at the pavement and kicks a stone with her toe.

'He's asked me out.' She glances up at me, her head to one side. 'I said yes.'

'Your dad won't approve. Ali's so much older than you are.'

'Age doesn't matter,' she says naively. 'Look at Clare and Jim.'

'It matters when you're only thirteen.'

'Very nearly fourteen.' Jade smiles in spite of herself, then returns to wronged and misunderstood teenager mode with a wobble of her lip. 'Ali will never want to see me again after today,' she says dramatically.

If he really loves you, he will . . . I don't say it.

'Oh Jade, come here and give me a hug.' Grudgingly, she lets me put one arm around her shoulder and kiss her cheek.

'Do I have to go to school, Mum? There's hardly any afternoon left.'

'Yes, you do,' I say firmly.

I divert on the way home to see if Jacqui's in. She seemed very down when we left swimming the other day. Clare says that it's because Fern stayed underwater for longer than Ethan, and Jacqui would have expected Zara to have awarded him his ten-metre badge by the end of the first session.

Jacqui's car is outside the house. Tony's van is parked in front of it, offside wheels on the pavement. There's a bath in the skip. I pick Chloe up in her carryseat and knock on the door.

Jacqui seems a little distracted.

'Hi, I was passing,' I say, 'and I thought I'd pick up those supplements for my knees.'

'Yes, yes, of course. Come in.' Jacqui looks pale. 'Tony's dropped by too, to talk about the hot tub.'

How much is there to say about a hot tub? As if reading my mind, Jacqui tells me that Tony's trying to sort out an electrician to fix the wiring, and Jim to make a flat, level base. The bathroom installation is in progress.

Tony comes through from the kitchen.

'Hi, love,' he says. He moves forwards and kisses me on the lips. This expression of affection takes me by surprise. I was about to blurt out what happened to Jade today, but decide better of it. It can wait. 'I was just leaving.'

'You'll stay, Lisa?' says Jacqui. 'You can come up and see the new bathroom.'

'Okay. Why not?'

'I'll see you later.' Tony nods to Jacqui, unsmiling. 'I'll be in touch.'

'How are you?' I ask, once Tony has left. 'You didn't seem terribly happy on Tuesday.'

'Oh, you know how it is.'

'I don't.' I smile. 'That's why I'm asking.'

Jacqui smiles back. 'I was worried about Ethan, but he's fine. I took him back to the clinic to have his head remeasured. Apparently the last health visitor misread the charts. He's perfectly normal.'

'Oh, thank goodness for that.'

'Katya's taken him to the park to give me a break.'

'Where's Greg today?'

'York, I believe, and I don't know when he'll be back.' Jacqui sits down on the sofa, hugging a cushion to her chest.

'Do you . . .' I begin. 'Don't you ever worry? I mean, do you wonder if he's . . .' I mean, he's away on his own, and I know myself that I sometimes open the door to the courier with no more than a towel clasped about my person.

'If he's having an affair?' Jacqui's lips curve into a small smile.

179

'He doesn't have the imagination for that. You don't think that Tony's . . . ?'

'It's crossed my mind.'

'Oh Lisa, your husband wouldn't dream of doing such a thing.'

I sit back, reassured that Jacqui doesn't know my Tony as well as she thinks she does. If he is plumbing new depths of disloyalty, it isn't with Jacqui then. 'Are you still looking for the perfect man?'

Jacqui stands up, turns and stares out of the window where the patio is marked out now with sticks and string, instead of streamers.

'No,' she says quietly. 'I've already found him.'

I smile to myself. The old platitude has some truth in it. Sometimes, when you're searching for something, you find there's no need to look further than your own backyard.

The clock, modern mahogany with a gilded finish, ticks loudly during the silences when we seem to run out of conversation. I begin to see that Clare has a point, that maybe we're only friends because we have babies. If I'd met Jacqui before I had Chloe, we wouldn't have had anything in common, no reason to continue our acquaintanceship.

'I can't stay long,' I say. 'I have to get back for Jade.'

'I thought that children became less dependent on their parents as they grew up,' Jacqui says wryly.

'It's a myth.' It isn't until I get home with Chloe and Jade that I realise that I've left the supplements behind at Jacqui's. I try phoning, but there's no reply. I phone Tony. He promises to be home at five, and he is. He makes up Chloe's bottles, then hangs about in the kitchen.

'Go away, Tone,' I say. 'I feel as if Gordon Ramsay's looking over my shoulder.'

'What are you cooking?'

'Butternut squash.'

He reaches over my shoulder, dips a finger into the mouli and tastes the purée.

'Ugh. That needs more salt.'

'It isn't for your dinner. It's for Chloe. Yours is in the oven. Shepherd's pie and peas.'

'Thanks, love, I don't know what I'd do without you.'

'That's the second time you've called me love today.' I start spooning the vegetable purée into an ice-cube tray. 'Have you got a guilty conscience or something?'

'You're not still going on about that anniversary present?' Tony pinches my bum, and breathes against my ear. The hairs on my neck stand up on end. 'I'll buy you something to make up for it . . .'

'Chloe broke my necklace the other day. I lost it in the swimming pool.'

'Is that a hint?' He loops his hands around my waist.

'What's all this in aid of?'

'I've been looking at those books you borrowed from the library.' He pauses. 'We could ask your mum or Clare to have the girls so that we can spend some time together.'

'What about your mother?'

I can feel the tension in Tony's body. 'She will babysit as an emergency.' He pulls me back against him, moulding his body to mine.

'Is that a screwdriver in your pocket?' I ask softly.

'No, I'm just pleased to see you . . .'

I hear Jade pick up the phone in the hall, turn and push him away gently.

'We have to talk. About Jade.' I tell Tony about the audition at the Whitgift Centre. I don't tell him what she wrote about Ali in her diary. I think that's enough information for one day.

'Chloe can have her first sleepover with Fern, the first of many,' Clare says enthusiastically at lunchtime the next day. 'Jade must come too.'

I accept Clare's invitation on the girls' behalf, feeling more confident about leaving Chloe with someone else now that she is older.

Clare and I are in my kitchen with every surface covered with plastic as if we're about to redecorate. I've laid a mat on the floor and a wipe-clean cloth on the table. Chloe sits in her highchair, dressed in one of those bibs with sleeves. Fern sits in her carryseat, swaddled in a towel with only her eyes, nose and mouth visible. I sit, tapping my feet on the floor.

Clare stirs carrot purée in a bowl. The spoon sticks then slips, flicking purée up the wall.

'Oops, this weaning process is harder than it looks.' Clare slides the spoon between Fern's lips. Fern sticks the tip of her tongue out and dribbles it down her chin. 'I don't think she's ready, do you?' Clare decides to leave introducing Fern to solids for a while longer.

'That's probably a good idea. You should see what carrot does to the nappies.' I change the subject. 'Has Jim sold the bike?'

'No, it's in the paper again. I can't understand why a machine that's supposed to be in so much demand doesn't sell.'

I bite my tongue. It's up to Jim to make his confessions to Clare, and I wish he'd get on with it.

'Perhaps he should consider reducing the price?' I suggest.

'No way,' says Clare. 'Yesterday, he came home with a coffee machine.'

'One of your own? With a heated milk frother?'

'Yes, but I don't want it. There isn't room in the kitchen for all these gadgets that he keeps turning up with. They're supposed to be timesavers, but it would be much quicker to chuck a bit of instant and boiling water into a mug.'

'Where did he get the money from?'

'Tony paid him for the work he's been doing for him. I think he's been over-generous.'

'That's typical of Tony.'

'Anyway, enough of me and my husband. You and Tony will be able to have that romantic night in, after all.' Clare hesitates. 'Why are you tapping your feet?'

'I'm wearing the pedometer you gave me,' I confess. 'I'm trying to reach the daily target for a healthy lifestyle, but I've only managed three thousand out of the recommended ten thousand steps so far today.' I check the device at my waist. 'I'm sure it doesn't work properly. It can't possibly register *every* footfall that I make.'

'You're making excuses, you lazy cow.' Clare grins.

When Clare goes home, I walk with her so that I can pop up the High Street for one or two bits and pieces, and add on a few more steps. A man in a vest and shorts runs past us up the hill.

Clare nudges me. 'That was Dr Hopkins.'

I look back, frowning. 'I didn't recognise him.'

'See you tomorrow,' Clare says, and I watch her divert off along Sundale Avenue. I set myself up for some serious multi-tasking as my mobile rings. I continue pushing the pram, making up a shopping list in my head, with the mobile tucked under my chin.

'Hi,' says Jacqui. 'I'm outside your house.'

'I'm out.'

'I realise that. I've brought those supplements for you on my way back home for lunch. I thought I'd see how Ethan was.' She clears her throat. 'Actually, I'm going to have a word with Katya. I've just checked up on her, and she's missed Ethan's Mini-Musician session.'

'I'm sure there's a good reason for it,' I say, trying to dismiss a picture of Katya and Peter together on the sofa, and Ethan sitting neglected in front of the telly.

'Shall I leave these things outside your front door? You can send the money round with Tony.'

'Yes, thanks, I'll do that.' I pause, then go on: 'That stuff I talked to you about the other day? It was just me being silly. Paranoid. I've realised that now.'

'What made you change your mind?'

'You know I said that Tony isn't romantic? I was wrong. He's planned for us to have a night without the girls at the weekend.' I squeeze my elbows against my ribs, partly from excitement, partly to get a more secure grip on my mobile. I can't help recalling Jacqui's competitive airs at Clare's coffee mornings, and the fact that she lied about the carrot cake. 'Are you and Greg doing anything special on Saturday?'

'There's no need to rub it in.' I think from the tone of her voice that Jacqui's smiling . . . I'm not sure. 'We're going to visit my in-laws in North London.'

'Sounds fun,' I say insincerely. 'Look – I have to go. Bye.' I can't keep walking and speaking at the same time, and it's imperative that I keep walking very quickly because Manda is striding along on the opposite side of the road, coming towards me with her long hair flowing behind her. She carries a patterned Bag for Life from Tesco on her arm, and a purple purse in her hand. She wears flat ballet-style pumps and grey socks, black trousers, a red blouse and, over the top of this ensemble, a short denim-blue pinafore dress, yet she looks incredibly stylish.

I keep my head down and walk on, but it's too late. Manda waves and calls across the road.

I feign deafness like Mrs E, but Manda isn't put off. She stops briefly at the pedestrian lights halfway up the High Street, neglects to press the button and wait for the green man, but crosses when there's a gap in the traffic. The distance between us is closing fast. Manda is fitter than me, and isn't in charge of a buggy. Although it's favoured with the option of swivelling wheels, my mum has locked them into the fixed position so that they only go straight, and I can't manoeuvre around the various obstacles in the way: the enormous planters on the pavement that are filled with flowers; the signs knocking around outside the estate agent's; a woman delivering bags of clothes to one of the charity shops.

I'm losing ground. There's only one thing for it. I head into the dry-cleaners to hide.

'Hi, Sue.'

'Lisa, how are you? And Chloe?' She comes round the end of the counter and bends over the buggy. 'What can I do for you?'

'Oh, I just thought I'd pop in and say hello.' I'm aware out of the corner of my eye that Manda is outside with her back to the window.

Sue grins. 'You came in here because Clare sent you to find out about the current status of my love-life.'

'No, not really.' I do a couple of pelvic squeezes. I promised myself I'd do an exercise in every shop I go into. What with this strategy and the odd pumpkin seed, I'll be insatiable on Saturday night. 'But if you'd like to tell me, you can.'

'Neville and I had an interesting evening. We set out to sample this Mediterranean cuisine, but the place was closed for refurbishment so we tried the Tapas Bar.'

'Was that any good?' I ask nervously.

'That was shut as well,' Sue continues, to my relief. 'Environmental Health closed it down, so Neville brought me back here for a kebab from the takeaway.'

'Did he kiss you?'

Sue purses her lips into a skewed pout, and shakes her head.

'Did he ask you out again?' I say.

'He didn't ask me out in the first place. Clare arranged it, didn't she? The poor guy had no choice.'

'So it was a disaster?' I say sadly.

'Not exactly. He's sent me the most beautiful bouquet of flowers.'

'Oh Sue, how exciting!'

'It's early days. I'm not sure exactly how arresting Neville can be.' She smiles wryly. 'I suppose we'll find out eventually – he's been accepted to join the Police, subject to passing a medical and some other checks.'

I glance out of the window. Manda is still waiting.

'You know, you ought to go home, Lisa. You look shattered.'

I am grateful to Sue. She is the first person to have noticed, let alone offered me any sympathy. I go back outside. The shoulderstrap on my handbag tangles with the door handle as Manda holds the door open for me.

'I hope you don't mind, Lisa. I'd like to talk to you.'

I rearrange my strap, recalling how kind Manda was when I left Chloe at the chemist's. She deserves a few minutes of my time.

'Go ahead. You can talk as we walk.' I head up the hill towards the supermarket.

'I'm really sorry about the other night. I thought you knew.'

'Well, I didn't.'

'Listen, I'm not asking you to be friendly for my sake, but for our daughters'. Kimberley and Jade are like sisters.'

I don't respond.

'Jade is singing in Ali's band.'

'Was,' I correct her.

'All right, but please don't stop her coming to my classes. We're rehearsing the summer show and she's my star dancer. She has amazing potential. It would be such a waste of talent if she gave it up.' Manda pauses while we cross the road. I bump the buggy down the kerb. 'Please, Lisa. Blame me. Blame Colin. Don't take it out on the kids.'

'How can I let my daughter mix with people who encourage promiscuity, who think so little of their partners that they're willing to let them sleep with strangers?'

'The swinging?' says Manda. 'I thought you were cool with it. I must have misunderstood something you said, about Chloe and the swings.'

'You thought I was using my child and the playpark as a

185

metaphor for your bizarre social arrangements?' I can't help grinning. Suddenly, I feel so much better. Manda is laughing too. 'You're mad, did you know that?'

'Colin is very upset about what happened. He hates to offend people.'

I keep walking up the hill. Manda is still with me. I'm out of puff, and Manda hasn't raised a sweat. I take a quick glance at the pedometer at my waist. I have to have taken more than four thousand steps today . . .

'Isn't it dangerous?' I ask. 'I mean, don't you ever fall in love?'

'There is that risk, I suppose, but Colin and I have rules that we stick to.'

I am no clearer as to how Manda and Colin cope with their unusual relationship, and all the jealousies that it might inspire. Tony is more than enough man for me.

Chapter Twelve

What strikes me most when the girls aren't at home is the silence. I've looked forward to this golden moment for ages, yet when it comes, I feel lost: a hen in an empty nest.

Tony's out too, helping Jim shift a sofa for a mate of his, so I busy myself, preparing for my husband's pleasure . . . and mine.

I bathe in fragrant bubblebath and lounge about in no more than a squirt of perfume and a dressing-gown. I move Chloe's carrycot into the nursery. I change the sheets, air the bedroom, arrange tealights and candles around the bed. I hoover underneath the bed, and discover not one, but two packets of condoms and a tiny blue velvet box. I snap the box open. Inside is the most beautiful necklace, a silver chain and droplet with a dazzling sapphire in the centre. With trembling fingers, I pick it up and drape it around my neck. Tony has hidden this gift in the one place he thought I'd never look.

The hoot of a horn makes me jump. I throw the necklace back into the box, snap the lid shut, and put it away where I found it, then wait on the edge of the bed for Tony to come upstairs.

'Lisa?' He calls softly from the hall. 'Have the girls gone already?'

'Don't sound too disappointed,' I call back.

'I'd have liked to have kissed them goodnight.'

'You can come up here and kiss me all night instead,' I say, my tone hoarse and, I hope, seductive.

Tony's head appears around the door.

'Come here, love.' I prop myself up on one elbow, allowing my dressing-gown to slip and reveal one nipple.

'Why aren't you dressed yet?'

'I haven't got any clothes,' I say with mock gloom. It's all very well going on a diet, but the clothes I have got are falling off me, and I still couldn't squeeze into Jade's with any decency, even if I did want to go out all in black like a pallbearer.

'What time's the booking at the restaurant?'

'It doesn't matter if we're a little late.' I smile. 'We don't have to go out at all.'

'I really fancy a Thai tonight.'

'You're supposed to say that you fancy me.'

'That goes without saying,' Tony says smoothly.

Say it though. Say that you adore me. That you want to make love to me all night long . . .

He steps forward, chucks his mobile on the bed and glances at his watch. Does time matter when we're together? I can recall, in the dim and distant past, occasions when we let time drift. Who cared if we missed breakfast, lunch or tea, or all three? We feasted on each other. My stomach rumbles, reminding me that I have survived the day eating only three Ryvita and four spoonfuls of carrot and butternut squash.

'I need a quick shower before we leave,' Tony says, and I lie back for a moment, disappointed. When he returns, he sits on the edge of the bed with a towel around his middle. He looks completely knackered. His eyes are tired and his cheeks are dark with stubble.

'Are you sure you wouldn't prefer to stay in?' I ask quietly. 'I could make us an omelette.'

'I don't want you to have to cook tonight.'

'*You* could make us an omelette then.' I move around the bed and sit down beside him.

How do I seduce my husband? He didn't used to need any encouragement. I shouldn't have been so quick to send that waitress outfit off to the charity shop.

I rest one hand on Tony's back, absorbing his warmth. I lean across, press my lips to his shoulder and give him a gentle nip. My breasts swell, and my nipples chafe against the towelling fabric of my dressing-gown. I twist awkwardly to bring our bodies into contact – my knees click and I am, literally, aching for him.

Tony slides one arm around me. It feels different, as if he's forgotten how we fit together, as though we've forgotten how to be a couple. He turns his head. I think he's going to kiss me. I reach my lips towards his and close my eyes, but there is no answering pressure. Instead, he rests his head on my shoulder and gives me a bear hug.

'Is everything all right, Tone?'

'Yes, it's fine. I'm fine.' He sighs. 'I'm so tired.'

'Lie back and relax then. I'll give you a massage.'

As I push my husband back so that he's lying on the bed, a mobile rings. It's Tony's ringtone, Kelis's, 'Trick Me'. Once. Twice. Three times. Tony's hand creeps towards the handset.

'Leave it, Tone.'

'It might be important.' Tony picks it up and checks the number display. 'It's Jacqui.'

'She can call back during working hours like everyone else.' I don't think that the favours endowed by our friendship stretch to disturbing us on a Saturday night. 'She'll only want to talk about hot tubs,' I continue, but Tony has answered the phone.

I sit back on the bed, my hands fidgeting in my lap as I watch him talk. He frowns and scratches his head.

'I'll be right over.' He turns to me. 'I'm sorry, Lisa. I've got to nip over to Jacqui's.'

I freeze. 'Why? Why now?'

'There's a leak from one of the pipes under the bath. She has water dripping through the ceiling.' He groans. 'I shall never hear the end of this.'

'She isn't supposed to be there,' I complain. 'She and Greg were going to stay with his parents.'

'They must have changed their minds.'

'Can't Jacqui switch the water off at the stopcock? Can't Greg do it? Can't he stick a bucket underneath it for the night?'

'I don't understand why there's a problem,' Tony says. 'I checked everything.'

'Oh, don't go,' I plead. 'Jim'll fix it.'

'He isn't a plumber.'

I bite my tongue. If Tony had accepted that fact in the first place, then Jim would never have helped him out with the work at Jacqui's, and there would be no leak to fix.

'I really am sorry, Lisa. Could you ring the restaurant and see if you can delay the booking? I shouldn't be long.'

Famous last words. I lift the corner of the curtain and watch my husband go. How can we work on our marriage if we never see each other? If we never talk about anything deeper than who put the cornflakes back in the wrong cupboard or left the lid off the toothpaste?

Part of me is furious with Jacqui for bothering us with a pipe on our one night alone together. Part of me is restrained and reasonable. Tony doesn't have any alternative but to go and fix it. Bringing customers' ceilings down isn't good for business.

I toy with the idea of ringing Clare, or going over there to bring the girls back. I open a bottle of wine instead and sit with a book, munching on pumpkin seeds. Indigestible memories start to resurface once I'm alone, of a time not long after Jade was born. It took longer, but I became obsessed with her, like I am with Chloe, so I missed the signs. I didn't notice anything until I caught Tony in bed with Her, one of his customers. While my neglected husband had been repairing her pipes, she had been restoring his neglected ego.

'You know, I can't help wondering if there's something going on between you and Jacqui when you're back so late.' It's past midnight when Tony turns up, and I'm half-teasing, half-serious.

'Of course there isn't, Lees,' Tony sighs.

I stand up, grab onto his T-shirt and pull him towards me.

'If I ever find you've been lying to me . . .'

Tony's lips curve into a rueful smile. 'I can recall our marriage vows even if I can't remember the date we made them on.'

We're wasting what's left of the night, and Tony hasn't given me my present. A double disappointment since, when we do curl up in bed together and I slip my hand between his thighs, he's almost asleep in both mind and body. Quiescent.

'I can't,' he mutters thickly.

'It doesn't matter.' I lie awake in the dark, watching the crescent moon between the gap in the curtains. 'Tony?'

'Goodnight.' He leans across and kisses me without any passion, as if to shut me up. My frustration is two-fold – I was going to tell him about Chloe not being an accident tonight.

*   *   *

190

'Has Tony given it to you yet after your disastrous evening in?' Clare's eyes twinkle as we park outside Jacqui's house the following Tuesday. 'That, and the necklace.'

'I've hardly seen him. He was out late last night, having a drink with Jim.' I say this almost as a question.

'Sitting around, a pair of Grumpy Old Men, mulling over their midlife crises with a pint.' Clare smiles. 'Jim was late too.'

So, if Tony is by any chance having an affair, he's having one with Jim! I am reassured. They are both hotblooded, heterosexual males. Hotblooded? Maybe not.

Clare is right. I do have an overactive imagination, and I assume that it's still working overtime when we walk in on Greg, who is sitting in the kitchen in a tartan dressing-gown with Ethan on his knee. There's wholemeal toast on the table, and organic strawberry jam all over Ethan's face.

I shouldn't be miffed, but I am. Greg has every right to be here, in his house, but his presence will cramp our style.

'I'm supposed to be at work,' he says, 'but Jacqui's having a natural facelift session today, and she can't possibly cancel because it's the first of a course of six. I've had to stay at home holding the baby, so to speak, until she returns to take Ethan back up to the clinic for weighing, because she's sacked the au pair, and she won't have her mum or her gran up here to mind Ethan because they insist on smoking indoors.'

'Katya's left?' Clare says. 'What happened?'

'I wish I hadn't gone along with it. It sounds really bad, but Jacqui borrowed a CCTV from her uncle. The man with the clothing stall next door to his at the market uses it to keep an eye on the stock in the back of his van.' Greg runs one hand through his hair, sticking it up with strawberry jam. 'I feel like a Peeping Tom.'

'You spied on Katya?' I say quietly.

'I didn't want to do it, but we couldn't be sure what she was up to while we were both out. You understand that we did it to protect Ethan. You would have done the same if it had been Chloe or Fern.'

I glance towards Clare. Would we?

'What did she do that was so bad?' Clare asks.

'She took a lunchbreak?' Greg says.

'Gasp,' Clare cuts in sarcastically.

'She left Ethan unattended in his cot so she could canoodle

with that boyfriend of hers.' Greg tries to distract Ethan from grabbing at the plastic wrapping of a long-life, ready-sliced loaf on the table.

'Oh, but that's hardly a crime, is it?' says Clare. 'Especially if Ethan was asleep.'

'She was supposed to be at Mini Musicians. Ethan missed *Beethoven for Babies*,' Greg says dramatically. 'It isn't the fact that we've paid for the class in advance that annoys me. It's that Jacqui and I want our son to have the best possible start in life. Some people might look down on my wife for being a pushy mother, but she's right. Ethan won't thank us if he ends up with no qualifications like me.'

Clare and I have a break before we start, while we absorb this information. I make tea for all of us, Greg included.

'We're going to put Ethan into a nursery,' says Greg. 'Jacqui considers that he's more likely to develop the necessary social skills to survive in today's urban society if he's in a group of babies his own age.'

'We could have Ethan for you, just for today,' I offer.

'No, it's okay. I've got to be here – we're having a new fridge delivered.'

'What happened to the breadmaker?' I ask. 'I couldn't help noticing . . .'

'Jacqui car-booted it. It was too much hassle.'

The conversation falters. Like Jim, Greg isn't naturally chatty, particularly with women. I don't suppose that his parents were as concerned about his social skills as Jacqui is about Ethan's.

'Tony did an excellent job on the bathroom,' he says. 'We're looking forward to our hot tub next.'

'Jim did most of the work,' I say, wanting to give credit where it's due.

Greg frowns. 'No, Jim only did a day and a half. He and Jacqui had what she described as a personality clash so Tony took over. I thought Jacqui would have told you.'

'I expect Tony said, and I've forgotten.' I bite my lip and grab my mop.

'Did you know that Tony was working here on his own?' I ask Clare, when we're inspecting Jacqui's new bathroom. Even though I keep my voice down, it echoes.

'I'd have told you if I did.' She runs her fingers across the marble tiles on the wall.

'Surely you'd have noticed if Jim wasn't going out to work in the mornings?'

'You know what Jim's like. He's always popping in and out, here and there. Jim didn't say anything, but then he rarely does.'

'Do you think he kept quiet on Tony's behalf?'

'Oh Lisa, he didn't say anything because he didn't think it was important. Did you know that you've cleaned that tap three times already?'

'Have I?' I pause, wondering why Jacqui failed to tell me either. The bitter scent of lemon and salt stings the lining of my nose. Did she have some ulterior motive for keeping quiet, and when she said she'd already found her perfect man, did she mean Greg, or Tony? What exactly is Jacqui capable of? 'You don't think that Jacqui's been filming *us*?'

Clare goes as white as the bathsheets that hang from the heated towel rail. 'We'd better have a look, in case the whole house is wired up.'

I drop everything – bathroom cleaner and cloths into the sink – and scurry after Clare. We do an incredibly thorough clean, dusting up behind curtains and around all the photo frames, but we don't find any cameras, just a video marked *Katya – evidence* in red pen in the bedroom on the dressing-table.

'I think we should stop cleaning for Jacqui,' I say, as Clare slips it into her bucket. 'I don't feel comfortable here any more.'

'I need the cash. Jacqui pays well, and reliably, unlike Della Ramsay,' Clare says thoughtfully. 'If Jim had sold his bike, I'd give her notice.'

'We never did hear from Della, did we?'

'I thought she might have chased us up – these earrings cost a small fortune.'

Clare has hardly stopped wearing the earrings we took from Della's house as payment in kind. She misread the sales ticket when she picked them out from Della's treasure trove of jewellery. When she discovered that they were £125 not £12.50, she almost felt obliged to go back and put a few more hours in for Della. Almost . . .

'The house has never been so clean,' Greg says admiringly on our return to the kitchen.

'Energy and attitude – that's our slogan.' Clare grins.

'You've just made that up,' I say.

'I know, but it'll look great on the side of our van when we can afford one – unless you can think of a better one,' she smiles.

'Talking of vehicles,' says Greg, 'has Jim sold his bike yet?'

'Would you like it for work?' Clare says quickly. 'It would be great for nipping through the traffic in Central London.'

'I like the van for work,' says Greg. 'I was thinking of it for me. For fun. Jacqui says that as she's going to have her hot tub at last, I can have a motorbike. Do you know how much Jim wants for it?'

Clare tells him. Greg whistles through his teeth.

'What is it, goldplated? I've been checking out the used prices, and that's way over the top. Jim'll never sell it for that.' He pauses. 'It is a Honda CB500?'

'I'm not sure,' Clare falters. 'I know that it's red – I've had it parked it in my living room for long enough. And there's no good you looking down your nose at me, Greg. I know what you're thinking: "Silly woman, fancy not knowing the make and model".' She puts a hand on one hip and waves a duster at him. 'I bet you can't tell me what make and model this fridge is that you're having delivered?'

'*Touché*. All I know is that it's stainless steel to match the rest of the appliances.' Greg grins. 'Listen, if Jim really wants to sell that bike, get him to give me a call. I am interested – at the right price.'

We don't stay much longer. That video is burning a hole in Clare's bucket.

'We'll go to mine after we've picked Chloe up, and have a quick butcher's,' says Clare. 'I'll do lunch – tuna and pasta salad with low-fat mayo.'

Later, we sit down to feed Chloe and Fern. Clare aims the remote control at the video-player, and we are transported into the world of Jacqui's domestic arrangements.

The camera is in a fixed position, set among the greenery and candles in Jacqui's sitting-room fireplace. We see Jacqui's face when the video comes on, see her exit the room in heels and close-fitting trousers. We hear her open the front door, greet Katya and give her a list of instructions in shouted pidgin

English. The door slams. We watch for ten, fifteen minutes. Nothing happens. I prop Chloe up, burp her and wipe a string of dribble from her chin with a muslin cloth. Clare winds on a little.

Katya and Peter are on the sofa kissing. That's all. Oh, and he might have his hand down her top. Apparently, Katya is a virtuous girl.

'Please,' Peter urges hoarsely.

'Not till we marry,' she smiles. 'I want to be a Mrs. I want to stay in England. I love England.'

'Do you love me?'

There's a moment's hesitation – not long enough for Peter, but long enough for me and Clare to pick up on it.

'Yes,' says Katya, at the same time as Clare says, 'No, she doesn't. She's lying.'

'Poor Peter. He's infatuated.'

'I think someone should tell him,' says Clare indignantly.

'Not us. It isn't any of our business. If you tell a man not to do something, he always goes and does it anyway.'

'Will you marry me, Katya?'

'I don't know ...'

'Is that a maybe, or maybe not?'

'It's a yes.' Katya strips off her T-shirt, and Clare covers Fern's eyes with the flat of her hand.

'Don't look, Fern,' Clare chuckles.

I lean forwards. 'What's happened?' The screen goes grey, the voices muffled. I'd guess that Katya's top has landed in the fireplace and covered the lens.

'Great,' says Clare.

A pattern of zig zags covers the screen, and we're back to watching an empty sofa. Clare fast-forwards through the rest of the tape.

'At least we don't star.' I am both relieved and disappointed. If we did, then we'd have reason to sack Jacqui, and I'd have an extra morning free each week. I don't often ponder the Theory of Everything, but I do wonder if I might have more chance of fulfilling all my obligations, including cleaning my own house, if I existed in triplicate in separate, parallel universes.

I am seriously time-challenged, yet I still find myself agreeing to attend the Baby Clinic with Clare in the afternoon. We wait

195

in a disorderly queue in the room where we had our postnatal support meetings.

'Hey, it's Di and Nadia.' Clare nudges me and pushes towards the front. 'We're not pushing in, really.' She pauses. 'Oh, look at Emily and little Harry. Haven't they grown!'

Nadia nods to acknowledge us, then turns her back and starts talking to another mum in the queue. I suppose she's a bit sore that Clare and I went off and formed what she perceives as a clique with Jacqui. Dippy Di is more than happy to chat.

'We've found this wonderful Toddler Group that meets at the church once a week,' she says.

'Aren't the babies a bit young for that? I mean, none of them will be toddling for a while.'

Dippy Di gives a proud smirk. 'Actually, Emily is already sitting up. She's very advanced for her age.'

A case of rapid evolution, I wonder cruelly, or did the good genes skip Di's generation?

'How's the perineum, Lisa?' she asks brightly, at which the rest of the queue falls silent. 'Those exercises Patsy suggested have done wonders for mine. Anyway, I was telling you about the Toddler Group. Nadia's taken over the reins of chairperson and I'm her assistant. There's always room for new members, if you're interested.'

'I'm rather busy with work,' I say, but Di won't be put off.

'It really is great fun. We chat over tea and biscuits, and sing.'

I find that I am losing the will to live at the very thought. 'I'm not much of a singer.'

Dippy Di rattles on. 'We keep the cost down by organising a rota of helpers and, once a term, we leave the babies at home and have fun, cleaning and disinfecting all the toys over a glass of Blue Nun, or a non-alcoholic alternative for those who don't drink.'

'Clare and Lisa won't be interested,' Nadia cuts in.

'Not in the non-alcoholic alternative,' Clare agrees.

'Jacqui's invited as well,' says Dippy Di. 'Everyone's welcome, regardless of their age, colour or creed. You don't even have to bring a child.'

My mobile bleeps. The health visitor flashes me a furious glance.

'Can't you read?' She points towards the wall, then frowns.

'Somebody's taken the notice down,' she huffs. 'All mobile phones must be switched off.'

In my panic, I drop Chloe's spare nappy. Clare and I try to pick it up at the same time and clash heads. When it's my turn, I strip off Chloe's clothes. She takes offence at being naked in front of so many people and wees on the scales.

'Have you started weaning her yet?' the health visitor asks imperiously. I haven't met her before. I think she must be a locum.

'Oh no, of course not.' I try to mop up the wee with the tiniest piece of paper towel that she gives me. I know that the NHS is supposed to making cutbacks, but this is ridiculous.

'So that wasn't carrot juice on her vest?'

I can't deny it. Chloe's too young to have been playing with an orange felt tip pen.

'You do realise that the current advice is to feed breast or formula milk exclusively right up until your baby is six months old?' the health visitor goes on. 'It's especially important if you have allergies in your family.'

'The only allergy Lisa has is to work,' Clare says from behind me.

'I started feeding Chloe on solids because I thought it might help her sleep.'

'Has it helped?'

'Well, no, actually.' My face is burning. My hair is in rats' tails. I am a bad mother. Chloe is too light for her height. If she carries on growing at the same rate, she'll be six foot four and skinny as a bamboo cane by the time she starts at primary school. The health visitor hands me a sheaf of leaflets on how to feed your baby – with milk. 'Oh Clare, what have I done?'

'Do I detect some hypocrisy here?' Clare says. 'You said you weren't bothered when they told you about Jade's head measurement. You told Jacqui not to worry about Ethan.'

'Well, I don't want Chloe to end up taller than her dad. How will she ever find clothes to fit her? A boyfriend? She'll never be able to wear heels.'

'You don't, and you don't approve of Jade wearing them.'

'I'm talking about the future.' I wonder what the future holds for my family, as we pack up and head down the corridor towards Reception. Clare suddenly turns very pale and reaches out one arm to the wall. She lowers Fern's seat to the ground.

'Are you all right?' Silly question. I grab a chair from the hall. 'Sit down and I'll fetch a glass of water. I'll find someone medical.' I dash in and yell at the health visitor to come and help. She bustles after me.

'I'm all right,' Clare insists. 'There's a Mars Bar in the changing bag. I can eat that.'

'Mars Bar? You're on a diet. You promised me you weren't buying any chocolate.'

She looks up and smiles weakly. 'Jim bought it for me.'

'Remember to come to Toddler Group for your free session,' calls Dippy Di as she passes, and Clare passes out completely.

'Can't you see that she's in the middle of a faint?' I say dramatically.

'Give her some air.' The health visitor shoves me out of the way. 'Is there a doctor on the premises?' She bangs on the desk at Reception.

The receptionist ignores her. She's on the phone, shouting at someone. 'No, you can't bring your dog! This isn't a veterinary surgery.' She turns and glares at me. 'Do you mind? This is a private conversation.'

'Lisa?' Clare is coming round. I kneel beside her and hold her hand.

'Shall I ring Jim?'

'Don't do that – you know how squeamish he is.' She straightens and stretches out her legs. 'Anyway, I'm not ill.'

'You could have fooled me.'

Clare smiles. 'I think I just did – I'm pregnant.'

'Panic over, cancel the doctor and the ambulance.' I leap up and broadcast Clare's news. 'It's all right. She's up the duff, that's all, got a bun in the oven. Oh my . . . a sister or brother for Fern. Clare, that's fantastic.' I pause and lower my voice. 'Can I tell Tony?'

'I think you just have. I imagine the entire population of South Croydon heard that.' Clare nibbles the end of the Mars Bar that I dig out from beneath a pile of clean reusable nappies in the changing bag. 'I haven't told Jim. I've only just put two and two together.' Clare looks up towards the window. I follow her gaze. Jacqui is parking the Jeep, aligning it perfectly between Clare's car and the wall at the edge of the car park. 'I'd rather that she didn't know just yet. I need time to get used to the idea myself.'

Jacqui is unloading her luggage when we walk past.

'I like to have Ethan weighed once a week,' she says cheerfully. 'Greg thinks I'm fussing, but you can't be too careful, can you?'

'We'll have to meet up for coffee sometime,' I suggest.

'I can't make next Tuesday. I'm finding it difficult to fit everything in with being back at work.'

'Too busy to see your friends?'

'A true friend understands,' Jacqui says. 'You do understand, don't you, Lisa?'

'I do. I know how it is. I expect that it's much harder to cope without Katya, isn't it?' I pause. 'Greg told us about the camera. It seems a little mean . . .'

'You'd better watch that film, *The Hand That Rocks The Cradle*, then you'll realise why we did it. Of course, I had to tell the other family, and the agency. I doubt that Katya will ever work as an au pair again.'

'I thought you said that she was leaving in a month or so?' I say.

'She changed her mind because of Peter's proposal. Foolish boy,' Jacqui sniffs.

'Come on, Lees, we must go.' Clare hassles me.

'Clare isn't feeling too good,' I add, half-hoping that Jacqui will want us to elaborate, that Clare will let her news slip out. It's great gossip. On a scale of one to ten, reporting a pregnancy is a ten.

'I'm fine now,' Clare says firmly. 'Why on earth did you ask Jacqui about meeting for coffee, Lees?' she asks, when we head home in her car.

I can't answer. Clare won't like it. She'll tell me that I'm being ridiculous for even imagining that Tony is having an affair, let alone expecting Jacqui to confess that he's having one with her, over a cup of coffee at my house. I remember my phone. I have a text from Colin.

Lisa. Happy days. Manda sez u have forgiven us. How about sleepover? Not 4 u and Tony! 4 Jade? Salutations, Colin.

I text back.

Will think about it, give u a date. Lisa.

I'm inclined to tell him not to text me again, but it doesn't seem fair. How can I ask Colin to back off without sounding extremely rude, without explaining that I'm only asking because my daughter thinks that because I'm receiving texts from a member of the opposite sex, *I* must be having an affair.

I leave it at that and call Tony, once Clare's dropped me and Chloe off.

Immediately, he assumes that I'm ringing about Jade.

'Our eldest hasn't been skipping school again?' he says.

'No. Just thought I'd give you a ring, to see how you are.'

'I'm fine.'

'Will you be back at the usual time tonight?'

'I might drop over to see my parents first.' If I could see Tony, I know that he'd be frowning. 'Are you checking up on me?'

'No, not at all. Love you,' I add hopefully, but the phone cuts off. The battery's flat.

I'm still recharging it at six-thirty. Tony's late. In the kitchen, Chloe is transfixed by a television news article about rolling sheep. How else are they escaping over cattle-grids to raid village gardens in Wales? It's an inescapable conclusion, like mine that Tony has lost interest in me . . .

'Baaa!' I say.

Chloe looks up at me wide-eyed, and grips her rattle tight.

'All right, I'm no good at sheep.' I smile. I'm aware that I'm looking like a sheep myself, one that's been dragged through a hedge backwards, my top and jeans spattered with formula milk, toothpaste and dribble. I glance at my reflection in the window. My hair is more wild, more exuberant than any of Clare's mops.

I am whizzing up a toad-in-the-hole when Jade arrives home after her dancing lesson.

'Mum, why are you swaying while you whisk the batter?' she asks.

I glance down, feeling foolish. It's automatic. I'm so used to holding Chloe in my arms, gently jiggling her to keep her quiet, that I rock even when I'm not holding her.

'What's this stuff?' Jade looks in the fridge.

'Courgette and potato. It's Chloe's.'

'Can't you give her some decent food?' Jade takes out the cheese and tomato ketchup and puts them on the worktop. She squeezes most of the bottle of ketchup onto two pieces of white

200

bread and arranges slices of cheese on top. Hang on a mo. Didn't I give Jade a healthy diet when she was a baby? Didn't I bring her up to crave fruit and vegetables? What happened?

'Hey, stop that. It's toad-in-the-hole for tea.'

'Sausages give me a headache.' She looks up at me and wipes ketchup across her face. 'You give me a headache, keep going on at me.'

'I'm sorry that I'm an embarrassment to you sometimes.'

'All the time.' Jade is surly. 'You know, that might have been my one and only chance, my only break, and you ruined it, not just for me, but for Kimberley, Ali and Shifty too.'

'You're not still going on about the audition?'

Jade falls silent.

'While we're on the subject of Ali . . .' I continue.

'Ali will never speak to me again after what you did, so you've got what you wanted.'

'I'm sure he will.' I am confident that he'll do no such thing. I'm delighted that he hasn't been in touch since the audition. 'It might seem like the end of the world if he doesn't, but it'll be for the best. Ali's too old for you.'

'But boys my age are *soooo* boring.'

Everything is black and white to Jade. You don't appreciate the shades of grey until you're my age.

'Dad's agreed to buy you that phone for your birthday, and I thought you'd like a small party to celebrate this weekend.' I pause, hoping to find something that will cheer her up. 'Is there anything you need for your dancing?'

Jade shrugs. 'I don't care, Mum. Do what you like.' She bites into her sandwich. 'You always do what you want.'

My conscience pricks again. I suppose I do railroad people into doing things they might not have chosen – like making Tony father Chloe. I'm not sure I'm looking forward to Tony coming home now. Our relationship is like tea without caffeine, baked beans without salt, rice pudding without nutmeg – the spice has gone.

The door opens. Slams.

'Da, da.' Chloe thumps her palms down on the plastic tray on her highchair.

Tony strides into the kitchen. He smells of drink.

'You haven't been to your mum and dad's then?'

201

'I ran into Jim.'

'You said you wouldn't be late.'

Tony rolls up his right sleeve and checks his wrist. 'I've lost my watch.'

'Try your left arm.'

He looks up and grins. 'Gotcha,' he says. 'Just tricking your mum, Chloe.' He picks her up and holds her. She smiles adoringly. How can I compete with that?

'Kiss for your dad, Jade?' Tony leans towards her, but she turns away. Tony raises his eyebrows in my direction and I shrug in response. Jade hasn't forgiven him over the Kimberley episode yet.

'Jim and Clare are having another baby,' I say. 'Did Jim tell you?'

'That's why I'm so late. He's recovering from shock.'

'I don't know why Jim was surprised. He was very much involved in the process.'

'He was relying on breastfeeding being a natural contraceptive.'

Jade, I notice, is picking at her fingernails, trying to ignore this conversation.

'I have a surprise for you too, Lisa.' Tony heads out to the hall again with Chloe, but instead of going upstairs, he goes out to the van and returns with a bunch of red roses.

'For you,' he says.

'Thank you.' I try to sound grateful. I bury my nose in their dark, velvet scent. I *would* be grateful if I didn't know that the necklace was still up in our bedroom, under the bed.

'I've been neglecting you.' Tony moves close to me, and our foreheads touch. 'I'm trying to make amends for the other night, even though it wasn't my fault.'

'That isn't strictly true. It was your handiwork, your pipes that leaked.' I look up to check that Jade has left the room. 'Why did you lie to me about Jim doing the work at Jacqui's?'

'I didn't lie. You didn't ask.'

'You didn't say.'

'I didn't think it was important. You're making out that it is a lie. It wasn't. I wasn't hiding anything from you. I *can't* hide anything from you. You're too bloody nosy.' He changes the subject. 'You haven't seen my keys, have you? I had to use the spare for the van this morning.'

'I'll put these in water.' I hug the roses. 'I'll dish up your tea, then I'll help you look for them.'

He eats, manfully chewing each mouthful of sausage as if it's a piece of rubber, and gagging as he tries to swallow.

'Is it all right? Would you like ketchup with it?'

'I'm not hungry,' Tony confesses. 'I had a kebab on my way home.'

I snip the ends of the rose stems, pricking my finger on a thorn. He can have his toad-in-the-hole tomorrow, when the gravy's soaked through into the batter and it looks and smells like a dog's dinner. I stab the remaining sausage through with a fork and transfer it to a clean plate, then I help him look for his keys.

'Where do we start? Have you any idea where you might have left them?'

Tony shakes his head. 'They could be anywhere.'

Taking him literally, I open the freezer.

'My keys won't be in there, will they?' Tony opens the cupboard above the fridge where we keep a spare key for Clare's house. He finds a tin of lychees two years past their use-by date, and a historic photo of me and him at a swimming gala. He's wearing tiny blue trunks, and I'm in a red tracksuit with white stripes up the sleeves. I never swam. I just wanted to look the part. I laugh. Tony laughs. We can't stop laughing. Chloe joins in, and Jade turns up again to find out what's so funny.

'Look at this photo. Not at me, at your dad.'

'So you've always been not cool,' she says scathingly.

'That was a trendy tracksuit back then,' I argue.

'And they were my lucky trunks,' Tony chuckles.

'I think we should display this on the mantelpiece,' I say.

'No, you can't, Mum!' Jade cries. 'If any of my friends see that, I'm dead. That's if you'd let me have any friends,' she adds morosely. 'What kind of birthday will I have if you won't let me invite Kimberley?'

'I can see that it won't be much fun for us either,' Tony says.

'Does that mean I'm allowed to see her again?' Jade throws her arms around Tony's neck without waiting for his response. 'Oh, you're the best dad in the world.'

Tony glances towards me. I can see that his desire to make Jade happy has overruled his protective streak.

'Soft touch,' I mouth. I slip the photo back into the cupboard. 'Shall we have a look for your keys in the bedroom, Tony?' I suggest in what I hope is a seductive tone. 'Keep an eye on Chloe for us, Jade. We won't be long.'

'I'm not your babysitter,' I hear Jade moaning behind me. I run ahead of Tony up the stairs, and dig around under the bed.

'What on earth's this?' I say, feigning amazement as I lift out the velvet box. 'Oh Tony, is it for me?'

'I was waiting for the right time,' he says bashfully. 'Your birthday.'

I open the lid. 'Oh Tony, it's beautiful.'

'Here, let me put it on for you.' He picks the necklace up and drops it around my neck. He fastens the clasp, and it's here that he should have brushed my hair aside, pressed his lips to the nape of my neck, and slid his hand around to cup my breast . . . Instead, he's like a fire-breathing dragon.

'You had the chili sauce, didn't you?'

'I don't see why that should upset you.'

'I'm not upset,' I say curtly. 'Tony, have you gone off me? I mean, you've bought me this lovely present—'

'Oh, don't tell me that it isn't enough,' he interrupts. 'Flowers and jewellery, what more can you want?'

'Affection? A cuddle? Like we used to.'

'You're so busy cuddling Chloe that it seems as if you don't want me to touch you,' Tony says, exasperated. 'How is a man supposed to know what to do? One minute you don't want me near you, and the next, you're all over me.'

'You could hold me now. I'd like that.' I turn to him and put my arms around the back of his neck, press my body against his.

Tony holds my forearms, as if he's resisting my embrace. 'I have to find my keys.'

Reluctantly, I keep looking.

'This place is such a tip, I'm surprised that you can find anything,' Tony complains. 'I don't know what you do all day.'

My back stiffens. I'd like to wipe away the sweat that's trickling down his brow with a Brillo pad. 'I'm always busy. I don't sit on my bum, if that's what you're thinking.'

'Oh, don't keep going on about how tough things are for you. At least *you* wanted another baby.' Tony looks me straight in the eyes. '*I* didn't.' Immediately, he slaps his palm across his mouth. 'I'm sorry, I didn't mean that. Lisa, it came out wrong. Of course I want Chloe now that she's here. I wouldn't want my life – my family – to be any different.' Tony puts his arm around my shoulder and gives me a rough hug. 'Go downstairs, sit down and I'll fetch you a cup of tea.' I hesitate. 'Go on.'

'Everything is all right, isn't it?' I ask softly.

Tony forces a smile. 'Apart from not being able to find my bloody keys.'

I sit downstairs, wondering. Tony's always wound up in August, but this is July, and it's far too early for him to be worrying about the transfer market at Highbury.

Chapter Thirteen

Nothing's changed since my teenage days – you'll still find me in the kitchen at parties. It's Jade's birthday, and she can't have just one celebration. She has two: one for the relatives; one for Kimberley.

'Have you taken that necklace off since Tony gave it to you?' Clare asks as we finish making sandwiches in my kitchen – or rather as *I* finish making the sandwiches. Clare doesn't have morning sickness; it's all-day vomiting this time. Slicing cucumber is about all she can manage without having to rush to the bathroom.

I finger the pendant. 'It's only been three days.'

'Has he found his keys?'

'Can't you tell from the mood he's in?' If, as recent scientific studies have shown, men do have a monthly cycle like women, Tony has to be in the seven days before his period.

'He seems a little quiet,' Clare observes.

'Of course, he might be lulling me into a sense of false security.'

'You're beginning to take this joke about Tony having a fling far too seriously,' she says.

'It's what I'd do if I were having an affair, be very attentive to my spouse to put her off the scent.'

'Lisa!' Clare throws a piece of cucumber at me.

Laughing, I chuck it back. 'How's Sue?'

'She's going out with Neville again this weekend. Tonight. And he's been bombarding her with gifts – a bracelet, chocolates and champagne.'

'I shouldn't buy that bridesmaid's dress for Fern just yet,' I warn. I'm still sceptical about Clare's matchmaking efforts. I change the subject. 'Any news on the bike?'

'I didn't understand it. We'd tried all the papers – the *Croydon Guardian*, *Dalton's Weekly* . . . I was wondering whether to go up to the library and post it on eBay, till Greg turned up and enlightened me as to the going rate for a bike of that age.' She sighs. 'Sometimes, I could kill Jim.'

'You're so understanding.'

'Well, he said he couldn't bear to let it go. Sentimental old sod.'

'Did you agree that he could keep it?'

'I did, but then Jim suffered a crisis of conscience when I told him I was pregnant and that I'd soon have three children to support – Fern, the new baby, and him. He said he'd sell it after all. If Greg can find the money, he's going to have it.'

Chloe sits in a highchair, examining her fingers. Fern is nodding off in her carryseat. Jade pops into the kitchen with Kimberley and takes a snap of the babies with her new mobile. She shows off the photo. It isn't brilliant, one blurred baby indistinguishable from the other, but Jade is delighted.

'Mum and Dad gave it to me for my birthday,' she says.

'Along with a twelve-month tariff,' I say.

'Was that wise?' Clare asks me, but Jade goes on about her birthday treat, how she and Kimberley are going to the cinema, before I can respond.

'After the film, we're going to eat at Dezzie's,' she continues.

'Where a burger costs more than one at McDonald's because it's served up on a plate,' Tony cuts in. 'I'm bringing the order for teas.'

'You'll have to make them yourself. The kettle's boiled.' I look up from buttering the last slices of bread. 'Where are you going, Jade?'

'I'm going up to my room with Kimberley.'

'You're supposed to be mingling with your guests.'

'Jade!' Tony yells after her as she disappears out of the door.

'Oh, leave her, love. She's happy,' I say. 'Hi, Mal. Come on in.'

My brother wanders into the kitchen with his camcorder dangling from his shoulder and starts grazing on the sandwiches.

'Hey, stop that.' Clare taps him on the hand. 'Your sister's just made those.'

'All right, I'll have a sausage roll instead.'

'They're in the oven on emergency defrost,' I say. 'I don't think they'll be ready in time.'

'They'll be fine,' says Clare.

'Yes, but will *we*?' Much as I dislike my mother-in-law, I don't want to be held responsible for her demise.

'I'll test them for you,' says Mal.

'You'll be all right – you have a cast-iron stomach.' Bunny's is more delicate. She once accused me of trying to poison her when I served up home-made mayonnaise. She was in hospital for three days with suspected salmonella.

'Where is the birthday girl anyway?' says Mal. 'Carlton wants to give her a present. Carlton? Come here!'

'Yoo hoo, we're here!' Bunny and Philip enter the kitchen, closely followed by my parents. Mal's son rushes in too, and starts opening and shutting the cupboard doors. I glance at Clare. It's getting a little crowded . . .

Carlton opens the door under the sink. Out rolls a rotten cabbage, stopping right at Bunny's feet. Philip bends down and picks it up. He unwraps the dark, slimy outer leaves and squeezes the heart.

'I was going to use it in the next couple of days,' I say quickly, my face burning.

'What for?' Philip says. 'Compost?'

'What a dreadful waste,' Bunny joins in.

'Have you a plastic bag?' Philip asks me. 'I'll have to take it back to the allotment to feed the worms.'

'You'd better take all those spring onions as well,' Bunny adds. 'Really, Lisa, if you bothered to prepare a few fresh veg, you wouldn't have to work to pay for convenience foods, instead of spending time with your baby.'

'I appreciate Philip's thinking of me when he has a glut, but he doesn't ask me if I can use the extra fruit and veg before dumping it here. I'm not keen on cabbage, or spring onions, and I hate rhubarb.'

Bunny sucks a swoosh of air past her false teeth. 'I don't know what's wrong with today's women. They don't seem to know what they're doing.'

'I know exactly what I'm doing.'

'Life's too short to skin a tomato, isn't it, Sis?' Mal says in support.

'Thanks, Mal.'

Tony tries to smooth things over, handing round cups of tea, while Mal picks Carlton up. Carlton is about to protest, but Mal silences him with a chocolate mini-roll.

'It's a lovely day for a birthday.' Dad smiles and kisses my cheek. 'The barometer's rising here, and falling over Iceland, and the only cloud in the sky is high cirrus. Mares' tails.'

Mum whispers aside to me and Clare as he starts to explain the science behind the formation of different types of cloud to Mal, that Dad's weather-watching is getting out of control. 'It's a matter of finding a happy medium,' Mum says, looking towards Mal, 'not one of the kind who looks into crystal balls.'

'What do you mean?' I ask.

'Hasn't your brother told you? He's just become engaged to a fortune-teller.'

'No, he didn't say anything. Congratulations, Mal.'

'A fortune-teller, did you say?' Bunny grimaces. 'Have you asked her to see into the future to see how long *this* marriage will last?'

'She doesn't bring her work home,' Mal says.

'Obviously,' says Bunny sniffily. She blows her nose into a hankie embroidered with violets.

'A summer cold?' Mum enquires.

'No, there's a distinctive smell of onions,' she says, turning to me. 'While I remember, Bridget says that she's sorry she couldn't be here today. Sally and Joanne are busy too.'

'That's fine,' I say. 'Tell them that I really don't mind. Maybe next year.'

We eat outside, and cut the birthday cake, then laze around, chatting and enjoying the sunshine. Bunny has Chloe. Mum is in charge of Carlton. Jim has disappeared with Fern, and Clare is talking to Mal. I sit on a blanket with my legs stretched out and Tony's head on my lap. I stroke his hair . . . I love him so much.

'How's your guilty conscience?' I ask.

Tony frowns. I can feel his pulse beat harder and faster.

Clare's right. I can't just come right out with it. 'About what you said the other night – about Chloe?'

'Oh that.' Tony sighs. His pulse steadies. 'I feel really bad about that.' His fingers twist around mine. He raises my hand to his lips and kisses it.

My skin tingles. My body grows warm. 'Did you find your keys?' I say huskily.

'Not yet.'

I am disturbed by the sound of retching from the bathroom window. I excuse myself, sneak upstairs and listen at the bathroom door. Someone is in severe distress. Either I've served up some dodgy sausage rolls or the girls have smuggled alcopops into the house. I knock. The door swings open. Jim is on his knees on the bathroom floor. He holds a babywipe in one hand and a stinking, swollen nappy in the other. Fern lies on a changing mat beside the bath, kicking her legs and smiling.

'Are you all right?' I ask.

'I offered to do my bit.' Jim retches. 'Poor Clare can't even open the fridge without throwing up.'

When Clare told me last time that she was pregnant, I was insane with jealousy. This time, I'm relieved that it isn't me.

'Let me do that,' I offer.

Jim stands up and backs out of the bathroom to let me finish off.

'Was Tony with you at the pub the other night?' I ask.

Jim thinks for a moment, then grins. 'Not all night. We didn't go to bed together.'

'He was very late home.'

'It was a good evening, I guess.' Jim is staring at me very hard with those grey eyes of his. Unflinching. I should be reassured, but I'm like Jade with her new phone – I can't put it down.

At breakfast the following Wednesday morning, Jade is still playing with her mobile.

'If you aren't calling someone, you're texting,' Tony says, but Jade isn't listening. 'Perhaps I should have signed up for a different tariff.'

'There isn't one for continuous free call-time.' I have Chloe in one arm, and Tony's sandwich box in the other. 'You'll have to put that phone down while you eat, Jade.'

'All right. I know.' She puts it on the table beside her plate of Marmite on toast, but it buzzes before she can take a bite. She grabs it. 'A text message,' she says, her voice tense with anticipation. 'Oh, it's only Kimberley.'

'Were you expecting someone else?' I ask. 'Ali, perhaps?'

'I have texted him. I've texted *all* my friends,' she says to make it clear that Ali hasn't received preferential treatment.

'Men aren't good at taking hints. They need to be told things straight, don't they, Tone?'

'Er, what's that?' Tony says, looking up from his notebook.

'No, Chloe. How many times do I have to tell you, no, you mustn't play with Mummy's necklace?' I hold her hand clasped around the pendant. She burbles happily, then, when I won't let go, starts to whinge with frustration.

'I'm not bothered anyway,' says Jade. 'I don't really fancy him. He's just a mate.'

'Okay.' Do I believe her? 'If you want to talk any time . . .'

She looks at me. Of course not. Silly me. I'd never have talked to my mum about boys when I was in my teens.

'You do realise that if you exceed your allocated minutes on your tariff, you have to pay the excess with your allowance?'

Jade yawns theatrically. 'Oh Mum, I'm not stupid.'

I extract the pendant from Chloe's grasp, tuck it safely under the neckline of my *Maids 4 U* top. Gone. She kicks her feet against my tummy, then throws herself backwards as if to fling herself out of my arms. Out of sight and out of mind. The principle works for Chloe, but not for me.

Once Tony has left the house, I drop Chloe at Mum's and set out for work at Jacqui's. Jade is staying home alone for the morning as the school summer holiday, the bane of all working mums' lives, has begun.

My knees ache and my face, I notice in Jacqui's cheval mirror in her bedroom, could do with some emergency resuscitation. I bend down and start grovelling around in the washing basket to make up a load for Jacqui's machine. There's something hard, clinking at the bottom. I know exactly what it is. A shiver runs down my spine, as if someone's dropped a bunch of cold keys down my back.

I plonk myself down on the gold velvet throw at the end of the bed, clutching the teddy bear keyring that I bought for Tony one Valentine's Day, and a pair of Jacqui's black tulle shorties. I can hardly breathe against the constriction in my throat.

Tony and Jacqui? There is no other explanation. I picture him too easily, lying on top of her, caressing her cheek and whispering her name. Did he think of me? Did he feel even a twinge of guilt – before? During? After? I bite back tears and fight the crushing pain in my chest.

How could Tony do this to me? After last time? After promising on his life that he'd never stray again?

'Lees, where are you, you lazy slapper!' Clare's clogs come clopping across the laminate floor, then fall silent on the rug in front of me. The mattress sinks as she sits down. 'What's wrong?'

'I've found the keys that Tony claims he lost at the pub.' I can hardly speak. 'He's been here in her bed. With her . . .'

'Oh Lisa.' Clare gives me a hug. She smells of bleach and vinegar. 'There must be some mistake.'

'They were caught up in her knickers.'

'So? Tony probably dropped them when he finished installing the hot tub.'

'When they were testing it together, you mean?'

'Lisa, think about it.'

I am. That's what's so terrible. The coy glances that Jacqui gave my husband, the flashes of breast and glimpses of thigh were all calculated to seduce him.

Clare shakes my shoulder. 'Tony would never in a million years shag That Woman.' She sounds like President Clinton did when he denied any liaison with Monica. 'Oh yes, Jacqui's a calculating bitch. I wouldn't be surprised if she didn't filch Tony's keys and plant them in her washing basket.'

I can't speak.

'It makes sense,' Clare goes on. 'Look at how she dragged him over here once she knew that you were going out for a romantic evening together.'

'She would have had to create a leak in the pipes,' I say doubtingly.

'Was there ever a leak?' says Clare. 'Have you noticed any patches in the ceiling under the bath where this torrent of water is supposed to have poured through?'

I shake my head. When people speak, I assume that they are telling the truth. What else have I missed? There have been those late nights, the odd phone calls and Tony's sudden lack of interest in the bedroom department ... I look at the mirror again, expecting to find the word MUG tattooed across my forehead.

'Tony's been seeing her. I'm sure of it.' My nails rip angry red lines across my throat. My fingers catch in the chain around my neck. The pendant flies across the room, hits the dressing-table and slithers down to the floor. 'The necklace. It wasn't for me, was it? It was for *her*. He bought it for Jacqui.' Hot tears burn my eyes. I have convinced myself of Tony's guilt. I seem to have convinced Clare too.

'I never did like That Woman,' Clare says.

'You did at first.' We both did. She seemed so normal, so like us.

'I didn't like her,' Clare insists. 'She has a smile like a split water melon, and a bum like the back of a number sixty-four bus.'

'Yet Tony still fancied her.' I stand up. 'What does that say about me?' I can feel tears streaming hot and wet down my face. Jacqui never made any secret of the fact that she planned to ditch her husband and find another one, but she didn't warn me that the one she had her eye on was mine.

'What are you going to do, Lisa?'

'Do?'

'You can't sweep this under the carpet and forget about it.' Clare pauses. 'You aren't going to let Jacqui relieve you of your husband without putting up a fight?'

'I d-d-don't know,' I stammer. I can't take it in.

'Come on, Lisa. Get angry, will you!' Clare snatches the pair of shorties from my clammy grasp and heads for the dressing-table where she rummages through Jacqui's make-up bag. Out comes a pair of nail scissors. With a few vicious snips, fragments of black tulle come floating down to the floor.

It's nothing, an empty gesture, when I'm cut to pieces, beyond repair.

'You're in shock,' Clare says more gently. 'Let me take you home.'

'I'm not going anywhere,' I murmur.

'I don't think that confronting Jacqui is such a good idea,'

214

Clare says. 'We don't know what time she'll be back, Jade and Chloe will wonder where you are, and you really should have a chat with Tony first.' She rubs my shoulder, and I realise that Clare remains to be entirely convinced that my husband has been having an affair. 'Now let's go home.'

Home? What's the point? The house doesn't feel like home any more, yet nothing's changed. Yesterday's newspaper is spread open on the living-room carpet; a pair of Jade's trainer socks lie rolled up in a ball on the coffee-table; her music throbs like a pulse through the floor above. I sit down once Clare's gone, absorbing all this normality. Chloe lies underneath the baby gym, batting her favourite dangling monkey, the one with the smiliest face.

I tip my head back and close my eyes. I sit very still, trying to make sense of it all. With one act, maybe more than one – I don't know how many times Tony had the opportunity to screw around with that slag – the man I thought of as my husband, lover and friend has altered the course of my life for ever. I sit tossing the keys from one hand to the other, clenching my fingers around the metal until my knuckles go white.

I don't ring Tony at work. I want to see him face to face, otherwise how will I tell if he's lying? Not that I could tell before. Obviously.

Jade wanders downstairs, her mobile pressed to one ear.

'Oh my God, Kimberley. Oh my God.'

'I wish you wouldn't blaspheme, Jade,' I cut in, but she ignores me. I'm not religious, but I feel uncomfortable with anyone taking the name of the Lord in vain. If there is one . . .

'I've got my very first spot.' She points at her chin, even though there's no chance of Kimberley seeing it, unless she takes a photo. 'It's enormous.'

The spot really isn't very big. In fact, it's so small that I'm surprised that she's noticed it. When Jade had finished ranting at Kimberley, she starts to dial again.

'You do remember that you have to pay for the minutes you go over your talk-time?' I say for the fiftieth time. 'I don't know why you're wasting it, talking about spots.'

'Well, look at it. It's, like, hideous, and I've got to practise for the dance show later. I can't go looking like this.' Jade pauses for a moment. 'Are you all right, Mum?'

'I'm fine,' I say curtly.

'You look old. You've got wrinkles round your mouth.'

'I'm tired, that's all.'

'Would you like a cup of tea?'

Am I hearing right? Is this my daughter or some benevolent alien beamed down from another planet, taking on Jade's form?

'Please.' I allow myself a small smile. 'You do know how to use a kettle?' I wait for some time, until Jade returns with a cup of tea, cheering me with the fact that it's full of antioxidants that are supposed to slow the ageing process. I believe that this is misinformation put about by the tea companies to sell more tea. It hasn't worked before. Why should it now?

Jade sits down beside me and I am obliged to drink it. The teabag must have broken because brown crud floats on the oily surface. The milk is off, and I don't take sugar any longer since I'm on a diet.

'Don't you like it?'

'It's just what I needed, thank you.'

Jade's eyes widen. 'Mum, can I have an advance on my allowance?'

'Yes, Jade.'

'*Pleeease.*' Then she hesitates. 'Did you say yes?'

I nod.

'Really?'

'Yes, just don't keep hassling me. My purse is in my bag in the hall. Help yourself.'

Jade stares at me. 'Are you sure you're all right?'

'It's just a migraine, nothing to worry about.' I have a burning sensation down the back of my neck and an ache in my right temple. The pain builds, like a boil under pressure and many times the size of Jade's first teenage spot. I head for the kitchen, force down some painkillers and start cooking the tea: fish pie and frozen peas that scatter across the floor because I'd forgotten that the packet was already open.

'Mum?' It's Jade again. 'Um, did you know you've left Chloe alone, only she's managed to wriggle across the floor. She's chewing on one of Dad's trainers.'

'Oh no, I forgot her!'

'I'll get her.' Jade brings her into the kitchen and straps her into her chair. 'How's my naughty little sister then?' she coos.

216

I serve Jade and Chloe their tea.

'Aren't you having any?' says Jade.

'I'll wait for your dad.' I couldn't eat a thing. However, when Tony does turn up at six, it isn't the right time because he has to take Jade straight up to the dance school. Manda has scheduled rehearsals for the summer show for every day this week.

Tony returns at seven, when I'm on my knees in the bathroom, drying Chloe after her bath.

'Hi, Lisa.' He speaks so softly that tears come to my eyes. The sound of his voice is heartbreaking, or would be if my heart wasn't already broken. 'Jade said that there was fish pie for dinner.'

'There was.' I tickle Chloe's tummy. 'Where did you get to?' I try to keep my voice under control. 'Does it really take an hour to drive into Selsdon and back?'

'I waited to see Jade dance,' he says. 'Why do I always have to explain myself to you? Is it necessary for you to know exactly where I am every minute of the day?'

'Depends on *exactly* where you are.' I pause. 'Guess what I found.' I dig around in my pocket and dangle his keys in front of him.

'My keys?' As he makes to reach for them, I snatch them back.

'Any idea where I might have found them?' I slide a nappy beneath Chloe's bottom and fasten it across her hips, slipping two fingers inside the waistband that's covered with grinning lions to check that it isn't too tight. I pick her up and stand up. 'Excuse me.' I push past Tony and head for the bedroom to find Chloe's pyjamas.

'I've been looking everywhere for those,' Tony says.

'Is there anything you'd like to tell me? Any confession you'd like to make?'

'No.' Tony grips his top lip between his finger and thumb, and shakes his head.

'Only I'm wondering how these keys which you claim to have lost at the pub, came to be wrapped up in Jacqui's dirty knickers. You tell me how they got there. Go on! Go on!'

'How can I if I have no idea?' Tony glares at me. 'You must have made a mistake.'

'*I've* made a mistake!'

'Keep your voice down, Lisa. There has to be a perfectly good explanation.'

'You'd better think of it bloody quick then.'

'I must have left them at Jacqui's when I was collecting my tools.'

'I found the keys in your lover's bedroom. They didn't get there by teletransportation. You dropped them when you dropped your trousers, you bastard. You fucking bastard!' I throw the keys at him so hard that I can hear metal making contact with flesh and bone. His face goes grey. A red mark flares on his forehead.

'I haven't. I didn't,' Tony stammers.

'You think you're such a man, but you're not man enough to admit that you've been shagging someone else.'

'That's because I haven't! You're making it up. You're a jealous, paranoid, bad-tempered, spiteful old cow!'

'That necklace wasn't meant for me, was it? You bought it for your lover!'

'I was saving that necklace for a special occasion – for your birthday – and you railroaded me into giving it to you when you wanted it.'

'I don't believe you. You promised to forsake all others.'

'You said you'd always love me.'

'I do.'

'You've had a funny way of showing it recently.'

'So it's all my fault?' I stare at him.

'I've been working all hours, keeping my business going for you and the girls. I'm too bloody knackered to be carrying on with another woman.' Tony scratches his head as if we're merely talking at cross-purposes, not that he's betrayed our marriage for a second time. 'I thought you'd forgiven me, even if you couldn't bring yourself to forget what happened. Oh Lisa, it was years ago, and you're still letting it eat you up.' He tips his head to one side, all superiority and serene understanding.

That look infuriates me. Pompous git!

'It isn't me. It's you!' I'm yelling. Chloe is crying on the bed.

Tony's shoulders collapse. 'Oh, what's the point in arguing with you, Lisa? You're always right. Yes, I've slept with Jacqui. I've been having an affair.'

'Say that again.'

'You heard. You always hear what you want to hear.' He turns away and heads out of the room.

'Where are you going?'

'Out.'

'That's right. Coward!' I hear him slamming doors about downstairs. 'It's only what I'd expect.'

Except I wasn't expecting him to walk out. My stomach churns like an overloaded washing machine. I pick Chloe up and hold her to my breast. She pushes herself away with her hands. My heartbeat must be deafening. Tony's van starts up outside and pulls out of the drive, and then there is a terrible silence. One by one, sounds of life return.

'Da da da,' Chloe burbles. A car goes past outside. The phone rings. It's Mum, her voice light and bubbly.

'I wondered if I could have a word with Tony. Dad and I have a favour to ask, a small plumbing job. It shouldn't take long.'

'He isn't here.'

She doesn't ask why, and I don't correct her assumption that he's still at work.

'Poor Tony, he works far too hard. I'll probably pop up tomorrow after I've been to the shops.'

'Okay.'

'Oh, Dad would like a word.'

'Hi,' I say.

'We had forty-two millimetres of rain last night.'

'Oh, that's ...' I search for the right word, any word '... great.'

'Not for those people living beside the River Wandle or in other low-lying areas.'

'I suppose not.'

'But excellent for anyone with an allotment, like Philip.'

For a moment, I assume that he's teasing, then I realise that he's serious.

'Make sure you take your coat or a brolly if you're going anywhere tomorrow,' he adds.

'I will. Thanks, Dad.' I put the phone down, more concerned about the forecast for my family's future than the weather. How am I going to tell Mum that the son-in-law she worships has been having an affair? How am I going to tell Jade? I won't tell her – not yet.

It isn't Manda, but Colin who drops Jade back from the dance rehearsal.

Jade pushes past me on the doorstep. 'I need a shower.'

219

'Don't be long in there.' I'm on autopilot. It's what I always say. It's normal, reassuring.

'Asking a teenager not to spend too long in the shower is like asking two buses not to come up the High Street at once.' Colin grins, bobbing up the steps behind her. 'Manda is still up at the school dealing with a temperamental diva. The princess is refusing to perform a *pas de deux* with Manda's chosen frog.'

I'm confused.

'They've fallen out.' Colin hovers as if he wants to stop and chat.

'I would ask you in, but . . .'

'It's all right. I understand. My reputation goes before me.' Colin is downcast. 'I'll see you at the performance on Saturday. You and Tony will be there?'

'Of course.' I bite my lip as I push the door shut. Will we be there? Will Tony go, if I go? Will I be able to go, if Tony goes?

I burst into tears and I am still crying when I hear the sound of the van. Tony's home. In spite of all that's happened, my spirits lift slightly. He wants to talk it through. He's going to explain why he shagged That Woman. Will I let him, though? Will I let him cut at fresh wounds with words of apology and regret?

A key turns in the lock, and I wish that I hadn't thrown his keys at him because now he has access to the house. He switches on the light in the hall. The bulb pops.

'Tony?' I watch him hunting around in the dusky shadows. 'Aren't you going to change that, so you can see what you're doing?'

He doesn't respond. He can't face me, I suppose. My resolve hardens.

'You're not coming back,' I say quietly.

'I wouldn't want to. I've just come to collect my wallet.' He pushes past me and picks up his wallet and change from the windowsill.

'Is that it then?' My heart is beating in my mouth as he heads back into the black hole of the night. 'When will I see you? We have things to discuss.'

He shrugs. 'Whenever.'

'Dad. Dad! Is that you?' Jade comes hurtling down the stairs in her pyjamas. She's too late. Tony slams the door in our faces. Jade opens it, and flies out to the van. 'Dad!'

'Talk to your mother,' he growls, and then he drives away.

'Mum, what's happened?' Jade's face is pale and pinched. 'What's wrong?'

'Nothing.' My voice comes out as a squeak. 'Everything's fine.'

'It doesn't sound like it,' Jade says slowly. 'Where's Dad going?'

I don't know what to do, what to tell her. It'll break her heart knowing that her father's left home.

'He's been called out to an emergency, a burst pipe. Some poor old lady is up to her neck in water.'

Jade folds her arms. 'I don't believe you,' she says stubbornly. 'Dad was angry.' She stamps her foot. 'Mum, I'm not stupid.'

I realise that. I also realise that as much as I want to, I can't shield Jade from the truth. By morning, when Tony doesn't return home, she is going to guess what's happened. I take a deep breath. I'll have to tell her sometime and it might as well be now . . .

'Dad's left home. We had a row.'

'You kicked him out, you mean.' Jade thinks I'm a heartless bitch. She is not happy.

'He was . . .' How can I put it to make it any easier? 'He's been having an affair.'

'You're just saying that to make me hate him as much as you do.'

'You can believe what you like, but it's true. He admitted it.' I'm not sure how much I want Kimberley and her parents to know about our dirty washing when we've always made ourselves out to be the respectable married couple with moral values that other people should aspire to.

'Lots of people have affairs.' Jade tries to justify her dad's behaviour.

'It doesn't mean that it's right,' I point out.

'I always knew my parents would end up divorcing,' Jade says quietly. 'At least I won't be one of the odd ones out at school any more.'

'Divorce?'

'Well, you're always arguing, nagging at Dad, and you're always more interested in Chloe and cleaning than anything else. No wonder Dad's going off with someone else. Who is it?'

'I can't say.'

'One of your friends?'

I shake my head. I can't count Jacqui as a friend. Friends

221

support each other and exchange ideas. What Jacqui committed, selling those supplements at extortionate prices, and snatching my husband, was robbery.

Jade's eyes glint in the darkness, but she won't let me give her a hug with Chloe. My arms are aching. I have been holding her for ages. She is almost asleep, so I follow Jade upstairs and put Chloe to bed, telling her how she is a poor little scrap to grow up without a dad because, even though I know what's best for her, I shan't be able to let him see her again. I couldn't bear it. She looks up at me, eyes wide, sobs a little, then falls asleep.

I stumble back downstairs to perform my very first duty as a single parent because I will never take Tony back. I shall never forgive him for what he's done to me.

I fetch a new light bulb, and a chair which I place beneath the light-fitting in the hall. I close my eyes and step onto the seat. As soon as both my feet are off the ground, I feel as though I'm flying, circling and swooping through the air like a drunken seagull. I touch the back of the chair with one hand, and reach up to the light socket with the other. I'm all right. If I keep my eyes closed and work by touch, I can do it.

I step down from the chair and flick the switch. The hall floods with light that dazzles me momentarily, until I recall that, not only has Jacqui robbed me of my self-respect and my faith in human nature, she has stolen the light of my life. It is her fault that I am fumbling around in the dark.

I pick up the phone and dial her number to tell her so, but the answerphone cuts in and I find that I can't compose a message that will adequately convey what I think of her. And then I wonder, What's the point? What's the point of telling her to keep her hands off my husband if he's gone straight round to see her? The more I consider it, the more likely that scenario seems. In fact, I can picture Tony standing behind Jacqui with his arms around her waist, while she listens to her messages. I can hear his mocking laughter as she mimics my voice. How humiliating is that?

Chapter Fourteen

I didn't sleep at all last night. At least, I don't think that I did. The clock reads nine thirty – I must have switched it off in my sleep, the sleep I didn't think that I had. Jade must have slept in too.

I pick up Chloe. Her nappy weighs more than she does, so I strip her down quickly and carry her to Jade's door.

'Jade, are you okay?' I knock. No answer. No music. Nothing. I push the door open. The bed is empty, the duvet cast back. The desk diary is gone. I glance in the wardrobe – clothes too. I start to panic. 'Where is your sister, Chloe?'

'Ooh. Ooh.' Chloe grins, quite unconcerned that Jade has done a runner.

I try her mobile but there's no answer, so I text from mine, but after five minutes there is still no response. Where is she? What can I do? I said that I'd never speak to Tony again, yet our mutual responsibility for Jade, plus a spurned wife's curiosity maybe, forces me to call his mobile.

'Jade's gone missing,' I blurt out, as soon as he answers.

'This isn't some trick to persuade me to come home, is it?'

'Of course it isn't. How can you imagine that you're so special to me that I'd want you back?'

When Tony responds, his voice is flat and very controlled. 'Let's save the arguments and recriminations, and concentrate on finding our daughter.'

'I thought she might be with you, that she might have found out where you spent the night.'

'Why would she want to see me? I expect you've poisoned her against me with tales of my infidelity.'

'Now you're wasting time,' I snap. 'I'll try my parents. You try yours.' I cut Tony off and dial Mum's number.

'It's Lisa.' I hear my mum talking to Dad. 'I'll tell you in a minute. How do I know what she's ringing for? I haven't had a chance to speak to her yet with you chattering on in my ear.'

'Mum?'

'If it's about having Chloe for you this morning, I'd love to, but—'

'Jade's run away from home. I wondered if you'd seen her.'

'Jade?' My mum's breath catches. Her voice fades slightly as she snaps at my dad. 'No, it isn't about the tap! I'll have to live with the drip for a while longer, won't I?'

'I'll try her friends. She might be with them.' I cut Mum off. I haven't time for idle chat. I need to know that Jade is safe. I try Manda.

'Hi, Lisa,' she says. 'I'm so sorry. I should have thought to ring straight away, but I didn't like to interrupt her. Jade's been telling me all about it.'

My knees sag with relief that she's safe; I don't even care that she's been blabbing about the collapse of my marriage. 'I'll be right round to pick her up.'

'Is that a good idea? Wouldn't it be better for her to stay with us for a couple of days until things settle down at home? It would give you time to sort things out with Tony.'

I'm finding it difficult. Not only do I have to confess that I've lost my husband, but also accept that my daughter prefers to live elsewhere.

'I left home when I was thirteen,' Manda continues. 'I could have done with somewhere to go, where I had time to sort my head out. We aren't bad people, Lisa. Staying with us is better than being on the streets.'

'I know. Thanks.'

'Colin will come round and collect some of her clothes.'

'Hasn't she brought enough with her? Her bedroom's been stripped.'

'She says she hasn't brought her pyjamas. Look Lisa, Ali's here – she can kick about with him and write some more lyrics.'

'I'll drop her pyjamas round to you. I'm going up to the High Street later – I've got a couple of books to take back to the library.' Suddenly, I realise how bad that must sound, me being concerned with something so trivial when my marriage is on the rocks and my teenage daughter has left home. 'Tell her that I'll call her later,' I add.

I phone Tony to tell him that Jade is safe. I don't say where she is; he doesn't ask. However, I can't resist asking him where he stayed last night. Not knowing is torture. The truth may be a whole lot worse.

'Oh, let me guess,' I continue in the face of Tony's silence. 'Screwing your whore like some alley cat.'

'Think what you like, Lisa,' he says icily, and cuts me off.

Chloe grabs the phone from me and stares at it, smiling in triumph.

'You're not having one of those until you're at least eighteen, young lady.' Something warm and wet trickles down my leg. 'Oh Chloe . . . That isn't what young ladies do.' I have just finished clearing up and dressing her when Mum turns up.

'I've found Jade,' I tell her, as I let her inside the house. 'She's gone to stay with Kimberley for a few days.'

Mum frowns. I can see lipstick on her teeth. 'But why? I'd never have let you stay at Clare's during the week.'

'I know.' I break down.

'What's happened, Lisa?'

'Tony's walked out.'

'Why would he leave you and the girls?'

'He's having an affair.'

'Tony? Having an affair? Don't make me laugh.' However, Mum isn't laughing. 'You must have made a mistake. Having a baby plays havoc with your sleep patterns and hormones, until you're in such a state that you can dream up anything.'

'I wasn't dreaming when I found his keys in his lover's dirty washing basket.'

My mother's world is rocked. Her perfect son-in-law. 'Where is he now? Where's he sleeping?'

'I don't know and I don't care.'

Mum wraps her arms around me and pats my back. 'Poor Tony.'

'How can you say that?'

'He must be in a terrible state.'

'Oh, and I'm not?' I say, pulling away. 'What about me? What about Chloe? And Jade?'

225

'I'll put the kettle on,' Mum says, as if a cup of tea will solve everything.

It seems cold, but I must have read too many books about the consequences of affairs, for it seems as if I know exactly how to proceed. I close our bank and building society accounts and call a locksmith, while Mum sits with Chloe as if she's afraid that I'll neglect her in my preoccupied state.

'How much did that locksmith say it would cost to make the house secure?' she asks.

'It's all right – Tony's paying. When I sue him for divorce, I'm going to take him to the cleaners.'

'I hope it doesn't come to that. Do try to save your marriage. Please don't throw it all away.'

'Tony's done that already. It's too late. I'll never forgive him.'

'You say that now . . .'

'Mum!'

'What about the girls?'

I told Chloe last night that I wouldn't let Tony see the girls, but I've had time to reconsider.

'I shall let him see them, if he wants to.'

'Of course he'll want to. He adores them.' Mum sips at her third cup of tea, and I wonder, idly, if we're running out of teabags. 'Every marriage has its difficult times. The arrival of a new baby is one of them, especially one so unexpected.'

'This has nothing to do with Chloe,' I snap. 'Tony slept with another woman. He was unfaithful to me.'

'Who was it?'

'Someone I thought was a friend.'

'Not Clare?'

I laugh drily. 'I might feel a little better if it was.'

'I doubt it, love,' Mum says sensibly, and I agree with her. My emotions are all over the place and I can't think straight. 'Won't you just talk to him?' she goes on.

'Through a solicitor.' I couldn't face him. I'm angry, disgusted. I hate him.

I feel Mum's expression pricking me like pins. Any moment now and she's going to tell me that it's all my fault, that my lethargy and slovenliness, and neglect, drove Tony to it, but we are interrupted by the arrival of Jezza from a local locksmiths.

He's short and blond and cocky. He says that he's used to

dippy women locking themselves out, and he does a lot of domestics, but he doesn't seem terribly professional to me, jemmying the lock out of the front door so that the uPVC cracks.

He has a floppy fringe that falls over his eyes when he's examining the new locks, and I wonder how he can see what he's doing. The idea that I'm paying for him to spend half the time flicking his fringe makes me seethe.

'Haven't you finished yet?'

'You can't hurry a proper job.' He tests all the keys, demonstrates the use of the deadlock, gets me to sign his timesheet, and leaves a prepaid envelope for the company's customer satisfaction survey. I screw it up and chuck it on the floor. He stares at me as if to say, No wonder your old man left you . . . and swaggers out.

Mum agrees to my suggestion that we head out for some fresh air, although I suspect that she considers my behaviour irrational and irreverent. All the way up the High Street with Chloe in the pram, she repeats unhelpful platitudes like, 'It'll all come out in the wash,' and, 'He'll come round. They always do.'

I know that Mum means well, and that she's worried about me, but I can't bear to hear any more about 'Poor Tony'.

'Are you going to come along to the show?' I ask, trying to change the subject. 'Jade would love it.'

'Oh no, I'll stay at home and look after Chloe.'

I realise that this entails supreme grandparental sacrifice, and I almost forgive her for all that she's said this morning.

'I'm sure that Tony will want to go along too,' she adds.

I've had enough. 'You take Chloe into Sainsburys,' I suggest. 'I've got to return some books to the library and drop Jade's pyjamas up at the dance school.'

'Oh *you*, you're always reading,' Mum says in a tone that suggests that, if I'd read just a little less, my husband might not have gone off with another woman.

'I'll see you soon.' It takes me a couple of minutes beside the superloo on the Triangle to compose myself. I slip in through the library doors, hoping that Ted might have taken a day off – I've been unable to face him since Manda and Colin's party – but he's manning the BOOKS IN desk. I am about to turn and run for it, when he waves me over.

I realise that if I don't return the books today, they will end up hidden in a box at the back of the garage, and I'll never be able to borrow another volume from Croydon's library service ever again.

'Hello, Lisa.' Ted smiles. 'I've kept a book aside for you, a self-help manual for serial hobbyists.'

'Oh thanks, that's very kind of you.'

'It's a joke. I thought it would amuse you.' He hesitates. 'You didn't come to my party. In fact, hardly anyone turned up. The evening didn't go swingingly at all.'

'I'm sorry.' I'm not really, but I don't know what else to say.

'Even Colin – I mean, the Emperor – and Manda backed out at the last minute.' Ted drums his fingertips along the desk, raising a shush of protest from behind a set of shelves. 'Colin said that he had a headache and wasn't in the mood.'

I'm not in the mood to talk. I slide my hand into my bag where my fingers engage with a mass of soggy material from which emanates the faint scent of chlorine. My swimming costume? The books will be ruined. Mumbling some pathetic excuse that I've forgotten them, I turn and flee.

Up at the dance school, the doors are locked, yet I can hear a piano playing. It could be a brilliant virtuoso performance of some modern composition with a basic animalistic rhythm but no tune – or a toddler bashing the keys at random. I walk around the back of the building, climb onto some rubbish – tins of paint and wooden planks left over from making the scenery for the show next week – and peer in through the window. Manda and the piano player are performing a duet. They are both naked. I feel sick at having seen this performance.

How can Manda do this? I hurry round and leave Jade's pyjamas at the entrance to the hall. Manda will know who they belong to. My heart races. So does my mind. Is this part of the swingers' society, or some extracurricular activity on Manda's part? Should I tell Colin?

Should I tell Colin? The question troubles me long after my mum has gone home. Does he already suspect that Manda is having a fling? Is that why he pulled out of Ted's party?

I try Jade's mobile again.

'Hi, love,' I begin.

'It's your brother, fruit of the seed of the loins of Julius, Emperor of Rome.' The voice, a male one, hesitates. 'That *is* you, Kimbo?'

'No, it's Lisa.'

'You want to speak to Jade?'

'Well, yes.'

'She doesn't want to speak to you,' Ali says. 'She's very upset.'

'Just hand her the phone,' I insist. 'Please.'

There's a crackling sound, then the quiver of strings on an electric guitar.

'Jade? How are you?'

'Fine,' she says, but I know that she isn't.

'I thought I'd let you know that I left your pyjamas up at the dance school with Manda.'

'Trust you to think of such a trivial thing at a time like this.' Jade pauses and, just as I assume that the conversation is over and she isn't missing home at all, she comes out with, 'How's Chloe?'

'We're just about to make a start on some housework,' I say. 'I'll phone you again tomorrow. Take care, won't you?'

To my surprise, Jade says goodbye without telling me how boring I am, and I head off with Chloe to tidy the sitting room. I vacuum the floors and iron the library books' sodden pages, and spread them out to dry. Now what? I have a sudden desire to watch my wedding video, to exorcise all memories of that day. I try to slide the tape into the slot in the player, but it won't go. There's something sticky on the flap.

'What do you think that is?' I ask Chloe who is batting at her baby gym.

She pauses and gives me a 'how should I know' look. I squat down and press 'eject'. Out comes a squashed sandwich.

'I think your Cousin Carlton's going to be a postman,' I say, once I've returned from throwing the remains of the sandwich out for the birds. I pick Chloe up and sit with her in my arms. I call her 'my small comfort', my main reason, apart from Jade, not to curl up and die. She falls asleep, her head warm and heavy against my shoulder, and I wallow with my wedding video. I'm not sure it's a good idea, but I want to see what went

229

wrong, if there are any clues as to if and how our relationship was going to end . . .

Mal has the camcorder – it's his voiceover. There's a shaky view of the church, a flash of the bridegroom looking pale but very handsome, just inside the porch where he waits for the bride. Then Mal forgets to switch off so there is a long, unedited sequence of close-ups of various pavements, paths and feet: Bunny's practical black court shoes; Mal's trainers with a hole in the toe; Miriam's – Mal's wife back then – bare feet.

Mal's feet scrunch back and forth across the gravelled car park, escorting guests as they arrive. There are eavesdropped snatches of conversation.

Beth, one of Tony's nieces and a bridesmaid, is talking to Clare.

'I'm jumping on a dead body.' She's laughing – until Mal does an impression of a ghost from behind a gravestone.

Bunny's voice. 'Who does she think she is in that hideous hat?'

'The mother of the bride,' says Philip matter-of-factly. 'It's Jeanette's day almost as much as it's Lisa's. Don't forget that you've already had three hats.'

'I had one, Philip,' she says stiffly. 'I adapted it for each of our daughters' weddings. Tastefully, I should point out.'

I have to confess that, for once, Bunny was right. Cinderella's Ugly Sisters, or some other panto dame, would have lusted after Mum's confection of deep-green velvet piled high with imitation cherries.

'You haven't switched it off, you idiot.' It's Miriam this time, examining the camera. She aims it at Mal. Mal looks sheepish. 'Your big sister is late.'

'Do you think she's changed her mind?'

'About Tony? She won't let that one go.'

Are there any signs that our marriage wasn't going to last, like the tells in the great fairytale wedding of Charles and Diana that we've seen playing over and over at Mrs Eddington's, who claims that she knew it would all end in disaster right from the start?

During the ceremony, the best man, one of Tony's mates, Ian, who's since emigrated to find a better life in Australia valeting cars, fumbles as he hands the ring over. Tony slips it on my finger, then presses my finger against the ring. It's a tiny gesture, but highly significant. He had good intentions. He loved me then.

The video flicks on and off from now on: people lining up for photos; me in an ivory strapless dress; a lingering shot of my pregnancy of six or seven months, partially hidden by a carefully draped cream shawl; red faces and a view of a waitress's stockinged thighs at the reception. Mal must have kept charge of the camcorder.

The wedding speeches are unedited. Bunny frowns as Ian recounts tales of Tony's previous girlfriends, while I grin inanely at my new husband. I didn't care about the past. Clare says that you shouldn't marry a man you can live with. He should be someone you can't live without.

Ian toasts the bride. 'If anyone can keep Tony on the straight and narrow, it's Lisa.'

That's me. That *was* me, and I failed.

I look down at the ring on my finger – there's no chance of it falling off now. I try to slide it off, then use half a tub of Lurpak and washing-up liquid in a solution that's more soapy than an episode of *Coronation Street* to budge it over my knuckle. After a panicky moment when I'm convinced that it's stuck, and I'm going to have to drive myself and Chloe to the hospital to have it cut away, it suddenly slips off. I drop it into one of the kitchen drawers as if it's just one of those loose nuts or screws that I sometimes find lying around the house.

Clare comes over to check that I'm not lying around as well.

'What on earth are you doing?' she asks when I eventually answer the door to her, after much rattling of the letterbox. 'I thought something had happened to you and Chloe.'

'I'm wallowing. I don't want to see anyone, Clare. It's nothing personal.'

Clare steps inside, regardless. She brings me a quiche, still warm from the oven, and sits over me in the kitchen, making sure that I eat it. Her mouth works as I chew on each forkful that I manage to force between my lips. I feel like a baby.

'I think the whole world's gone mad. I caught Manda making music with the piano player at the dance school. What do you think I should do? Should I tell Colin?'

'Forget Colin and Manda. It's *you* you have to concentrate on. Have you heard from Tony?'

231

I shake my head. 'Jade's with Manda, and Tony's gone.'

'I know. He came round to see Jim just as Greg turned up to collect the bike. Jim kept Tony talking on the doorstep while I took the bike out through the back garden and down the alley with Greg to avoid any confrontation. I don't know how much Greg knows about Tony and vice versa.'

'I was right, Clare,' I go on. 'I just wish I'd realised what Tony had been up to earlier.'

'I still can't believe he did it.' Clare pauses. 'You *are* sure?'

'He admitted it.'

'He told Jim a different story then,' she says thoughtfully.

'I'm sorry. I can't eat any more.' I throw my fork at my plate.

Clare takes it away. 'You can keep the rest for later.'

'What's life all about, Clare? Tony's changed. I don't know him any more.'

'He sees Jade starting out. Everything's new and exciting for her, yet the young women don't look at him any more, apart perhaps to compare him with their dads. Men cope with the midlife crisis in different ways.'

'Jim buys himself a motorbike and nearly kills himself.' I grab a piece of kitchen towel and blow my nose. 'Tony has a fling with That Woman. Pathetic, isn't it?'

'If that, indeed, is what he's done,' says Clare. 'Was throwing Tony out such a good idea?'

'I told him that if he ever did this to me again, I'd kick him out and I've kept my word, even though he never kept his.'

'Yes, but you can't keep an eye on him if he's goodness knows where.'

'I don't want to keep an eye on him. I never want to see him again.'

'You should at least sit down together to talk this through.'

'He won't be coming back inside this house. He can't. I've had the locks changed. You still believe him over me, don't you?'

'I don't know what to believe,' says Clare.

'I'm going to kill him. And her.' My fingers tighten on my disintegrating piece of kitchen towel. (I knew that I shouldn't have listened to Jade, advising me to buy cheap recycled paper to save the world.) 'I want to get round to her house and punch her in the face.'

'Don't be too hasty,' Clare says. 'Vengeance is a dish better eaten cold.'

Clare's quiche isn't, I discover later.

However imaginative my excuses for not going to work become, Clare insists that life goes on. The break-up of a marriage is no reason to stay in bed all week.

When we arrive at Neville's, Clare armed with a broom and me with a box of cleaning solutions, there is no sign of the occupant himself, although there is evidence of some recent action in the bedroom.

'Naughty, naughty,' Clare grins. 'Look what my sister's left behind.' She waves a slip of scarlet lace on the end of her broomhandle. I pick it off with my nails. It's the tiniest string. Clare snatches it back. 'I shall return it on our way to Mrs E's. I can't wait to see the look on her face.'

The look on Sue's face when we stop off at the dry-cleaners changes from one of welcome to one of confusion as Clare stretches the string out to its full extent in front of her.

'Look what we found in your boyfriend's bedroom,' she giggles. 'You dark horse, you.'

'Me?' Sue's mouth contorts in horror.

'There's no need to be embarrassed,' Clare says.

'It isn't mine!'

Clare swears softly and puts her arm around Sue's shoulders. 'I'm so sorry.'

'I should reserve your sympathy for Neville's new woman,' Sue says. 'I finished with him last week when he proposed to me.'

Will Neville ever learn, I wonder?

'It was the last straw as far as I was concerned. He wouldn't leave me alone. He even joined the same exercise classes as me at the gym. Can you imagine Neville, dressed in Lycra, the only man in "Legs, Bums and Tums"? It was so embarrassing!' Sue flexes her biceps. 'He wasn't even a good kisser.'

'So who is Neville seeing now?' I ask.

'He's doing more than seeing her,' Clare remarks.

'She's called Hannah. She works in the café at the gym.' Sue smiles suddenly. 'Promise me that you'll never try to set me up again, Clare.'

'I promise,' Clare says, but I can see that she has her fingers crossed behind her back. I suppose that she'll keep trying until Sue is happily married, like she is, and I am not.

Slightly subdued, Clare and I head for Mrs E's.

'I hate to say I told you so,' I say on the way in the car.

'No, you don't,' Clare smiles. 'Getting Sue and Neville together was worth a try. I might have failed in finding a partner for Sue, but I've found one for Neville – indirectly. I seem to recall that you thought that Jim and I were a complete mismatch at first.'

'That's true.' I pause. 'Look – why won't you let me confront That Woman?'

'Think of your children, Lisa,' Clare says dramatically. 'How will Jade feel if you end up going to prison? Who will look after Chloe?' She turns into Mrs E's road and parks. 'Anyway, I'd like you to listen to Jim before you do anything rash.'

'Jim?'

'I know that he's a man of few words,' says Clare, 'but you can rely on him to say what needs to be said. No more, no less. Now, come on, let's go and stir up Mrs E.'

We can't rouse Mrs E. She's never let us have a key because she doesn't go out on Tuesdays. Clare bangs on the door. I knock on the window. I can't see past the elaborately patterned net curtains, but I can hear Prince whining.

Clare tries ringing Mrs E on her mobile. There's no reply, and Prince's whining becomes increasingly desperate. I almost feel sorry for him.

'She hasn't gone out.' Clare peers through the letterbox. 'Her shopping trolley's in the hall. Mrs E! Mrs E!'

'Do you think we should call the police?'

'Don't you ever read a newspaper? Haven't you seen the latest response times? Stand back!' Clare grabs the mop from me and bashes the glass on the old front door with the end of the handle. 'We'll have to break in.' The glass shatters. Clare thrusts the mop back into my hands, gingerly reaches her arm inside and opens the door. Prince comes trotting up and growls his usual greeting. Seeing that we are undeterred, he turns tail and strolls off into the kitchen. We follow.

The kettle is whistling on the stove. Mrs E is sitting at the table, reading a magazine. I look at Clare. She looks at me sternly, then her lips curve and the corners of her eyes crease up. She wraps her arms around her ribs, throws her head back and starts laughing.

Mrs E eventually looks up. She raises one white eyebrow.

'If you don't hurry up and get that hearing-aid fixed, Mrs E, I will,' says Clare.

'Harry and Will? It's Prince to you, dear.' Mrs E frowns. 'My memory isn't what it was. I don't recall letting you in.'

'You didn't,' Clare confesses. 'We broke in.'

Mrs E twiddles the hearing-aid behind her ear. It makes an earsplitting whistle, but she appears oblivious. Prince scarpers. Clare takes Mrs E's arm, helps her up from the table and leads her through to the hall to show her the broken glass. Mrs E clutches at her chest, and for a moment, I think she's having a heart-attack.

'What a royal mess,' she mutters. 'My home has been vandalised.' She turns to Clare. 'What is the world coming to?'

'It was me,' Clare shouts. '*Me!*' She points to herself.

'You?'

'You didn't answer the door. I thought something had happened to you. I thought you might have had a fall.'

I adopt my Customer Services role, apologising for our error and offering compensation. Fortunately, unlike Queen Victoria, Mrs E is amused.

'How many breaches of security have there been here, compared with Buckingham Palace?' she says, smiling. 'You'd better tidy up while I finish reading the Court Circular.'

Clare calls Jim. He can't get hold of a frosted pane to repair the door, so he uses a clear piece of glass.

'It's lucky I haven't got a proper job,' he says, 'otherwise you'd have had to have paid for labour on top.'

'If you had a proper job, I'd be able to afford the labour,' Clare says crossly.

Once he's finished, Clare tells me, 'Jim's got something to say to you, Lisa.'

She leaves me in the sitting room while she chats – or shouts – at Mrs E in the kitchen. I sit on one chair; Jim sits on Prince's Union Jack blanket. One minute passes. Two. I sip at a cup of tea.

'What is it that you want to get off your chest, Jim?' I ask finally.

Jim clears his throat. 'He didn't do it. Lisa, he didn't do it. Tone was always in the pub with me.'

I don't believe him. He's Tony's best friend. Of course he'd lie for him.

Why is everyone on Tony's side? I'm the wronged party here. Why am I being made to feel as if *I'm* the one who was unfaithful?

It's only been three days since I kicked Tony out, yet everyone knows about it. Clare and her big mouth . . . Some people greet me as though nothing's happened, commenting on how fantastic the weather is, as if I'd notice in the state that I'm in. Others speak softly with a mixture of horror and sorrow, empathy tinged with a hint of accusation – that it must be at least partly my fault that I didn't hang on to my man. How am I coping? Fine – as long as no one asks.

Manda greets me at the door to the dance school on the day of the performance. She's dressed in a costume that owes more to Bollywood than *Fame*. A jewel sparkles from the middle of her forehead, her hair is down, and she seems to float across the floorboards in layers of multicoloured silk.

'I'd hate to have to take sides.' She squeezes my hand. 'It wouldn't be good for Jade.'

'Is Tony here?' I can't help asking. I was going to play it cool, but I need to know. I won't be able to relax and enjoy the show if he *is* here, and I shall sit, seething about how he has let Jade down, if he *isn't*.

'He arrived a few minutes ago,' Manda says.

'Lisa.' I feel someone tugging on my bag as I push through the rows of seats towards the stage. I shall try to get a good view, although I'm not good at seeing things even when they are right in front of my face. 'Lisa?'

I look down. It's Bunny. She smiles nervously. 'We've saved you a seat.'

Tony is sitting right beside her. He nods to acknowledge me. The muscle in his cheek tautens and relaxes. He looks tired, yet cleanshaven. Feeling sick and panicky, I clutch at the back of a chair.

'Are you all right?' Tony asks quietly.

'What do you think?' I turn away to hide my tears and look for a seat as far away from him as possible. However, if I'd hoped to be alone, I am disappointed. Colin, carrying a large black shoulderbag, sits down beside me and pats my thigh.

I try to ignore his presence, gazing at the stage, at the crooked columns that I believe are supposed to represent a temple, at the painted trees, scrubby and dark, and the lake behind, a splurge of black and blue.

'Those are authentic copies of Corinthian columns,' Colin says. 'Manda borrowed them from the Re-enactment Society. The trees are the pines on the hills outside Rome.'

'Very nice.' I am wondering what can be authentic about a copy. What else can I say? 'Does the show have a Roman theme then?'

'Oh no, it's deliberately eclectic – to relieve the boredom of watching sixty or more children perform various dances, generally very badly.' Colin leans closer. 'These shows go on for an inordinately long time. Manda tried a selection procedure one year, but it almost caused a riot. I've brought refreshments – marmalade sandwiches, ginger beer and grapes. Would you like to share?'

'I'm not hungry.'

He stares sympathetically. 'I'm so sorry. Here's me gabbling on while all you want is some peace and quiet, and no mention of the split. Which I've just gone and inadvertently mentioned when I promised myself that I wouldn't.'

'It doesn't matter, Colin.'

'I said, "Sweet Fanny Adams, that isn't possible!" when Manda told me. Of course, I've been through something similar before when Manda . . . Actually, I'm going through it again.' His eyes drift towards the piano at the side of the stage where a man is sitting down, adjusting his stool and his music. 'Lisa, you and I are united in having chosen unfaithful partners.'

'At least I didn't encourage my husband by inviting swingers to my house.'

Colin's mouth turns down at the corners. 'Manda's theory is that if you have an open relationship, these affairs of the heart, of lust, can run their natural course. It's true that they don't last, but the trouble with Manda is that as soon as one finishes, another begins.'

'I can't do that. I won't share Tony with anyone. I don't know how you do it.'

'I'd like to say that it gets easier, but it doesn't. I stay with Manda because I love her.' He looks up adoringly towards the stage where Manda is announcing the beginning of the show, and I realise that Colin loves Manda far too much to have ever been seriously interested in me. I relax into my seat as he rustles about in his bag, then thrusts a sandwich into my hand.

'No, thanks.' I give it back, but the bitter scent of oranges stays with me.

The piano player flips his black coat-tails over the back of his stool, raises his hands and starts to play 'Three Blind Mice' with feeling and panache. Three hefty little girls, in grey furry suits with whiskers and tails, thunder across the stage. There are fairies and daisies. There are group dances and solos. There's ballet, tap and contemporary freestyle.

I've often wondered how the Queen feels, watching *The Royal Variety Performance*. Now I know.

'When is it Jade's turn?' I whisper to Colin as the audience cheers some poor girl who remains on stage, oblivious to the fact that the rest of her troupe has tripped off into the wings.

'Oh, she won't be on until after the interval. Manda saves the best till last.'

So this is why my mum was so keen to stay at home and sit with Chloe.

'I didn't realise that these events could be so emotional,' says Bunny, who catches me crying in the interval, but I'm not crying for the dancers. I'm crying for me and Tony, for the man who was Tony, and who isn't any more. I'm not sure how much Bunny knows, how much Tony's told her. That I drove him into the arms of another woman, no doubt.

I make to move away, but Bunny's hand is on my arm. A paste jewel glistens on the lapel of her woollen coat. She carries a scent of camphor and roses.

'You might not believe me, after all that I said about you having chocolate sponge instead of fruit cake at your wedding reception, but now I'd be very sorry if you and Tony didn't get back together.'

I can hardly believe what I'm hearing. 'But you hate me. I don't keep the house clean, I don't bring up my children correctly . . .'

'I've not hated you,' she says, 'not since Tony told me that you were engaged. Oh, and when you gave me that trip in a hot-air balloon for my birthday that time. Tony loves you. He misses you.'

'If you love someone, you don't go and sleep with someone else.'

Bunny bites her lip. She doesn't believe me, does she? Tony hasn't told her *all* about our break-up. Bunny glances around us as if to check that no one is listening, particularly Tony.

'He hasn't told me the details,' she says, 'but if what you're suggesting is true, then Tony is more like his father than I ever realised.'

A light shines down from the stage.

'You mean?'

'Philip had an affair, several affairs, most of them carried out in his potting shed on the allotment.'

'I don't believe you.'

'Philip might appear to be a cold fish, but other women seem to find his reserve attractive. Perhaps they see him as a challenge. He does have a passionate nature, but not everyone sees that side of him.' She pauses. 'It isn't something I normally talk about, but I thought you ought to know that it is possible for a marriage to survive. It is possible to find forgiveness in your heart.'

I shake my head. It *isn't* possible.

'Give it time,' Bunny says. 'Think about the girls, Lisa.'

We are interrupted by the ringing of a bell and Manda urging the audience to return to their seats. The second half of the show is much less well-attended than the first as many parents have drifted off, having seen their little ones dance.

'Here's Jade,' Colin whispers. He has a whistle of orange peel on his goatee beard, reminding me of stories about Paddington Bear.

'Where?' There's a dancer on stage, a girl dressed in a tight cat-suit that's made of camouflage material. She kneels, curled up in a ball in front of one of the Corinthian columns. As the piano plays out of tune, her body gradually unfurls like a flower. It *is* Jade.

I join the rest of the audience in applauding my daughter. I have tears in my eyes again, but these are tears of pride. I glance towards Tony who is applauding her the loudest. Jade is *our* daughter. It's time that she came home.

Afterwards, I head for the side-room where the dancers are changing. It smells of sweat, of perfume and deodorant.

'What did you think?' Manda's face glows. 'Jade and Kimberley were fantastic, weren't they?'

'I'm no expert,' I say shyly.

'You should be very proud.'

'I am.' I hug Jade and congratulate her on her performance. 'I'd like you to come home with me.'

'Oh Mum,' she groans, but she puts up less resistance than I expected.

'Your mum needs you, Jade,' Manda cuts in. 'You can come round and see us at any time, but you can't live with us for ever.' Manda looks at me. 'It's difficult at the moment.'

'Manda was very kind to look after you,' I say to Jade on the way back to the house.

'It was just like being at home, with Colin and Manda fighting all the time. Kimberley wondered if she could come and live with us.'

'It wouldn't be a good idea.' I pause. 'Did your father speak to you?' I'm not sure Jade is really listening to me as she's texting at the same time.

'You know, I don't care if you argue as long as he comes back.'

'I don't know what will happen,' I say stiffly.

'I miss him.'

I turn away. Tears burn my eyelids which isn't good when you're driving in heavy traffic down the High Street. I miss him too.

Ten minutes after we arrive home from collecting Chloe from Mum's, Ali is on our doorstep, asking to see Jade. 'Is she here? She said she'd be here.'

'Er, yes, she is,' I say, frowning.

'Can I see her then?' he repeats.

'I suppose so.' I wonder where to arrange this tryst, if that is what it is. Should I respect Jade's privacy if Ali should turn out to be her boyfriend, or should I ensure that they meet where I can keep an eye on them?

The trouble with the latter plan is that there's ironing and paperwork all over the living room, and dirty dishes and bottles in the kitchen, and it's far too hot in the conservatory because I forgot to lower the blinds this morning. It isn't so much that I'm worried about them suffering heatstroke in there, as providing them with an excuse to take their clothes off.

I make my decision.

'She's in her room.' I yell up the stairs. 'Jade! There's a visitor for you.'

She comes to the top of the stairs. The change in her expression is amazing, as if she's been transformed from imminent death to ecstasy, confirming to me, even if she's denying it to herself, that she is head over heels in love with him.

'Go on up, Ali.'

'Are you sure?' His expression is one of apprehension more than delight, which isn't what I'd expect if he'd come here hoping to have his wicked way with her.

Jade hesitates, her mouth dropped open, as Ali ambles up the steps towards her. I suppose that she might well be gobsmacked. When I was fourteen, I wouldn't have dreamed of taking a boy into my room. Not true. I might have dreamed about it, but Mum would never have allowed it.

Ali appears to be putting on weight. He has a big, saggy bum and I wouldn't be surprised if he had lice in that long hair of his. I tell myself to stop criticising his appearance. He's probably a very nice person, not a chav, even if he is far too old for Jade.

I resist going upstairs to find out what they're up to for all of five minutes, then I take Chloe, and two glasses of Coke on a tray, and enter Jade's room without knocking. It isn't a popular move if the scowl on Jade's face is anything to go by.

'I thought you could do with a drink after all that dancing,' I say brightly.

'Thanks, Lisa,' says Ali.

'Ali would prefer a lager.' Jade is sprawled out on her belly on the floor, her head propped up on her hands. Ali is stretched out on the sofa, his legs splayed apart. Have I really set her such an example that she feels she has to grovel to men?

'He's driving.' I plonk Chloe down, and prop her up with one of Jade's pillows. 'I'll see you later then?'

My ruse fails. I get as far as the top of the stairs before Jade calls out, 'Mum, you've left Chloe behind.'

'Oh, sorry.' I pop back in for Chloe, and leave it ten minutes

241

before I return to collect the glasses. They've changed position. Ali is still on the sofa, but he's backed himself into the corner, and sits with his arms and legs crossed. Jade has taken up a seat beside him.

'What do you want now, Mum?' she says, glaring at me.

'I want to put the dishwasher on.' I push the door ajar. Someone – Jade probably – kicks it shut. I creep back with Chloe in my arms and press my ear to the woodwork.

I sit there for another five or ten minutes. Chloe fidgets while I listen to stilted conversation, muffled giggles from Jade and Ali's low growl. There's a strange gurgling sound, then a series of grunts that remind me of the piglet in the film *Babe*.

'Oh my God,' I say under my breath as Ali lets out a moan of satisfaction. How dare he lay a hand on my daughter! I fling the door open. Ali and Jade look up with mock dismay on their faces. They are sitting in exactly the same positions as they were when I left them. How did they do that?

Ali gazes at me. A lazy grin spreads across his face, and my scalp prickles with irritation and dislike.

'We were practising some singing techniques,' he says. He's lording it over Jade and she doesn't realise it.

'Oh, is that what you call what you do with that band of yours – singing?'

Ali pulls his foot towards him and starts picking at some fluff on the end of his black trainer sock.

'I doubt that Deep Purple and Status Quo did deep-breathing exercises while they were practising,' I say.

'Status who?' Jade raises her eyebrows.

'I'd better go.' Ali drags himself up.

'Do you have to?' Jade jumps up quickly, far too quickly if she's trying to play it cool, if she doesn't fancy him.

'Thanks for the drink, Lisa.'

'Goodbye, Ali.' I step back with Chloe and let them go downstairs ahead of us. I peer around the banisters at the top of the landing as they say goodbye. Ali leans towards Jade and gives her a peck on the cheek.

It wasn't really a kiss, I keep reminding myself later, when I notice how my daughter keeps touching her face with her fingertips, which is what I did after Tony's first kiss.

'I felt uncomfortable letting Ali up to your room, Jade.' There's an awkward pause as I consider how best to raise the subject of contraception. 'Do you understand why?'

'S'pose so. Mum, there's no way I'll ever let myself get pregnant, if that's what you're worried about. Chloe's enough to put anyone off.'

Impervious to this insult, Chloe reaches her arms out towards her big sister. Jade takes her from me, and Chloe clings on to Jade's hair and burbles.

'Da da da.'

'Daddy's not here, Chlo,' Jade says softly, 'but he will come back soon.'

I stifle a sob. The girls need their dad. I need him.

Chloe rests her head against Jade's shoulder, and Jade kisses her hair – and I have to turn away.

All these denials. Tony's, Jim's, Clare sitting on the fence . . . I am beginning to wonder if I really have misjudged Tony. If I have made a terrible mistake . . .

Chapter Fifteen

It's ironic, isn't it? The very first time that Chloe sleeps through eight whole hours, I am woken at dawn by the phone. I snatch it from the bedside table.

'Tony?' I breathe.

'Hi, it's me.' It's Clare.

I lean over Chloe's cot – she is lying on her back, smiling in her sleep, while Tigger watches over her. I pucker my lips against her cheek.

'Hey, are you blowing kisses at me?' says Clare.

'It's Chloe. She's irresistible.'

'Would you like to come over for lunch today?'

'No thanks, Mum's invited me.'

'Next weekend then. No, no, take it away.' I can hear Jim speaking in the background. Clare retches. 'Got to go, Lees. I can't bear the smell of bacon.'

'I'd better go too.' Chloe is stirring. I pick her up and hold her against my shoulder. She jerks her head, slowly focuses on my face, then yawns. 'Am I really that boring?' I fear that may be a rhetorical question, another reason for Tony to find other women more interesting than me. Chloe smiles anyway. 'You see what a good night's sleep can do?' I smile back. 'Just wait till we tell your daddy.'

Chloe gazes at me with wide blue eyes that remind me of Tony's, and I feel as if someone's come along and cleaned the shine that she has given this morning with an abrasive surface cleaner. Tony scours any that's left when he turns up on the doorstep a few minutes after I've fed Chloe her first bottle of the day.

245

'Lees!' He knocks on the door, rings the bell and tries his key in the lock. 'Lisa, what have you done? Let me in.' He bangs on the door with his elbow, swears and rattles the letterbox. 'We need to talk!'

I poke my head out of the window. 'I know.'

Tony looks tired. He has dark crescents under his eyes, and stubble shades his cheeks. He is dressed in black joggers and a grey sweatshirt which makes him blend into the shadows beneath the window, reinforcing my impression that he's just an illusion, this man who is my husband.

'I'd like to see the girls too,' Tony says quietly.

I feel rushes of love, and hate, and yearning.

'I tried to see Jade after the show,' he goes on. 'I waited, but Manda said that you'd already left. Please, Lisa . . .'

'Please, Mum . . .' I turn. Jade has come downstairs in her pyjamas. She's been listening. How can I refuse her?

'Go and open the door,' I say. I sink down onto the sofa with Chloe and wait. When Tony walks in with Jade, Chloe wriggles with excitement. He puts out his arms and picks her up. His fingers brush against my bare arm, making a tiny shiver run down my spine.

'Hi, darling,' Tony says, kissing Chloe.

'I'm surprised she still recognises you,' I murmur.

'It's only been three or four days,' Jade points out.

'I should have come round sooner.' Tony pauses. 'You were great yesterday, Jade. What was the dance called again? *The Demon Stick Insect*?'

'It was *War Flower*. I choreographed it myself.'

He grins. 'Only joking.' Tony looks at me in the eyes for the first time. 'Your mum and I need to talk. Jade, do you mind?'

Jade makes her way upstairs, and I guess that she is hoping that he's going to move back in. However, I don't want Tony here. I don't want him any more, and if he's come begging, pleading with me to let him back, I shall at least have the satisfaction of turning him away.

Tony stands facing me, with Chloe in his arms.

'I was glad we were both there for her,' he says.

'Yep.'

'How are you, Lisa? Are you coping okay?'

'Yep. No problem.'

Tony takes a deep breath. Here we go.

'I suppose everyone knows. I expect you've told Clare, your mum ...'

'What do you expect? It's impossible to keep the fact that your husband's moved out a secret around here. And why should I? I haven't done anything wrong!'

'I have,' he says, 'and I'm sorry. I shouldn't have said that I had a thing with That Woman, when I didn't.'

'Ha ha.' That is supposed to be a mocking laugh, but I'm aware that I sound more like a screech owl with a sore throat. 'First you did, then you didn't.' How am I supposed to find out the truth of what happened between Tony and Jacqui when he doesn't appear to know himself? 'I think you should leave now.'

'What about the girls?'

'You can have Chloe and Jade to stay over with you for one night a week.'

'Stay with me?'

'You didn't think of that, did you? That I might want to share the childcare?' I put the squeeze on him, as Jade does on her new spots. 'It isn't a problem, is it?'

'I thought I might have them for the day, rather than overnight. The van isn't big enough for one, let alone three.'

'I thought you were staying with your parents?'

'Mum's kicked me out, being more inclined to believe you than me. I don't know what you said to her yesterday, but I feel as welcome as potato blight at my dad's allotment.'

'I'm sure that That Woman will have you.'

'How many times do I have to tell you? I didn't sleep with Jacqui. Nothing happened. I love *you*, Lisa.' He stares at me, beseeching. 'How am I going to make you believe me?'

'You're very convincing, but you've had plenty of time to plan your defence, and nothing you say can change the fact that I found those keys. I held them in my own hands.' I swallow hard. 'Now get out!'

I become aware that Jade is behind me, brought back downstairs perhaps by the sound of raised voices.

'Dad says he loves you, Mum.' Her voice trembles. 'You can't send Dad away again. *Please.*'

Tony places Chloe under the baby gym.

247

'You can't go, Dad,' Jade begs. 'I hate it when you're not here.'

'I'm sorry, love.' Tony gives Jade a hug, and I watch her cling on to him. 'Right, I have to go.' He disentangles himself from her embrace. 'I'll be back soon though.'

'Promise?' Jade whispers.

'I promise.' Tony leans down and plants a kiss on her cheek, and Jade follows him around the house with bedraggled locks of hair sticking to her face, while Tony collects a few bits and pieces, a couple of clean shirts and his razor.

I can't begin to imagine how poor Jade is feeling. If only Tony and I could sort this out between ourselves. If only we didn't have to hurt our daughter . . .

Once Tony's gone and Jade has hidden herself away in her room, I phone Clare. I have to talk to someone otherwise I'll go mad.

'Who is it?' Clare says rather sharply. I assume that she must have been having a nap with Fern.

'Me.' I pause. 'Tony came round.'

'And?'

'And nothing. He's living rough in the van because his mum's kicked him out. He saw the girls, told me that he didn't do whatever he said he did, and left.'

'I wish you'd cheer up,' says Clare. 'It won't last, you know.'

'What, my bad mood?'

'No, this situation. Tony didn't have an affair. He didn't even have a one-night stand.'

'How do you know?'

'I trust him, Lisa. Tony couldn't lie to save his life.'

'Hang on a mo. You're supposed to be on my side.'

'I am. I'm on both sides. I straddle the fence of suspicion and pigheadedness that divides you and your husband. I've appointed myself as your mediator since you probably won't agree to going to Relate.'

'No way. That's for couples who have some hope of reconciliation. I have none.' I sniff.

'Well, you'd better raise your expectations,' Clare says. 'First of all, you need to work through your anger.'

'How do I do that?'

'If you won't accept help, you'll have to decide for yourself.'

Clare puts the phone down on me. Revenge – is that what she's talking about? I look out of the window where Tony's van is still parked on the drive. I fetch a net of mouldy oranges and throw them one by one onto the roof of the van from my bedroom. It doesn't make any difference to the way I feel. All it does is make a mess on the herringbone block paving. I am still livid.

On the way to my parents' house in the car with Chloe and Jade, I cringe at the memory of what I have just done. Would I condone Jade throwing oranges at Ali's convertible if she felt he had slighted her?

Jade cringes too, at my mother's kiss when she welcomes us into her home.

'Hello, Jade, darling. I've made your grandad go up in the loft and bring the old games down. We have Draughts, Snakes and Ladders, and Bagatelle.'

'Oh Gran, can I put the radio on instead?'

'Course you can, love.' Mum turns to me. 'Lisa, let me have Chloe.' She takes the baby from me and carries her through to the kitchen.

I follow, expecting her to mention the subject of my marital breakdown. She wants to – I can tell from the deepening vertical lines above her top lip that she's trying desperately to keep her mouth shut. 'Where's Dad?'

Mum falters slightly. 'Oh, he's outside.' She nods towards the kitchen window. In the garden, my father is fiddling about with some wooden structure that resembles a bird-table. 'It's his new weather-station,' she explains. 'I wish he'd taken up poetry instead of meteorology. He's never at home.'

I scratch my head. 'I thought that was what you wanted.'

'I'd like him to spend a couple of hours a day with me. I'd like him to help with the shopping occasionally.' She pauses. 'I've had to book him an appointment with the doctor because he cricked his neck looking at the sky for too long.'

'So he's gone from being a pain in your neck to having a pain in his own?'

'You may smirk, Lisa, but it's perfectly true. Oh, that must be Mal.' Mum looks at me. 'I invited him to lunch. He's bringing Carlton and this new fiancée of his. He wants to introduce her to us.'

'Does Mal know about me and ... ?' My voice tails off.

'I told him on the phone,' Mum says awkwardly. 'Have you heard from Tony?'

'He's been in to see the girls.'

Mal interrupts any further conversation on the subject, handing Mum a bouquet of gypsophila and white roses.

'Oh, you shouldn't have wasted your money on me,' Mum says.

'It's probably mine,' I mutter.

Mal casts me a glance, meaning 'keep quiet', then goes on to introduce us to Rosie. Mum hands her a glass of water and Mal a glass of lager – she won't let him drink it out of the can. Rosie is beautiful, tall and slim, with dark tumbling curls and a pale complexion. Her shoulders are bare above a duck-egg blue sun-dress.

'Mal's told me so much about you that I feel as if I know you all already,' Rosie smiles. 'I understand that you're a cleaner, Lisa. That must be an interesting occupation.'

'That's the first time anyone's said that to me before, but you're right. It can be.' I think of Mrs E and her gas leak, of Neville and his love-life, and of Clare on Dr Hopkins's tread-mill.

'I'm a fortune-teller,' Rosie goes on.

'That must be useful,' Mum cuts in. 'Lisa, would you finish off those potatoes for me? Carlton is up to something – I can hear him upstairs.'

'I'll get him,' says Mal.

'No, you have Chloe. I'll go and have a chat with Carlton.'

'I'll have the baby,' Rosie says. I still get that pang of anxiety when a stranger takes Chloe in their arms, but it isn't quite so acute now that she's getting older and bigger. At least Rosie appears to have stronger arms and quicker reflexes than Mrs Eddington.

'Let's go up and find your granny and Carlton.' Rosie heads off out of the kitchen with Chloe.

I turn to the sink and start peeling potatoes. The first one that I pick up is irregularly shaped with a knobble at each end, making it look like a human head and body. The skin is freckled and it reminds me of That Woman. I gouge out two eyes with the peeler then, casting a glance over my shoulder to check that no one is looking, I take a knife and run it through the midriff of the body. I don't believe in Voodoo, but it does make me feel slightly better. Maybe Clare is right about working through my anger. I stab it again. And again.

I find Mal's hand on my arm.

'I'll do that, Sis,' he says softly. 'I'm sorry about, you know . . .'

I can't look at him. I might burst into tears.

'What do you think of Rosie?' he asks.

'The Happy Medium?' I smile in spite of myself. 'She seems very pleasant. I can't believe that you're thinking of marrying her, though.'

'I just fancied the idea of another disco.' Mal winks. 'No, I'm very fond of Rosie. I can't help hoping that, this time, I've got it right and she's the woman I shall spend the rest of my life with. She loves Carlton too – well, most of the time, when he isn't writing on the walls with her lipstick, or filling her shoes with breakfast cereal.'

'He posted a sandwich into my video during Jade's party,' I say. 'I ejected it last week.' As we're alone in the kitchen, I go on to ask Mal for my money. I'm a single parent now with two daughters to support.

'Won't Tony contribute?'

'Like you do for Carlton?'

Mal gazes towards the floor. I've shamed him, I suppose. He left Bernadette, his third wife, to bring Carlton up on her own from when my nephew was a baby not much older than Chloe is now.

'I'm sorry, Lisa, but I'm skint.' He makes a show of patting his pockets.

'If you don't start crossing my palm with silver, Mal, I can see a dark future for our relationship. A very dark future indeed.'

He smiles. 'I'll get it to you as soon as I can.'

'I've heard that before – I won't hold my breath.'

'Tony and you splitting up? It wasn't anything to do with him finding out about you lending me money?'

I shake my head.

'Mum wouldn't say exactly,' Mal continues, 'except that she gave me the impression that Tony was the injured party.'

Mum chases Carlton into the kitchen, interrupting our conversation.

251

'That's my nightie case. When I catch you, I'm going to give you a roasting, young man,' she laughs.

Carlton giggles, holding a teddy bear above his head. He takes a step back, and, in the way of small children, trips on thin air, falls and bumps his head.

'On second thoughts,' Mum sweeps him up in her arms, 'I'll roast those potatoes instead.'

'Where's your camcorder, Mal?' I ask. 'If you'd been filming just then, you'd have had a clip to send to *You've Been Framed*. You could have made two hundred and fifty quid.'

'I've never known anyone so unfortunate with money as you, Mal,' Mum cuts in fondly, and I smile to myself at the way she excuses his careless, spendthrift ways as bad luck.

Once lunch is ready, Dad hands over the carving knife to Mal and disappears.

'I thought it was supposed to be a traditional roast, not Chinese shredded beef,' I observe as Mal starts hacking at the meat.

'Dinner's ready, Don,' Mum calls.

'I'll be back with you soon.' Dad's voice is drowned out by the sound of the telly in the room next door.

'He's watching the farmers' seven-day forecast,' Mum explains to the rest of us. 'How am I going to get my husband back?' She gazes at the table. 'He's in a world of his own. Look, he's laid an extra place.'

I know who it's for – for Tony – and I think of him, sitting in his van with a takeaway. Unless, of course, he's with That Woman. I am too choked up to eat. Mum's roast beef and Yorkshire puddings might as well be witchetty grubs on my plate.

After lunch, we sit in the garden. Chloe lies naked on her back, her skin dappled in the light and shade under an apple tree, while Jade blows raspberries at her.

'I hope you're not teaching her bad manners,' Mum says, laughing. She keeps reaching down from her garden chair to tug on Chloe's toes.

'Oh look,' Jade squeals. 'Chloe's doing it. What a clever baby!'

Chloe concentrates, goes almost cross-eyed, puckers her lips, sticks her tongue out, takes a breath and blows.

'Thanks, Jade,' I groan. 'She'll be blowing raspberries at the health visitor and Dr Hopkins next.'

252

Jade's phone bleeps. It's at her side – never far away, I notice. She picks it up and presses a couple of buttons.

'Is everything all right?' Mum asks. Now, if I'd asked that question, Jade would have told me to mind my own business, but because it's her gran asking, she explains that she's received a text from Ali. The band has been *dis*banded due to artistic and musical differences.

'That's very sad,' says Mum. 'Can't you find another group?'

'I doubt it,' says Jade. 'Ali's going to Uni, Shifty's working at the petrol station, and Kimberley – well, she's, like, decided that black doesn't suit her and she's more into techno than rock. Oh, I don't mind really. It was getting boring, playing the same thing over and over again.'

I notice that Jade doesn't text back.

Rosie joins the conversation. She tucks her sundress tight around her knees and hugs her legs as she sits down on the grass.

'I was at a Psychic Fayre in Croydon yesterday,' she says.

'I've always wanted to go to one of those, but Tony's always been rather sceptical.' He didn't want me wasting money on cranks. It's changed though, hasn't it? I can do what I like. Tony has no say in what I do any more, yet . . . it's going to be difficult to break the habit.

'You'll have to come to the next one with me, Lisa,' says Rosie. 'I'll let you know when it is.'

'Don't you know then?' Dad cuts in. 'I thought you could see into the future.'

'I can,' Rosie says, 'but I don't do dates, or weather. I predict significant life events and emotions. I help people.'

'How do you do it?' asks Jade. 'Do you use a crystal ball?'

'I pick up vibrations from personal items like watches and jewellery. I use Tarot, and I read palms.'

'Would you read mine?' Jade asks.

'I'll read your mum's,' Rosie says.

'Yes, read Lisa's palm,' Mal says. I flash him a glance which means, If you think that's writing off your debt . . .

She tells me that my life-line suggests that I will live until I'm at least ninety, and that my heart-line indicates that I am lucky in love and will remain in a longterm relationship. There are a couple of interruptions to the line that mean trouble, but the partnership lasts for ever. She's wrong though, isn't she? I won't have Tony back even if he does come sneaking round here, trying to tell me that he didn't have an affair with That Woman after all.

'How about you, Dad?' says Mal. 'Can you predict snow at Christmas? I might like a little flutter.'

Dad rubs his chin. 'I don't know yet, Mal. I'm not Michael Fish.' He stands up and draws me aside to demonstrate his weather-station.

I admire the graduated funnel for measuring rainfall, the plastic weathervane and the maximum and minimum thermometer. I read the notes that he's copied from Merle, an Oxford clergyman who kept details of the weather from 1337 to 1343. He doesn't mention Tony. He's treating me like a toddler, using the distraction technique to take my mind off my marital difficulties.

'You mark my words – those pitches along the road to West Wickham will be flooded by mid-September,' he says. 'There'll be ducks playing rugby on the fields.' He gives me a small smile and rearranges his hair.

I understand what he's saying. Life goes on.

'August will be pretty similar to July,' Dad goes on. 'September will be dismal and October will be much brighter.'

I don't know what he's referring to – the weather, or my relationship with Tony. I forecast heavy cloud for the rest of this year, and the years to come. Lots of it. I might see flashes of sunlight in the halo at the edge, but that's all. Glimpses of what other people are enjoying. Of the sunny days that we could have had together . . .

Rosie's prediction of trouble turns out to be correct. If yesterday was Bloody Sunday, today is Black Monday. I nip out with Chloe to take Jade up to Kimberley's. Manda is in bed, making the most of her summer break. Colin is at work. Ali is playing electric guitar. My guts knot in response to its mournful cry.

As I arrive home, I find that there's a cat-fight going on in my drive, and I don't mean of the feline variety. It's Clare and That Woman. Clare is trying to drag Jacqui up to my doorstep by the sleeve of her coat. I don't know why she's wearing a coat on a warm summer morning. I don't know why they're arguing outside my house.

I stop the car on the road and leave Chloe inside. She's asleep anyway, and I don't want her to hear me lose it, because that's what I'm going to do. My fingers tighten on my keys. I am about to commit murder . . .

'I brought someone to see you,' Clare says, looking up as I slam the door.

'What the hell for?'

'She has something to say to you.'

Jacqui doesn't look well. Her lips are pale, and pink patches highlight her cheeks. Her puffy eyelids look as if they require structural correction.

'We'll come inside,' says Clare. 'We don't want to disturb the neighbours.'

'I wish you'd shown the same regard for mine,' says Jacqui. 'I'm a bloody laughing stock.'

'They need to know how to protect their husbands,' Clare hisses. 'Now, can we go inside? Lisa tried to befriend you. She deserves an explanation.'

Out of the corner of my eye, I see a movement out on the road. A streak of metallic blue. My car . . . I didn't check the handbrake!

'Help me!' I run for it. 'Chloe's inside!' Clare runs after me. And Jacqui. It's like a horror film in slow motion. The car will accelerate down the hill, hit another vehicle at the junction at the bottom, unless . . . Jacqui overtakes me and Clare. The car is moving very slowly, but Jacqui can't quite catch up . . . She's gaining on it, she has her hand on the doorhandle. The door opens and Jacqui dives in. Slowly, the car comes to a stop with its front tyre on the pavement.

'Kelly Holmes, eat your heart out,' Jacqui says when I reach her.

'Chloe? Are you all right?' I lean into the back of the car and pull her out of her seat, still half-asleep.

'She looks fine, thank goodness,' says Jacqui. Her voice wavers. She's shaking as she gets out of the car. So am I. She could have been caught up in the wheels. She could have been seriously injured. I stare at her. She's ruined my life, yet her actions have saved Chloe's.

'I think we should go inside,' Clare says gently. 'We could all do with a drink.'

'I'm fine,' says Jacqui. 'I want to go home. Lisa won't listen to me.'

'Oh, she will,' says Clare.

We assemble in the sitting room, Clare with a tot of rum topped up with plenty of water, and Jacqui and I with double measures. Chloe lies beneath the baby gym. Jacqui and Clare sit on the sofa. I stand with my bottom perched on the windowsill and my arms folded, and I stare at the evil cow who stole my husband from me.

This is bizarre. This kind of confrontation only happens on *EastEnders*. I don't know what to say. I don't know how to kick off the conversation. Yet if I don't, we could all still be here at midnight.

'The council really ought to do something about that hill.' As soon as I open my mouth, I realise that I sound incredibly stupid.

'*You* really ought to do something about your handbrake,' says Clare.

'I suppose that I should be grateful to you for saving my daughter's life,' I go on. I'm torn. If I'd had any arsenic in the house, I would have poured it into Jacqui's glass, and I don't feel too well-disposed towards Clare either. 'This is ridiculous.' I point at Jacqui. 'I don't want to hear anything that That Woman might want to say. Why should I let her offload her guilt on me?'

'I stole Tony's keys. I planted them to make you think that there was something going on between us.' Jacqui looks up from her glass and flashes me a strange look, full of resentment. 'Your marriage was in trouble before I came along. I just hoped that when you kicked Tony out, he'd come to me.' Her lips flatten and curve down at the corners. Tears glint in her eyes. 'Only he didn't.' She passes me a ball of paper. 'If you don't believe me, perhaps you'll believe him.'

I open the paper. There is Tony's handwriting in pencil, his letters unrefined and open because he never did concentrate in class.

J – leave me alone. I am not interested. I AM MARRIED.

'Well?' says Clare.

Incontrovertible evidence. I screw the paper up and jam it into my fist. Tears well up in my throat, threatening to choke

256

me. The room, Chloe's face, and those damned smiling monkeys that dangle from the baby gym, swim in front of my eyes.

Jacqui flees from the house. Clare stays.

'Why did she do it?' I blubber.

'She was jealous. She wanted what you have.'

I realise that Tony must hate me for what I've said about him. What a mess! I shall never smile or laugh again.

'I thought I'd have to threaten Jacqui with telling Greg exactly what she'd been up to before she would agree to see you, but she'd already confessed.'

'Why did she come with you then?'

'Because I made her realise how badly she had treated you after you had been so kind to her.' Clare runs her fingertip across my mantelpiece and examines the end of her finger. 'It's clean!'

'I wish you wouldn't sound so surprised. I've been dusting. If I sit around, I brood.' I grab the phone and start dialling. 'I have to speak to Tony.' I try his mobile, but it's switched off. I try Bunny, but Tony isn't there. I confess what has happened. I made a mistake: I'm very sorry. I wait for Bunny's tirade, or for her to slam her receiver down – she's unintentionally retro, still using a Bakelite model with a coiled cord.

'Oh dear, Lisa,' she says. 'If I see him, I'll tell him to call round. I'm not sure he will though. We fell out.'

'It's all my fault,' I groan. And then I think, Stop being such a bloody mouse, Lisa Baker. 'Actually, it was just as much Tony's fault as mine,' I continue. 'If he hadn't betrayed our marriage once before, I'd never have suspected him of having a fling now.'

'Let me guess – it was after Jade was born. I thought something was wrong.'

'It preyed on my mind. I thought I was over it, but when we were both tired and he was working long hours, and he'd lost interest in, you know . . .'

'In the bedroom department.' Bunny helps me out.

'I thought he was avoiding me. I thought he was with someone else.'

'He was working for you and the girls, Lisa. He said that you were exhausted, that you hated your job but felt obliged to carry on with it for Clare's sake. He thought that if he could bring more money in and find more work for Jim, then you'd be able to stop.'

'You'd love that, wouldn't you? You've always wanted me to be a stay-at-home mum.'

'I don't think this is the time or the place to rake up past disagreements,' Bunny says.

She's right. Clare passes the bottle of rum, offering me a top-up once I've put the phone down.

'If I drink any more, you'll have to book me into the Priory,' I say, forcing a smile.

'Can I take Chloe off your hands for a while?' she offers.

'No, thanks.' I need Chloe with me. Her presence gives me great consolation. I take her up to the library where she blows a raspberry at Ted, who laughs in that restrained manner peculiar to librarians. He might wear loud shirts – a Hawaiian one with beach scenes today – but he knows how to keep quiet at work.

'Her big sister's been teaching her bad manners.' I take my books out of my bag. They still smell of chlorine, but Ted seems happy to scan them in.

'How much do I owe?' I am aware from the heat in my cheeks that I'm probably the colour of a raspberry.

'I think we can overlook it this time,' he smiles.

'I don't need you to do me any favours.'

'Pity.' He gazes at me. 'Colin mentioned that you and your husband have separated.'

'It's none of your business.'

'I know, but I wanted you to know that Colin feels responsible—'

'Colin didn't break up my marriage,' I interrupt.

'It isn't uncommon for couples to break up after being introduced to our Society. It's very difficult when one of you seeks the safety and tedium of monogamy while the other craves variety.'

'What do you mean?'

'Well, it's obvious, isn't it? Tony couldn't wait to drag you away from Colin and Manda's that night. You, Lisa, would have stayed.'

'You've got it all wrong. Me and Tony – it has nothing to do with the swinging.'

'Keep your voice down,' Ted whispers. 'I don't want my colleagues to know about my hobbies outside work.'

'I'm sorry,' I say quietly, even though it should be Ted who is apologising to me.

'I misread the situation,' Ted says. He changes the subject. 'We've had some new novels in if you're interested.'

'No, thanks. I'm rather busy at the moment. I haven't time to read.' Now that I've discovered that Tony wasn't lying about the affair, I consider that I don't need fiction to feed my imagination. It's fertile enough already.

Clare has a better imagination than mine when it comes to schemes for revenge. She has always carried out revenge on my behalf. I've never had to deal with it myself.

'Greg didn't ask for the key back to their house,' Clare says gleefully on the morning when we should have been cleaning there, if he hadn't terminated our contract after Jacqui's revelations about the games she had been playing. 'This is the perfect opportunity for you to get your own back.'

I am reluctant. I know that nothing I can do, no amount of graffiti in the new bathroom, or dead fish hidden on the canopy of Jacqui's four-poster, or yanking the plug out of the power supply to her fridge-freezer could make up for what she has done to me and my family.

'What if Greg or Jacqui are at home?'

'Why should they be? Look, if their cars are outside the house, we'll go back another time.'

'All right, I'll come with you,' I agree eventually. 'But I don't want to do anything that will hurt Greg or Ethan.'

There's little sign that anything has changed. Greg's toothbrush remains alongside Jacqui's in the bathroom, although his tartan dressing-gown hangs in the spare room, not the master bedroom where I find myself examining Jacqui's belongings. I squirt a mist of perfume – *Poison* – into the air, and slip the bottle into my pocket. There's a shoebox on the floor, marked with the name of the manufacturer of some cheap brand of footwear. Inside, however, is a pair of high heels from upmarket shoe shop Russell & Bromley. Jacqui's deceit permeates her whole life . . .

Did she intend to wear these shoes to pull my husband?

I take them to the bathroom and drown them in hot soapy water in the sink. I pour the perfume down the toilet. I didn't plan to do anything. It just feels right.

'Coffee or champagne?' Clare calls up the stairs. 'Or both?'

'I don't care.'

'Champagne it is then.' I wander downstairs to find Clare's bum sticking out of the cupboard as she inspects the wines that Greg brought back from his last trip on Eurotunnel. She brings out a bottle of champagne. 'It's warm, but I don't suppose that matters.'

I follow her into the back garden.

'We're going to try out the hot tub,' she says. 'That Woman did promise us we could.'

'Oh, I don't think so.' The tub is in the shade, and it isn't terribly warm at nine thirty on a weekday morning, even if it is the end of July.

'Give us a hand, will you?'

'You're not going in there in your condition, are you?'

'I'll sit on the edge.'

I help Clare haul the cover off. She fills the tub, then pours several tens of pounds' worth of Inaglow spa products into the water. She flicks the switch and it becomes a steaming blue cauldron of bubbles. She shakes up the bottle of champagne.

'I've always wanted to do this.' She's laughing, fiddling with the wire around the cork. 'I think Michael Schumacher's had more practice at this than I have.' The cork explodes out of the top of the bottle, followed by most of the contents. Clare hands it to me. 'You'll have to drink it out of the bottle. Go on.'

I take a gulp. 'Now what?'

'It's time to get your kit off, Lees. Come on, Greg will be out for hours.'

I slench another mouthful of fizz. I haven't eaten breakfast, and it goes straight to my head. At Clare's insistence, I strip to my pants and jump into the tub, where I sit and drink champagne while the bubbles froth and foam, and slide over the edge, forming a white puddle across the patio slabs.

'What does it feel like?' Clare sits on the edge, dangling her feet in the water.

'Like I'm in *Big Brother*, but without the cameras.'

'You hope,' Clare giggles. 'Shh. Can you hear something?'

'Not Greg?' I jump up in a panic and start looking around for a towel, except there isn't one.

'Can you hear whistling?'

I strain my ears. Yes, I can. Oh hell. Why do I always let Clare lead me on with her wild schemes? I could be in Croydon shopping while Mum looks after Chloe and keeps an eye on Jade, not here. I could be having a wander around IKEA.

A man in dark trousers and a pale blue shirt appears round the corner. He's young and overweight, with a faint blond moustache. When he sees us, he stops and stares through frameless lenses, his jaw dropped somewhere down around his paunch. His fingers go white on his handheld computer device.

I sit down sharply. Rather hard.

'I came to read the meter,' he stammers. 'I heard a noise, thought I'd investigate. I'll . . . er . . . leave you to it.'

'No, don't!' Clare shrieks. 'What's your name?'

'Er . . . Nick.'

'Jump in and join us.'

'Oh no, no.'

'Go on.' Clare tips her head to one side coquettishly. 'There's no need for a cossie with all these bubbles.'

He walks backwards, knocking into a flowerpot. Fragments of terracotta lie spinning on the patio amongst spilled peat and fronds of decorative grass as he turns and runs away.

'What did you do that for, Clare?'

'I was messing around. I knew he wouldn't dare – I wouldn't have invited him if I thought he'd say yes, would I? I'm not that stupid.'

'How can you be sure?'

'I'm a good judge of character,' she beams, 'always have been.'

I sink back into the bubbles and close my eyes.

'There's no hurry. I rang Mrs E and left a message on the royal answerphone to say we'd be running late today.' Clare stretches her legs. 'This gives a fantastic foot massage. I love it.' She begins to sing Abba's 'Waterloo'. An echo comes back, an unwelcome ricochet of two more voices. Benny and Bjorn?

Nick the meter reader appears around the corner of the house once more, his recording equipment in one hand and his shirt in the other. Another man – I say 'man' although he can't be

261

more than nineteen – accompanies him. He's tall and skinny, and has an eager smile. Too eager.

The singing stops.

'I fetched my mate.' Nick unfastens his belt.

'Oh no, there's been a misunderstanding.' I stand up, but I can't run for it until I've helped Clare who's stranded on the edge of the tub. I grab my clothes from the puddle on the patio. Clare slips her feet into her sandals.

'I told you it was too good to be true,' says Nick's mate. 'They're old enough to be my mum. Older,' he adds as Clare and I tear across the patio and barricade ourselves inside the kitchen, dripping scented bubbles all over Jacqui's laminate floor. I said I'd never laugh again. I was wrong. I can't stop.

'See?' says Clare. 'Revenge can be sweet if it's carried out in the right way. I told you that you'd feel better.'

It's true. I feel a whole lot better about my situation, until Tony's van appears on the drive at home at about seven in the evening. My spirits lift slightly then fall again. This is my opportunity to apologise, to grovel, to go down on my knees. I rush across and open the front door. Tony stands on the step.

'Where are the girls?' he asks. He looks exhausted. He smells of smokey-bacon crisps and ripe brie, and his shirt is filthy.

'Jade's at the park with Kimberley. Chloe's having an afternoon nap. Oh love, I was so worried about you . . .' I pause. 'Let's get you out of those clothes. While you're in the shower, I'll cook you up an omelette.'

'Don't bother.' He rubs his eyes. 'I've eaten.'

'Tony, I'm really sorry for what happened, for all those things I accused you of.'

He shrugs. 'Don't waste your breath. This is the first time I've ever done what my mother told me. I've come home to claim what's mine: my share of the house, my kids . . .' His voice tails off.

'And?' I say hopefully.

'And nothing.' He straightens. 'You didn't think I'd come home for you, did you?'

'I thought—'

'You thought wrong. I don't understand you. I haven't so much as looked at another woman since, you know . . . Well, I have looked, but I haven't considered being unfaithful to you,

Lisa. I thought we'd got over it. I thought you trusted me, and I've been thinking while I've been living out in the van, that a relationship isn't much good without trust.'

'Tone . . .' I am in tears again. My eyeballs ache.

'I am moving back in, and I shall sleep in the spare room.'

'Don't the past fourteen years mean anything?'

'No, I feel as if I've wasted them being with you.' Tony stares at me. 'Yes, I knew Jacqui was after me. That's why I didn't want to get involved with working on her bathroom, but you sucked me in, being friends with her, although how much of a friendship that was, I do wonder now. I said there was something odd about her.'

'I should have listened to you. You should have made it clear how you felt.'

'You said you'd forgiven me, but you obviously haven't forgotten, and if you haven't forgotten after all these years, you can't blame me for thinking that you never will.' His voice is hoarse and angry.

'Tony, it takes two. If you hadn't forgotten our anniversary, if you hadn't kept turning up late, if you'd just *talked* to me, I wouldn't have jumped to conclusions. The wrong conclusions.' My heartstrings feel as if they are stretched to breaking point. 'So can we try to make it right? Please.'

He shakes his head. 'I'm always being propositioned at work by women who fancy a bit of slap and tickle with a tradesman. Sometimes, I have to take Jim as protection.' He steps up very close. I can feel his breath hot on my face. I can see the pulse throbbing at the side of his neck. 'I'd be the first to admit how difficult it is to resist the temptation of an attractive lady in skintight jeans and a thong.'

'A tart, you mean,' I cut in.

'But I have done, Lisa,' Tony goes on, 'because I loved you and respected you.'

Respected? Loved? All in the past tense.

'Jacqui makes the most of her figure. She's ambitious and flirty, and I flirted back, but I never liked her. No man will ever be good enough for her. She'll always be craving someone smarter, richer, more romantic than the one she's with. I feel sorry for Greg.'

I can feel tears running hot down my cheeks. Tony remains

impassive, the muscle in his cheek flickering. All I want is for him to take me in his arms and hold me for ever, but he turns on his heels and heads down the steps.

'Where are you going now?'

'To fetch my shopping in. I hope it isn't too much trouble for you to give me a key that fits the new locks.' He unpacks a load of food and toiletries out of the back of the van. He labels his milk and yoghurts with a T and puts them in the fridge, and makes the bed up in the spare room. The territorial lines are drawn. Battle commences. The Battle of the Bakers.

Chapter Sixteen

It feels like the equivalent of the Seven Year War, but I've been living in a state of siege for only seven weeks. Clare and I are sitting in her car outside Neville's flat. Clare's car has been renovated by a company of panel-beaters whose slogan is *We Can Lift Your Depressions*. Clare said that she'd send them round to my house.

'I don't want to be alarmist, but it's only ninety-nine days till Christmas.' Clare passes me the bag of doughnuts that we've just bought on the way here.

'We haven't had Hallowe'en or Guy Fawkes night yet, and it isn't going to be much of a Christmas for my family, is it?'

'At least Tony's back and you know where he is,' Clare soothes. She looks well in the second trimester of her pregnancy. Her hair shines and her skin glows. 'There must be plenty of opportunity for conversation when you're both living in the same house.'

'Oh, he won't talk to me. We have bizarre games of Chinese Whispers, using Jade as intermediary. I sent him a message accusing him of stealing the last of my cream crackers, and he thought I was casting aspersions on the size of his Jacobs.'

'Joe Pasquale has much to answer for,' Clare grins. 'How is Jade?'

'It's difficult to say. She loves having her dad back, but deep down she's very unhappy.' My eyes prick with tears. 'I can't persuade her to talk to me about her feelings. She blames me for what's happening to our family.'

'It must be very hard for her, not knowing whether you and Tony'll stay together.' Clare raises one eyebrow. 'Or split up?'

'Jade says that when we divorce, she'll live with Tony.'

'Oh, she's only saying that,' says Clare. 'Divorce? Did you say the word?'

'It's the only way I can see out of our situation. I mean, Tony's sleeping in the spare room, and we're living like Steptoe and Son in that episode where they divided the stairs in half. Even the cutlery holder in the dishwasher has separate "his" and "hers" sections.' I pause. The idea of divorce appals me, the division of one life into two. 'If Tony wants a divorce, I shall make him fight me for it. I shall work on the principle of what's mine is mine, and what's his is ours.' I bite fiercely into my doughnut. Jam splurges down my chin. I grab a clean duster out of the bucket at my feet and wipe it off.

'I don't think the courts operate that way,' says Clare. 'The only people who win in a divorce are the lawyers.'

'Don't worry about my bank balance. How's yours?'

'Jim's applied for a job.' Clare leans forward conspiratorially. 'Actually, he doesn't know about it yet. I've applied on his behalf. I'll tell him if he gets an interview.'

'Clare!'

'Then I'll coach him in exactly what to say,' she goes on. She's laughing. I almost allow myself a smile. 'If Neville wasn't so much taller than Jim, I'd ask him if I could borrow his suit.' She looks out of the driver's window, still miffed that someone has parked their car outside Neville's in what she considers to be *our* space.

'What do you think is going on in there?'

I don't like to imagine. The curtains are drawn. 'I don't think we should—'

'We'll be breaking the terms of our contract if we don't clean in there this morning.' Clare dangles the keys in front of me, and I have to confess that it's tempting. Very tempting.

'I thought Neville had started his training.'

'He goes away next week,' Clare says.

We head inside and make straight for the kitchen, following the sound of voices. A woman is in there, with Neville. From her tousled appearance, she hasn't dropped by on her way to work. Her blonde curls form a frizz across her forehead, and she isn't wearing make-up, which makes her appear very young, although I suspect that she is in her early twenties. Neville pats

266

her on her bottom which is encased in stretch blue denim.

'This is Hannah,' he says. 'Hannah, these are my cleaners, Clare and Lisa.'

She radiates heat and it isn't because she has her back to the grill.

'Nice to meet you.' She smiles. 'I must go.'

'I'll drop in and see you at work.' Neville leans down and kisses her. The kiss goes on and on . . .

I clear my throat. Clare taps the handle of her broom against the bin.

Eventually, Hannah tears herself away.

'I could come to work with you,' Neville suggests.

'No, Nev,' Hannah giggles. 'I wouldn't be able to concentrate.'

'But I can't live without you, not for a minute, my sweetest honeybunch.'

'Oh, I give in.' Hannah throws her arms around Neville's neck. 'I'll take you with me. You can help me take orders and clear tables.' She presses her lips against Neville's, at which I tug on Clare's sleeve and we withdraw to the living room where we tidy up to the sound of Il Divo on CD, until Hannah and Neville go out and leave us to get on with cleaning the rest of the flat.

'I can see why Neville didn't suit Sue. He's far too soppy,' Clare says, yanking the grill pan out of the cooker and slamming it into the sink.

'Perhaps Hannah will start a new trend, an annual *Take Your Boyfriend to Work Day*.' I pause from twisting up the neck of a bin-liner stuffed with rubbish. 'Do you think it'll last, or is she only after his truncheon?'

'That's better,' says Clare. 'You can smile after all. I was beginning to think that you'd forgotten how to.'

I test Neville's bathroom scales – I've lost weight in spite of our return to the Doughnut Diet.

'That's something to celebrate then,' Clare says.

'It doesn't make me feel any happier. At one time, I would have been over the moon to have lost five pounds, but I don't care any more.'

'This is because of Tony, isn't it? You aren't going to give in, are you?' Clare asks.

'I might as well.'

'You can change things, if you try.'

'What's the point?' I pick at the pile on one of Neville's new bathroom towels until it's bald. 'It's over. Tony's made that perfectly clear.'

'How would you feel if he went around accusing you and telling all your family and friends, and anyone else who'd listen, that you were having an affair when you weren't? If you were washing your clothes to help out, not to remove the stains of an illicit liaison? If you were going to the pub to wind down for a while before returning home to a partner who screamed at you, louder than the baby?'

'I never screamed,' I counter.

'Oh, stop bloody wallowing!' Clare's eyes flash with anger. She shoves me aside, then batters the mop over the floor. She dunks it in the suds in the bucket and screws it dry. 'You aren't going to give Jacqui the satisfaction of beating you, are you, because she will have won if you let your husband walk away.'

'I wish you'd stop telling me what to do. You even choose which type of doughnuts I should eat. Don't you ever wonder if I'm fed up with jam, that I might yearn for ones with a chocolate topping instead? You're always arranging my life for me.'

'That's because you don't seem capable of organising it yourself.' Clare pauses. 'I choose your doughnuts because you stand there at the counter, unable to make your mind up.' She flushes the toilet. 'Don't let your marriage go down the drain, Lisa. Decide whether you want Tony back, then go for it! What have you to lose?' She looks me in the face. 'You *do* want him back?'

I think of Chloe. And Jade. I think of myself, alone without Tony for the rest of my life. I do want him back – of course I do – otherwise what will these past fourteen years have meant?

I hate to admit it, but Clare is right. I have to try to bring my family back together again. I have to win Tony back, not just for me, but for my children. It won't be easy when I've left the hot-pink bikini that was my marriage at the bottom of a drawer of ordinary, everyday clothes – nursing bras, mumsy fleeces and frumpy tie-waist jeans. Can I rescue it? Can I retrieve my *va va voom*?

Clare has hundreds of suggestions for how to do it, some better than others. The following weekend, she organises Jim

268

to look after Fern and my mum to come over to sit with the girls while she takes me out. Tony has gone to work, not because he has to work on a Saturday, but to avoid spending time in the house with me.

'I don't want to go anywhere,' I protest.

'You go, love,' Mum says. 'You could do with a day off.'

'Don't forget your credit card,' Clare says. She has a wicked glint in her eye. 'Come on, Lisa. Trust me.'

Clare drives like a bat out of hell into Croydon.

'What's the hurry?'

'Your first appointment is at ten.'

I find myself in front of a mirror in a hair salon with a towel wrapped around my head, and my scalp tingling.

'This is Alberto.' Clare introduces me to a skinny man in black. 'He's the top stylist.'

Alberto unwraps the towel and examines my hair, running his fingers through to check the length and condition. He has kind eyes, but I'm not sure that I trust him with my locks.

'She wants a complete restyle,' says Clare. 'Something that's young and wacky.'

I open my mouth to contradict her, but she's rattling on about how coppery highlights would look fantastic too.

'What did you say that for?' I hiss at Clare while Alberto's off fetching a sample book and tubes of colour.

'You need to make drastic changes if you want to catch Tony's attention.'

'I don't want to look like someone else.'

Three hours later and I resemble Sharon Osbourne. My hair is cropped shorter than I've ever had it before and the fringe is run through with red – not copper – streaks. Do I like my new look? I'm warming to it, but that may be down to the vodka that Clare slipped into the coffee that Alberto offered me earlier.

I find myself looking at my reflection in shop windows on the way through town.

'We don't have time to hang about.' Clare nudges me. 'I've booked you a facial and then we're going to buy you new clothes.'

The relaxing effect of the facial is soon wiped out by the stress of shopping with Clare, who revels in doing impressions of Trinny and Susannah. I am standing in a changing room in Debenhams, dressed in a low-cut turquoise top and hip-skimming black trousers. Clare grabs my breasts, lifts them and pushes them together.

'Hey, what are you doing?'

'You need a decent bra to keep those boobs up where they used to be.' She moves round and slaps my bum. 'Nice butt though. Why don't you try the red halterneck next?'

'I like what I'm wearing,' I say quickly. 'Why don't I pay for these so we can go home?'

'We're not quite finished yet,' says Clare. 'If you're going to buy that top, you're going to need a tan.'

'I can't afford anything else.'

'We'll buy one you can apply yourself.' Clare tidies the changing room, slipping the outfits I rejected back onto their hangers, while I dress.

I can't wait to get home to put my feet up, but Clare has other ideas. We collect Fern from her house on the way back. Clare and Mum drink tea and play with the babies while I exfoliate and apply fake tan upstairs in the bathroom. I trot downstairs to show off the result.

'What do you think?'

Mum hesitates. 'If you want my honest opinion, you remind me of Chloe when she had jaundice for those few days after she was born.'

'You need a second coat,' says Clare.

By the time I've finished, my skin has a healthy glow. Mum heads home to cook tea for Dad, and Clare leaves with Fern.

'Knock him dead, Lees,' Clare yells from her car just before she accelerates off down the hill outside my house. 'You look amazing!'

I am inspired. After I've fed Chloe and cooked a pork chop and noodles for Jade, I plan my seduction technique. I put Chloe to bed early and offer Jade a fiver to stay in her room for the evening. I would have offered her more, but she described my new hairdo as 'mingin'' which I thought was rather a mean thing to say.

I change into my new outfit, light a couple of tealights in the sitting room and leave a bottle of wine, glasses and some spicy nibbles on the coffee-table. I sit on the sofa in the dark with my feet up and my arms hugging my knees.

270

The sound of Tony's van turning onto the drive sends a shiver of apprehension down my spine. Tony will notice me all right, but what if he doesn't want me any more? His key turns in the lock and I hear him fumbling around in the hall.

'That's all I need, a bloody powercut,' he mutters.

With the click of a switch, the sitting room floods with light. I jump up and cross the floor to greet him, swaying my hips in what I hope is a seductive manner.

'Hi, Tony.'

'What's going on?' He stares at me. 'Are you all right, love? I mean, Lisa, what's happened to your skin! I didn't know you suffered from vitiligo.'

'Vertigo, you mean?' I don't suffer any more. I went up in the loft the other day, clinging to the ladder, keeping my eyes closed and groping about for the next size up in Jade's old baby clothes for Chloe, because I didn't want to ask him.

'I'm talking about your arms. And your face!'

I rush to the mirror above the mantelpiece. The fake tan has darkened over the past few hours just as the instructions on the product said it might do, which makes the areas that I missed appear much lighter. I look like a marble cake.

'And what on earth have you done to your hair?' Tony says over my shoulder. 'Did you let Jade loose on it?'

'I had it done professionally.' I don't think he approves. My cheeks burn. My new top clings to my sticky armpits.

'You paid money to look like some street entertainer?' Tony starts laughing. He's laughing at me. I flee and lock myself in the bathroom where I spend the next hour scrubbing at my skin with a flannel, trying to even out the fake tan. I scrub so hard that I make my arms bleed, but it doesn't hurt as much as the fact that my attempt at seducing Tony failed. I made him notice me, but not in the way that I intended.

So much for retrieving my *va va voom*. I wonder if I ever had any in the first place.

It's October, and it's National Courtesy Day, according to the radio news. We're experiencing an Indian summer, although Dad's been on the phone this morning to warn me of an imminent cold snap. 'Make sure you lag your pipes,' he says. I thank him and write it on Tony's To Do list on the fridge door.

271

There's a mound of washing on the utility-room floor – there's Tony's pile and a heap for the rest of us. Occasionally, I put them together, but Tony always sorts them again, a sign of how he's keeping our lives apart. We share the same house, but we might as well be living in parallel universes. Sighing, I load the machine and press the buttons. The lights on its display flash. There's an eggy smell of water that won't drain.

I think of adding 'repair washing machine' to Tony's list, then change my mind. I'll do it myself when I have five minutes. When I'm a divorced single mum of two, I won't be able to rely on him, so I may as well make a start now.

Chloe's like a baby sparrow today, bright-eyed and chirping. I take her upstairs to Jade's bedroom and sit her on the floor, surrounding her with pillows so that, if she should have a sudden hissy fit and throw herself backwards, she won't hurt herself.

I climb onto Jade's bed and tangle with her undersheet as I change the bedding.

'Where's Mummy, Chlo?' I lean over the edge of the bed and drop the sheet from my face. 'Boo!'

Chloe grins, revealing two white teeth. I do it again. And again. By which time she's laughing so hard that I fear that she may be sick.

'That's enough for now.' I try to stop laughing myself and tug at the last corner of the sheet that's still tucked under the mattress. An envelope flies out, landing on the floor beside Chloe. She squeals with delight.

'That isn't part of the game.' I clamber gingerly down the ladder and gently extricate the envelope from her soggy grasp without tearing it. It's addressed to Mr A. Baker, and it's open. 'How did this get up here?' I examine the contents. It's an invoice marked 'Overdue' from the mobile phone company: Jade's run up a bill of over £700.

On the basis of a rough calculation, that means she must have been on the phone for six or seven hours a day since her birthday. I don't believe it. There must be some mistake. However, I realise that if there *had* been a mistake, Jade wouldn't have tried to hide it.

Chloe attracts my attention by turning her beaker upside down. The spout is supposed to be drip-proof, but there's water all over the carpet.

'Oh Chloe,' I groan. 'Why do you two girls make so much trouble? Haven't I got enough trouble of my own?'

It might be National Courtesy Day, yet I am in the mood to be anything but when Jade returns from school. She lets herself in and wanders up to my bedroom where I am running through my daily beauty routine in case Tony should be home early from work. I run some gel through my fringe – short hair suits me, and the red streaks have faded a little. I grimace into the mirror and press my forefingers into the corners of my eyes, feeling for the bones of my nose.

'Mum, what on earth are you doing?'

'Facial gymnastics.'

Jade picks up the bottles on the dressing-table one by one: rejuvenating anti-wrinkle creams, body lotions that contain aloe vera for good health, a spray fake tan.

'I thought you didn't believe in all this stuff,' she says.

'I don't believe in waxing my legs, that's all.' Tony did his once, to prove that it didn't hurt. He didn't do it again, or carry on going on at me to wax mine. He bought me an electric Ladyshave razor instead. Tony again. I don't think that he's noticed my efforts to tart myself up. 'When you get to my age, you want to believe anything.' I smile regretfully.

'What does Dad think?'

'I'm not doing this for your dad. I'm doing it for myself.' I lean back and massage my brow, trying to induce a feeling of calm. 'You are developing the same bad habit as your father – hiding things from me.' I take the envelope out of my jeans pocket and wave it in front of her. 'I wonder what this could be?'

Jade's face pales.

'How can you spend so much time on the phone? What happened to old-fashioned face-to-face communication?'

Jade shrugs and folds her arms.

'You can speak to your friends for hours every month on that phone of yours, but you can't take five minutes out to talk to me.'

'I need to speak to my friends, and Ali's away at Uni.'

'I thought he'd be too busy to have time to talk to you.' I can see from the expression on Jade's face that I've hit a nerve.

'I don't always get through to Ali. Sometimes I end up chatting to his friends, and then there's Kimberley.'

'What about Kimberley?'

273

'I lend my phone to her when she runs out of her Pay As You Go.'

'That's very generous of you, but have you thought about how you're going to pay this bill?' I'm being unreasonable. Jade is only a kid, fourteen, too young to take responsibility for so much cash.

'I'll ask Dad.'

'Is that wise? He'll be furious.'

Jade's upset. She thinks that Tony and I owe her something for splitting up, and not trying hard enough to get back together.

'I could give up dancing lessons for a while,' she says.

'That's a noble offer, but we'll try to find another way.' I don't want Jade giving up her hobby to hang around in town, and the friendship with Kimberley has been good for her, I can see that now.

Jade has an early night, but Chloe is still up at eleven when Tony gets back from the pub. He must make a pint last a long time because he's never drunk. Chloe is in her chair, chewing on a piece of raw carrot.

Five minutes to repair a washing machine? I underestimated. The machine is in pieces on the utility floor. I have my sleeves rolled up, a spanner in one hand and a screwdriver in the other. I have the instructions for repair on the worktop. They read: *In the event of failure, contact manufacturer's approved agent.*

'Chloe, what's your mum doing?' Tony asks. 'She should have told me that it wasn't working.'

'I did,' I say. 'I told Chloe, but she obviously didn't give you the message.'

Tony smiles ruefully and runs his hand through his hair. 'Okay, your sarcasm isn't wasted. It is ridiculous, you and me communicating through the girls – well, Jade anyway. *You* should have told *me* that it wasn't working.'

'I'm dealing with it myself.'

'Are you determined to keep me shut out?'

'In the circumstances I thought it was for the best. You've made it clear that this is only a temporary arrangement.'

'Give me the screwdriver. Go on. Go and put the kettle on.'

Tony reassembles the machine, removing soggy wads of tissue paper from the pipes and filter in the process. 'Don't you ever empty your pockets?' he says in a holier-than-thou voice.

'It isn't me. It's Jade – she uses things to pad her bra.'

Tony raises one eyebrow.

'I used to do it too, to make my boobs bigger.'

'You wouldn't believe that now.' Tony smiles appreciatively at my chest, and a shiver runs up my spine. It's instantaneous and erotic, and I wonder if he feels the same. He turns away quickly, as if he's been caught out doing something he shouldn't, which he has, if he's living here as a stranger . . .

He shoves the first load of washing into the machine and switches it on, then I follow him to the sitting room with Chloe, and we sit and drink tea in front of the telly.

'I thought Chloe had overcome her hypnophobia,' Tony says as Chloe chats to us from her chair.

'She'll nod off as soon as I put her in the cot,' I say. 'Now that she sleeps all night, I stay awake, worrying about why she hasn't woken up.'

Tony smiles, and I recall that I haven't told him about Jade's phone bill. I pull it out of my pocket and hand it over.

'That much?' Tony whistles through his teeth.

'Jade's agreed to give us a percentage of her allowance each month to pay us back. I told her that we'd pay the bill outright, that we'd go halves.'

'What do you mean?'

'I'll pay my share from my cleaning wages.'

'You don't have to do that. The girls are still my responsibility,' says Tony.

'I want to pay my own way.'

'Oh, but that isn't fair. You can't work the same hours that I do because you look after Jade and Chloe.'

I stare at him. It's hard to believe from his recent behaviour, but Tony's still concerned for my well-being.

'What are you thinking, Lees?'

'That it's impossible to fight with someone who's being so bloody reasonable.' *That I want to take you by the hand and lead you upstairs to the bedroom, to our bed, to have you make love to me all night long . . . I want to wake in the morning with your arms around me. I want you to chuck your rolled-up pyjamas at my face* . . . My throat constricts – I feel as if I've swallowed a cherry tomato whole – and I can hardly breathe. Is there any chance that we might get back together again?

*   *   *

'Just because Tony talked to me doesn't mean that our marriage is back on track,' I say to Clare as we turn up on Mrs E's doorstep. (She gave in and let us have a key after the break-in.)

'It's a start,' Clare says. 'Rome wasn't built in a day.'

'That's a strange expression, isn't it?'

'I wonder if it's true.'

'Colin would know. He was there, allegedly. He probably dealt with the planning application for the Coliseum.'

Clare laughs and pushes the door open.

'I had a text from Colin – well, several texts actually,' I continue. 'He's asked me out.'

'On a date?' Clare stops dead in the hallway.

'For a drink, that's all. He assumes that we're two wronged spouses in similar situations, except that we aren't, because Manda really is having an affair.'

Clare gazes at me, one eyebrow raised.

'It's all right. I said that I wouldn't go.'

'Maybe you should. It might force Tony to reconsider his stand-off.'

'No, I couldn't risk it.'

'You wouldn't do anything to win Tony back then?'

'I'll have my bikini line waxed and I'll enrol at a gym, if I have to, but I won't do anything that might hurt a third party.' I change the subject. 'Have you found work for Jim yet?'

'He has an interview next week,' Clare says. 'I didn't say anything because I don't want him to feel bad if he doesn't get the job. It's for the post of school caretaker just down the road. It would be perfect.'

I feel slightly sick. 'Does that mean that you'll want to give up work, that you'll want to pack in *Maids 4 U*?'

'I thought you'd be pleased.'

'No, I'd hate it. What else would I do?'

Clare grins. 'I'm teasing you. I'll still need to work part-time to make up the money and pay off the debts. The salary isn't that good.'

'Thank goodness for that.' It's true, isn't it, that you don't realise what you have until you think you're about to lose it? I'd miss all the scrubbing and polishing. I'd miss chatting to Clare. I'd miss our array of varied and peculiar clients.

We head for the sitting room where Mrs E is watching a

276

report by a royal correspondent on the news. Mrs E turns the television right down.

'You can leave it on if you like,' Clare shouts.

'I beg your pardon?'

'You can leave it on!'

Mrs E frowns.

'Haven't you replaced the batteries in that thing yet?' Clare points to her hearing-aid.

Mrs E twiddles with it.

'I'll commit battery if the silly old bat doesn't go up to the clinic and have it fixed,' Clare mutters.

'There's no need to be disrespectful, nor intemperate with your language, dear.' Mrs E sighs and, for a brief moment, I wonder if she's going to dismiss us. 'I expect you're out of sorts because of the baby,' she continues. 'Mind how you go with the duster.' She picks up the newpaper from beside her. She isn't reading it. How do I know? Because she's holding it upside down.

I keep half an eye on Prince while I clean the mirror above the fireplace, squirting vinegar from a bottle in one hand, and polishing with a cloth in the other, until it shines. Multi-tasking. Clare vacuums with the hose attachment while sorting through a heap of envelopes to make sure that Mrs E hasn't inadvertently thrown away any important correspondence.

'Has Jim said anything? About Tony?' I ask.

'Not much. You know what Jim's like,' Clare says, but I know that she's making excuses. Jim and Clare are torn between us. Their loyalties are divided.

'I hate myself for what happened. I still love him. I still fancy him to bits.'

Mrs E's newspaper may be upside down, but the photo on the page is very clear.

'Hey, Clare.' I point towards it. 'Do you recognise those people?'

'Katya and Peter,' she says, moving closer.

'Hasn't anyone told you that it's rude to read over a person's shoulder?' Mrs E says.

'Yes, but we know them. They've just got married.' Clare squints at the paper. 'Oh, and Peter's received a reward from a local traders' association for his help in apprehending a shoplifter. "When arrested, Mrs Della Ramsay was in possession of goods worth three thousand pounds . . ." Wow!'

'No! Who'd have thought Della Ramsay lived a double life? I suppose that explains why she didn't have any receipts for all those clothes,' I say. 'You realise you're wearing stolen goods?'

Clare fingers her pearl earrings. 'Do you think I should give them up to the police as evidence?'

'I imagine that they will have more than enough evidence at Della's house, and anyway, you can't return earrings once you've worn them. It wouldn't be hygienic.'

'You've salved my conscience, Lees.' Clare grins, and I realise that she never had any intention of giving up those earrings. She likes them far too much.

'I wonder how Della managed to smuggle those vacuum cleaners out of the shops,' I muse.

'Under one of her ponchos.' Clare giggles as she gently removes the paper from Mrs E's hands and turns it the right way up. 'Mrs E, have you considered buying a pair of reading glasses?'

'I shouldn't want to be married to you, young woman,' Mrs E says. 'You must nag your husband to death.'

'Jim loves it,' I say, but I don't think that Mrs E hears me.

'I shall be leaving Selsdon in the New Year,' she says, 'as long as all goes to plan.'

'What plan?' says Clare. 'You said something about a plan.'

'Anne?' Mrs E grimaces. There's a twinkle in her eye that I haven't noticed before. 'What's Princess Anne been up to? Who's she marrying now?'

'I didn't mention her,' Clare says, exasperated. 'I was talking about what you're going to do in the New Year.'

'Oh, I can hear, dear, don't you worry.' Mrs E smiles, revealing the remaining pegs of her teeth.

'She needs new ears, eyes and teeth, and now her mind's going too,' Clare says later on our way home. 'Poor old thing.'

I feel sorry for Mrs E. I feel sorry for myself, and I'm still moping a couple of months later, approaching Christmas. I have no energy to feel sorry for anyone else, but I do sympathise with Jade.

On the last day of the school term, she arrives home, having received a text from Ali to inform her that they're finished before they began! (How do I know? She told me, out of the blue and without prompting.) My relationship with Jade might be on the mend, but Ali himself hasn't got time for a relationship right now. He's still finding himself. He's too old for her. He's as good as saying that he doesn't fancy her. Jade is devastated, but I know that grief doesn't last long when you're a teenager and you've only had an imaginary relationship. It lasts for ever when you've been married almost fifteen years.

Jade and I go shopping. Retail therapy in the local supermarket – I think that may be a contradiction in terms. With all those couples pottering about, causing gridlock in the aisles with their trolleys while they try to decide what brand of cheddar to buy, I need to go into therapy – proper therapy with softly spoken counsellors – by the time I've reached the check-outs.

I strap Chloe into a trolley and push it towards the entrance to the shop. Being in possession of a baby is definitely a passionkiller. Jade walks some way behind me, chewing gum. Her eyes are red and her mascara is smudged, yet she turns heads. The youth working in the car park turns his head, but forgets to turn his line of trolleys, crashing them into a bollard.

My chest tightens with pride and envy. Jade is beautiful, and oblivious to the effect she's having, and she is my daughter. I correct myself. She is my daughter and Tony's daughter too. Like it or not, we will always have contact with a part of each other through Chloe and Jade.

'Bling, bling,' says Jade as we stroll through the shop.

'Could you say that in English?'

'Oh Mum, you're sooo . . .'

'Boring,' I finish for her. 'You'd be pretty boring if the subject uppermost in your mind was the price of nappies.'

'Yeah, I would.' She pauses. 'Can I buy you something for being such a good mum? Chocolate?'

'What a lovely thought, Jade.'

'I'll have to borrow some money till next week. My allowance doesn't go very far when I'm still paying that phone bill.'

I can't help smiling. 'I'll treat us then.'

'And Chloe?'

'She can have white chocolate buttons. You go and find them while I continue to addle my last remaining brain cell choosing nappies.' I take a quick guilt trip past the Christmas decorations, change my mind and pick up a box of tree-lights, tinsel and some chocolate Father Christmases for Jade and Chloe before I head up the For Baby aisle. Will Chloe really notice if her nappies are no longer printed with cute animals? I pick a different brand which is much cheaper. I have to economise if I'm going to be a single parent.

I stroll along in jeans that are far too tight – I bought them in a sale, assuming that I would slim down into them, but I haven't. They crush my crotch and squeeze every ripple of flesh as I walk. My new boots have a higher heel than I'm used to, and pinch my toes, but it's worth it when the man at the check-out gives me an appreciative smile.

'You two sisters?'

'I wish.' I can't help grinning. I feel good. So what if he has a patch over one eye? If he can see my sex appeal, there's no reason why Tony should miss it. He does give me the odd glance now and then, so I am quietly optimistic.

As the weather grows colder, the atmosphere in the house warms up – and it isn't all down to the central heating. I hang a garland on the front door (Philip gathered the holly and ivy, and Bunny wired them together) and prick my finger, drawing blood. Typical! In spite of small suggestions of a truce, the fact that Tony no longer labels his food in the fridge, and is less particular about sorting his washing, there is still the thorny question of Christmas.

Tony finishes early on Christmas Eve. Plumbers are welcome for emergency repairs only over the Christmas and New Year period.

'I'd finished installing a new shower for Mrs Angry from Arthur Gardens. I thought she'd be grateful, but she told me to pack my tools and get out from under her feet so I thought I'd come back here and get under yours instead.' Tony winks, and my heart turns over. 'Shall I open a bottle of wine?'

'Yes, thanks. I was just about to cook tea. Can I do some for you?' I dig around in the fridge. I have the top shelf, Tony has the middle one and we share the vegetable container at the bottom. 'I thought I'd bought some sausages.'

'They're mine.' Tony examines the label and smiles. 'This is mad, isn't it? I'm fed up with making deals, like you can have some of my sausages in return for a chocolate muffin. Let's pool our resources.'

I agree. Jade, Tony, Chloe and I sit round the telly, eating together and watching *Mickey's Twice Upon a Christmas*. Jade says that she's chosen this video especially for Chloe, but I'm not sure that I believe her. She may be fourteen, but she seems just as excited about Christmas as she did when she was four.

After tea, she scoops Chloe up and sits her beside the fireplace to show her how to arrange the goodies for Father Christmas.

'Don't let her drink the vodka, Jade,' I warn. We have no sherry for Santa. We have no mince-pies either, so he will have to make do with a muffin. The reindeer will have to share an apple. Jade fetches a pillowcase for Chloe's presents and starts to decorate it with tinsel.

I sit back and watch the lights on the tree, spangling stars of colour. When Tony takes the plates out to the kitchen, I find myself eavesdropping on Jade's conversation with her sister.

'You can have red, gold or silver, Chlo,' Jade says. 'Which one is your favourite?'

Chloe reaches out and grabs the tangle of tinsel on Jade's lap.

'A piece of each then?'

Chloe looks up at her big sister and coos adoringly before stuffing the tinsel into her mouth.

'No, no, you mustn't eat it.' Jade prises it out of Chloe's grasp. 'Yucky yuck.' Jade tickles Chloe's cheek before she can start crying over not being allowed to chew the tinsel. She giggles instead.

'That's better, Little Sis,' Jade whispers. 'You know, I think everything's going to be all right now. Mum, Dad, you and me are going to be one happy family again.'

A lump forms in my throat. I hope that Jade's right. I really do.

Tony returns from the kitchen and sits beside me on the sofa. He gazes at me, his eyes dark with lust. I haven't seen that look for a very long time . . .

We sit there, not touching. I am aware that my breathing is quickening in time with the rise and fall of his chest. In spite of everything that has happened, my lips are burning for his kiss.

281

It is Jade who breaks the spell. 'So, what are we doing tomorrow?' she asks. 'You haven't said.'

I haven't said because Tony and I haven't discussed it.

'I thought I'd take you girls to Gran and Grandad's for lunch. Mum did include you in the invite, Tony. Did you want to come?' I hold my breath. Jade looks at him expectantly.

Her face falls when he shakes his head.

'You don't want to come to my parents' at teatime, Lisa?' It's a challenge, a gauntlet thrown down, and the white flag that I believe we have just erected will be torn apart if I refuse. He'll sulk about how my response is only what he expected. If I accept, on the other hand . . .

'I'll come,' I say. 'I'd like to.'

'Oh? Okay.' Tony stands up. Chloe starts to whinge and Jade points out that she has a dirty nappy. At this, Tony says that he has to ring his mother immediately. Happy Christmas, I think.

I don't sit down again until I'm at my mum and dad's the following day. Okay, maybe that's an exaggeration . . .

'I can't sit down at home,' I tell Mum. 'There's an elephant on my sofa.'

Mum frowns.

'Tell it to shove off then.' Jade grins. She's wearing her new trainers indoors. They are red and white. She appears to have completely recovered from her black phase. 'Dad bought it for Chloe, Gran.'

'Is he trying to make up for the terrible year you've all had?' Mum says aside to me.

'He's gone completely over the top. Chloe's petrified of it.'

'It's a pity that Tony couldn't come along,' Mum goes on. I've noticed that, out of deference to my feelings or because she feels let down, she no longer describes him as poor Tony.

Dad doesn't come inside from his weather-station until Mal arrives late for lunch with Rosie, or the Happy Medium, as Dad insists on calling her to her face. She doesn't mind. She laughs every time.

Mal brings a CD voucher for Jade and a woolly hat with antlers for Chloe. He also brings me my money.

'It's all that I owe you, with interest and more,' he says, handing it over after dinner.

'Thanks, Mal. So what did you have to sell to get this – not your body, I hope?'

He rubs at the back of his head. 'Actually, my numbers came up on Saturday night. It's only a few thousand pounds, but enough to pay off my debts and treat Rosie and Carlton. Rosie predicted that I'd come into money and she was right. You look well, Sis,' he goes on. 'I love the dress.'

'Thanks.' I am touched by the compliment. I just wish that it had been Tony who'd made it. I love the dress too, a coffee-coloured satin, embroidered with a darker thread, run through with gold. It hugs my curves and emphasises the fact that I have reacquired a waist.

'I hear that Jade has a boyfriend.'

'Has she? She hasn't mentioned anyone to me.' I start to panic. 'I suppose that Ali's back from Uni.' Perhaps he has found himself and realised that, in spite of the age difference, Jade is the girl for him, after all. Perhaps he's decided that it would be convenient to toy with her affections while he's home for the Christmas holiday.

'She said that his name is Jack.'

'Thank goodness for that. I mean, that's wonderful!'

'Have you met him, then?'

'No.' Although the name rings a bell for some reason.

'I'd reserve judgement in that case,' Mal grins. 'Don't you remember how you described Peter Wrigley as a David Essex lookalike? Mum was so disappointed when she eventually saw him: she said that he reminded her of one of Ken Dodd's Diddymen.'

'Thanks for that, Mal,' I say. 'Talking of little people, I'd better fetch Chloe from Mum, if she'll let go of her. I've agreed to go to Bunny and Philip's for tea.'

Mal raises one eyebrow. 'Is that answering the call of duty, or pleasure?'

'I'm trying to bring my family back together.'

I'm slightly concerned that Chloe isn't enjoying her first Christmas. She hates Mal's hat. She grizzles and pulls it off when Jade puts it on her head to show it to Tony as we arrive at my in-laws'. Her cheeks are as red as Rupert's nose, and she didn't eat her lunch.

It turns out that she has a second chance. Tony didn't make

it clear that the girls and I are expected to eat a second Christmas dinner – four courses this time, not three.

'I'm sorry,' he mouths across the table.

So much for my diet . . .

However, Chloe won't touch her food. She even refuses chocolate from the tree, which Jade eats for her, in preference to her grandfather's sprouts.

I pick Chloe up and hold her. She's hot, so I take off her cardigan.

'She doesn't look well, poor little mite.' Bunny fetches a wet flannel and spreads it across Chloe's forehead, which makes her cry louder.

'I'm sorry about the greens, Jade,' Philip says. 'I could have done with some frost around my brassicas to harden them off.'

I am aware of Jade choking back either chocolate or an attack of the giggles, I'm not sure which. I flash a glance at Tony, who thumps her on the back.

'I think we should call the doctor,' says Bunny.

'For Jade or Chloe?' Tony is laughing. Jade appears to have recovered from her choking fit, although her face is flushed, and I'm sure Chloe is merely suffering from a lack of paracetamol. I give her a dose of Calpol from the changing bag, and sit with her.

'Has she got a rash?' Bunny says.

'No. She didn't have this morning.'

I strip Chloe down to her vest and nappy to find every parent's nightmare, livid red spots on the back of her neck.

'Tony, look at this.' I try to suppress the panic in my voice. Tony's head is close to mine.

'What's that test for meningitis?' he says. He drains his glass of lager, wipes it out with a tissue, and presses it against Chloe's neck. She sobs then sniffles. We aren't sure.

'Shall I call the doctor or take her straight to hospital?' I say. 'What do you think, Tone?'

'I'll drive.'

'I'll drive. You've been drinking. That's why I don't drink.' I watch his face. His lips tauten; I've hurt him again. He thinks I'm blaming him.

'I'll come with you,' Jade interrupts, her face tense with worry.

'No, you must stay with Nan,' I say gently. 'We'll be in touch as soon as we have any news. I promise.'

Jade stays with her grandparents, and Bunny makes up a spare bed for her.

At the hospital, Tony paces up and down with Tigger in his arms. I hold Chloe on my lap. She grows heavier and floppier. Her cheeks become so hot that I can hardly bear to touch them. When she begins to cry, I'm torn between hugging her tight to console her and pushing her away to keep her as cool as possible.

I feel sick. Shaky. My hopes of reuniting my family are beginning to fade. I think Chloe is going to die . . .

'Oh, your mum's a real worrier, isn't she?' The nurse who comes to check up on Chloe's condition smiles, says that her temperature is too high, and gives her a drink. A happy Rastafarian comes along and sings to Chloe. She doesn't find him amusing. She likes the doctor though, and so do we, when he diagnoses an ear infection and gives Chloe antibiotics.

'That was the best Christmas present I could have had,' I say when Tony and I are back at home, sitting on the sofa side by side as we used to. My body is weak with relief. Chloe is asleep upstairs, oblivious now to the anxiety she has caused us.

'Me too,' Tony says. Reflections of the tree lights dance in his eyes. The radio plays music in the background. George Michael and Mary J. Blige sing 'As'. Tony gazes at me. My heart lurches. No matter what happens, if he should stay or if he should go, I'll be loving him always. His face moves closer to mine. I feel the pressure of his lips. As we kiss, my body floods with fire.

'Let's go upstairs,' Tony murmurs. He unzips my dress and slides his hands inside the fabric. His fingers massage my buttocks. I close my eyes and surrender. This has nothing to do with pumpkin seeds . . .

Afterwards, I lie in Tony's arms, holding onto the moment because it may not last. He strokes my arm and kisses my hair. My skin – my cheeks, my chest and between my thighs – still tingles from the pricking contact of his stubble. I smell of his scent – of aftershave and hospital disinfectant overlaid with musk.

'I suppose that you're going to tell me that this was an aberration, a moment of madness,' I say shakily.

'Lisa . . . I realise that I've been a complete idiot, going around in a sulk, but I can't live without you. I don't want a divorce.

I want us to be back as one happy family. I love you, Lees.'

I reach out and touch his face. 'I don't want any more secrets between us.'

'I'm not hiding anything.' Tony spreads his palms. He's completely naked. His face falls slightly. 'What about you? Is it Colin?'

'No, but I do have something else to confess.'

'That you washed my new shirt with Jade's games kit and turned it green? That you're going to leave your cleaning job? I've always said that you don't have to work as long as you can square it with Clare.'

'It isn't that.' I pull away and perch on the edge of the bed.

'You've had a change of heart? I thought you hated cleaning other people's houses.'

'I've realised that the job kept me sane when I could easily have gone mad. I like to go out to work, and have a laugh with Clare.' Life would be so much less if I didn't.

Tony strokes my thigh.

'Chloe,' I begin.

'Our little accident,' Tony smiles.

'Not exactly.'

Lines appear on Tony's forehead. I hadn't noticed how deep they were before. His eyes darken.

'I missed a Pill, or two.'

'I know. It happens.'

'I missed taking it for three months.' There, that's something I haven't been able to admit to myself before. 'I wanted another baby. I planned it.'

Tony sits up sharply. 'Without talking it over with me? When you knew I didn't want any more children?' His voice hardens like molten toffee dropped into iced water. 'How could you?' He stands and grabs his clothes. He slips into his trousers and sweater, leaving his shirt on the floor.

'Don't go,' I beg. 'Please . . .'

'Give me one reason why I should stay with you.'

'Because I love you.'

'You manipulated me. You played with my life – and Chloe's. That isn't love.' He turns on his heels and leaves the bedroom. I pick up Tony's shirt and follow, trying to persuade him to stay, but he won't listen. He collects some clothes and bits and

286

pieces, and drives off into the darkness in the van. I stand on the doorstop, hugging Tony's shirt. A few snowflakes scurry past, spangling in the light from the street-lamp. It must be very cold, but I can't feel it. I can't feel anything.

Chapter Seventeen

Tony will never come home now. My confession was like a stick of dynamite. I've blown my family apart and I can't see any way of picking up the pieces and putting them back together.

While I wait for Philip to drop Jade home the following morning, the radio plays BandAid's 'Do They Know It's Christmas?' What have I done? How will Jade react? At least I don't have to face Bunny – she's at home cooking a Boxing Day meal for Tony's sisters and their families – and Philip has to hurry back to polish the sherry glasses before they arrive.

'Where's Dad?' are the first words Jade says to me as she's kicking off her trainers in the hall. 'Where's the van?'

'He's gone, love. He's moved in with Clare and Jim.' I am all psyched up to grovel, to comfort her. 'I'm so sorry. I tried so hard . . .'

'Obviously not hard enough,' she says sharply. She stares at me, eyes brimming with tears, fists clenching at her sides.

'It's all my fault,' I whisper.

'I'm not surprised. You're hopeless. I hate you!'

I move towards her, but she pushes me away.

'Don't touch me!' she screams, and runs upstairs. A door slams.

'Don't wake Chloe!' I yell, but my voice is drowned by a storm of thudding and hammering. Chloe starts wailing, and I have to change and settle her before I venture into Jade's room, carrying Chloe on my hip, to try to console my eldest daughter.

'Oh Jade, what have you done?' I step across the rubble of broken CD cases, books bent open, and clothes ripped and strewn across the floor. Shreds of paper flutter down from Jade's

289

bed where she lies on her stomach, tearing up the last pages of her diary.

'You've ruined your diary!'

'I don't care. I don't want to remember *anything* about this year. I *never* want to be fourteen again.'

'You don't mean that. Here, I'll help you clear up.'

'Oh, go away!' Jade turns her face to the wall and sniffs. I do what I can with Chloe's assistance, making a pile of items that are irretrievably damaged and putting the rest away.

'I'll buy you a new diary, Jade,' I say, but she doesn't respond. Leaving Chloe on the floor, chewing on a rattle that I found in my pocket, I brave the ladder up to Jade's bed. She is asleep, exhausted perhaps by last night and the effort she put into trashing her room. Even though she is still dressed, I pull the duvet over her shoulders to keep her snug. I lift a lock of hair away from her face and tuck it behind her ear.

'Poor Jade,' I murmur as I stroke her forehead. She takes deep, stuttery breaths as if she is crying in her sleep. When she was born I vowed that I'd never let anyone hurt her. I have broken my promise. I must be the worst mother in the world.

Nothing happens in the next few days to change my mind. On Jade's first day back at school, I give her a lift to the bus stop. I can't make up for her dad's absence, but I can try to mend our shattered relationship. On my return home, I give Chloe her last dose of antibiotics and take her upstairs to change her nappy. She's much better. She hasn't had a hot flush for days, and she's eating properly again.

However, I can't have been paying her enough attention. Perhaps I've forgotten to dry her thoroughly after her baths, or I haven't been changing her as often as she needs because she has nappy rash for the first time in her life.

'Spotty bott.' I lean forwards and kiss her tummy, making her giggle. I force a smile in return. 'How did I let you get in that state?' I let her kick about on the changing mat with no clothes on. It sounds mean in midwinter, but the bathroom radiator is on. She isn't cold.

Dr Hopkins and his wife don't believe in keeping the fabric of their house warm while they're out at work. Clare turns the thermostat up as soon as we arrive, referring to the *Maids 4 U* Working Conditions Directive Number Three, which states that management will not clean in ambient temperatures of less than 20 degrees Centigrade. Okay, we've just made that up.

There are chocolates and fondant fancies on the kitchen worktop, alongside a jar of coffee and a note from Mrs Hopkins telling us to help ourselves, and she's very sorry but one of the boys has been sick on the bedroom carpet, and she didn't have time to clean it up properly before she went to work.

'I suppose the offspring of health professionals are just as likely to fall ill as the rest of us,' Clare says ruefully.

'I'll do it.'

'I'm fine. I haven't felt sick for ages. Do you want to eat or clean first?'

We clean.

'It was useful having Tony at ours this morning,' Clare begins. 'If he hadn't been banging about at seven o'clock, Jim wouldn't have got up in time for work. It's his first day. He's really looking forward to not having to look over his shoulder for the benefit police.'

'How is Tony?' I twist up a duster and jab the point behind a radiator valve to remove some dust. 'And don't go on again about how I should have kept my big gob shut.'

'You should have kept mum on the subject of the Pill,' says Clare.

'I didn't want any more secrets between us.'

'Occasionally, ethics have to be adjusted to suit the occasion. It was a stupid thing to do, like taking stitches out too early after an operation.'

'He'll never come home now,' I say mournfully.

'Tony's like a kid. The idea of a sleepover for one or two nights, maybe a week, is fun. Any longer, and he'll be desperate to sleep in his own bed.' Clare pauses. 'Actually, he seems very down. He isn't a happy man. Come on, let's have some Abba.'

'I'm not in the mood.'

In Dr Hopkins's study, Clare twirls her duster to 'Gimme Gimme Gimme (a Man After Midnight)'. I take a volume entitled *Dermatology* off the shelves, open it on the desk and flick through. It isn't much help. Every condition ends in –itis or –ans, and I can't find a picture that resembles Chloe's spots.

'What are you looking at those for?' Clare peeps over my shoulder. 'Ugh, that's disgusting.'

'Chloe's got a rash. I thought this might save me rushing back to the surgery.'

'It has to be those new nappies,' Clare says. 'You should ring the manufacturer to ask for your money back. You're good at customer complaints. You deal with them very well on the rare occasion that a client is less than satisfied with our service.'

'I'm good at appeasement, but not so good at causing a stir myself.'

'I'll phone them for you when we've finished.' Clare takes a sharp intake of breath and rubs her stomach.

'Are you all right?'

'The baby kicked me. Isn't that great?' She takes my hand and presses it against her stomach. I can feel something, a tiny knee or elbow, pressing back. 'It must be a boy.'

Clare doesn't know for sure. She and Jim decided that they didn't want to know the sex of the baby when she went for her twenty-week scan.

I head off to clean the cloakroom before we stop for coffee. The Man of the Month Slimming Certificate is still on the wall, but the chart of Dr Hopkins's weight has stopped falling. Before Christmas, it had levelled off. The latest week's entry is absent. I smile to myself in spite of everything. It isn't easy keeping fit, and I should know.

I make coffee, and Clare phones the nappy company for me. They are very apologetic. They'll send vouchers to cover my costs and a little extra in way of compensation for Chloe's distress.

A few days later and, in spite of changing the nappy brand, I'm back at Dr Hopkins's surgery with Chloe and her rash. I make for the last empty seat in the waiting room, turn the buggy round and plonk my bum down. The air is hot and still. My damp coat steams. I sit back slightly, aware of a baby on its mother's lap beside me. It's a big baby with a double chin. It catches my eye and grins.

A pain cuts across my chest. It's Ethan. I swivel my eyes without turning my head to discover that my neighbour has strawberry-blonde hair. It's Jacqui, and I can't escape from her most unwelcome presence unless I leave the surgery. I try to console myself with the thought that I'm in the best place if I am about to have a heart-attack.

'Da da da,' Ethan burbles.

Chloe's spotted him. She starts to whinge in the buggy. I pick her up and hold her on my lap. She and Ethan sit and smile at each other, and reach out their hands. Chloe grabs onto Ethan's Bob the Builder dungarees. Ethan grabs the fur on Chloe's winter coat and forces it into his mouth.

'Oh, it's you,' says Jacqui. 'Lisa.'

I turn. How am I supposed to react to the woman who tried to steal my husband – and Chloe's reluctant father – away from me? Should I give her a good slap, or sit here making polite conversation as if nothing ever happened?

'Are you and Chloe well?' she asks.

'Of course not. Why do you think we're here?'

A couple of people look our way with interest.

'I'm only asking.' Jacqui herself doesn't look too good. She's wearing sunglasses, even though it's the beginning of January, and her skin is very pale.

'How about you?' I say grudgingly.

'I've been off work for a while.'

'Oh?' I start to wonder if there is anything in Voodoo after all.

Jacqui lowers her voice. 'I'm being treated for postnatal depression.'

I should have guessed. Jacqui's diagnosis explains her mood swings, her almost manic determination to return to work and her bouts of tearfulness.

'I wanted to be the perfect mother,' Jacqui says. 'I lied to make people believe that. When I told everyone I was going to have my birth story printed in a magazine, they were so impressed that I couldn't bring myself to admit that it wasn't true.'

'Was the part about eating the placenta a lie as well?'

'No, of course not. Give me some credit, Lisa.' I fight a wave of nausea as Jacqui continues, 'I want to say how sorry I am for what I did.'

Grudgingly I accept her apology, recalling that she did save Chloe's life when my car ran down the hill, and realising that I can't keep going around blaming Jacqui for killing off my marriage when I was the one who struck the final blow.

293

'How is Greg?' I ask. Clare will want to know, and I don't want to let her down by not finding out.

'Did he stick by me when I told him about how I tried to seduce your husband, you mean? Yes, he did. I can't believe how supportive he's been.' Jacqui sniffs back a tear. 'And I'm doing everything I can to make it up to him. I've been such a cow.'

I don't feel comfortable with Jacqui unburdening herself to me. I do feel sorry for her, but I know we could never be friends, and I'm more than a little relieved when I'm called away to the consulting room. Dr Hopkins checks Chloe's ears, then examines her rash.

'It's just a reaction to the drugs she's been on.' The buttons on Dr Hopkins's shirt are straining across his belly. 'Now that she's stopped taking them, it'll clear up on its own.'

I sit opening and closing my mouth like a frog. He watches me.

'Have you done something to your hair?' he asks. 'You look different.'

'I've lost weight.' I run my fingers through my fringe.

'Excellent,' he says, tapping a quick note on the computer. 'How on earth did you do it? You must give me some tips.'

Diet, Exercise and Divorce. Presumably, Dr Hopkins failed in his aims because he has a happy marriage. Perhaps I should write a book on the subject. Those other books on marriage and men didn't do me any good, did they?

I buy a new diary for Jade at the stationery shop before I head for the library. Why shouldn't I? I've paid my debts. I hunt around the shelves for some light reading to take my mind off my troubles. Ted is at the BOOKS OUT desk, dressed in a purple shirt.

'Hi, Lisa. I haven't seen you for a while.' He grins. 'You are now talking to the new leader of the Roman Empire. Colin's resigned.'

'Er, I didn't know.'

'I beat him in a chariot race, impaled him on my spear and threw him to the lions. It was all symbolic, of course.' Ted straightens and puffs out his chest, then looks at the titles of my selection – *Houseplants To Brighten Your Home* and *How to Build and Decorate a Doll's house*. I thought that Chloe would like one for her birthday – her sixth or seventh by the look of the complexity of the designs.

'You're still as busy as ever,' Ted says.

'Oh yes.' Ted doesn't know the half of it. How my husband is about to divorce me. How I'm in the middle of defrauding a multinational babycare company. What am I going to do?

I ask Clare a couple of days later. 'Should I confess or keep quiet?'

'I'd keep quiet if I were you,' she says, stroking her belly, 'considering what happened the last time you made a confession.'

It won't be long, I think, before we have to discuss what is going to happen to *Maids 4 U*. Clare is already tired with looking after Fern. She isn't going to be able to carry on working like she did during her last pregnancy. She'll need to take maternity leave.

'Have you thought about what you're going to do about giving up work?'

Clare looks at me, aghast. 'I can't give up. I mean, I ought to have a break for this baby's sake, but we have clients who rely on us. We can't let them down.'

'What if I carry on while you're on maternity leave? I can keep the business ticking over.'

Clare's face lights up. 'Oh, that's fantastic! But what about your knees?'

'They've been better since I've lost weight. Listen, we haven't many clients left. I can manage those, and we'll take on new ones when you're ready to start back.'

'I've been so worried about what's going to happen.'

'Why didn't you tell me?'

'You have enough problems of your own. I didn't want to force you into something you didn't want to do.' She smiles wryly. 'Tony doesn't seem to want to leave my house. Jim said he could stay a while longer. He knows that you'd do the same for him if it was the other way round.'

Would I? Two months pass, then three, and Tony appears to have embedded himself into Clare's household. Clare fears that Fern is going to grow up believing that she has two dads, whereas my children might as well have none. That isn't entirely fair. Tony has been over to see the girls, but he won't stay or

295

talk to me. It's as if I don't exist, as if he's blanked out any part that I've played in his life, whereas I ask Clare how he is whenever I see her.

How am I coping? I don't know if I am. Jade copes by feuding with me, although our fights are becoming less frequent. I'm not sure whether it's because she's coming to terms with our situation, or whether she is secretly optimistic that her dad might move back in with us one day.

One evening, the girls and I are eating tea in the kitchen. Chloe sits in her highchair, splashing about in a bowl of chocolate mousse with a plastic spoon. Jade picks at pasta and pesto with a smile on her face. I should have noticed before, but that smile has been playing on her lips ever since she got up this morning. I don't question it. She's already told me that she's arranged to meet Jack at his mum's house tomorrow. I've met her briefly. She's a single parent like me, and seems very ordinary, exceedingly normal, but then I've thought that of people before. I shall therefore reserve judgement.

Jade tips her head to one side and gazes at me quizzically. She looks fresh and young, her hair back to its old colour, streaks of blonde run through hazel, apart from the ends which are black, like the hairs on a tabby cat. She's wearing lipgloss and some foundation to cover an almost invisible – to me, anyway – outbreak of spots on her chin. Her jeans are blue. Her top is pink with soft cream stripes.

'Have you talked to Dad about coming home?' Jade looks me straight in the eyes.

'Of course.' We've skirted the subject once or twice, when Tony's visited the girls. He always makes a real effort to appear cheerful, blowing raspberries at Chloe and cracking jokes with Jade as he helps her put posters of her pop idols up in her room, but he doesn't fool me.

'I mean, have you talked to him properly? Without me and Chloe in the way?'

'Jade, you don't understand.'

'I do.' She tears a pasta shell in half with her thumb and fingernail. 'You're both too bloodyminded to admit that you're missing each other like mad.'

'Jade!' I can tell that she's made up her mind what the problem is, and nothing I can say will change it. 'Will you eat that with a knife and fork? How is your little sister going to learn any table manners?'

Jade grins. 'She's just dropped her spoon.'

'Oh, Chloe,' I groan. I bend down and follow the spatters of chocolate on the floor to find it. By the time I sit up again, Chloe is wearing the bowl on her head, like a hat. Chocolate mousse drips through her hair and onto her face. She looks at me, wide-eyed and innocent, and I am doing very well at forcing my face to remain straight as I decide how best to scold her – until Jade giggles. Then I lose all self-control and fall about laughing. Chloe joins in.

Clare isn't quite so amused when I recount my tale of Chloe and the chocolate mousse. She doesn't like Fern to make a mess while she's eating. She's also less than happy that Tony's still living at her house.

'It's time he left,' Clare grumbles when we arrive at Mrs E's the following morning to clean. We find her packing her ornaments into boxes.

'Are you going somewhere, Mrs E?' I ask.

'My niece is taking these to a car boot sale. I'm selling my doubles.'

'What's this?' Clare picks up a tatty photograph album. A handful of sugar-paper pages and photos slide out.

'Be careful, dear.' Mrs E's hands tremble as she opens the album and replaces the pages. Her gaze lingers on a black and white picture of a woman in a white coat sitting at the front of a formal line-up of men in suits and tweeds.

'Is that you, Mrs E?' I shout into her left ear, making her jump.

'That's me at the research laboratory,' she says. 'Did I ever tell you that I used to be an atomic scientist?'

I glance towards Clare. I feel pretty bad now for doubting her, and from the other photos that I can see of Mrs E dressed in evening gowns and strings of black pearls, I wouldn't be at all surprised if she really did dance with the Prince of Wales.

Mrs E sits down with the paper while Clare and I get started. Clare is sporting a new pair of earrings, red marbles on green metal rings. Jim bought them – still wrapped – from one of the charity shops up the High Street. He's more careful with his money now that he's having to earn it.

297

Clare returns to the subject of Tony. 'One man is more than enough for any woman, I can tell you. It's all very well, but Tony and Jim are like an old married couple themselves. I don't get a look in.'

'You'll have to get tough with him. It is ridiculous, all of you being squeezed up like a tin of sardines, while I live with the girls.'

'Perhaps I should move in with you.' Clare is joking, of course, but it isn't such a bad idea. At least I understand her.

'Jim and I can't have a good row,' Clare complains. 'Tony's stayed long enough. He's been very good doing the ironing and stuff, but the baby's due any minute, and we need his room. I want to redecorate it and make it into a proper nursery.'

'Ironing? I didn't think he knew how to.'

'He didn't. I had to give him a couple of hours of instruction.'

'I could help – with the decorating, not with evicting Tony. He doesn't listen to anything I say.'

'You could offer to have him back at yours.'

'I'm not having him back just because he's homeless, not if he doesn't want me any more. I'm not that compassionate, but I will try to speak to him if you like.' I am aware that Mrs E is peering over the top of her paper, watching us.

'What exciting lives you two lead,' she says.

I look at Clare. 'How does she know?' I mouth.

'Errant husbands, financial difficulties . . . You've kept me amused these past few weeks.'

Clare and I stare at her, uncomprehending.

Mrs E taps her hearing-aid. 'I was going to tell you, but I didn't get round to it. I made an appointment at that clinic, and it wasn't much fun hanging about waiting with all those ancient fuddy-duddies, especially as the receptionist wouldn't let me take Prince in with me, but they syringed my ears and fixed my loose connections. They even gave me a new battery pack.'

'So you *can* hear?' says Clare. 'You've been earwigging on our conversations!'

'Forgive me, but I shan't be listening in for much longer. I have to give you this.' She hands Clare a slip of paper. 'I'm afraid that I am terminating my contract with your company. It's nothing personal. I'm giving this house up to a letting agency and moving away.'

'Where are you going?'

'I shall rent a small place in Windsor to be near my niece, Elizabeth.' She smiles. 'She's arranging for someone to come in and cook my meals and Prince's, as well as clean. I'm going to be waited on hand and foot.'

By the end of March, Mrs E has moved to a flat that she says is fit for royalty, Neville has dispensed with our services because Hannah, now his fiancée, has moved in with him and taken over the domestic chores, and I have become sole worker for *Maids 4 U*. I do my two hours at Dr Hopkins's house, then drop in to see Clare. Tony should be out working, but his van is parked outside. I hesitate, but Clare sees me from her window and waves at me to come on in.

There are holiday brochures all over the living room.

'Sue's planning an escape to the sun,' says Clare.

'My sister thinks that I need time away to mend my poor broken heart,' Sue says sarkily. 'Oh, you needn't worry about me, Clare, or you, Lisa. I didn't fancy Neville anyway. There wasn't that spark between us, not like there is between you and your husbands.'

I realise that Sue is speaking as though Tony and I are still together, as if nothing has happened. Tony and Lisa. Lisa and Tony . . .

'Where's Chloe?' Sue asks.

'At my mum's. Jade's there too because school's closed for a teacher-training day. I have to pick them up by two because my parents are going to some meeting about manual versus electronic methods of measuring rainfall. Mum's decided that if she doesn't see much of Dad at home, she'll have to go out with him. Actually, she's been hooked by this weather-forecasting hobby too.' I turn to Clare. 'Are you all right?' She rubs her swollen belly. 'That baby's dropped, hasn't it?'

She gazes fondly down at her bump.

'You mustn't come out yet.' She jabs her finger towards it, emphasising each syllable. 'I haven't packed my bag.' She looks towards me. 'Would you have Fern for us when I do go into labour, Lisa?'

'You don't have to ask.' I hesitate. 'Are you sure you wouldn't like me to take her home with me now?'

'Oh, I'm not in labour. I'm just having a few of those Braxton

Hicks contractions.' Clare smiles weakly. 'Don't worry, Lisa. I have had a baby before.' She massages the small of her back with her fists. 'My babysitter is playing with Fern in the kitchen. Tony said that he couldn't face going to work today. I told him that if he was having a break, he should use the time to clear the spare room instead of his head.' She offers me a cup of tea and heads off to make it.

Sue carries on making notes from her holiday brochures.

'I need a break too.' Clare is talking to Tony in the kitchen. I strain my ears, but decide that I have a better chance of hearing their conversation if I sneak out and stand behind the kitchen door.

'This baby will be born soon,' Clare continues. 'It's kicking like Thierry Henry.'

'I'll be out as soon as I can find somewhere to stay.'

'I know of an excellent place, a semi-detached house that's convenient for the High Street.'

At first I assume she's talking about Mrs E's house, then I realise that she's talking about mine, about *ours* . . .

'You have your own children to play with. There's no need to waggle your ears and stick your tongue out at mine.'

Tony's voice hardens. 'You don't have to remind me. I do see them, you know.'

'Two or three times a week,' Clare counters. 'It's time you stopped messing about feeling sorry for yourself. At least try. Lisa loves you. She always has.'

'She lied to me.'

'I'm not saying that I agree with what she did, but I know how deep the desire for a baby can be. And don't say, "Oh, but she's already had one with Jade". Lisa always wanted two kids. She wanted another child to complete her family. *Your* family!'

Tony begs Clare to keep calm. 'I don't want you going into labour.'

'Maybe I should, then you'd have to move out.'

'Clare!' There is just the suggestion of panic in Tony's voice. 'Shall I go and fetch Jim from school?'

'No,' Clare says firmly. 'Just pack your bags and bugger off, will you?'

'I can't go home. Lisa won't want me back.'

'If Lisa had wanted anyone else, she'd have found him by now. She's had plenty of offers.'

There's a moment's hesitation. 'Has she?'

Why did you tell him that? I think. It isn't true, but it's a great tactical move. There's nothing like a little jealousy to spur on a decision.

Clare takes a sharp intake of breath. 'Now, get out of my house.'

'Give me a couple of days.'

'Twenty-four hours, then you're out on your ear.'

I suppose I'd hoped that Tony would listen to Clare and move back in here with me and the girls, but twenty-four hours pass and he doesn't appear. It's Saturday afternoon, and Jade is kicking about in the sitting room while Chloe naps in her bouncing cradle, and I catch up with some ironing.

'Aren't you going to see Kimberley today?' I ask Jade.

'She's having a sleepover at hers tonight. I did tell you. Ages ago.'

'Did you? I can't remember.'

'Colin's picking me up at six.'

'I could have dropped you over there.'

'Well, it's easier for him. He doesn't have a baby to consider.' She wanders over to me and rests her hand on my shoulder. 'You know, you do so much already, Mum. You're the best mum in the world.'

'Oh, thanks.' I'm touched. Jade hasn't compared my mothering skills with Manda's since her stay at the Kennedys' house when she learned of Manda's affair with the piano player, and discovered that Manda can't cook. My eyes flood with tears.

'Please don't cry again.' Jade gives me a hug which only makes the tears overflow down my cheeks. They drip and make small marks on a *Maids 4 U* top that I've spread across the ironing board. 'I wish you could be happy like you used to be,' Jade continues. 'We're having a takeaway at Kimberley's, but I wondered if you'd like me to cook tea for you to cheer you up?'

I frown as I press the tearstains out of the fabric.

'I don't want anything in return,' Jade says quickly. 'Honest.'

'If I'd known you weren't staying for tea, I wouldn't have defrosted the mince. I was going to make chili con carne.'

'I'll make it, if you'll show me how to.'

I could almost get used to being a single parent, I think, as

301

Jade and I cook together. Almost. What is the point of going to all the effort of preparing a meal when there is no one to share it with? Chloe will have macaroni cheese. I shall have two portions of the chili con carne that is simmering on the hob to myself.

Jade disappears off upstairs to pack her overnight bag while I mooch around with Chloe in my arms, showing her the daffodils that Jade has picked from the garden and arranged in a vase on the kitchen worktop. Chloe's attempts to eat them are foiled by the doorbell, and I traipse out to the hall with her on my hip to answer it. There's an Audi parked across the entrance to the drive.

It's Colin. He thrusts a bottle of wine into my free hand. I glance at the label. Casa Kennedy.

'Jade asked me to bring it over,' he says. 'I didn't realise how much you'd enjoyed it that night at the party.'

'Oh?' I am aware that a white van has drawn up, bumper to bumper with Colin's car. 'Oh thanks, Colin. That's very . . . er . . . kind of you.'

Colin beams and bobs forwards to kiss me on the cheek, just as a door slams out on the road. Out of politeness, I peck Colin's cheek in return.

'Hey!' There's shouting, and a man – Tony – appears on the driveway. He hurries towards us, one shoulder dragged down by the weight of the toolbox in his hand. 'How dare you touch my wife!'

I push past Colin and plant myself and Chloe between him and Tony, whose eyes are glinting dangerously.

'Tony, please,' I say as calmly as I can.

'I've come to collect Jade, not pick up your wife,' Colin blusters.

'But the wine,' says Tony, 'and you were kissing her. I saw you.'

'It was a gesture of friendship, that's all.' Beads of sweat have appeared on Colin's brow, drops of spittle on his goatee.

'Dad!' Jade turns up at the front door too, holding a backpack and a sleeping bag, still unrolled from the last time that she used it. 'I'm going to Kimberley's for a sleepover.'

'Okay,' Tony says. 'I'm sorry.'

'No harm done.' Colin proffers his hand, and they shake in the spirit of mutual understanding.

'I'll collect Jade tomorrow lunchtime,' I say.

'I'll do it,' Tony interrupts.

Chloe and I watch Colin drive away with Jade and Kimberley waving out of the rear window, and I realise that Tony is still standing beside us. He looks more handsome than ever in dark jeans and a blue fleece that matches his eyes. A shiver runs down my spine.

'We'd better go inside,' Tony says after he's tickled Chloe's toes and given her a kiss. I return indoors, and he follows, but I'm not cold. It's the effect of his presence.

'The quicker I fix the boiler, the better,' he adds.

'Boiler?' I frown.

'Jade texted me. She said that you hadn't got any heating.'

'If I hadn't, I wouldn't trouble *you* with it. I'd pay someone else to repair it.' I fold my arms and squeeze my ribs as a mixture of love and hate, pain and anger wells up inside me. 'I wouldn't want you glowering about in my house.'

'It isn't *your* house,' Tony says, 'and as you're so sure you don't need my services, I'll just pick up the video Jade said that she left out for me, and go.' He heads for the television and picks up a tape that I hadn't noticed before from the top. He scans the label. 'Oh? It's for both of us.'

'You'd better watch it here then.'

'Do you mind?'

I do, but my curiosity is piqued. I watch Tony slip the video into the player and fiddle with the remote control. It won't play. He kneels down and thumps the machine with his fist.

'Don't do that – it belongs to me,' I protest.

'You're welcome to it.' Tony sits back on his heels. The TV screen flickers in black and white, then full colour, and there is Jade sitting in a big blue armchair with Chloe and Tigger on her lap. They stare earnestly towards us from my parents' sitting room.

'First, I'd like to thank Uncle Mal for giving up his time to help us,' Jade begins.

'It's a pleasure,' Mal says from behind the camcorder.

'To Mum and Dad, this is a message from your daughters, Jade and Chloe Baker.'

'Carlton, will you sit down,' Mal cuts in and the camera pans across to where Carlton is jumping up and down on a set of plastic powertools. When it returns to the armchair, Jade is retrieving Tigger from the floor, but she is soon hidden from our view by a close-up of Carlton's nose that leaves a sticky mark on the lens.

'Carlton!' Jade wails. 'How will Chloe and I ever get our parents back together if you mess up this recording?'

'Calm down, Jade,' Mal says. 'Start again . . .'

Jade sits up straight and takes a deep breath. 'Mum and Dad, please stop fighting and arguing and being horrid to each other. Me and Chloe want you to know that we love you both and wish you were happy again. That's all. That's all we want to say . . .'

The television screen goes blank, but Tony and I continue to stare at it for some time.

'I feel dreadful,' Tony says quietly. 'We've been behaving more childishly than our children.'

I turn towards him to meet his gaze. 'We must talk. We owe Jade and Chloe that.'

'Especially as Jade took so much trouble to fit us up. There's nothing wrong with the boiler, is there?'

I shake my head, plonk my bum down on the sofa and close my eyes. I am aware of movement, and the sofa sinking beside me. I am aware of the scent of aftershave. 'You first, Tone.'

'Okay. I'm not sorry for walking out on you when you told me about Chloe.'

I open my eyes, sensing that this isn't a good start.

'However, it's given me time and space to think about us – about me,' Tony goes on, 'and I've made a decision.'

My heart knocks against my ribs. The sound echoes around my skull like a waterhammer. What is it to be? A trial separation, or straight into the divorce? I turn to face Tony. The muscle in his cheek tightens. He takes a deep breath and speaks.

'I want us to live together again. Properly.'

'Oh?' I stare at him.

'As husband and wife, doing all the things that married couples do, like shopping at IKEA, ferrying their teenage daughter about town and visiting the in-laws. All the ordinary things. I've missed them. I've missed doing them with you.'

'Are you sure?' I have to ask. 'I don't want you back because you think we should be together for the girls. It isn't enough. I don't believe that we should rub along as a couple so that you can be here to waggle your ears and stick your tongue out at Jade and Chloe.'

'That's what Clare said the other day. You were listening, you nosy . . .' Tony's lips curve into a slow and sensual smile. 'Oh, I can't forget what it's like to hold you in my arms, to hear you laugh, to make love to you. I love you, Lisa. I've always loved you.'

'That's the most romantic thing you've ever said, Tony Baker.' My cheeks are burning from the heat of his caress, and he's hardly touching me. His fingertips brush the back of my hand, like a lover's breath.

'I've been such an idiot,' he says.

'Once you're on a high horse you have a habit of staying on it for a very long time.' I bite my lip. 'I can understand. I betrayed your trust. I know what it's like.'

'I've put it all behind me.' Tony's arm curves around my waist.

'Me too.' I lean towards him and slip my hands around the back of his neck. I tilt my head. His eyes shimmer. His lips touch mine, very softly. 'I love you,' I murmur, and I don't know how we get there, but we're on the floor and my bra is dangling from Chloe's baby gym, and Tony's going to make love to me, and I just know that Clare is on the other end of that phone that's ringing out in the hall, and, if I don't answer it quickly, Chloe will wake up, and howl the place down . . .

'Leave it.' Tony grabs my arm as I pull away.

'I can't. I said I'd look after Fern.'

Tony smiles ruefully and runs his hand through his rumpled hair when I tell him that I have to fetch Fern from Clare's house so that Jim can drive her down to the hospital.

That night, Fern refuses to go to sleep, assuming, I guess, that if she's having a sleepover at her friend's house, she should make the most of it and stay up all night. She wakes Chloe too, and Tony and I, having dined on Jade's chili con carne, end up spending the night cuddled up on the sofa, drinking coffee while they play in the sitting room.

Chloe pulls herself up to a standing position and cruises the room via the furniture. Fern doesn't stop chattering.

'She doesn't half go on,' Tony observes. 'She takes after her mum. Clare drove me mad while I was staying there.'

She's driving me mad right now, keeping me in suspense. Jim doesn't phone until six in the morning. It's a boy. Charlie. 8lbs 2oz. Mother and baby are doing well.

'We'd better plan a double celebration,' Tony says. 'A party to wet the baby's head, and celebrate our anniversary.' He looks at me, a smile dancing on his lips. 'It's at the beginning of next month. I won't forget this time. I'll never forget again.'

I put my arm through his. 'I won't let you.' We kiss, and I feel as though the sun is coming out again.

The sun is still shining on the morning of our anniversary celebration, and I am dressed to dazzle in a sheer lilac dress that has a subtle, sparkly thread running through it. Chloe is sitting on the bedroom floor at my feet, dribbling over my toes as she examines my painted nails. Jade is sprawled across the bed, texting Kimberley who turned out to be less of a bad influence on Jade than Jade was on her. On my dressing-table is a photograph of Jade dancing. She's doing very well at school too. She won't have to resolve customer complaints or clean other people's houses.

'Is Jack coming today?' I ask her.

She blushes furiously and keeps staring at her phone. 'Yes, and Kimberley.'

'I'm really looking forward to meeting him.'

'You've met him already,' she sighs.

'I've seen him in passing – on the way to the bus, and on the doorstep.' He's about Jade's height and he has pale blond hair – sometimes it's spiked up with gel, sometimes it's flat. He wears jeans and T-shirts, and if they are designer label, I don't recognise the names. I haven't heard him speak. Jade does all the talking for him.

I check my make-up in the mirror. Tony's reflection appears beside mine.

'Happy Anniversary, love.' He smiles and pinches my bum. 'How long does it take you women to get ready for a party?'

'I'm ready.' I look him up and down appreciatively. He's nicked himself shaving, and stuck a piece of tissue to his chin. He's dressed in a shirt and tie, and dark trousers. His socks are blue, with Father Christmases on them, a present from Jade back in December. It was all she could afford with what was left of her allowance, and Tony is still delighted with them. Press them in the right place, and they play 'We Wish You a Merry Christmas'.

We head downstairs. Tony carries Chloe who chats and wriggles in his arms. She wears a glittering tiara and a white dress with fairy wings – Jade chose it from a catalogue. It isn't a proper party dress, but one for playing dressing-up. It's hitched up over her nappy, and I tug it back to cover her modesty. In response, she tugs the tiara off her head and drops it.

I leave Tony to sort her out while I duck into the kitchen where Mum and Bunny are in charge of catering. I pick up a knife and a cucumber, but Mum takes them back from me.

'No, no – you go and entertain your guests. You don't want to ruin that lovely dress.'

Bunny looks at me through narrowed eyes. Will I pass her scrutiny?

'Well, Lisa, you're still just about young enough to wear it.' She smiles warmly, and I take her comment as a compliment, not criticism.

The doorbell rings.

'Go on,' says Mum, 'answer it.'

I get there at the same time as Jade. It's Jack.

'Hi,' I say.

He nods and smiles, and I wonder, as I watch him and Jade disappear off to the kitchen, if he's ever learned to talk. I join Tony in the sitting room. Chloe is sitting on the floor, dropping wooden bricks into a trolley. I gaze out of the window, just as Colin's white Audi pulls up outside. I invited Manda and Colin, expecting them to decline, but they accepted. They are still together, but their relationship is not my kind of relationship.

Manda sashays across the drive in a floral dress and white ballet pumps. Colin strides behind her in a short-sleeved shirt and green trousers. Kimberley follows them in tight hipster trousers and a cropped top. She's taken to wearing a jewel in her bellybutton, but Jade assures me that it's a stick-on.

'Jade and Jack are in the kitchen, Kimberley,' I say when I let them in. Manda and Colin join Tony in the living room while I fetch a tray of sparkling wine and orange juice. As I serve them, I warn them not to do any recruitment at our anniversary celebration.

'It would be highly inappropriate,' Colin agrees. He winks at me. 'Anyway, Manda and I have given up ...' he pauses '... that activity that you forbade me to mention ever again in your presence. We gave it up for Lent, and just carried on.'

Manda sits down on the sofa and smiles as Chloe bumshuffles up to her and hands her a brick. 'We didn't want to be known as the oldest swingers in town,' she confides. 'Of course, I told Colin that he'd have to give up his membership of the Re-enactment Society too, and he has.'

'Ted told me,' I say.

'I can still be Emperor in private,' Colin says, touching an imaginary sword at his hip.

I head back for the kitchen to return the tray. Jade, Jack and Kimberley are eating sandwiches faster than Mum and Bunny can make them. Mum covers the plates with clingfilm and puts them in the fridge.

'That's it then,' she says. 'Is it time for the ceremony yet?'

'We're waiting for the Master of Ceremonies.'

'That's typical of Mal,' she says, gazing out of the kitchen window where Philip is sitting at the garden table. On the table is a lettuce from his coldframe, and a bunch of radishes wrapped in newspaper – he did phone to ask me if I'd like them before he brought them along. In spite of the sunshine, he's wearing his blazer and Allotment Society tie. 'Mal will be late for his own funeral,' she goes on. 'Are you expecting anyone else?'

'Clare and Jim. Sue couldn't come – she's blagged her way onto an Eighteen to Thirty holiday with her girlfriends. It's ironic really. Sue finds herself a man without any help from Clare, and promptly leaves the country.'

'Anyone we know?' asks Mum.

'I don't think so. He's called Paul. Sue booked her holiday with him, and he's going to collect her from the airport on her return. Clare and I popped into the travel agent's where he works to check him out. I picked up some brochures for the Greek Islands too – I promised Jade that we'd have a proper family holiday this year.'

'Where's Sue gone?' asks Dad.

'Ibiza.'

'Sue is no stormchaser then. She won't see any hurricanes out there.' Dad clings on to the brolly that he brought with him. I don't know why. It's a beautiful, still day.

'Don't worry,' says Mum. 'Your father always errs on the pessimistic side. That way, people don't mind if he gets the forecast wrong. You can always use a brolly as a parasol.'

'Actually, I'm more interested in global longterm forecasting than trying to interpret local conditions,' Dad says.

Tony links his arm through mine. 'It means that when the time comes, if you get it wrong, people will have forgotten what weather you forecasted.'

'Oh Tony, you do make me laugh.' Mum chuckles to prove her point, and Dad, who looked a little hurt at Tony's lack of faith in his abilities, relaxes and picks at a bowl of crisps.

'Jim will have to take over the role of Master of Ceremonies,' Tony whispers aside to me when Jim and Clare arrive with their brood. 'It's midday and everyone's starving.'

'You are, you mean! You can't inflict that responsibility on Jim – you know he hates speaking at all, let alone in public.' I chose Mal because he's the expert on wedding ceremonies – he's taken those vows often enough. He's agreed to let Rosie take over his camcorder while he officiates. 'Don't worry, Mal will be here any minute.'

Tony drops his arm around my shoulder and runs his fingers down my bare skin, raising goosepimples. I shiver at the contact, recalling how he made love to me last night, not once, but twice, which is pretty good going for an old married couple like us.

Someone shouts from the hall. Jade. 'It's Uncle Mal, and Rosie!' Her voice isn't quite so animated when she adds, 'And Carlton.'

I don't care if Carlton posts sandwiches into the video, and he can open as many cupboards as he likes. There are no more skeletons inside them, no rotting vegetables, and no secrets. There's no wedding ring either – I took that out of the drawer and put it back on my finger. Now that Mal is here, Tony and I can repeat our wedding vows on the lawn in front of our family and friends.

'Forsaking all others,' Tony says, loud and clear.

'To love and to honour,' I say.

309

'Till death us do part.' Tony squeezes my hand, and turns to Mal. 'Where is it then? I gave it to you.'

Mal fumbles through his trouser pockets, then grins and pulls out a small box. 'Only joking.' He snaps the box open. A ray of sunlight catches a row of diamonds on a band of gold. I can't believe it. I wasn't looking for any present. You see, I've learned many lessons during the past year, including the fact that presents aren't important.

Tony takes the ring and slips it onto my finger. It fits perfectly.

'Oh, it's beautiful, Tone.' I am choked.

'I love you, Lisa,' he murmurs.

'You may kiss the bride,' says Mal, and Tony's lips claim mine to the applause of our friends and family.

No one is in a hurry to leave. Dad, Mal and Rosie are playing a modified game of rounders with Manda. Colin keeps score with a pencil and paper. Carlton is making mud-pies, using a trickle of water from the outside tap and earth that he's dug up from one of the flowerbeds. Jim sits snoozing in the shade of the apple tree with a can of lager in his hand. Bunny and Philip wander arm-in-arm around the garden, examining the plants that I have left to grow unchecked. Every so often, Bunny turns and says, 'Lisa, that one will have to go. Philip says that it's poisonous. When it comes to weeds, your father-in-law certainly knows his onions.'

Chloe and Fern sit on a picnic blanket with my mum who's making daisy-chains. Chloe squeezes a jam tart between her fingers. It's everywhere, in her hair and all over her face. Not to be outdone, Fern stuffs a splinter of breadstick up her nose. Clare kneels down beside her to extract it. She's holding baby Charlie in her arms at the same time, trying to balance him on her lap. I walk over and take him from her to help her out. He's wearing Arsenal colours. He smells milky and sweet. His hair is very soft. I press my nose to his forehead.

Tony joins us. He looks at me. 'Don't tell me that you want another baby.'

I shake my head and smile. 'You'd better rebook that appointment you cancelled, and have the snip after all. Don't get me wrong, Tone. I love babies, but I've had my two. I don't want any more.'

'It's nice to be able to hand them back, isn't it?' Mum says, as I return Charlie to Clare.

'I dream of having a good night's sleep,' Clare says. 'Fern was such a quiet baby. I can hardly wait to get back to work for a rest.'

'I can't wait either. *Maids 4 U* isn't the same without you. Twirling a duster to "Winner Takes It All" on my own in Dr Hopkins's study is no fun.'

'I could bring Charlie with me next week. My mum will have Fern.' Clare winks at me. 'I hope you haven't missed those hard-to-reach places.'

'I've been very thorough, and I've thought of a fantastic company logo. How about *Maids 4 U, On the Dazzle*?'

'I love it,' says Clare. 'It's snappy.'

'It sums you two up.' Tony grins as Mum tries to place a chain of daisies around Chloe's neck. Chloe won't have it. She pulls it straight off and stuffs the daisies into her mouth. Mum is laughing as she takes them away and distracts her with Tigger.

Tony reaches out his hand and leads me towards the bottom of the garden, where Jade is perched on the edge of the old swing. Kimberley stands, holding onto one of the supports, and Jack sits on the grass in Bermuda shorts with his legs outstretched, gazing adoringly at Jade. Kimberley says something. Jade giggles. I don't feel envious that she's just starting out. I wouldn't want to go through all that uncertainty and angst again.

Tony turns to me. 'What's this?' he says, gently wiping a tear from my cheek. 'You're crying.'

'I'm not,' I sniffle. 'The sun's in my eyes.'

He raises one eyebrow. My heart lurches. I throw my arms around his neck, remembering my promise to myself. No more secrets. Everything out in the open.

'Oh Tony, I *am* crying, and it's because I've never been so happy. You, Jade and Chloe. You're all I've ever wanted.'